Butterflies Set Free

Breaking the Chains of 21st-Century Slavery
By Bringing It into the Light

Authored in Spanish by:
José Pedro de la Cruz

Revised and Adapted by:
Katie Gallaher

Edited by:
Mary Nell Sorensen

Translated to English by:
Accent Network, LLC

"The most powerful art in life is to make pain a talisman that heals, a butterfly that is reborn, blooming in a festival of colors."

Frida Kahlo

"Truly, truly, I say to you, unless one is born again he cannot see the kingdom of God."

Jesus of Nazareth

"How does one become a butterfly?" she asked. "You must want to fly so much that you are willing to give up being a caterpillar."

Trina Paulus

"Many small people in small places doing small things can change the world."

Eduardo Galeano

Butterflies Set Free: Breaking the Chains of 21st Century Slavery by Bringing It into the Light

Original Text Published in Spain 2021
Adapted Text Published in the United States of America in 2022

de la Cruz, Jose Pedro.
    El renacer de las Mariposa: Una luz para romper las cadenas de la esclavitud del siglo XXI / Jose Pedro de la Cruz. –
Layout: Lidia Del Pino Merino
Printing: Christian Bookstore Project Logos
ISBN: 978-84-09-36406-0
Legal deposit: MA1610-2021

Gallaher, Katie.
    Butterflies Set Free: Breaking the Chains of 21st Century Slavery by Bringing It into the Light / Katie Gallaher. -
Second Edition
Published by On Mission Press
Seattle, Washington
ISBN 979-83-56-90372-4

All rights reserved. No portion of this book may be reproduced, stored in an electronic retrieval system, or transmitted in any form or by any means – electronic, mechanical, photocopy, recording, or any other – except for brief quotations in printed reviews, without the prior permission of the publisher.

José Pedro de la Cruz Cortés and Katie Gallaher have assigned all copyrights to the Papilio Association. All proceeds from the distribution of this literary work go directly to the organization to support the continuing fight against sex-trafficking.

      For more information or to contact the authors/publisher:
                  ButterfliesSetFreeSpain@gmail.com

Printed in the United States of America

Author's Note

We all know they exist. Most of us have seen them. They are here, much closer than we would care to believe. Prostitutes. Sometimes, it is enough just to turn your head. Our minds fill in the blanks with stereotypes and clichés. Most of the time, we reach those conclusions without actual data at hand and don't go beyond the headlines.

To assuage our discomfort, we make rationalizations such as assuming the women engage in such activity by choice and therefore it would also be by choice that they could leave that life behind. However, the truth of reality is far different, and each woman has her own story; and as is the case for most women engaged in prostitution, it is often a cruel and devastating one that began with poverty, deception, desperation, and abuse.

Slavery has existed for as long as humans have lived on this planet, in some periods with greater cruelty than in others. Still, it has always been present in the use by some people for exploitation, whether labor, criminal or sexual. Some enslaved people were from the same culture and geographical area, but others were taken by force from other regions of the known world; that is what human trafficking consists of.

According to a 2019 report by Spain's Office of the Attorney General, the victims are "sold, assaulted, beaten, branded, humiliated, threatened and coerced in every conceivable way to overcome their resistance to being exploited." They come from a multitude of countries and regions, including Nigeria, Morocco, Romania, and South America. Trafficking in women for sexual exploitation in Spain is a 5.5 million euros a day business, which amounts to almost 2 billion euros a year. The United Nations estimates the global economic value of trafficking in women at five to seven trillion dollars annually. Hence it is called "the business of trafficking" but it also must be understood as slavery of the 21st century.

The International Labour Organization puts the worldwide number of victims of forced sexual exploitation at 4.5 million. Approximately 90 percent are women and girls. According to the NGO Anesvad, eight out of ten women who work as prostitutes in Spain do so against their will.

Suppose we stick to the numbers and reduce everything to profits, percentages, statistics, prevalence, or any other quantifiable evaluation of this issue. In that case, we can appreciate the magnitude of the problem just from the sheer numbers. However, it's much more critical to dig through the surface and learn the stories of enslaved women to truly appreciate the injustice.

There are organizations that make every effort to help these women with legal, medical and emotional support and access to the resources necessary in case they decide to attempt to escape from this living hell. Currently, approximately 35–40 organizations—large, small, official, and private—work in this field in Spain. They are to be admired, all of them.

This book is about one of those organizations—small in number but large in their work with enslaved girls. Furthermore, it is about them—the women who lived in their homeland in precarious economic situations, who were deceived in different ways, depending on the area they came from, and converged at a shared destination: sexual exploitation. It is the story of those who believed that a way out was possible, to offer a new life to these girls, to allow them to take back the helm of their lives that were destroyed by mafia networks and pimps who profited from their pain and suffering.

I cannot forget the first night I accompanied the team to the industrial park. At the end of the visit that night, a leader asked me if I could summarize in one sentence what had struck me most. Once I could put in order the inner turmoil caused by that first contact, I could answer without hesitation. It was the countenance on the faces of the women; they were hollow and empty, despite the smiles they attempted to display.

That night I felt useful. I could recognize in myself the capacity to be able to help. More nights came, and more activities followed. I dived deeper into the most terrible stories of these women, some of them almost children. And I found meaning in the possibility of helping the girls see a way out and voluntarily decide to take a step towards freedom. I wanted to do what I could to help fill their eyes with life again. These women exist, they are enslaved, and we can and must do something to stop them from being so.

The purpose of this book is to show the inside of this problem and to value the work of small organizations that are not afraid to go to battle for the lives of these women by taking a stand against the giants before them. I have seen first-hand those who never lose their determination, energy, and, especially, their soul in this endeavor to help these broken butterflies be re-born.

For security reasons, none of the names that appear on the following pages are real, although the people who support them are.

When you turn the last page of this book, I hope that you will join me in acknowledging that once seen, you cannot unsee the prevalence of such evil, and that you would be compelled to do what you can to also help.

José Pedro de la Cruz
August 18, 2021

To all those women who had the courage to give their lives to the the first step towards freedom.

To all those who are still afraid to leave.

To the people who initiated, maintain, and put forth their souls and energy to make all this possible.

Our Story

We met each other in 2011 and quickly became best friends with a sister-like bond. Over the years we've mutually encouraged and challenged one another to look for opportunities to be stretched outside our comfort zones, believing that it is in that space that we experience the most growth and purpose.

Similar in many ways yet very different in others, we share a common passion to live out our faith in a manner that reflects the love of Jesus Christ. As this story well illustrates, once we saw the injustice and suffering experienced by so many vulnerable women, we knew our own lives would forever be changed because we "could not unsee what we had seen."

Those who have had the privilege to meet the real life "Sara and Diego" are quick to see their sacrificial service and to recognize the anointing on their lives. They too are compelled by the love of God to be shepherds that care for and even risk their own wellbeing to save and rescue the lost sheep that come their way.

While our partners in Spain are doing the greatest work on the frontlines, here in the United States we seek to recruit others to bring their fish and loaves, to offer what they have for the benefit of others - not just our neighbors, but for the refugee and the stranger, even a world away.

Una vida.
Each of us can use our one life
to make a difference in the life of another.

"Laura" and "Amy"
November 1, 2022

We long for justice to run like a mighty river but more often than not, it begins with a trickle.

Be that trickle.
Do your part.
Start where you're at.
Listen to the stories around you.
Grow in empathy.
Be a good neighbor.
Seek justice.
Love kindness.
Walk humbly.

Pastor Eugene Cho

Foreword

Northshore Community Church in Kirkland, WA has a long-standing history of supporting global missions work. Faithful and dedicated volunteers lead these initiatives and support our ministry partners around the world. Hundreds of congregants have participated in short-term mission trips, including "Sara's" 2013 trip to India featured in this book. Those who engage in such trips often return with new perspectives and a desire to continue serving at home and abroad. At Northshore we believe that Jesus can change everything for anyone, and we are committed to supporting the work of organizations such as *"Mariposa"* as they fight for the freedom of those enslaved in such injustice.

NCC Global Missions Outreach Team
https://northshore.church

The Call

At ages 58 and 64, Sara and Diego were living a rather typical life for a recently retired Spanish couple. They rented a modest home in an area filled with many other retirees just a few blocks from the Mediterranean Sea in a small town in Southern Spain. And while they enjoyed the slower paced life that allowed them more time with family, friends and being involved in their local civic and church communities, their contentment was mixed with some degree of restlessness. Diego had served his entire career in ministry, most recently as a pastor of an evangelical church and Sara had a successful entrepreneurial career running her own salon and providing massage and esthetician services. After all these years in such highly relational and service-oriented jobs where the well-being of others was often at the forefront of their hearts and minds, the simplicity of their retired lives left them missing the purpose and fruitfulness they had known for so long.

Just when monotony was about to set in, some unexpected excitement entered their lives in the form of a phone call from Diego's brother Damian who lived in the United States. Looking back, Diego should have known that it would be Damian who would be the one to introduce a new adventure into their lives, a pattern that had persisted since childhood.

Like Diego, Damian also had served in ministry in his younger years and then went on to study nursing so he could help heal both body and souls. He had met Janis, an American girl born in Morocco, the daughter of missionaries, and they fell in love and were married. They relocated to the United States where he finished his nursing training and started working in a hospital in Seattle. As a couple from two different Mediterranean cultures, it was challenging to acclimate to the American lifestyle, but they made a commitment to adapt, especially as their three children came along.

They began attending an evangelical church in the area and quickly became involved in the community. The church had a long-standing tradition of involvement in global missions and Damian soon found himself as a translator on one of the trips to Nicaragua. Although Diego and Damian had grown up in a rather poor family, for Spanish standards, he had never seen such poverty before. He was known to many as a man of great compassion and of action so Janis was not one bit surprised when he returned from that first trip a changed man, determined to do what he could to care for others in such dire need.

A year later, the Global Missions Pastor of their church unexpectedly passed away and both the staff and lay leaders saw Damian as the perfect candidate to step in and lead the global ministry, and so it was. In the following years the outreach continued to grow and church planting partners were established in Central America, Morocco, the Philippines, and India. It was in India that Damian met Ramchand and the church joined efforts with the Indian nationalists to create centers to help the children leprosy patients and to take in girls of the lowest social castes who were destined for either an arranged marriage at an unthinkably young age or sale by the family into prostitution.

Damian knew his brother and sister-in-law were interested in getting involved in humanitarian work in this new season of retirement so as the latest trip to India was being planned, he called to extend an invitation. While both were excited at the prospect, funds in retirement were limited. Diego had traveled the world during his time of ministry, even working with the legendary evangelist, Billy Graham, so he deferred the opportunity to Sara, who said yes in a heartbeat. Little did Diego and Sara have any idea that answering that phone call would forever change their lives and lead to an unexpected calling.

Sara Visits India and Sees So Much More

The Charles de Gaulle airport in Paris was such a bustle that one could barely attend to one's own thoughts. Thousands of people were looking for their departure gate, the boarding gate, or any kind of gate that would take them somewhere in the world. We were going to Delhi on a direct flight that announced its landing at Indira Gandhi Airport eight and a half hours after takeoff. The focus of the trip was to visit and help as much as possible in the daily life of a school that cared for the children of leprosy patients—either the mother, father, or both.

It was ten o'clock at night when we landed in Delhi. I had boarded the plane already not feeling 100%, so after more than eight hours locked in the aircraft, my body was not cooperative on many levels, my mind was racing back and forth, and the fatigue was adding to my already strong emotional state. I said a little prayer and reminded myself that Diego had given his blessing for me to come on this trip, both of which brought me comfort. Not only was this my first trip to India, I was also the only non-American on the team as the other six had all come from my brother-in-law's church. My limited English skills made communication challenging but Damian was a strong and sensitive leader that brought unity to our team. We spent the night there, as the next flight, which would take them to Indore, took off at 9:30 the following day.

We were taken to the school, full of deaf and leprous children. The first thing was to change our clothes. In my heart I was open to new experiences and change on the trip, but I never imagined it would be so much, or that it would start with my outward appearance. We packed away our clothes and they gave us ones in Hindu style: large white pants, an unbuttoned blouse with a wide yellow geometric drawing in the center, and a red veil to cover the head. At that moment, I began to feel like one of them, perhaps because of the enthusiasm of my mission or because of a feeling of having crossed the border of my daily life in the West to a new identity in the East. Little did I know that this was just the beginning of how my life would change.
"Here, we take care of deaf and hard of hearing children, children of parents with leprosy, and children with mental problems."
I said the building reminded me of centuries old farmhouses in rural Spain and our guide replied, "Shelter schools are almost all like that in this area, there is no money for more; it is what it is."
The children were filled with infinite curiosity as they approached us with smiles that were impossible to look away from. But I also noticed some of the girls expressed a smile that seemed to hold both joy and fear behind it. I did not understand that duality at the time, but the harsh truth of their previous realities would soon provide the heartbreaking reason.
"Let's move on to the rooms where we will be working."
I expected to see benches, desks, or tables, but everything was done on the ground. Some areas were well kept but in most places it was difficult to walk calmly around and through the undefined magma - a mixture of mud, water, and who knows what.

From the very moment I set foot in those facilities—if I can even call them that—until I left that country, I was overwhelmed at the deepest level of my very being. Every act, every gesture, every image, and every story I discovered was like a battle between the beauty of those faces and the tragedy inside them, the laughter and the pain, the colorfulness of their clothes and the darkness of their lives, the heaven of their souls and the hell of their destinies. The girls, who just by being born already have their future written in those areas of India where poverty, caste system, ancestral traditions of a society in which women are worth less than nothing, and mafias that take advantage of culture and people to make money off them for the maintenance of the rest of the family for years.

All the young people were excited; they approached us with smiles on their faces, I did not understand anything of what they were saying, but I immediately understood the joy caused by our arrival. However, one girl remained squatting, covered with an orange sari that only allowed us to see big, brown eyes, eyes whose gaze was filled with emptiness and sadness. Despite all the activity surrounding me, a shiver ran down my back because that look pierced my soul; it was the expression of nothingness reflected in the eyes of an innocent young girl.

"What's wrong with that little girl?" I asked our Spanish/English/Hindi speaking guide, Vijay, as we entered the next room.

"Her name is Saniya, and her story is terrible," he replied, his smiling expression shifting to a serious and deep one.

"Can I come closer to her?"

"Of course."

She asked Vijay to translate what he was going to tell her. In a soft voice, full of gentleness, she tried to convey compassion and a safe presence.

"My name is Sara. I'm here to learn from you. Are you willing to teach me?"

The Remarkable Ramchand

Sara's learning was just beginning and one of the most influential teachers was Ramchand, the Director of the School. At the end of that first very long day the team gathered with their hosts and Ramchand shared his story and how the school came to be.

Ramchand was born an upper-class boy who lived with his parents and three brothers, descended from a family lineage far superior to most who lived in his community. Indore was the most populated and the largest city in the Indian state of Madhya Pradesh and, from its foundation, was the commercial center between Deccan and Delhi. Ramchand's paternal grandfather was a businessman who had excelled at connecting foreign investors with some of the industries developing in that area. Ramchand's father dutifully and successfully followed in his footsteps. It was not a subject for discussion that his son was to follow in the business, even though he had not yet started his university studies, which is essential for navigating the turbulent waters of the technology industry.

While Ramchand's family was prosperous, he grew with an acute awareness of the extreme poverty within his community. He used to sneak out when his father was in the office and join two like-minded friends. They would cycle to those places to help in whatever way they could, even if it was just to bring some joy to their desperate lives, but they brought fresh food, clothes, hygiene items, and so on whenever they could. Images of boys and girls living in those filthy conditions were never far from his heart and his mind.

His father was focused on the future of his business, so he arranged for Ramchand to go to the United States to study finance and economics at Seattle University. He did not want to go against his father so he accepted without opposition and because he knew that the experience would prepare him to develop a project that had been on his mind for years: residential schools to take in children discarded by society and care for girls out who were destined to be sold by their own families to prostitution mafias.

He successfully completed his studies and graduated at twenty-four. His parents were proud of him, although they could not help but notice a discontentment in their son's eyes. At first, he downplayed it when his mother asked him what was wrong but eventually he worked up the courage to discuss the subject with his father.

"Can you accept that I don't want to go into business?" he asked directly.

"What are you saying? Your grandfather passed the business on to me, and I want to—"

"And what I want doesn't matter?" he interrupted his father.

"I can't believe what I'm hearing," said his father with obvious signs of nervousness at the turn the conversation was taking.

"I want my life to have significance. I do not want to be a manager or run companies. I want my life and my effort to serve to improve other people's lives. So many children are suffering and that is the death of a country; I want to prevent the death of the children and to bring change to our harmful traditions. I want to build schools to take those kids off the street, give them a livable presence and a better future."

His father struggled to control his anger and keep his composure, "Give me some time and space to digest what you just told me."

Ramchand gave his father an honoring nod and then left, knowing he had made his purpose clear.

Two weeks passed and they had not spoken of it again, in fact very few words were exchanged as the tension in the household was intense. Ramchand was pretty sure that at any moment his father would strongly oppose his projects and forbid any further consideration. Ramchand guarded all his ideas and plans in his mind as he knew where, how, and how much it would take to realize his dream. The only thing missing was the money to carry it out, and of course he greatly desired his father's blessing. One morning, after breakfast, his father told him to stay.

"I will advance your part of your inheritance."

"Thank you, Father. You don't know how much this means to me!" Ramchand attempted to get up and hug him, but he waved his hand and told him to remain seated.

"I don't agree with this, but, above all, I don't want you to think of me as someone who clipped the wings of your dreams as the years go by. My assistant already has the order to process the documents to give you that money; talk to him."

Ramchand went straight to his desk drawer, picked up his project folder, and pressed it to his chest. He couldn't stop a single tear from falling down his cheek.

Sara's Learning Continues

The next day we returned to the school and began the time together with introductions. We sat on the floor—everything was done on the floor— we formed a semicircular and the children began to say their names: Varsha, Hari, Narendra, Anjali, Arya, Harisha, Ishwar, Naisha, Jaya… Her smile captivated me from the very moment she pronounced her name—Varsha. Everyone smiled—some more than others, but her face expressed a contagious joy.

Ramchand had shared the story of his dream of building a well to supply water to the village. Many of the children in the school had parents who were lepers, and the authorities would not let them go near the school. After being denied any opportunity to reunite families, Ramchand and his collaborators proposed they would build a well for the village in exchange for permission for these parents to visit their kids. When the children heard the news, they were filled with joy as expressed w/ exuberant celebration in the form of squeals of delight and dancing. They would prepare the visit as if it was a feast dedicated to the god Brahma himself.

I was told the story of many of those families. They lived in the deepest poverty. Many days they did not even have enough to eat; the school helped relieve the anguish of not being able to feed their children. I was amazed by the contrast between those lives and what I could see. Despite their squalid living conditions, they wore brightly colored clothes, displayed frequent laughter, and had seemingly happy faces. It was all quite humbling.

While the conditions at the school were well below the standard Sara or her team had seen in the poorest areas of their own countries, their daily drive back and forth from the hotel in the city was beyond the pale. Dirt and dust covered everything and the streets—if I can even call them streets—were covered with layer upon layer of human and animal waste, resulting in a most intolerable stench. Many of the people were naked, with skin so wrinkled that it was impossible to guess their age. Our guide, Hari, told us this was the plight of the untouchables.

"The caste system divides the Hindu population into distinct groups according to their work and life duties. It was established about three thousand years ago and persists," explained Hari. "It is difficult to understand for a foreigner, but I will try to explain the best I can."

"The oldest texts recognize and justify the caste system as the basis of the order of society. It divides Hindus into four groups: Brahmins, Kshatriyas, Vaishyas, and Sudras. The Brahmins were mainly teachers and intellectuals and are ascribed an ancestral origin from the head of the god Brahma. The Kshatriyas, or warriors and rulers, supposedly came from the arms of Brahma. The Vaishyas or merchants were created from his thighs. The Shudras constitute the lowest caste of all and are recognized to have originated from the feet of Brahma, which is why they do the most menial jobs.

This system is very complex since within each group there are many subgroups and others that do not fit into this classification. For example, the Pariahs or the Dalits oversee the most marginal jobs such as leather workers, poor farmers, landless laborers, street artisans, folk artists, clothes washers, and others.

The Dalits are the ones you will know as untouchables. Dalits are oppressed, outcast, and rejected, hardly considered human beings, completely without dignity. I am ashamed to tell you this as if it is something normal, but the reality is that half of India's population belongs to this caste. They do the domestic work that others do not. Their living conditions are often deplorable, as you have already seen on this road. Many of them live in houses like the ones on the right," everyone turned their heads towards that area and saw poor, dilapidated yet very colorful dwellings with people standing on their doorsteps. The problem is that, if someone is born a Dalit, they die a Dalit."

"The next day we accompanied several school workers on an outreach that was discouraged by the authorities. We went to the street of the untouchables that had impressed us so much the previous afternoon. It was an uncomfortable experience for all of us, but we were sustained by the firm conviction that something had to be done for them and we were reminded by Pastor Damian that Jesus was willing to touch and heal the lepers of his day, two thousand years before. Then Damian put on his medical hat and began to instruct us on how to treat what we would encounter. The goal was to cut away the gangrenous skin and disinfect the ulcers, wounds, and lumps as we saw deformities of the hands, feet, and face, the lack of skin sensitivity and the inability to move the limbs. We put on latex gloves and performed this care with scalpel in hand.

With us came a tall, serious guy who treated the lepers with special compassion. He was always present, helping and controlling everything so that it would run smoothly. I had observed him as our guide at the school, always willing, kind, and careful, and always rather serious. I asked who he was, and they told me his name was Vijay Chowan. He was one of those children that Ramchand rescued when he opened the first school in Indore."

The Curse of Being a Girl

It had quickly become apparent to me that the plight of girls in India was far worse than their male counterparts. To understand what it meant to be a girl in India I was given a document produced by the United Nations entitled 'Sexual Exploitation in India, a Scourge to Be Eradicated!' The first paragraph alone defined the core of the situation:

Women are vulnerable and are subjected to forced marriages, trafficking, and exploitation, in addition to a myriad of social inequalities that make it impossible for them to fully realize their rights as persons and places them in a position of inferiority in relation to men, as they cannot choose and live by themselves, but are dependent and subordinate to them.

I spent that night immersed in reports, documents, and handwritten stories dictated by women who described their lives.

As the trip was nearing its end, Ramchand knew how interested I had become in learning all I could about the plight of these vulnerable girls in this culture, so he made secure arrangements to take me to one of the houses…to give me a glimpse into what hell on earth looked like. That image will never be erased from my memory: a large bed, somewhat rickety, with a brightly colored bedspread, gaudy decorations, and on both sides of the bed, two girls with big eyes, looking lost in some distant place or maybe nowhere, standing, waiting for another man to arrive, pay their parents, and do with them whatever he wanted. Yes, it was their own parents who prostituted their daughters. The mother was the one who taught the girls what men liked in bed; the father was the manager of the business.

"There are mothers who refuse to sell their daughters, but they might be threatened and assaulted. They cannot lose the meager profits generated by the prostitution of their own daughters," Ramchand explained.

"What do these mothers do?" I asked with concern.

"They flee, they confront their husbands, but they always lose. Those who leave have no way to survive; those who confront may even be killed to get their daughters as a source of money."

"Are the parents the pimps?" I asked, indignant at the possible answer.

"They also sell them. I have already told you about the case of Saniya…"

When Dharma was born, her parents did not show the joy that is supposed to fill a family that welcomes a new member. They knew perfectly well that this child's life would be very complicated. Twelve people lived in that home, including her parents, her paternal grandparents, an older brother with his wife and two sons, her father's sister, two brothers who had not yet married, and herself. The women, four of working age, and her grandmother, who was bedridden and unable to move, oversaw all the unpaid work: taking care of the house, the children, and the elderly. They had to always obey the orders and whims of the men.

Dharma's parents worked in the fields, earning a wage that barely provided for food and basic sustenance. Dharma was seven years old when her parents felt the need to initiate arrangements for their daughter's future marriage. They betrothed her to an uncle of hers in the second degree, forty years her senior. When she reached the minimum age for marriage, twelve years old, she got married. The newlywed husband was fifty-two years old and had already been widowed once but had never fathered a child. He was about to divorce his wife for this reason when it so happened that she was assaulted in an alley, raped by strangers, and left to die. A year after that tragic event, he married Dharma.

The first years of marriage seemed strange to her. Her husband showed no sincere affection towards her and instead would constantly order her to do chores and scold her daily because the young teen did not do them to his satisfaction. His primary goal in the relationship was to produce an heir, preferably as many boys as possible, and indeed, not long after they were married, young Dharma became pregnant. He did not show happiness nor congratulate her; he simply told her to implore the gods for the child not to be a girl, as they were useless and brought many problems. To his dismay a daughter was born whom they named Saniya.

Her husband worked on a plantation and one day he had the misfortune of stumbling and one leg got caught between some barbed branches that dug into his foot. The muddy ground and the wounds made his leg gangrenous and within two weeks he was dead. Dharma became a fifteen-year-old widow with a daughter who was not yet two years old—someone that no one would want for a wife. Her husband's parents would not accept her back, but a still unmarried brother-in-law in his thirties, Renjy, spoke to her parents, and they agreed that he would marry her.

Dharma and Renjy had three more children, all boys, who worked in the fields as they grew up. Saniya devoted herself to housework. Renjy and the boys took every available job they could find even if it paid just a few paltry rupees, but the family was still struggling to provide for their basic needs. Through their employers, they met a man named Darshan. He offered to "invest" in their daughter: he would give them a sum of money that would support the family for years, at least enough to eat daily, and when she turned twelve, he would take her, as he said, to work for him. Dharma knew perfectly well what that proposal meant. She knew it from other families, but she had to save her family from starvation.

Little by little, Dharma was teaching her daughter about life, people, and the evil inhabiting the villages and cities. She was instructing her on how to deal with relationships with men, in all its aspects, because she knew that she would have to face this reality in one way or another. She gave her lessons on how to dress according to who was in front of her, how to behave, and how to obey.

The day after their twelfth birthday marked her inevitable departure. They were ready. A simple "we'll be in touch" from Darshan's emissary, a "goodbye, Mom" from Saniya, and a "good luck" from her stepfather sealed the farewell. Later, silence. Dharma's deep, silent weeping came as her daughter got into the car. Saniya's anguish was mixed with a hope for a better future...a hope that would soon become a living nightmare.

Ramchand could only do so much for so many girls who suffered just because they were girls. There were hundreds of thousands of them, but he became aware that each one that he could help, each one that could take her out of that hell, even if they were few, was worth it. Faced with this thought, he always said that the sea is made of infinite drops; if we take just one, it is a tiny part of the ocean, but that drop carries a sea within it, and that is what is important.

Saniya was one of those drops, one precious life worthy of being saved. Ramchand's team had learned that a young girl, Saniya, was in the hands of a local gangster, that her parents had sold her two weeks earlier when she was only twelve years old. They found out where she was and took turns watching the entrances and exits; they chose the moment when every day she went out to the toilet behind the house; they acted quickly. Before she entered, they took her and told her quickly that they were going to save her; although they knew she would not believe it, she would think it was another beast that would do the same to her as so many others had done every day and every night.

They got into a van waiting for them in a side alley, afraid they might come out of the house and be seen, but they were lucky. They hid Saniya under a blanket in the back of the vehicle and, without accelerating too fast so as not to arouse suspicion, drove out of the neighborhood and out of the city. That had been just a month prior to my first day at the school when I saw Saniya under that orange sari, and now I understand the source of the indescribable pain held in those big, brown eyes.

On to Kharwa Kala

As our time in Indore came to an end, we traveled to Kharwa Kala by car. The temperatures were beyond what any of us had previously experienced and one could almost cut through the humidity in the air. It felt so dense. After eight hours of driving on all kinds of dirt roads, expertly navigated by our driver, Hari, we arrived in Ujjain, eighty-five kilometers from our destination. There, Vijay Chowan led us to a leper colony. It was in a rural area with the property distributed in two large areas: one served as a school for the children of the sick and for boys and girls who, if it were not for this institution, would be homeless in Madhya Pradesh. The other area was reserved as a medical office that specializes in treating the wounds of leprosy patients.

In that place, I realized that there was another way of life different from mine, from ours in our countries. I was moved by how these people dedicated their lives to helping those in need, they took care of them as if they were their own family. They provided those suffering with leprosy with all kinds of health care as they took care of their feet, their hands, and their wounds. Most of the patients went barefoot, and the sores were easily infected due to direct contact with the earth. They did manicures on the women, but how different I saw that act from the one I practiced at my own salon for so many years! Different hands, different intentions, different results. You could see in their faces the gratitude for being cared for, considered as people, and being shown intentional touch.

This experience also opened the eyes of my soul. In India I was doing the same thing, facilitating the care and beauty of the body, as I had done in my work. In my vocation, I received money for it, but here, the payment was manifested in thankfulness, a sincere smile, and a nod of the head that wanted to convey gratitude. That was priceless; it filled my whole heart without the need of a single coin.

We also did activities with the children which were again done on the floor but at least here there were carpets. They showed unusual interest in whatever was proposed. The beginning of a sentence with "Who wants…" was the signal for everyone to raise their hands to offer to do anything. Other women in our team joined the staff in leading sewing groups and made ornaments and accessories for the home and dresses. I was struck again by the joy expressed by so many we encountered, despite all the suffering they had experienced and were still living through.

Providing relaxing massages was another thing I had done in my job. These lepers had known very little physical contact, let alone a safe, soothing touch. When I ran my fingers over their faces and massaged their heads or arms, I noticed the response of their trauma-filled bodies, although the real response, I am convinced, was from their souls. As I touched with my hands it was as if I was touching each person with my very heart. Even as I gave the many massages, I knew in my mind that an irreversible course for my life was beginning and though I did not know the route or even the destination, my new journey, my new purpose, had already begun.

There I was told many stories, unbelievable in the light of modern and Western thinking, that is, for people, who live our daily lives comfortably, calmly, and with our daily needs more than met. As we passed groups of girls, Vinjay would discreetly point out different girls and summarize the hell they had gone through.

"What about the women who help you?"

"Some have gone through similar situations. That one," he pointed to a young woman who was playing games with a group of children, "her name is Naisha. Although you see her young, she was married to a man twenty years older than her. She had three daughters, and her husband decided to sell them to get a good sum of money. She refused, which is unusual in this area, and ran away with her daughters, chased and threatened by her husband and his family. Ramchand rescued her and placed her under his care at this school. Now, her girls are safe and being trained. She has become a leader among the caregivers. She also gives lectures so that people know what is happening and tries to raise awareness that women are human beings and should be treated with dignity, something not easily accepted in this society." Once again, I noticed a young girl who stood out to me and when I asked Vinjay he told me Sanji's horrific story...

It was called the "thousand-year war." It was not new; since the time of the Western Middle Ages, there had been a direct confrontation between Hindu and Muslim radicals. When one attacked, the other responded in kind, so a spiral of unrestrained violence was established. Sometimes it was initiated by Hindu radicals and sometimes by Muslims, but it was always the same. No part of India was spared, although towards the north, possibly due to the proximity of Pakistan, confrontations were even more frequent. The international press highlighted the harsh clashes in New Delhi but ignored those occurring in the towns and villages where the suffering inflicted was even greater. A single allegation from one side against the other served as sufficient cause for retaliation. The authorities spoke of peace, fruitful dialogue, and brotherhood between religions...but nothing could be further from the truth.

Orchha was a city in the heart of the Madhya Pradesh region. Like so many others, it had temples, palaces, gardens, and suburbs where poverty was part of the air that circulated through the streets. In one of these neighborhoods lived Sajani and her family in a dwelling where it seemed that the walls could collapse at any moment. Many window openings were covered with cardboard or plastic to imitate glass. The floor of each house was made of wood and was high from the ground, as floods were frequent at certain times of the year. The roofs hardly stopped the heavy rains filling the narrow streets with mud.

In Sajani's family's living quarters lived her parents and three siblings, two girls and a boy, as well as her father's sister, who lived with them after her husband disowned her for not getting pregnant. Life was monotonous. The father swept streets in the city; the mother was busy taking care of her children, and together they were barely managing to survive.

It had been two days since Sajani had turned seven. She helped her mother and oversaw keeping clean the latrines they shared with three other houses. The families that were closest to each other formed close knit communities. There were barely fifteen long steps between one house and another.

It was seven o'clock in the evening, and the daylight was beginning to fade. Sajani had been playing with her neighbor friends and each were just returning home. The light bulbs were turned on, one per house. Father had not yet arrived, and mother was beginning to prepare their typical dinner of flour porridge and rice.

Five days earlier, in the heart of Orchha, a group of Hindu radicals attacked Muslims gathered around a table for tea. Without saying a word, they approached them simultaneously from two streets and, without any provocation, riddled them with bullets. Everyone knew that sooner rather than later Muslims would launch a counterattack to this massacre; they always did. Those filthy neighborhoods like the one in which Sajani and her family lived were usually too insignificant to be a meaningful target and because the extremists that devised the attacks on both sides did not live in such poverty but in areas with a higher standard of living.

Sajani's mother was stirring the butter in a pan that had been patched several times when she perceived a strange silence as if the sound that came every night from the Western part of the neighborhood had been muffled. There followed shouts, wailing, shrieks, running, and more shouting. Barely a minute or two had passed, and dozens of men in dark clothing, a knife in one hand and a lit torch in the other, emerged from nowhere.

"Run, hide wherever you can!" she yelled at everyone in her home.

"What will you do?" asked Sajani with anguish on her face.

Her mother knew exactly what was going to happen. She could see them through one of the windows: they would throw the lit torches through the windows so they would run away from the fire; then, they would take boys, girls, and adult women and rape them right there, in front of the men. Then they would slit the throats of the men so that they would take with them to the next world the image of their wives and daughters being humiliated, assaulted, and raped. The damage was threefold; they destroyed with fire their few possessions, took revenge on the men, and brought shame to the Hindu society by raping and killing their children.

Sajani encouraged her siblings to leave and told them where they could hide. She knew the area very well. But she did not intend to leave her mother alone as she planned, intending to serve as bait for the revenge-hungry killers. Her siblings ran away, and she heard their screams amidst those of so many children who were running away just like them. At that moment, a lit torch entered through one of the windows, and everything began to burn quickly. It was a premonition of what the house could become—a real funeral pyre. The whole neighborhood was on fire—hundreds of pyres, hundreds of people would die that night.

Sajani and her mother did not want to go out. They knew they would meet death or worse. They soaked themselves with water and lay down on the ground near a window to try to take from the outside the little oxygen that was lacking inside. Two Muslims stormed in and saw an adult woman with a piece of wood in her hands attempting to protect herself and the young girl. The assailants went to grab her, assuming that the girl was dead, possibly suffocated, but just as they were about to push the mother into the street to rape or, who knows, kill her, a piece of burning wood fell on Sajani, causing her to move and get the embers off her exposed skin. The men immediately let go the woman and went for her. They were infamous for raping daughters in front of their parents. The mother, seeing what was about to happen, jumped toward them as if it was the last thing she would do in her life, managing to push them away and separate them from the girl. Immediately, without thinking, she grabbed her daughter, semi-conscious because of the smoke from the burning wood that made the air unbreathable, and with all her strength got her up and through the window and shouted, "Run, Sajani, run!"

Two blows were enough for the mother to fall unconscious on the floor of the burning house. The two men quickly went in search of Sajani. They could not allow her to escape; it would be a humiliation for them. The girl barely managed to get up and, limping from the fall, tried to run away - anywhere but there. It was no use, they caught up with her, knocked her down, and right there, in the light of the bonfire her house had become, with her mother being burned alive inside, they raped her with all the crudeness imaginable. After they brutally tore her innocence apart they didn't know if she was alive or not. They didn't care about that detail. They left her there, covered in mud, her childhood destroyed, almost dead. Almost.

Ramchand explained that in their outreach to neighborhoods, the teams not only provided food, comfort, and basic health interventions but also tried to find out if in that area there were any girls in likelihood of being sold to pimps, abused by family members, or subjected to a young, arranged marriage. In this way, they were able to rescue many girls, who were incorporated into the children's schools, where they tried to give meaning to their lives, knowing that not all of them could change their destinies.

They knew that after an attack of extreme violence between radical Hindus and Muslims, not only were their direct victims but also orphaned, abandoned, or lost children which easily became targets to predatory pimps. So immediately after hearing of the attack in Orchha they formed a team. Upon arriving they looked around and found that there was nothing left, no one alive. They came across Sajani's naked, bleeding, and burned body, at first believing she was dead, but miraculously she managed to blink. She was carried away with the utmost care, given all possible medical attention, and thus, she began the long process of restoring her body and soul at the Kharwa Kala School for displaced children.

Returning Home, Forever Changed

I never imagined anything could impact my very existence as much as this trip had. Here, shocked by everything I have experienced, in the seat of the plane that was taking me back to Spain, all the images I have lived through, all the faces that have spoken to me without words, all those smiles that enclosed real tragedies, went through my mind.

I would like to close my eyes and imagine that it was a dream, an unreal sequence belonging to a film not yet shot. But no, I cannot close them. I cannot unsee that which I have seen. On the contrary, I want to open them and start a new life, trying to help those who, like the Hindu girls, suffer degradation in so many ways, just because they are female. We believe these tragedies only occur in distant, remote, almost exotic places, where poverty is the modus vivendi of the population. In short, in places where we are not; we are not forced to see or acknowledge the reality. But I am also convinced that we have voluntarily placed a self-imposed blindfold over our eyes so we can more easily ignore the pain that does surround us in our own cities and neighborhoods. We pretend we do not perceive, and we go about our lives protecting ourselves from the pain and poverty of others, accepting that the lot in life for some is simply to be less fortunate.

I am convinced that in my city there is a Varsha who, abandoned to her fate, laughs so as not to show the hell inside her; sick in body and soul, praying for good, dedicated and efficient people to help her; many girls like Saniya, marked by prostitution, are taken through the trafficking and enslaved; girls like Sajani are raped, destroyed, broken in body and soul, who has lost any sense of self; and also women like Naisha, who rebel against this criminal barbarism against girls, risking their own lives to prevent as many girls as possible from falling into the mafia's nets or saving them from the chains that already have them inhumanly imprisoned.

Nothing is the same from today. I cannot continue my way as if nothing had happened. These human beings deserve a chance to be restored full of hope and enthusiasm to know and feel another way of existence, a chance to be redeemed, a chance for beauty to rise from ashes.

I don't know how, but I must try. As soon as this plane touches down, with everything I have experienced and learned in India from Ramchand's organization, I plan to save as many girls as possible from their living-hell. My compassionate humanity compels me to action and my faith demands it.

Brainstorming Begins

The trip had come to an end and outside the airport Sara said her goodbyes to her Indian hosts, her new American friends, and her brother-in-law. Overwhelmed with emotions from the whole experience, she reached up, took Damian's cheeks in her hands, looked into his eyes and at the time could only offer a single word, "Gracias."

As the only traveler from the team headed to Europe, Sara was alone with just her thoughts as she sat in the terminal awaiting her flight. Already she had ideas swirling in her head, places where she wanted to go and things, she could do for those women who were victims of trafficking for sexual exploitation. If there was one thing she knew for sure, it was that this was the twenty-first century version of slavery.

Enslaved people were part of history: Egypt, Greece, Imperial Rome, the Middle Ages, the Renaissance, and the Modern Age... always. In each era, they were designated with different statuses, different considerations, and legislation adapted to each culture. Still, there was a common factor invariable throughout the centuries: exploitation of human beings for different purposes, sometimes the result of poverty, sometimes the living casualties of war, and sometimes simply dehumanized due to the color of one's skin.

Boarding was delayed by several hours. Known as a woman of action, Sara found a Wi-Fi zone and set to work. She began to download on her laptop all the news, documents, stories, and information she could find on human trafficking. She quickly learned that trafficking was a complex issue and included several kinds of forced labor, but she focused her research on articles related to sexual exploitation.

Sara was downloading all that information on her computer, aware that it would be impossible to have an Internet connection during the flight. She bought a notebook and began to write down ideas, phrases, data, impressions, and notes...hopes of what she might implement when she returned to Spain. At the time there was little order or construct but she was content knowing that for now she was just brainstorming.

"From the 12th to the 19th century, twelve million Africans were enslaved."

"In the last thirty years, thirty million adult women and girls have been sexually exploited by international mafias."

"<u>No demand, no supply.</u>" She underlined this phrase as a key idea.

"Prostitution is the oldest craft in the world." "Craft? Profession? Dignity?" wrote Sara next to the phrase.

She quickly went to look for a document prepared by a Spanish ministry:

"90 percent of the prostitutes who work in Spain are victims of trafficking in women". Next to it, she scribbled five exclamation points, a mixture of astonishment and indignation: "!!!!!"

"World Health Organization report: 62 percent of prostitutes who are victims of international trafficking were raped when they were minors." Every time she wrote one of these sentences, she had to stop, take a deep breath, and look out the airplane window. How vast the land that reached her sight was; under those gray clouds how many women were enslaved as victims in a life they could not escape?

"It's not a professional issue. It's not even a money issue. It's a human rights issue."

"Ninety-four percent of the world's countries have something to do with trafficking women, either as a source of women, transit, or a destination for exploitation."

"They told me that I had a debt with them of 600 euros, that in a year it would be paid off, for sure. I've been in debt for five years, and they still don't consider it finished; now it's 3000 euros…"

"Mirta (real name hidden) came to our organization and told us that she wanted to get out: right at that moment, her new life began." This sentence, taken from the statement of a victim of trafficking who decided that she could no longer stand it all and had bravely found a way to escape. She wrote underneath: You can get out! There is a way out!

She closed her notebook and laptop, stared through the window towards the horizon, and thought that this was her mission: to try to get as many women as possible out of that hell, to give them the possibility to start a new life, to give them back the ability to decide, to become people again. She closed her eyes, and her mind was already plotting a plan of action. When she landed, the priority was to tell Diego. A new life would begin for both.

"And what can we do?" asked Diego.

He had listened sympathetically as he had been bombarded with ideas, non-stop, for the past hour. Sara scanned her notes and went from one page of her notebook to the next with sincere passion. Her arguments were all aimed at the same goal: to give these girls back the dignity that had been ripped from them; to treat them as people, not objects.

"It's just you and me. Do you think we can take on these mafias alone? It's David against Goliath," said Diego.

"Who was the defeated one?" challenged Sara in return.

"We need help."

"Of course! I have some ideas for it…"

"Hold up, let's go slowly!" interrupted Diego. "The first thing will be to see if there is anyone else doing anything about it and contact them."

"Red Cross. I've already looked it up," said Sara enthusiastically.

"So, let's talk to the people in charge, and we will continue to come up with ideas to carry out, but we have to start with them."

Reaching Out to the Red Cross

We came out of that first meeting with two things clear: there were many things to learn and there were many safety protocols that must be followed. On the other hand, we realized from the very first moment that we could insert ourselves into that network of help, focus on serving the enslaved women, and be another source of support that would complement the great work of the Red Cross. We saw people who put real soul into what they were doing, and we believed we could contribute our own practical support and genuine love that was essential in the task.

"We want to be part of this, immerse ourselves in this world, and participate in everything that will help get the girls out of this hell," said Sara.

"You will have to take a training course to prepare you as a volunteer."

"We will do whatever it takes."

"We see you are very enthusiastic. Your intention is praiseworthy, but we have to face reality. We can take care of the girls in their environment, bring them hygiene items such as condoms and wipes, some food, and even some clothes so that they do not get cold on those winter nights outdoors in the industrial parks. We can inform them of the procedures they must follow to legalize their refugee status in Spain, since many of them do not have a passport, and we can tell them where they should go if they need our help…"

"Are you exploring the possibility that they might want to get out?" interrupted Sara.

"It's up to them, but practically speaking, there is little we can do about it. Sara, it is extremely difficult for any of these girls to get out of that world."

"Do you have the budget that funds your expenses?" asked Diego.

"A very limited one. I'll give you an example—we don't have the money to buy a big thermos to bring hot cocoa."

The following week they started the volunteer course. At the end of the course, Sara and Diego went for a coffee at a nearby cafe.

"We have to get them out, as many as we can, even if they are few, but those few will have a new, dignified life," Sara began to say.

"You've heard them—it's very difficult."

"But not impossible." Diego already knew that Sara was going to do whatever it took to make her dream, her personal conviction, a reality. He recalled all the years that she had supported his own efforts in serving those in their community and decided then and there that he would adopt an equal commitment to whatever this new endeavor would look like, that they were in it together.

In the months that followed they continued to train with and learn as much as possible from their mentors at the Red Cross.

Diego recounts, "We were received with all the kindness in the world. Our intention was to gather information but also to propose things, to try to be part of a caring community where everyone would play his or her role with the goal of saving young women from slavery."

"We were given precise details of all the protocols that served as the basis for their work. The team gathered in what looked like a special ops room where everything had its proper procedure, even with abbreviations, signs, symbols, and flow charts. Nothing was left to improvisation; everything had a place in those protocols. We would ask about possible scenarios and they would tell us what bureaucratic protocol to initiate…Plan 462, Paragraph 3, Point #5, and so on…

We realized the importance of these protocols. They were essential for everything to go well. But we also imagined that not everything could be accounted for in a procedure manual, but rather there needed to be room for flexibility and timely responsiveness.

"We were extremely nervous as we prepared to go out with the Red Cross for the first time. At the organization's headquarters, there was a van with the unmistakable cross symbol; we were given red identification vests with the Red Cross logo bordered by a double white line. Our objective that night was to observe, take notes, and get an idea of how it all worked. We helped pack the kits that would be given to each girl: wet wipes, lubricating gel, condoms, and a small bottle of mouthwash. In addition, several boxes were loaded with juices, muffins, croissants, and fruit smoothies."

"We have brought something," said Diego to the person who had guided them in their successive interviews.

He went to his vehicle and removed a large package from the trunk, a box approximately one meter high. They helped him unload it. When they opened the lid, they saw its contents: a thermos with ten liters of liquid capacity. They looked at each other in amazement, not knowing what to say.

"With the cold weather, they could use some hot cocoa," said Diego.

"Thank you very much, but—"

"It's a gift, don't worry," interrupted Diego so the recipient didn't have to say anything.

With the van loaded, they started their journey. It was 10:10 at night, and the destination was an industrial park. Everyone knew prostitutes, pimps and customers inhabited the area in the evening, but everyone looked the other way.

Luisa, who oversaw the operation that night, explained that the young women tend to gather together in certain areas based on their national origin and that they always follow the same predictable route through the industrial park.

They first approached a group of three young women clearly of African origin. The women moved toward the vehicle and the volunteers got out and opened the cargo doors of the van. Sara and Diego watched everything, how Luisa and her partner acted, how long they were at each stop, everything. The volunteers distributed the clearly coveted hygiene kits and asked each girl if she wanted anything to eat or drink. Luisa tried to engage with each young woman to learn what she could and always ended with the same sentence, "Well, take care, and you know where we are."

After only a few minutes had passed they went to another area where the Romanian women were located and the scene repeated itself, though this group was less extroverted than the Nigerian women. Finally, they ended the route with a stop at a corner that was filled with native Spanish speaking women that they later learned were from various Latin American countries. While communication was easier with this group, in general they seemed more reluctant to reveal much personal information, either real or fictitious but rather tried to retain as much anonymity as possible while still receiving the handouts.

At 2:05 a.m., they finished the route through the streets of the industrial park. They returned to the headquarters to unload all the leftover material. They promised they would wash the thermos Sara and Diego had given them the next day.

"What did you think, Diego?"

He tarried in answering. He knew that that world existed—everyone knew it—but it was the first time he had entered that jungle, and the evening had taken them deep inside. He could not put words to what he had seen and, above all, to what he had felt.

"Why were they smiling?" Sara asked herself, putting voice to a thought she had when she saw those girls, knowing their terrible plight, but they were smiling.

"Their smiles, Sara, were empty," answered Diego, still looking straight ahead, holding the steering wheel of his vehicle, trying to find the emotional strength to make the solemn drive home.

Brave Baby Steps

They continued to go out with the Red Cross on several occasions. Having given it much thought and prayer, they were increasingly convinced that they could use all that they had learned from the Red Cross volunteers and design a similar systematic approach to serving the women. While the work of the Red Cross was solid, consistent and well executed, they saw that bureaucratic and organizational limitations hindered the agency's ability to take that vital next step in seeking a way to assist women who were ready to find a way to leave the life of slavery. So, while they knew they were making a difference in caring for these women on the streets, it was not the lifesaving rescue that Sara was so passionately pursuing.

They devised a strategy based on the protocols they had learned but without so much bureaucracy. To set out on their own also meant they had no other option than to fund the activities out of their own meager retirement funds; a sacrifice that seemed insignificant in comparison to the suffering Sara had seen.

And so came the first outing alone, previously communicated and agreed upon with the Red Cross. Nerves were once again tightening their throats. They had learned much but still felt unqualified to take on such an endeavor on their own. But despite their doubts they loaded the van with croissants, muffins, juices, hot chocolate (they had also bought a large thermos for themselves), and hygiene kits. At 10:00 p.m., they began the first chapter of a story whose consequences they had not even imagined that night.

When they arrived at the industrial park, they followed the same order they had learned. First, they entered the area of the Nigerians and stopped the van on the corner where the ladies were. When they saw Diego at the wheel, they thought he was a client so several of them approached to offer their services. When they saw Sara, they were surprised, but they had already experienced all kinds of situations and assumed the clients came for a threesome or some other sexual fantasy. When Diego and Sara emerged from the van and opened the back doors the girls understood they were Red Cross volunteers. It was cold that January night, and the girls appreciated the gifts.

Beyond providing the practical relief, Sara was determined to do all she could to make a connection with each girl that might lead to a willingness to trust.

"What is your name?" asked Sara to a girl as she filled a cup with hot chocolate.

"Julia. And you?"

"Sara. And this is Diego. How are you holding up the night?"

"For now, all great. It won't get lively until twelve o'clock or so," said Julia as she glanced sideways at her companions.

"Have you been here long?" Sara's voice was gentle, with no hint of an interrogation.

"One year, but some of them..." she pointed to three others, "have been here for more than two years."

At that moment, Sara had a spontaneous idea pop into her head and before she knew it, the words spilled from her mouth, or really, her soul. While not planned, the action would be key for the future.

"Write down my phone number. You don't need to give me yours." Sara wanted to gain the woman's trust without Julia believing that she was being controlled. "If you need anything or if you want to talk to me about anything, don't hesitate to call me, at any time."

Julia was somewhat surprised. Someone, possibly for the first time since she arrived in this hell, was offering her something in exchange for nothing, simply giving away help. She didn't know what to say. She looked at the other girls, who had heard everything. They each put forth a skeptical look. They were suspicious of everything and everyone. Since they left Nigeria, no one had been trustworthy, in fact, everything had been violent, deceitful, demeaning.

"Here." Sara handed them a piece of paper with her cell phone number on it since she could see that Julia was not taking the initiative.

"Thank you." She took it and tucked it into a fold of her scantily attired look.

"Take care, girls!"

They got into the van and headed down another street. Diego stopped the vehicle in a place where there didn't seem to be any girls.

"We have taken the first step, Diego; we cannot stop. I don't know if what I have done will have repercussions, but we have to try. I hope they call! It would be a way to open the door to give them something they are surely missing: the opportunity to be free again and regain their dignity." Diego had his concerns, but in his heart, he could not argue against Sara's actions because he knew it was the right, loving thing to do. Diego had been a man of faith all his life and in this moment, he knew that to continue this work would require more trust in God's protection than he had ever imagined. Sara clearly was full of faith and without fear, so he resigned himself to match hers.

For the first few months, they went out in coordination with the Red Cross volunteers but as they became more confident in the field, they moved more and more independently. They also learned much more about how the sex industry worked and the role that pimps and the mafia played in the lives of the girls. From time to time, they saw a suspicious car, half-hidden behind a fence or a container, always with one or two men inside, watching their area of influence. They decided two things: to identify themselves with red vests and white banners attached to the side mirrors and to stay inside the van for as long as possible. It was important for Diego to be seen as a man who did not want their services, but someone friendly, even paternal. From the driver's seat, he could see if there was a car prowling the area. He copied its license plate number in case something happened, to be able to report it to the police or get out of there as quickly as possible.

Little by little, they gained the girls' trust, regardless of their nationality or shared language. They were coming to understand the characteristics of each group of girls and realized that the ways of talking to them, approaching them, and earning their trust were somewhat different.

The first sign that they were doing well was on that night when they arrived at the traffic circle where four Romanian girls were working.

"Hi, Mommy!"

That word boomed in Sara's ears like a thunderclap that told her she had taken another step closer to them.

"Poppy, aren't you getting out of the car? Are you cold?" they teased him. Immediately Diego got out to share in the fun that the Romanian girls were having.

Sara had given her phone number to the girls she saw most willing to talk, but she learned that they had distributed it among their companions. And they did call. Some ask about services available, others ask for some medication, and one even asked her to accompany her to the doctor. Sara answered all of them, and they did everything within their means to provide for every request.

But they still needed to find a way to help them get out of that world of slavery. And not just off the streets themselves but to get them help to recover from that hellish existence and begin to rebuild their lives. The words of the Red Cross volunteer were still echoing when he explained to them all the existing legal protocols:

"Do you explore the possibility that they may want to leave?"

That was the key question Sara asked them.

"It's up to them, and there is little we can do about it. Sara, it is extremely difficult for any of the girls to get out of that world."

This was the recognition of powerlessness and a lack of infrastructure to provide a future for women who decided to leave.

Sara and Diego were very clear in their resolve: they had to know more about how to get to the point of rescue, how those girls became enslaved in the first place, and investigate if there were other people helping girls in other places, even in other countries.

"Multidisciplinary Conference on Trafficking in Europe. Bucharest, Romania, April 2015."

"Look, Sara, Damian sent it to me." Diego read an email to her. "He says that it would be interesting for you to attend, that we could learn a lot about the subject."

Diego had kept his brother up to date on all the progress they had made since Sara's return from the trip to India where this passion was first ignited.

Sara read the information carefully and did not hesitate for a moment.

"How do I register?" she asked with readiness in her voice.

The opportunity to attend the conference and learn more adding even more enthusiasm to Sara's disposition. Registration, flights and a hotel were booked less than 24 hours later, and she continued her online research, especially reading European legislation on the subject of trafficking, guidelines from some governments to try to prevent it, etc.

An Unexpected Interruption

The couple continued their weekly trips to the industrial park and Sara was focusing on preparing for the conference that was just days away when a newspaper headline brought an unexpected interruption. As was his morning routine, Diego enjoyed his coffee while scrolling through the news on his tablet.

"Sara, look at today's newspaper!" exclaimed Diego.

Sara read the words and at the same time began to tremble:

"Man arrested for trying to strangle a prostitute he robbed in the industrial park" Not waiting for her to read the entire article, Diego quickly commented, "From the area they describe, she is one of the Romanian girls."

Sara automatically picked up her phone and called the number of one of the girls.

"Oh, my! It was Lorena!" said the young woman between tears and sobbing sentences that were almost impossible to understand.

"Don't worry. We will go to meet her and help. That scoundrel cannot go unpunished," Sara reassured forcefully.

They knew Lorena and had learned bits and pieces of her story from their many visits. Lorena's circumstances were different from the others who gathered at that traffic circle. She was brought in deceived, like the rest of her companions, but she had already finished paying the supposed debt that the pimps had established. She was now with a man, quite a bit older than her, who, also according to her somewhat disjointed account, was protecting her. She had decided to continue sending money to her parents. She hoped to buy a piece of land, build a house for them, and return to live there. Sara and Diego were both unclear and skeptical about that story, but they neither challenged her nor did they expose their doubts about the man who was allegedly taking care of her.

They informed the Red Cross who the victim of the assault was and then were able to inquire by various means and eventually located her. They were shocked to see how she was, both physically and emotionally. They told Lorena they would support her through the entire process of pressing charges against the man, emphasizing that the assault could not go unpunished. Diego had many connections in the community, and he reached out to a lawyer he knew, and she agreed to take the case as an advocate for Lorena, who as a non-citizen had little legal standing.

Doors Open, Air Flows In

When Sara boarded the plane to Romania, she had the feeling that this could be another key point in the project she and Diego were creating. Her trip to India was the genesis, the spark that ignited the initial fire inside her. Now she was going to explore why the girls they visited in the industrial park left their countries, how they arrived in Spain and the details of their enslavement. She also wanted to know what European governments were doing to prevent this scourge. She would not accept that it was impossible for a woman to get out of that world. She knew there was a solution; she just had to find what it was.

The room was big. She didn't think there would be so many people. Sara sat in the middle rows to best see the projected images. The opening session began with a few words from the Conference Director, a member of the European Union's group on human trafficking in Europe. The first image projected struck the center of Sara's chest and she read the following:

"In the last year, 20,532 victims of trafficking were registered in the European Union. More than half (56%) of the cases of trafficking of human beings were for the purpose of sexual exploitation, which remains the most widespread form of trafficking. Women and girls accounted for more than two-thirds (68%) of the recognized victims; almost a quarter of the registered victims (23%) were minors; 44% of the victims were citizens of the European Union.
The top five EU countries by nationality of registered victims were Romania, Hungary, the Netherlands, Poland, and Bulgaria. The top five non-EU countries by nationality of recorded victims were Nigeria, Albania, Vietnam, China, and Eritrea."

She mentally reviewed the origin of the girls in the industrial park: Romanian, Nigerian, Polish, and others that declined to share their nationality. She quickly thought of something the Red Cross volunteers had told them: in the clubs, Moroccan and Latin American girls predominated; they had not yet visited these places, but they eventually would, no doubt.
The next presentation dealt with the types of exploitation of human beings in Europe, in addition to sexual exploitation: labor exploitation, marriages, forced begging, and criminal threats.
They described the routes of extraction from those countries, transportation in inhumane conditions, humiliation during the

journey, types of deception used to take the women away from their familiar environments, and the issue of the debts that the pimps demanded from the girls at the place of arrival and that they had to pay, using all kinds of tricks to make the amount owed grow larger and larger.

Another of the presentations defined the victims of trafficking for the purpose of sexual exploitation as a "commodity" that generates billions of dollars a year worldwide. In the document distributed among conference participants, Sara quickly looked up the data referring to Spain and opened her eyes in astonishment: the trafficking business for sexual exploitation in Spain moved between three and five million euros a day, more than drug and arms trafficking combined.

There was a break in the session —it was time for a coffee. Sara went out to the restaurant area; she was like a zombie. In her head, the data, the descriptions, the strategies of the mafias, the girls— yes, especially them—she could not avoid seeing the faces of the ones she was getting to know more and more in the industrial park parading in her mind. She was so absorbed in her own thoughts that she didn't realize she had expressed herself aloud:

"What a pity that it is so difficult for them to get out of that hell!"

"Excuse me, are you Spanish?" asked a female voice next to her.

"Yes, my name is Sara," she replied.

"I'm from Madrid. My name is Claudia." She kissed her twice by way of introduction. "Do you work in an anti-trafficking organization?"

"Well, my husband and I collaborate with the Red Cross, but we have some ideas of our own, which we believe could complement and expand what they are already doing. I could summarize it as 'less protocol and more soul.'"

"I like it. Besides, I can see in your eyes that you are excited about it." Claudia offered a broad smile. "Shall we meet later for lunch, and you can tell me about these ideas?"

"Of course, but what organization do you belong to?" Sara sensed that she was a woman with clear and strong convictions, she didn't know why, but she could see it in her face.

"I'll tell you all about it later. Come on, they are already calling for the next session."

The restaurant was small, on a discreet street with little foot traffic. They sat at a secluded table to talk in peace and quiet, with no prying ears around. A faint light was breaking through the clouds, which had been threatening to pour in all morning, and entered through the window next to the table, almost like a premonition of something extraordinary that would come out of the conversation that would soon take place.

"Like you, it was also my husband and I who started our project," Claudia began to answer the question Sara had asked at their first introduction. "I was very happy to hear your definition of your project because ours was and is very similar."

Her story caught Sara's attention immediately; she needed to hear those words. She was becoming more and more hopeful that meeting Claudia would be a milestone in her life.

"We created a team of volunteers, first a few people, both young and old, men and women, all united by a common desire to help. I explained our idea to them, and they embarked with us on a ship that would sail through turbulent seas, go through unyielding storms and gather in its cabins people who had been harassed, enslaved, humiliated, and abused."

Just then the waiter arrived and waited patiently for the decision of both women.

"Do you visit any industrial parks or go to clubs?" asked Sara, eager to know the details.

"We started with the industrial parks, but my heart from the beginning was to be involved in what we call after care. To create a safe place for the women who want to be rescued from slavery to get a fresh start at life through trauma counseling, legal assistance for their documentation, and ultimately skills training. So now I work on the receiving end of people like you who are more on the front lines.

These words landed so very well on Sara's heart; finally, another piece of this mysterious puzzle had been found. "I know we help the girls. We give them advice on hygiene and help to legalize their papers. Many of them do not have passports; the pimps took them away to keep them trapped in their net; we also give them the opportunity to talk, to unburden themselves if they want to, and we offer them the assurance that we care about them, that we will do everything possible for them. But if any of them say they want to leave, we don't have a way to get them out. We have even thought about rescue, but I don't know if it is more of a fantasy movie than feasible in reality?

"Most of the time rescuing the women does look and feel like something right out of a movie," said Claudia with a smile.

"Tell me, have you been involved in rescuing any women?" Sara asked.

"Yes, I have been involved in quite a few. We started by networking, talking to all kinds of people, officials, relief agencies, churches, and individuals. Non-governmental organizations (NGO's) got involved, people who, like us, were moved by all this, even some religious leaders have encouraged participation by their congregants."

"We established an action protocol that we adjust according to the circumstances of the woman being rescued. When our contacts tell us that there is a girl who wants to be rescued, wherever she is, we go and extract her from her environment. Perhaps this is the most critical moment of the process. It is the part of the 'movie' in which we must be most decisive and careful. Then the transfer. That is where discretion comes in, where it is essential not to always do the same thing, to have the route planned, but without giving clues to anyone, often not even to our own team; they know it and understand perfectly well the need to limit details."

"We take them to an initial safe house and give them time to decompress and in some cases, detox from substances. There we have doctors, psychologists, and social workers to assist and help guide them throughout the process."

"Once their physical and emotional needs have been addressed, the next phase consists of starting the process of legalizing their papers, so they have proper documentation to be in Spain. This takes much time, so it is necessary to begin as soon as possible. We then also begin the process of helping each woman imagine what a future in this culture and supporting herself independently would look like. We finance courses comparable to vocational training: hairdressing, sewing, design... From there, depending on each girl's skills and circumstances, we help them find a job. This is often the moment when they really feel free, when their life depends on themselves, and they know they are responsible for it."

Sara had listened with rapt attention to Claudia's summary description and then exclaimed, "That's what we're missing!"

"Well, there is always a possibility of collaboration, even of integrating you into this system, to combine our efforts of providing hope and life." Sara could not believe what Claudia was proposing, but she saw clearly that this was the way to go.

It became cloudy again outside the restaurant. The trees began to sway in the increasingly strong wind and a door behind them swung wide open from a big gust.

"Well, the door has opened," said Claudia with some astonishment.

And the air has entered...

A Front Row Seat

Sara returned with the same excitement and nerves she felt after her trip to India. She told Diego everything she learned at the conference, and, above all, what Claudia had told her and her proposal to adopt her system and work together. As she had sensed at the beginning of the trip, the conference and Claudia marked a before and after in their project. She believed they had found the missing piece of the puzzle; now, everything could fit into place.

Sara's enthusiasm continued to be contagious, and Diego continued to take on her passion and make it his own. He read everything he could get his hands on about trafficking and organized a computer file with everything that was published on the subject, whether from official or unofficial sources.

"Claudia invited us to go there so we can experience first-hand the whole process, the after-care homes, the people who work with them, and those groups of volunteers she always refers to as the team."

Once again, Diego was in full support and within a week they had decided to travel across the country for the visit, but the journey also symbolically set the course for what was to be the foundation of their lives from that moment on.

Claudia and her husband lived in a spacious, comfortable house, and they were a content couple, despite the many moving pieces in their lives. They sat in the living room and continued to talk about the work. Sara wanted Claudia to describe it again, in case she hadn't caught all the details, and for Diego to hear it firsthand. The next day they would go to one of the after-care homes.

It was a cozy dwelling where three Nigerian women lived. The first thing Diego noticed was the looks on their faces. He mentioned it to Sara when they separated from the group as the girls showed them what they were doing in their learning workshops.

"Have you noticed how different the eyes of these women are from those of the Nigerian women in the industrial park?" said Diego in a low voice.

"Yes, they transmit joy. They are not empty like the ones we see on our nights out," said Sara, accompanying her words with a sense of admiration and hope.

Claudia made the introductions of Sandra, Esther, and Doris and then in return, "Meet Sara and Diego, they are also helping girls like you. They would like to hear about how your life has changed since you came here."

Sandra was the boldest in the group and she felt safe in the presence of this older couple and so she began to share. Before she was rescued, she knew she desperately desired to escape her living-hell, but she did not have any idea how it might be possible. Diego wanted to ask her what led her to leave Nigeria and how she got to Spain, but Claudia had warned them beforehand that they should not inquire about their past because it would trigger trauma. Instead, she encouraged them to hear how they were looking to the future.

"They treat us very well here, like people. They accompany us to the doctors and legal appointments, so we do not have to go alone. It is like they have given me a key to a door that will lead me back to a normal life, something I thought had become impossible."

"I had always been very good at doing my friends' hair, and here they offered me a hairdressing course. Look, these are pictures of hairstyles I did during the training course." She proudly showed them the images as if they were works of art.

Sara said, "Those hairstyles are in fashion and very popular among young women." A beaming smile spread across Sandra's face as her heart soaked in Sara's words.

Seeing the success of Sandra's story, Esther began to speak, "I was the first of the three of us to arrive here. They taught me how to weave and make dresses, a lady came to give me sewing lessons, and..." She looked at Claudia for the Spanish word she wanted to say.

"Tailoring," prompted Claudia

"Yes, tailoring, it's just that I still find it hard to speak the language well. And what I'm most happy about is that I'm an apprentice in a clothing repair shop. The owner of the store has me on a trial basis and says that maybe she can offer me a permanent position. See this dress I'm wearing; I made it all by myself." Sara praised her handiwork and again, the young woman soaked up the affirmation.

"I came last," said Doris, "I still don't know what I can do well, I'm pretty clumsy, but I'm trying." She looked down sheepishly.

"No, Doris," Claudia interrupted, "we are still finding out what you could do for a living, that's all. You know how to cook very well, you can prepare delicious dishes, and I think you could study cuisine. Sara and Diego will be here for a few days, so you can make them a recipe from your country."

"I'm going to make Jollof rice. I think I'll be good at it."

Claudia looked at Sara and Diego and said, "You will love it - it's finger-licking good!"

This time it was Diego who responded by jovially patting his belly and expressed his excitement over the impending feast.

Next, they spoke with the psychologist who worked with the home. She told them about the adaptation process and the guidelines she followed with them. Sara and Diego diligently took as many notes as they could, knowing they would bring order to it all when they returned home.

"Before making future plans," the psychologist tried to summarize, "it is necessary to pay attention to the crucial moment of the beginning of the process. From the moment they decide to leave, through the experience of rescue and the fear of being discovered, until they reach a new, safe environment it is like a non-stop race. It is imperative to give the women time to decompress, to allow the healing to begin organically, to just be in a state of living where nothing is required of them. After some days it will seem that they have come down from such a high state of alert and are beginning to settle but be prepared for re-bound occurrences of heightened emotions as their minds and bodies continue to relive the trauma and wrestle with doubts. It is not uncommon for women at this time to be tempted to go back. Psychologically there is a false sense of safety in returning to what they had grown accustomed to, as awful as it was, rather than facing the uncertainty of the future. And then there is the issue of helping them work through their shame."

This insight from the psychologist was incredibly helpful but also rather overwhelming to take in. But Sara was determined to glean as much as she could from those who had gone before her in this work, so she set aside the emotion welling up inside her and pressed on.

"Claudia, a question. You have told us that while they are going through the whole process, the legalization of their documents is being sought. Do the police know all this?" It was a question Sara had been wanting to ask for a long time.

"Of course, collaboration is of the utmost importance. Otherwise, nothing would go right. When an opportunity for rescue comes, we immediately notify them, and they are aware and supportive from the time we get her off the streets through the subsequent processing of their legal situation."

"What role could we play in all this?" Sara wanted to get to the heart of the matter as soon as possible.

Claudia had anticipated this question and readily offered a reply, "I think you should form a team in your area. We don't have anyone in that region to execute the girls' departure and integrate them into the usual rescue channels."

Sara and Diego looked at each other with eagerness, with that complicity that characterized them, both smiling with satisfaction: the puzzle was beginning to come together.

"Excuse me, I have a phone call. It's from one of our groups on the Eastern coast," Claudia retreated to an adjoining room and could be heard giving directions to initiate the rescue protocol.

Upon her return she said, "A girl is ready to leave, and this very night, the rescue operation has begun. It seems this is a Divine appointment; you will have a front row seat to see everything in action."

Nasha decided to get out of hell. She had suffered slavery in that industrial park for four years, night after night, humiliation after humiliation. The pimps imposed on her a debt of three thousand euros as the transfer from Nigeria had been very expensive. It was completely ignored how much she suffered during the journey, almost a year since she had left her city with the promise of a job in Europe so that she could send money to her parents and move them to live with her in the future. Repeated rapes, confinement in filthy camps, fear of being murdered, more rapes, mistreatment, abandonment, and kidnapping until she reached the coast of Andalusia after a crossing on a barge that was shipwrecked at sea just two kilometers off the coast. Half of those who were with her on that boat had died, drowned, the rest...she did not remember anything, not even how she was rescued from the water by some men and taken to that dive where she was placed in a room behind a locked door that both practically and symbolically began her enslavement.

In the wretched weeks that followed her debt increased. She was fined for low productivity, consuming too many medicines for her pain (the result of the violence suffered during her trip through Africa,) and the inflated prices of hygiene products imposed by the pimps. Soon her debt had reached five thousand euros.

The body has a limit, and so does the soul; she had almost been destroyed, but there was still a little spark left in her that remained simply out of self-preservation. She had received the comfort and support of volunteers many times at the industrial park. They gave her warmth and hope, they never forced her to choose, but they offered her a chance for a way out if she was willing to take it. One day that spark was fueled just enough for her to pass a handwritten note to Ana, one of the volunteers. I am willing, it simply said on the back of a bus ticket.

"How do you proceed now?" asked Sara, not wanting to miss a single detail.

"Our local team gets her out of there and takes her by road to a secret safe house where she will stay for one night to calm her down and prepare for her arrival here," Claudia told her.

"Do you take women out immediately when she proposes?"

"No. First, they inform us, and then we do an interview and a questionnaire to make sure their intentions and cooperation are clear. Keep in mind that some will try to use this way to evade the police for actual crimes committed or they can be trying to leverage one pimp or one faction of the mafia against another. It is a balance of making sure we understand their situation while at the same time extracting them as soon as possible before they either change their mind or their handlers become suspicious."

Mafia groups controlled the area where Nasha lived and worked, they knew who went in and out of it. After studying the times and patterns the team knew they couldn't pick her up there as it was too heavily guarded. They had confirmed with the authorities that she did not have any pending legal cases and informed them of the plan to pick her up as soon as she got off the bus at the industrial park.

Around six o'clock in the evening she would take a line 4 bus and get off at the stop just 200 meters from the industrial park. The nondescript car would be waiting just behind a grove of trees, ready to leave as soon as she arrived. Nasha was instructed to go quickly to the area of trees, get in the back of the car and lay down on the seat so as not to be seen.

The bus arrived at the established meeting point, but Nasha did not get off it. The pimp had received a warning from his contact inside the apartment. There was always a girl who informed the handlers of everything, and she had reported that Nasha was very restless and nervous and that morning she hugged her companions for no reason and told them that she loved them very much. That afternoon the pimp sent a controller to the apartment to drive her by car to the industrial park; she would not have to go by bus.

"Ugh, the extraction didn't take place," Claudia lamented.

"What happened?" Diego asked.

"They must have suspected something and put a lookout on her. She sent a telephone message to our group, who are already working on a new plan. They think that tomorrow they will try again. In these cases, we must act as quickly as possible, if not, suspicions will be greater and greater."

"This time they are going to try to rescue her in the middle of work. They don't think she has too much surveillance there. When a client arrives, they go to an area hidden from view. They are going to try to rescue her there. Our group in the area is well respected among the girls. They appreciate them a lot and trust them. They have never let them down; that is the key to almost everything."

That night, Claudia was restless, unable to sleep. She exchanged messages with her contacts on the coast, who informed her of the new plans and possible risks. They had already alerted the police of the changes in place and time. Even though this was not their own operation, and they had a lot to still learn before attempting to execute a rescue, Sara and Diego were attentive and engaged in the details and supported the effort through their prayers.

The following afternoon, the man from the previous day came to pick Nasha up again. The contact had already informed Nasha of their new plan - a young man would be driving-up to claim her services, and she would direct him to the usual place, where the extraction team would be with their vehicle. Obviously, the young man was an undercover accomplice.

Natasha took up her usual position on the corner and the controller was stationed in his car in the dark shadows where he could see the girls clearly. A car pulled up and all three of the women approached to offer their services. The decoy played his role perfectly, he even asked one of them to lower her bra. He pretended to wrestle with the hard choice and eventually chose Nasha. In a voice loud enough for her companions to hear she told him to follow her around back where they would have a great time. He parked the car in a place that could not be seen from where the controller was watching and then met her there.

A dark vehicle was waiting for her. She turned around and thanked the "hook" then literally threw herself in the back of the car. The driver pulled out the opposite direction and drove without drawing undue attention to himself but rather as if he and his companion were looking for girls to spend some time with. They pulled up near the Nigerian girls and the driver rolled down the window, positioned near enough to the controller's car, and could be heard perfectly well telling his companion that instead of Africans they would go for the Romanian girls this time. Nasha was trembling, cowering under a blanket in the back of the car. When she knew they had driven away from there she finally allowed herself to breathe, even though she was still nervous.

At an agreed upon location the driver got out, and Ana, the team leader, got in. It would not have been convincing to have a woman looking for girls with a man, so they did not take that risk. They went straight to the highway to get out of the city as soon as possible. They kept checking if they were being followed. On some occasions, they suspected it, but they changed lanes and verified that it was a false alarm. Without further incident, they set off for the safe house, where another team would escort her to Claudia's after-care home within the next 24-48 hours.

Upon getting in the car, Ana had instructed Nasha to give the phone to the original driver who would ensure that all location apps were disabled and wiped from the phone before she would get it back. Phones were used as a means of control by the pimps, so it was imperative that it not give her location away.

"That's it! She's out!" Claudia exclaimed with joy.
"Great job!" said the others with one voice.
"In a couple of hours, we will be notified upon arrival at the house. It will be another step on this ladder of liberation."
After two and a half hours, Claudia received the call she had been waiting for. Claudia always wanted to hear as many of the details as possible, so she was best informed to help the women that came into her care.
"They are already in the house, thank God. They have had no further incidents. Everything went very well. They told me that Nasha was exhausted, they are going to let her sleep as much as she wants, and tomorrow they will come here as soon as they see her willing and emotionally stable."
Sara began to live all this as if it were her own rescue, as if she were part of the network. Both she and Diego had experienced in real time the uncertainty, the anguish of waiting for news and, of course, the joy of success. They didn't even know her, but if she could have, Sara would have embraced Nasha with all her love. They were excited that the rescues were a reality. The opportunity for a new life was opening before these girls. It was possible, difficult, but NOT impossible.
When they returned to Claudia's house the next day, Nasha had already arrived. She was a beautiful lady, one of those that turned heads when she walked by. She was clearly tired, but there was a light in her, one they didn't see in the girls at the industrial park.
Nasha said little at first as she kept thinking it was all a dream. She wanted to believe she had been set free from her slavery but a

fear of being discovered by the mafia, remained. Among all the women there, including the three Nigerians, the psychologist, the social worker, Claudia, and her team, all of them were going to help Nasha accept her new reality.

"Form a team," Claudia told them before the return of Sara and Diego, "men and women, let the girls interact with men who are not looking to take advantage of them but who also want to help them. We have already talked about how to plan everything. Start the journey, and I am certain our paths will cross again sooner rather than later. Continue to partner with the Red Cross volunteers, coordinating with them, and helping each other. And you should contact the police units that deal with these issues; it is the SNP (Spanish National Police), a section that deals with trafficking in women and sexual slavery of women. And you can continue to reach out to me for advice, not that I know everything but we certainly have learned a lot over the years."

"Of course!" exclaimed Sara and Diego in unison. "This has given us just what we need to take the next steps forward. We can't thank you enough!"

Will Justice Be Served?

Sara and Diego had only been home from their trip for ten days before they found themselves even deeper in the pit of the world of trafficking than they had ever imagined.

The day came. Diego had already been awake since five o'clock; he didn't need an alarm on his cell phone; the accelerated beating of his pulse was the alarm. He got up carefully so as not to disturb Sara. She, too, had been awake for some time now, from thoughts about that day and many other things. Her mind was always in a state of brainstorming, each detail itself might seem insignificant but together it was a significant unseen weight she carried every day. She didn't move when she heard Diego arise; she let him think she was still asleep; it was the time of day when she could think without the constant buzz of voices, people moving in various directions, feeling consumed with all the people and all their needs. While sleep brought rest to her physical body, it was this time of solitude and spiritual reflection that brought restoration and readiness to her soul.

Diego made himself a cup of coffee and began his daily ritual of reading the news on his tablet, though that morning he went straight to the local news. It was the day set for trial against Lorena's attacker.

The oral trial was scheduled for February 24 and 25. They arrived at the Provincial Court and entered the corresponding courtroom. They kept their distance but close enough to see Daciana—that was Lorena's real name—scared, with an uneasy look; she did not want to see his face again; she did not want to meet his eyes. The courtroom secretary ceremoniously opened the door and announced the beginning of the oral trial.

"Judge Pascual Andrade presiding, please, stand!"

"You may be seated," said the judge, almost as a matter of routine. "The Secretary has the floor."

"We prosecute today the case coming from the Court of Instruction Number 4, with the pointing of the alleged crimes of attempted homicide and robbery with violence against Antón Villanueva Sánchez, in provisional prison for the present cause, represented by the Attorney Sr. José Antonio Zarauz Villalta and defended by Lawyer Sr. Augusto Gil Cruz. The Public Prosecutor's Office and the private prosecution, Daciana Gabor, represented by Attorney Sra. Cristina Almenara Rodríguez and assisted by Attorney Sr. Ángeles Beltrán Carrera."

"With Your Honor's permission, the Public Prosecutor's Office presents the facts that occurred and constitute a crime of attempted homicide, a crime of robbery with violence, and a minor crime of injury."

"The private prosecution agrees with the final conclusions of the Public Prosecutor's Office."

"The defense considers that his Defendant is culpable of a minor crime of injury or alternatively a crime of attempted homicide, with the extenuating circumstance of being under the influence of alcoholic beverages that caused a disturbance to his mental state and volitional capacity. These alcoholic beverages were not ingested with the intention of executing the said crime. Likewise, the Defendant requests resolution of these charges by paying for personal damages incurred by the plaintiff and the State in lieu of additional incarceration, given the extenuating circumstances in this case."

The trial began.

On the day of the attack, Lorena had provided six full services, as she had done every day for the past eighteen months. She was controlled by Pascual, a man who, although Lorena referred to him as her protector, both Sara and Diego suspected that he controlled more girls in or outside that industrial park.

Pascual was on his way to pick her up when a man approached on a bicycle. He was zigzagging down the street.

"That one is coming drunk, Pascual," she told him in hopes that he would allow her to pass on this prospective client.

"That one is not going to give you much work; he can barely function. He'd fall asleep while you undress him. It's twenty euros more; think about it," Pascual told her, without asking her opinion and leaving no room for her to object.

"I'll pick you up here in half an hour." He drove off in his car to a place somewhat distant from the traffic circle to wait for the completion of Lorena's last service.

"Please confirm that on the night of the case, at about one o'clock in the morning, at the traffic circle indicated in the map, you approached, riding a bicycle, BH brand, MTB model?" asked the representative of the Public Prosecutor's Office.

"Yes, I did," replied the defendant.

"Now, I ask you whether your intention was to solicit the sexual services of the plaintiff."

"Yes," Anton repeated without moving his gaze from the floor. It was clear his attorney had instructed him to reply with as few words and little information as possible.

Diego listened to the interrogation from the public seating in the courtroom. He had always been a man filled with a deep sense of justice and he was also a father and grandfather, so his body was filled with indignation and a desire to storm the witness stand and force the pathetic man to at least look at Daciana when he spoke. Really, he wanted to strangle him but his practicality and a hand holding his right leg, which kept moving, forced him to control himself and follow the proceedings.

"He'll go to jail, Diego. There is no other way for him," said Sara in a low voice while she told him to hold back and be calm.

When Anton had arrived at the place where Lorena was she didn't follow the expected acts of pulling down her bra or flaunting her thong because she had no interest in dealing with a drunk customer, even if it meant twenty fewer euros being deducted from her debt. With slurred speech and giving off an unpleasant odor, a mixture of alcohol and sweat, he dropped his bike and stumbled over himself to Lorena.

"Hello, beautiful!" he swooned over her as he scanned her entire body.

"What brings you here?" Lorena asked almost unwillingly.

"How much for a blowjob?" he went straight to the point, clearly struggling to formulate actual words.

"Ten euros."

"And for getting laid?"

"Twenty euros," Lorena replied as if she were reciting the price list of a supermarket.

Anton reached toward his trouser pocket, failing several times. Eventually he managed to pull out a twenty-euro bill and put it in front of her face, mockingly, contemptuously, and with an attitude of arrogance so unbefitting of his current condition.

They agreed on the service, and she led him a few meters from there to an area out of sight of passers-by, dark and hidden by a hedge. It was the usual place where Lorena provided her services. As she had done countless times, and five times already on this shift, she disassociated her actions from her sense of self and began to go through a variety of actions to stimulate the man, hoping to get it all over with as quickly as possible. Given his inebriated state his body was non-responsive other than running his hand over Lorena's breast, squeezing it.

Lorena didn't intend for it to last long, so she reached over and opened her bag, which she had left next to them. As she reached for a condom, Anton wrapped a green canvas tape around her neck and applied intense force, intending to strangle her. His grip tightened, pressure increased, and it was clear to her that his aim was to leave her without air, strength, or life.

Lorena kicked, trying to get away, but to no avail. He kept squeezing, his eyes filled with fury. He did not plan to loosen his grip—on the contrary. She could not scream; no air was coming in. She kept trying to make him let go of her, desperately grabbing the tape around her neck with the intention of putting her fingers between it and her skin to loosen it, but it was too tight. Her brain was running out of oxygen, her vision began to blur, and everything narrowed into gray and then black. She lost consciousness.

When Lorena gave up her resistance, and her arms fell limp on the ground, Anton straddled her back as she lay on her stomach. He held the green tape with one hand and continued to squeeze, albeit with less intensity. This caused some air to enter her lungs, and she was able to regain consciousness. Her instinct for self-preservation, strongly ingrained since childhood, led her to once again attempt to insert fingers between the tape and her neck. Since he had relaxed his grip there was just enough room for her to have success and she managed to pull the rope from her neck up to her chin, which reduced the asphyxia, but still was causing great, but not lethal, damage to her jaw. When Anton realized that she was still alive, with the other hand, he held her hair as if it were the reins of a saddle. He slammed Lorena's face into the ground again and again with all the force he could muster, at the same time continuing to tighten the tape. She lost consciousness again, no longer only from suffocation but also from the blows to her head.

"Confirm that you took advantage of the victim's unconscious state to steal the money she kept in her jacket and her cell phone."
Anton simply nodded his head.
"I require the defendant to state his answers aloud for the record," interrupted the Judge.
"Yes, I confirm."

He grabbed her by the shoulder and turned her on her back, straddling her so that she could not move. Clumsily and in a hurry, he checked the pockets of Lorena's jacket and found a cell phone with cash from the last service. She twisted around, trying to free herself from the pressure that Anton put on her, but she could not. What's more, he kept hitting her and squeezing the tape without realizing that it was no longer on the front of her neck but under her mouth.

Though convinced these would be her last moments of earthly existence, she did not cease in her defense and hoped that the influence of the alcohol would eventually diminish the stamina of her attacker. She waited for movement, a distraction that would make it easier to get rid of that demon and to run away if she still had some strength left in her legs. She could not give in; she had to try, even if it was the last thing she would do in her battered and complicated life. It could not end like this.

Her eyes were bloodshot because of the blows, and her eyelids swelled violently, but she felt no pain, only growing darkness that warned her of a final departure into nothingness.

She had lost track of time. It didn't matter. It was endless, eternal, and macabrely indefinite. She was an instant away from giving up and surrendering to the grim reaper. But something in that very moment gave her a small dose of hope for a miracle.

Pascual told her that in half an hour, he would come to pick her up, as usual, at the agreed place in the traffic circle since it was the end of the shift. And indeed, he showed up on time in his car but did not see Lorena at the meeting point. He was not upset; sometimes, it took a little longer to finish the service, or a new deal on something additional to what was agreed originally; there were as many proposals as clients. Nevertheless, he drove to the roundabout and stopped the car where he had said half an hour before.

As more time had passed, Anton saw a man approaching, sniffing around the area as if making sure that everything was under control. He didn't think twice: he dropped everything he had in his hands (green tape, money, cell phone, and Lorena) and ran to his bicycle, stumbling. Desperate and scared, he grabbed the girl's purse by the handles and went in the opposite direction to where the man was. The effort he had made further numbed his already alcohol induced senses.

Lorena summoned what little strength she had left, concentrating it all on her vocal cords and squeaked out, "Help!"

"Lorena, where are you?" He didn't have to walk far to see the result of atrocious violence—a body with bruises on more places than not, blood on the ground and soaking the little clothing she wore, and a limp body that looked more dead than alive.

"Are you officer number 4865 of the local Police Force?"

"Affirmative."

"I ask you to describe what you saw on the night in question and the actions that resulted from the events that took place."

"Our Mobile Unit patrols that area for the purposes of preventing and settling possible altercations, fights, quarrels, whether between the prostitutes, their pimps, or between any of them and the clients."

"We were passing by the traffic circle at 1:40 a.m. and noticed a man, known to us, waving his arms and pointing in a direction. We clearly heard him say, 'He ran that way!' while pointing his hand towards Gandarias Street. We radioed another patrol car to close off the opposite end of the street. At first, we did not see anyone, but as we passed through an area about 500 to 1000 meters from the traffic circle, we were able to identify a bicycle lying on the ground and a man in the adjacent bushes. Upon my initial evaluation of the situation, it seemed apparent that the individual had fallen off his bicycle and had landed, if I may say so, in those bushes. We quickly proceeded to get him out of there."

"Did the defendant put up any resistance?" interrupted the attorney for the Public Prosecutor's Office.

"None. His faculties seemed to be numb. He emitted a strong odor of alcohol, and we could not understand what he was trying to tell us. My unit partner retraced our route and found a purse and a cell phone. Upon further investigation, it was determined that the purse belonged to the victim and the cell phone belonged to the man we arrested. He possibly dropped it when he became unbalanced on his bicycle in his escape."

The members of the second unit went to the place where Lorena was. Although the officers had seen many horrific things in the course of their work, the youngest one was visibly shaken at the sight of that girl with an absolutely swollen, bruised, bleeding face, bloodshot eyes, and no clearly demarcated facial lines. They quickly called for an emergency medical response, which arrived on the scene after about fifteen minutes.

The health personnel who attended her were aware of the seriousness of the case. They asked her questions, but she could only emit guttural and muffled sounds. Her consciousness seemed to be moderately preserved, but she was dazed, in pain, and her gaze was lost somewhere.

"The clerk of the court, at the request of the Public Prosecutor's Office, will now read the medical report prepared by the doctors who attended the victim in the emergency room of the hospital."

What followed was a lengthy medical accounting of the injuries sustained by the victim. In a subsequent report, it was noted that the injuries took twelve days to heal, all of which prevented her from carrying out daily activities, and that there were no physical pre-existing conditions. The psychological report stated she also experienced feelings of fear, panic, and insecurity, which prevented her from freely developing her personality and daily life.

"I request the projection to the courtroom of the images taken by the medical staff on the night of the case in the hospital emergency department," requested the attorney for the Public Prosecutor's Office.

"Proceed," authorized the President of the Chamber.

When the images were projected, both the accused and the victim did not move their gazes from the floor. Silence pervaded the room. It was only broken abruptly, in anger, in an instant when a voice in the gallery shouted,

"Son of a bitch, look at the pictures!"

"Silence! Any further comments will be grounds for the eviction of the audience. The hearing is adjourned until 10 a.m. tomorrow."

The words may or may not have been those of Diego.

They couldn't eat dinner.

They did not want to call Daciana; she would have enough in her head with what had been relived in the trial. Instead, they phoned the lawyer to inquire how she was doing. The attorney was hopeful; the Public Prosecutor's Office had done an exemplary job, so hopefully there would be little else needed.

Sara and Diego were people of character and commitment who rarely rested, which often to their own detriment in physical fatigue, but added the joy of satisfaction to their days. Despite all that was happening with the trial, they never stopped planning new activities, new projects, and agreeing on how to plan the next weekend's outing.

And then came the second day. The preambles were repetitions of the previous day. Now it was the turn of the private prosecution who affirmed the material presented by the Prosecutor's Office and requested the maximum penalty available under the law, with no extenuating circumstances. Of course, the defense lawyer objected and requested an in-chambers hearing with the President of the Chamber, the private prosecution and the Public Prosecutor's Office. The President agreed. It was clear to the defense counsel that they could only try to reduce the sentence because the guilty verdict was not in doubt. They announced that 15,000 euros had been deposited in the bank account of the Court, on behalf of the defendant, to pay the civil liabilities that could be imposed on the accused. The President took note and made it known that, in any case, this deposit would not be admitted as a way of trying to mitigate the facts or the sentence.

"Call the first defense witness," ordered the Presiding Judge.

"The presence of Mr. Arturo Bienvenido López is required."

"Are you a friend of the defendant?" asked Anton's defense counsel.

"Yes, Sir."

"On the day of the incident, did you have lunch with the defendant and other friends at a downtown restaurant?"

"Yes, Sir."

"How many alcoholic beverages did the defendant ingest?"

"Around six or seven beers and a couple of whiskeys after lunch."

"Could you say that the defendant left the restaurant under normal conditions, for example, to drive?"

"Well, the truth is that he was pretty intoxicated, but he said he was on a bike, that nothing bad could happen."

"No further questions."

"With your Honor's permission," intervened the counsel for the private prosecution. "Did you force him to drink these beverages?"

"No, we just drank in company."

"In other words, he took them voluntarily."

"Yes, Ma'am."

"No further questions."

The waitress at the bar confirmed her friend's statement.

After some minor details, the President of the Chamber completed the protocol and ended the hearing,

"The trial is adjourned. Clear the courtroom."

The lawyer for the private prosecution conveyed to the client and to Sara and Diego an optimistic impression regarding the sentence.

"It took a long time, but everything is now closed," said the lawyer.

"Are you all right, Daciana?" asked Sara when she saw her so serious. She only nodded.

"You know we are here to help you. Whatever you decide…we'll keep in touch," Sara said, almost whispering.

When they said goodbye, Daciana approached Sara and brought her hand close to hers. A light touch as she tried to hold it, a subtle contact between their fingers, an unwritten signal that transmitted through her skin. They looked at each other from the corner of their eyes, mutually acknowledging a shared hope that Daciana would get not only justice from the court, but a freedom that would give her own life back to her.

A month later, the lawyer phoned them. Anton got his sentence.

"Five years in prison and 32,000 euros for physical and compensatory damages for attempted murder. He was also sentenced to a further three years for robbery with violence. In total, eight years. I am sending you the sentence by email."

"Thank you, Ángeles. We really appreciate it," answered Diego sincerely.

"We'll have to celebrate, won't we?" asked the lawyer in a more relaxed manner.

"We are very happy for Daciana, but this could not go unpunished. Our celebration is to continue the work, to continue helping, and to be, in a way, the guardian angels of these girls."

"I know you well, and I understand you. Thank you for all you are doing."

"Do not doubt that we will continue as long as we have breath."

Diego had put the phone on speaker so Sara could hear the conversation. A subtle smile appeared on her lips. They both looked at each other, and their eyes expressed satisfaction, incomplete always, but hopeful.

The Enthusiasm and Energy of a Team

Sara and Diego had continued to collaborate with the Red Cross volunteers and began alternating weeks to visit the industrial parks. They knew they were making a difference, but it continued to be apparent that there was no real commitment by the organization to develop a strategy that would lead them to that next step of helping women leave the streets and escape their slavery.

As the date on the calendar turned to 2016, they decided that the time was right for them to take that next step that Claudia had proposed…to create a team of their own. By this time many people in their social circle were aware of this project that they had undertaken, though few really understood it.

Diego reached out to his wide network in their community and got the word out that they would be hosting an informational meeting for those interested in learning more and perhaps becoming involved in joining the fight against sex trafficking. About thirty people came to that first meeting, the initial seeds planted that would soon grow into a committed team of volunteers.

"The best way for trafficking to continue is to sit still and do nothing."
"As you can see in this image, I wanted to start this presentation with a call to action, one given almost two centuries ago by the abolitionist, William Wilberforce:"
You may choose to look the other way, but you can never say again that you did not know."
"This is also our mission, to give visibility to the problem of trafficking for the purpose of sexual exploitation, to call on people's conscience and convince them that here in the Twenty-first Century slavery is still a scourge on this earth. Not only does slavery still exist, but it is also right here in our own neighborhoods – in the industrial parks, in the nightclubs, and clandestinely in private flats. Unknowingly we cross paths with the enslaved people in the street, even with their pimps, but we do not recognize the tragedy, the horror that these women live every day, that defines their entire existence."

The former preacher in Diego was evident as he gave what one might liken to an altar call at the end of a religious service, a call to action. And indeed, many in attendance were literally moved to their feet as one by one, most of them stood to show their solidarity for the cause. Through the stories that were shared that evening, those in attendance knew in their hearts that they could no longer say that they didn't know. In the years that followed some of the team's most faithful volunteers were those who had sat and listened, stood, and then took the next steps that were put before them and who would likewise recruit others to join the cause. The words of the evangelist that night fell on fertile soil and were indeed multiplied by the words and actions of others.

Thus, a working group was formed, made up of 13–-15 people. Sara and Diego knew they would need to provide adequate training for the volunteers before taking them out on the streets, so they began by assigning other efforts that supported the process.
Everyone on the team solicited used closing from their friends and some established connections with grocery stores, markets and restaurants to collect excess food. Once a week they would gather to assemble the hygiene kits that would be distributed every other Friday night.

Having a team assembled brought both new energy and new responsibility to the couple. What started as a project had grown to be the nucleus of what every other area of their lives revolved around. As the team grew the need for a functional workspace also became apparent. Sara still had a lease on a very modest room as part of a larger salon space that she kept for doing massage and facial services on a select number of clients. Sara had learned that asking with boldness often opened doors that otherwise appeared shut so she confidently approached the building owner and asked permission to take over an underutilized storage area in the back for the purpose of storing supplies for their humanitarian project. Between hearing of the work that was being done and Sara's compelling, if not guilt-inducing request, the man agreed to make the space available for a very low price, on the condition that it was a month-by-month arrangement, should a future customer require additional space.

Augusto's Gusto

One of the people at that initial meeting was a man Diego knew from their shared involvement in local civic matters. Augusto worked as a teacher and in his free time loved to engage in just about any kind of sport from handball to soccer. However, his real passions were extreme, endurance events as are often found in hiking and cycling. He was the kind of guy who knew how to persevere through obstacles and did so with a positive attitude. His demeanor was enthusiastic and as an educator he was an effective communicator. He also was known as one who advocated for others, so it was not surprising that he was quick to join his friend Diego's humanitarian work and in true Augusto fashion, he would do it with gusto!

He had dreamed of cycling across Spain for years and kept postponing it for various reasons. One day as he was doing a casual ride along one of his usual routes along the Mediterranean, he came up with an unusual idea. He saw in Sara and Diego's project the opportunity to fulfill his cycling dream while also using it to raise much needed funds to support their outreach work. As he had started volunteering on the team, he became aware that the expenses were all coming out of their own pockets. The idea was certainly unconventional, but so fighting against the evils of modern-day slavery was going to require interventions of all kinds.

Augusto was ending his ride in the city center and rode up to a café to enjoy a coffee before heading home. Next door, on the window of the Civic Center, he saw the poster announcing World Anti-Trafficking Day.

"People are not bought and sold.
Do not deal with traffickers."
Break the chains of trafficking."

Those words kept repeating in his head and he knew he had to talk to Sara and Diego.

The very next day he arranged to meet them and enthusiastically shared his idea:

"I will cycle across Spain, and we will raise funds from commercial brands, establishments, businesses, and individuals; each stage will be sponsored, and we will advertise the solidarity project." (Solidarity is a term used in Spain to describe the coming together of a community in a united cause.)

"We'll have to find a slogan," said Diego.

"I've already thought about it: Say no to trafficking. It's simple, but it carries the message and relates in some way to a bike ride."

Augusto embarked on his campaign that summer just as soon as school got out and before the temperatures peaked. Between his engaging personality and his intentional connections, he managed to gain the attention of local newspapers and even some television stations along his journey. The endeavor was indeed a success. Augusto got a fair degree of notoriety for his efforts in spreading the anti-trafficking message and over 6600 euros were raised to support the ongoing work.

After Sara and Diego had sufficiently organized, trained, and executed visits to the industrial park with the team members, an invitation was extended to Claudia to come visit and provide feedback.

Carmen had quickly risen to the surface among the volunteers as the one best gifted to bring order by implementing systems into what could easily spiral into chaos with all the moving pieces. Her talents were greatly respected and appreciated by Sara and Diego because Carmen's approach aligned so well with their own style. Soon she oversaw tracking the inventory of materials they distributed, coordinating the schedule for who would join a team on the streets on any given Friday night, and perhaps most significantly she kept impeccably detailed records of each woman they interacted with. This record of nationalities, names (always street names, not real names), and any other information that could become helpful if a rescue became possible. Carmen was indeed the heart and soul of the team as she led and inspired others which also allowed the couple to manage other aspects of the growing project.

On her visit Claudia also met and was impressed with the other team members:

Camila and her daughter, Sofia. As a single mother, Camila worked hard as a caregiver to elders, earning just enough to provide for her daughter but with little margin in her budget. Along with a strong work ethic she also wanted Sofia to grow up with a heart of compassion and care for others so volunteering together gave added purpose to both of their lives.

Marian was the wife of Sara and Diego's pastor, and she was the kind of person who did whatever needed to be done and did so not only without complaint but with real joy. She connected well with the girls, treated them as if they were her friends, cried about their sorrows, and was sincerely happy with their progress or that of their children.

Luis' was one of the few male members of their team. He often had a serious countenance as he sought to be as efficient and productive as possible with their time and resources. He was a businessman so the personality and approach that led to success in his work naturally translated to his part on the team. He had known Diego for many years, and it was out of his great respect for the man that he had stretched himself to be a part of the project. He also served as a back-up driver on the rare occasion that Diego was unable to go out.

María José and Miguel were a faithful but very soft-spoken couple who worked behind the scenes. They fixed some defective clothes, cleaned the thermos of cocoa for the next outing, washed the donated items and seemed to always notice the little things that needed to be done, often before Carmen could even task them with the duty.

Impressed with what she had seen so far, Claudia was anxious to see how the team managed from the trips to the industrial park, from beginning to end. Carmen decided that Camila and Marian would go out in addition to Sara, Diego, and Claudia. They prepared everything and loaded the van. They had a tradition of taking a group selfie to document the members of the team wearing their red vests, followed by a prayer of protection and blessing offered up by Diego. There was always a certain sense of joy on the way. It was like a sign of satisfaction that something worthwhile was going to be done, and who knows if that night some girl would say to Sara, "Mommy, I would like us to talk…" They arrived at the industrial park entrance and put the white flags on the van's external rear view mirrors. The tour began.

As usual, they started in the area of the Nigerian girls. The women eagerly approached the van, picked up the kits, and joked with Marian, who made conversation with ease and asked them how they were doing, how the night was going, and if they were cold. She also took note of their names knowing Carmen would expect a detailed accounting. Sara told them all should say yes to starting a new life, and some of them laughed, they thought she was joking, but really, she was planting seeds in hopes they would germinate into a phone call or a discrete conversation one day.

Next stop—the Romanian girls. The difference between the groups was often very apparent with the Romanian women being less expressive and more reticent to engage.

Those that did share their situation did so in a matter-of-fact manner. It was logical that they had to do it to bring some necessary money to their family and they did it to help their boyfriends, husbands, or relatives. They talked openly about their boyfriends who went to Romania with the money to start a business that was going to get them out of prostitution or who were about to find a partner in Spain to set up a financial company. Sara thought that many of them really believed these stories, although others looked at the floor as they listened to their companions give their personal accounts. Some had their supposed boyfriends sitting in a car or chair right in front of where they were offering their services, the money soon to line the pockets of their "beloved boyfriend."

"Has Violeta not come today?" asked Sara when she saw that a regular was missing, "or is she working?
"No, she had to go to the doctor the other day, and she hasn't come back here since," answered one of the girls.
Sara noticed something strange in the faces of the other women. She said goodbye after handing out the kits and giving them some juice and hot chocolate. As they resumed the route, Sara picked up her cell phone and dialed Violeta's number.
"Hi, honey, it's Sara. Are you okay? Call me as soon as you get this message. Kiss you, sweetheart."
"Something has happened to her, I'm sure, and it's not a cold. Diego, tomorrow we are going to see her at her house." Diego had learned that when Sara made her mind up about something in these kinds of situations it was best just to agree to go along...and that her intuition was almost always right.
"Maybe she has an infection, Claudia suggested, or she is pregnant and is going to have an abortion, or maybe she is recovering from a beating. We have seen this on many occasions, with all of them, but especially with Romanian women." She was not trying to lack compassion or concern, but she also wanted Sara to know the many possibilities that could exist.
None of these reasons brought Sara any peace and she became even more determined to find out what was going on with Violeta.
"Have you ever heard how these girls from the East arrive?" Claudia asked, looking at her companions.

A Note to the Reader

While each trafficking for sexual exploitation victim has their own circumstances and story, those that work closely to fight for their freedom have seen the common patterns and causes that can often be associated with each nationality. Deception, threats, and violence are certainly common threads that are weaved into almost every woman's personal account. These next four chapters contain composite vignettes that paint pictures of how a young woman from Nigeria, Romania, Latin America, or Morocco could end up as enslaved women on the streets and in the clubs of Southern Spain. Should the contents of these chapters be too intense, the reader is encouraged to rejoin the story of Sara and Diego on page 190.

    These accounts are graphic because the realities are even more horrific. And beyond the evil of the atrocities themselves, each of these stories represents literally tens of thousands of women who are currently trapped in sex trafficking in Spain alone, and hundreds of thousands across the globe.

    In the spirit of Wilbur Wilberforce, we can choose to turn away, but we can no longer say that we do not know.

A Long Journey from Nigeria: Aisha's Story, Part I

As was his daily routine, Diego was starting his morning with a cup of coffee in one hand and his tablet in another. A headline caught his attention; it was a translation of an article published in The Guardian and signed by Lucia Balducci. It was entitled "Shameful Nigeria, one of the most unequal countries in the world." The piece was an analysis of the inequality between classes in that country, basically between two—rich and poor. The last paragraph referred to statements made by a worker in a company owned by a very rich Nigerian, who ended his interview with the following sentence: "I prefer my life to that of millionaires because I am free. When they go out on the street, they must go out surrounded by police, but I am free. Nobody is looking for me. Yes, they have money, they have food, they can do whatever they want, but I have more freedom than them."

Diego closed his eyes and leaned his head against the back of the chair, unable to suppress a feeling of uneasiness after reading this article. An unenlightened man, a quiet, submissive worker, was talking about freedom in Nigeria, his freedom, something he had chosen and which he did not want to lose under any circumstances. He thought that, for this Nigerian, freedom was simply living without the daily, continuous risk of not having food in his house or that a stray bullet had not killed him. His freedom consisted in being able to return home every day, to go back to work the next morning. Diego quickly thought of all those Nigerians and, above all, women, who had no choice to feel freedom in their lives.

"Sara, do you remember Vanessa?" asked Diego without opening his eyes.

"How could I not?" she answered, surprised at the question.

Tafari was a peaceful, quiet, hardworking man. His parents had a small plot of land in Ekiti State. They grew cocoa and potatoes; with that, they subsisted and could even sell part of the production in the markets of the surrounding villages.

He had four siblings, all boys, who worked on his plot of land. His mother oversaw keeping the household chores in order and maintaining ancestral traditions, despite the invasion of foreign cultures that were increasingly closing the way to everything traditional. Looking for good women for his children was one of his father's unwritten missions. Tafari was the eldest of the brothers, so he had to be the first to take a wife. The future husband had no say.

He simply accepted the decision of his parents, who negotiated with another family. After evaluating all the options presented to them, Anatu was the best option.

The wedding consisted of three parts—the Urhobo ritual, the Christian ceremony, and the big feast. They tried to achieve a balance between tradition and modernity. The new foreign religion of Christianity was not allowed to entirely replace the Nigerian ones; that is why weddings were celebrated under the two rites. Spirituality was the magma that united the intimate being of a person; spirituality was innate in Nigerians and conditioned all their actions. That is why, when the ceremony was over, the officiant told Tafari: now you can take Anatu with you, but only in her feminine physical figure because her spiritual part will never leave what has always been her family home.

Both families purchased land adjacent to Tafari's parents' land. This way, they could make their own profits from tending the crops while continuing to help with his family's chores. Soon the first son, Daren, was born. Everything is going along well with the expectations of life in Nigeria: work, family, soul, and respect.

All was well until the regional government, unable to dominate the different areas of the country and unify the laws, customs, and tribes, did what rulers lacking in reasoning usually do... Expropriation - by a government law, all arable land became the property of the state. Tafari was now a hired hand for the government despots. He was to continue working as before, but a civic officer arranged what he would be paid for his labor. The problem was that often he received almost nothing for making the now state-owned land produce cocoa and potatoes. In the meantime, Anatu became pregnant for the second time. She had a baby boy, whom they named Mamadou.

The family's income dropped drastically, but they were able to draw on his father's savings for a while. A decision had to be made because the family was going to have a really hard time. Many of his neighbors had already made the decision to move to another state, Edo, where news was coming in that there were opportunities to work in the fledgling cement industry in the capital, Benin City. Eight months later, Tafari, his wife, and two children set off in the hope of the "promised land." Anatu was carrying their daughter Aisha in her womb.

Thanks to neighbors who had already settled in Benin, they were able to secure a house in a suburb of the city. It was an old, two-story house that had not been renovated or repaired since it was built. They had to share it with two other families, with two bedrooms for themselves. Aisha was born in one of the rooms.

Tafari got a job in a cement factory owned by one of the richest men in Nigeria. The problem was that this immense fortune, in addition to being a good businessman and participating in government corruption, was built upon the poor labor treatment of his workers. They were paid when he decided. Sometimes, months could pass without them being paid a single coin, and when they got paid, it was very little.

Aisha was four years old when Anatu became pregnant again. One more mouth to feed, and the income was not increasing. They managed along for the next several months just barely staying out of complete poverty when events unfolded that would change their lives forever.

"Tafari, this child comes different from the others. My belly doesn't grow the same," his wife told him worriedly.

"Tomorrow, we will call the midwife. You know what she says: 'this is not a job to earn money, but to help,'" Tafari told her in a hollow voice, imitating the midwife, "so it won't cost us any money."

"I don't know. Something doesn't feel right."

The midwife showed up two days later. Anatu felt a lot of soreness, and the midwife explained that the child was in an incorrect position. She prepared herbal tea for Anatu, to take every night before going to sleep. Two weeks later, a month before her due date, she cried out in pain in the middle of the night; she was sweating profusely, and the tremors made the whole bed shake. Tafari sent his eldest son to fetch the midwife. When the midwife arrived, Anatu was staring blankly, clinging to her husband's arms as if it was the last thing she could do in life. The midwife looked at Tafari and shook her head but began to prepare for a difficult delivery. As she set everything in place, she saw blood gushing profusely from Anatu. She tried to stop the bleeding, but to no avail. The midwife could not save her, although she was able to save little Anuar, who seemed to cry beyond that of a typical newborn but rather with wails of lament.

The siblings, huddled in the next room, were frightened. When their father began to cry with all the strength his soul was capable of, they instinctively hugged each other and cried inconsolably all night.

Aisha grew into a beautiful girl with deep, lively, sparkling eyes. She took care of her siblings and her grieving father; he never got over the loss of his wife. This time, he disregarded tradition and chose not to take a wife again. The other two families lived in the same house and helped as much as possible. Working conditions remained the same. Scarcity was the norm in the house, but they were able to get by, albeit very poorly.

Tafari was clear that his sons should work as soon as they reached the minimum working age. But Aisha was different. Many nights, when Tafari went to bed, he thought about what would become of her. He had no resources to arrange a wedding for her. Nor did it cross his mind to do what he knew other families in extreme poverty did: sell their daughters; he considered it a crime. Aisha was always tenacious to life and work, kind to everyone, and did all she could at her young age to ensure that her brothers and her father lived as comfortably as possible. And she was eager to learn. One of the families that shared a house with them could afford to take one of their children, the youngest, to school; when he returned, he recited the lessons to his mother. Aisha, hidden behind a dense curtain, paid attention without missing a detail. These moments were short-lived because she had to prepare the clothes for the men's work the next day, work real magic to prepare a half-decent dinner every night, and clean the little space where they lived, a thousand things that prevented her from focusing on studying or, at least, paying attention and concentrating on the simulated study she was doing behind the curtain.

In the meantime, she was growing. Her beauty became more and more evident. She had inherited from her mother that special, almost magical look and a smile that exhibited true joy. When she reached adolescence, she did not have her mother to ask about things she noticed and could not find an explanation for, so she turned to the mother of the family, whose son was her involuntary instructor. Her forms became rounder, and the little girl became a beautiful woman.

She made friends in the neighborhood, and almost every evening, the girls would meet in the hallway of the house of one of them when each family had finished their chores. They talked about their villages, stories told by relatives from other areas or states, and dreams, especially dreams. Although they assumed that it was their lot to live that life, they did not stop imagining what would become of them in other circumstances. The stories told by passersby from other lands, and, above all, the stories of other countries told by the more privileged school children, almost all of them boys, induced their adolescent minds to create worlds in which they could be princesses, teachers or magazine models. When a family had sons and daughters, if there was an economic possibility of sending one of them to school, they always chose a boy since girls had the primary purpose of being good wives, mothers, and souls of a family. This was the case with the boy she spied on every afternoon behind the curtain and who provided her with special nourishment—knowledge.

Little by little, children joined these evening gatherings. That is how Aisha met Okwonkwo. He was a handsome lad, two years older than her. He had a smile that hypnotized the girls, and she fell under the influence of his gaze and that curly hair that was so often a toy between her fingers. It didn't take long for them to become a couple. One night, behind one of the houses, he kissed her, and she felt an unknown and thrilling sensation. The excitement grew as the days went by, and the result was pregnancy. They talked to Aisha's father, and he did not reproach her. Anatu's death still weighed so heavily upon him that this lesser tragedy of an out-of-wedlock pregnancy seemed insignificant. They spoke with Okwonkwo's family and decided they should not marry until they were somewhat older and had enough income to pay for their union.

Despite the meager wages, he started working in the same cement company as Tafari. At that time, one of the three families that shared the house left for Lagos, the official capital of Nigeria, where relatives had settled and offered him the possibility of working in an oil company. Aisha and Okwonkwo occupied that part of the house, paying their share of the rent. There, their beautiful daughter, whom they named Anatu, in memory of her mother, was born. She was the doll of the house; her siblings, the other family who lived in the same place, and her friends from the neighborhood enjoyed making outfits for the girl; they took turns holding her, and Aisha believed that her daughter would have a beautiful family.

Though the day was her sixteenth birthday, Aisha knew that her family would not mark the day with any celebration, it was just not their way, though the practice had become more common in recent years, particularly in the city. She was lost in such thoughts when she heard a knock on the door.

"Is there anyone in the house?" It was a woman's voice, low but musical to the ear.

"Yes," answered Aisha, "come in."

She was a smiling, slender woman in her forties and carried herself well, differently than most women Aisha knew in her community.

"I am Mama Olawa," she said without being asked, "Is your father at home?"

"No, he's not back from work yet, but he should be back soon," Aisha replied with her characteristic gentleness. "Do you want me to give him any messages?"

"I'll wait. I'm in no hurry. "

"Come in and sit down," offered Aisha.

"We'd better stay out here. It's a nice evening."

"As you wish."

The woman gave no clues about the reason for her visit which left Aisha quite curious. She had seen her in the neighborhood on several occasions, always with a young lad in his twenties. He did not seem to have a relationship with her beyond serving as a companion. Occasionally, he saw her entering some houses, especially in the block before the market.

"I hear you're a smart, hard-working girl," Mama Olawa started the conversation.

"I am interested in learning, but circumstances have prevented me from going to school," replied Aisha, not without a regretful expression.

"How are you handling your daughter?"

Aisha froze.

"How do you know I have a daughter?" she asked in a trembling voice.

"Around here, everything is known. Is Okwonkwo being nice to her?" She arched an eyebrow at the question.

"Perfectly, he's a good father." She kept noticing the tremor in her lower lip.

"Well, I have come to change your lives, if your father lets me, of course," Aisha's face lit up, and she opened her eyes as if the whole universe was invited to enter through them.

"How can he do such a thing? Besides, Okwonkwo will have to give his opinion, as well."

"You are not married. It is your father who still decides here."

"But Okwonkwo will give his opinion on whatever you want to propose," she said without hesitation and with a degree of indignation at the woman's lack of regard for her baby's father,

"First, I must talk to your father. I'm sure he won't be able to refuse my offer."

First, she wanted to talk to Tafari alone. Then, they would gather the whole family together to tell them what they had decided. Mama Olawa presented herself as someone altruistic, doing well in life, having her own house, and her husband, whose name she did not want to say, was very important. Because of these economic comforts, she dedicated herself to helping the most disadvantaged families, choosing people in each neighborhood who could benefit from her philanthropy. Unfortunately, she could not meet the needs of all she encountered, but she could attend to those people she saw as having some special characteristic, which it would be a pity not to develop. He spent almost three hours with Tafari and then called the rest of the family, including Okwonkwo.

The father summarized the reason for Mama Olawa's visit, her altruistic mission in life, and the offer she made to them.

"You," she pointed to his three sons and Anatu's father, "have work, and you do it well, even if it is little earned, but it is enough to feed us and keep this house." They all nodded at her father's words. Mama Olawa had noticed that at that moment, all Aisha's muscles tensed. "Everybody talks of your sister's eagerness to learn and that she could not grow in her abilities here. She is still young and has many years ahead of her to be able to study and find a decent job. She has cared for us and looked after us in everything, every day and every night, since your mother went to God."

"What is the proposal?" Aisha interjected, anxious to hear.

"Mama Olawa has a sister in Europe. She lives alone. She offers to help Aisha by paying for her travel, her studies and so she can find a job that will develop her potential."

"How much does that cost?" asked the older brother.

"Don't worry about that," Mama Olawa said firmly. "I'll take care of the expenses, and when she finds a job, she'll pay me back. But in the meantime, she will send you money to help you...and her beautiful daughter. At first, her stay will be free since she will be living at my sister's house."

"It is a good offer," concluded Tafari, "we accept it. At last, something good is coming through the doors of this house, and a better future is in sight."

The silence that flooded the room was thick. You could almost cut through it. They looked sidelong at each other between the siblings. Aisha, with the child in her lap, took Okwonkwo's hand, and he squeezed it nervously.

"Let's hope so," said Aisha with tears welling up in her eyes.

The agreements were signed in the presence of a babalawo, a traditional Nigerian priest. Aisha defined herself as a Christian, belonging to the Evangelical Church (formed by the union of Presbyterian, Congregationalist, Methodist, Lutheran, and Waldensian communities). Still, like all her friends, she was not a devoted believer. From generations lost in the past, what always remained within Nigerians was spirituality; a link between them, their reason for being on earth, their actions, and the creator gods of the universe. A fundamental part of that inner state is voodoo; it is a way to make a deal between two parties, but using the soul as ink to sign it, a way to ensure before the gods that the person who is going to undertake something will fulfill it and that, if he does not, the divine punishment will fall on him or his family. So, whenever a Nigerian undertook anything, he went through the voodoo ritual to commit himself and to know the risks of non-fulfillment of the deal. But in some situations, black magic would come into play, and voodoo as a contract would become juju, where the whole ritual is focused on the macabre personal catastrophes that would befall if the contract was breached, including the death of family members, their own insanity, and the abandonment with which the gods would punish the defaulter.

Mama Olawa and Tafari had reached a financial agreement. The problem was that Aisha's father naively understood that she was speaking to him in the Nigerian currency, naira. So instead of what he believed was a debt of 450 euros, it was ten times that.

They met in a suburb of Benin City, in a sort of renovated shack to undergo the ceremony.

As guarantors, Aisha brought her father and Okwonkwo, in addition to the obligatory presence of Mama Olawa. In the center of the hut was a rudimentary wooden table, almost at the ground level; attached to the wall was a wooden representation of the deity Eshu. On the table were clay vessels containing secret herbs whose nature is known only to the priest, a white cloth, and a decorative nail.

Aisha placed on the cloth what Mama Olawa had asked her to carry—a piece of underwear, a piece of absorbent cotton soaked in menstrual blood, pubic hair, and a photo of her daughter. She went behind a curtain in the hut, where Mama Olawa helped her get naked completely and get dressed in a white, full-length robe. The priest wrapped Aisha's items in a cloth then used the nail to affix the offering to the wall near the representation of Eshu.

The priest took a large egg and proceeded to make a hole in one of its ends. He inserted some powders and some previously crushed herbs. He offered it to Aisha, and she drank the contents of the egg. Next, he took a chicken out of a box and decapitated it with a single cut, collecting its blood; he opened it and extracted its heart. He gave it to her to eat and then drank the blood, mixed with an infusion of herbs. Then, the priest approached Aisha from behind and made a scarification on the back of her neck, in the form of two curved lines crossing each other; it was an open door to the spirits that would accompany her on the journey. Then the priest recited the agreements made:

"You commit yourself before the gods who created the world to do what your guides tell you; to study and work at all times, without rest, in what they order you; not to talk to anyone about this agreement; not to tell anyone the identity of those who accompany and help you; to pay the debt established at the time you are required to do so; to obey in everything. Do you commit yourself?"

"I do," said Aisha tersely.

"As long as the package remains in the sanctuary, you will be bound to your promise, and it will only be returned to a family member when the account is reported settled. Do you understand?"

"I do."

"If you do not fulfill these obligations, talk to third parties about all this, or try to break your promise, the gods will cast upon you and your family all kinds of evils, incurable diseases, misfortunes, burning of their houses, suffering of your daughter and even the death of some or all of your relatives." All this he told her with a mirror in his hands, in which Aisha's face could be framed, as a symbol that, always, they could see where she was and what she was, or was not, doing.

The increasing volume of those words, as the priest stared at Aisha, made fear penetrate her through all her pores and remain inside her from that moment on. She could no longer release from her mind the commitment to keep her promises and, more seriously, the anguish of the consequences, personal and family, if she did not keep them. Her spirit had been imprisoned, and Mama Olawa held the keys to the prison for now.

In a week, she would leave Benin City. A simple bag with clothes for a few days and a bit of food. As a farewell, her friends in the neighborhood combined their meager contributions and together bought her a cell phone, a real treasure. She hugged her friends and cried for a long time. She agreed with her father and Okwonkwo that he and their daughter, Anatu, would move to Okwonkwo family's house and that her brothers and Aisha's father could visit her whenever they wished.

Her life was about to take a new turn, at least that's what she thought, but really, it was a turn not for a brighter future but rather a detour to a living-hell.

That night she could not sleep a wink. She had prepared the simple bundle the previous evening knowing her morning would start very early. As she sat with the baby on her lap, she ran her hand down Okwonkwo's cheek, and tears welled up in their eyes. Just before leaving, Aisha uttered a few words, almost imperceptible because of the tremor in her voice:

"Take care. I will be back very soon, and everything will be different, I promise."

It was like a combination of desire and fear, promise and panic, all mixed together.

By six o'clock in the morning, she was at the agreed place. She could not eat breakfast. A lump in her throat did not let her grab even a bite. Quite a few people began to arrive, almost all women, only about ten men, and all young. By way of consolation, she thought that, at least on the trip, she would be accompanied by people her own age. She was looking for Mama Olawa, but she was nowhere to be seen. Some young men began to herd the travelers into groups. Finally, one of them approached her with determination, and she recognized him at once: he was the one she had seen with Mama Olawa when she saw her in the neighborhood.

"Come on! Get on the bus!" he urged several girls, including Aisha.

"And Mama Olawa?" asked Aisha with some concern.

"I will be your companion on this trip. My mother is not coming with us."

At that moment, she discovered that the boy acting as Mama Olawa's shadow was her son, Ajani, about twenty-five years old. He did not come across as caring or considerate— he was always serious and spoke in a harsh tone. He never gave explanations, just orders. It was apparent that he was following a routine process in gathering the group. I guess it was not the first time he made this kind of trip, thought Aisha.

In addition to her small group of six girls, Aisha could see that fifty or sixty people were grouped just like them and with several other young men giving orders. They got on the bus, and he placed them in a certain area as if they had been previously assigned. It was like an organized trip, Aisha thought, remembering what her friends' relatives from other states had told her. It really was an organized trip.

She sat next to a girl whose face showed no sign that would allow one to guess the feelings that accompanied her. She did not raise her head, always looking down at her knees with a bundle in her lap. Her hands seemed to be trembling, although Aisha quickly realized that this trembling came from a contained cry that she did not dare to burst out. She noticed that her belly and chest were trembling. Instinctively, she grabbed her hand. At this act of comfort, she lifted her head, and her gaze met Aisha's. They said nothing. She leaned into Aisha and continued to weep for a while before finally managing to calm down.

"My name is Aisha, and I am going to Europe to study," she told her, trying to ease the tension.

"I am Deborah, and I am also going to Europe. I have been promised a job in a home for the elderly. With the money I earn, I will try to lift my family out of poverty. We didn't even have enough to eat."

They continued to hold hands for a long time. The bus was crowded, and the heat started to suffocate as the morning wore on. Aisha rested her head on the back of the seat and closed her eyes. Thousands of images were parading through her mind, jumbling together in no order. She mixed scenes from her childhood, laughing with her brothers, playing with her mother as they washed clothes, with more recent ones, of her father's aging soul since the death of his wife. She remembered the routine of her brothers, going to work with their father and returning in the evening, tired, sweaty, their skins dressed in a white patina of dust. She would tell them that they had been transformed into white men, but they didn't even have the strength to answer the joke.

She had dedicated herself entirely to her family, never allowing herself to even dream of the possibility of going to school. She had accepted it. Her mother's death had given her a strength unbefitting her age but a defining force to move forward. On that bus, she kept repeating to herself that this was the life she had to live, but at last, an opportunity had come into her life like a fairy godmother. The need to learn could finally be satisfied. Moreover, it would serve to improve the living situation of her family and her daughter's.

All of that was piling up in memories when a loud, booming voice came from the front of the bus. It was one of the boys accompanying the various groups of people:

"Attention! The trip is going to be long. We'll be making stops, so take care of your needs when we do. We don't want any complaints or protests. Remember that we have paid for this trip, and we are the ones who set the conditions. Each one of you has your guide. He will tell you what to do."

"We will pass through areas that are controlled by the army and others that are guarded by the police. We don't want you to say more than is minimally necessary. Keep your heads down, and never look at anyone who asks you: no last names, just your first name. Turn off your cell phones and hide them. We'll be taking back roads to avoid the checkpoints, so it won't be comfortable."

"If we are identified by any of you or the travel plan is canceled, you will pay a lot. Do you understand me? Like, a lot. From now on, we only want to hear from you when we ask you something."

And so, the trip went from being a formality to get to Europe to taking on dark overtones. Everything Ajani said to them was in a threatening tone; Mama Olawa's kindness was nowhere to be seen in her son. Some girl questioned Ajani for more information, and all she received in reply was a sharp smack on the back of her head. From the beginning, he made it clear: he was in charge, and they had to obey, or else they would pay.

Along the way, they were stopped three times, twice by the military and once by soldiers. On all three occasions, the guides would get off, and Aisha would see out of the corner of her eye that they were given envelopes and some unidentified packages. Then the bus would continue its way. They stopped a couple of times, fifteen minutes each time, to eat some of what they were carrying in the bundles and to relieve themselves. At these stops, the six girls that went with Ajani would gather. In addition to Aisha and Deborah, there were Nguba, Saratu, Awa, and Sarah. Not many details of their lives were given, but they all had a common goal: to get to Europe to work and earn money to improve the situation of their families. Aisha had a curiosity that she could not contain and brought it up at the last stop; indeed, they had all gone through a "juju" rite, they all had a debt to pay to the one who facilitated their journey, and they were all threatened by a priest with the consequences of not fulfilling their agreements.

At dawn, they stopped at the side of the road and were told they were at the border with Niger. They had to get off the bus and walk about five kilometers to avoid the border post, controlled by the state police. Getting out of the vehicle was partly a relief. They loosened their legs, stretched their limbs, and left the humid and oppressive environment. They breathed fresh air as if it were pure oxygen. The six Ajani girls grouped together and clasped their hands together as a kind of bond between them. During the trip they exchanged stories of their lives. It was as if they already knew each other a little more, like an invisible thread somehow held them together.

They went down a stony and dusty slope. In the end, they began a convoluted circuit of paths, sometimes smooth and sometimes among stinging, thorny plants without knowing where they were stepping. It took almost two hours, despite Ajani's verbal and sometimes physical pressure to move quickly. The words, always harsh and threatening, were repeatedly accompanied by pushing and shoving and the occasional blow. Finally, they arrived at a small, abandoned village, where another bus was waiting for them, different from the first one but just as uncomfortable and suffocating.

They stopped again on two occasions. In one of them, almost arriving at their destination, some men armed to the teeth, got into the vehicle and lifted the faces of all the girls, one by one. In each case, they were accompanied by the guide of each group. When they reached Aisha, the man looked at her carefully and smiled, showing his blackened and incomplete teeth. He said something to Ajani in a low voice. The same happened to Sarah. They got off just like that. Before that stop, another group of armed men stopped them and argued with the driver and the guides. In the end, a few bottles of liquor calmed the men's anger.

At last, they arrived in a neighborhood of Agadez, they were told. Houses of adobe, one or two stories high. They went down and divided them into groups, making them walk quickly through an infinite network of streets. The Ajani girls entered one of the houses—only six cots without mattresses were inside.

"We will be here for a few days, so get used to the place. You will not go out in the street under any circumstances, and only I will take you somewhere when necessary. Now sleep because tonight we will head out," Ajani ordered them with the usual harshness in his voice.

"Where will we go?" asked Saratu fearfully.

"You'll see," said the man sharply.

"When will we continue our journey?" Deborah dared to ask.

The question came laced with a slap in her face. The girl fell to the ground from the slap and immediately began to cry. The others surrounded her and formed a group as if defending each other. Ajani did not move a muscle.

"By the way, don't even think of telling anyone your real name, so make up one; if it's not African, all the better."

He left without another word. Once Deborah calmed down, they began to shuffle fictitious names. They looked at their cell phones for a source of inspiration but realized they had no reception. They reached for their memories in Benin City or the villages where they lived. They opted for names they had heard in their conversations as teenagers in their neighborhoods. Carla, Amanda, Victoria, Lilian.

"And you, Aisha, what names have you thought of?"

"Vanessa."

They were all exhausted, so they slept most of the day. Those infamous cots seemed a real luxury after the forty-five hours on the bus followed by walking along those roads. When night came, Ajani appeared again.

"You have seen that, since we left Benin City, we have stopped five times to pass controls of armed gangs and police. Each stop has cost money, which will be added to your debt." They looked at each other in astonishment. "But from here on, we can't give you any more money, so you will have to make the payments at each checkpoint."

"But we don't have any money!" exclaimed Aisha in surprise.

"You have your body, and that will be the payment," Ajani replied as he slowly shifted his gaze from one girl to the other. "Decide: either that or they will have no scruples about shooting you in the face."

That was not what they had been promised; that was not why they had undertaken the journey. None of them were virgins, they all knew what a sexual relationship was, but these threats sounded like something else.

"I don't think it will be hard for you to pay this price to go on to Europe. It will only take a few days and a few times each," he tried, unsuccessfully, to reassure them.

"Do we each have to sleep with a soldier?" Nguba wanted to know.

"You do what they tell you to do if you want to stay alive."

They arrived at the guerrilla camp in the middle of the night. Several men emerged from the canvas tents at the sound of the vehicle. The girls were terrified, together, holding hands.

"I'll come for them tomorrow morning," said Ajani. "I hope you like them."

Everyone burst out laughing, some with a bottle of gin or vodka in their hands. Without a word, they each chose one of them and took them to their tents. There was no preamble, no politeness, not even asking for their names. When Aisha entered the tent, without a word, he tore off her dress and left her completely naked. With a single push, he threw her onto the cot. Each one could hear the moans and the screams of the others as they tried to resist the assaults. Blows, insults, and screams in a language they did not know. There was no need to understand. They all knew what was happening to the others. When one finished, he would leave the tent and, without interruption, another would enter. There came a time when nothing could be heard—only the panting of monsters and the silence of shattered souls.

Ajani picked the girls up in the morning and took them back to the house. They had no strength. Almost all of them were badly wounded, with bruises, blood, and broken bodies. They were all silent.

"Wash yourselves and sleep well. Tonight, you will stay here, but any day, you will have to pay again to continue your journey," Ajani informed them without a hint of emotion in his words. It was just a warning about the plan of action. That night, he did not leave the house. He kept watch outside in case they reacted by trying to flee.

The next day passed almost with very few words spoken between each other. They were in pain, body and soul. They did not believe that this had happened to them. They had something to eat and, between them, managed to help Aisha to fix her dress, torn the night before. Amidst the silence of the afternoon, Awa prophesied:

"This is what awaits us. It was all a lie."

They lifted their gazes and glanced at her. She had summed up in one sentence what they had all been thinking since they left, but they didn't want to admit it.

"And the worst is the oath we swore before the priest in the voodoo ceremony. We are trapped by the gods. We and our families," Aisha concluded.

They remained in that house for ten days and were forced to make payments with their bodies three more times. They were different men, but what happened in their tents was always the same. What varied was that at any question, any request, Ajani would answer with a slap, a kick, a push, or by squeezing the neck.

Ajani reminded them that their debt had increased because of the payments they had to make at each checkpoint. What they had done in that place only served not to increase it even more. He told them that the next morning they would resume their journey. At least the route through Niger was safe from guerrilla attacks. The ringleaders had been satisfied, and that assured the girls of a certain security, at least until they reached Libya.

Any smiles that were seen in the first few days of the journey had faded completely. The silence, the slow, almost shuffling walk, became part of their daily life. Deborah hadn't eaten for three days; she couldn't even get a piece of bread in her mouth. She just cried non-stop. They all knew it was going to be a hard, tiring, suffocating trip, but they never expected this to happen to them. Sarah lived in a constant state of anxiety; her muscles were tense at all times, and she too could not sleep or eat. The others also struggled but were able to see these incidents as something temporary and they still held hope for a light at the end of the tunnel; a light that could make a difference in their lives. This was a price to pay, and they were paying it.

Crossing the Sahel desert was even worse. The roads alternated between burning sand and intricate forests. On some occasions, they had to get off the bus and walk several kilometers under a scorching sun to avoid guerrilla soldiers and catch another bus in a safer place. Everything was programmed as if it were a very well woven network, with its knots perfectly established. The guides knew the price of passing each knot and did not hesitate to use them as payment with violence.

On the bus were the same girls who had left Benin City, although Aisha noticed that the few men who had started the trip were not still with them, and she believed that eight or ten girls were also missing. At one of the stops, they were able to talk to some of them. Their guides had forced them to do the same as them, all of them. Some of them had visible marks from a beating, bruises on their cheekbones, freshly scarred lips, and the same darkness in their eyes that had settled on all of them. All of them.

Moreover, the whiteness of their teeth no longer contrasted with the tone of their skin, the brightness in their eyes had turned into a gray that barely reached the edge of their eyelids. Their minds were lost somewhere in limbo, although even they did not know where it could be, their hearts beat without the enthusiastic rhythm they had experienced when planning the trip. Their souls were wrapped up in packages with their personal belongings, the one that remained on the wall of the temple where they underwent the "juju" ceremony, an eye that always watched them. It had them wrapped in a cloak of atrocious, ancestral fear of one of the gods who would avenge all the evil they could inflict on them and their families. A chain was used at will and without mercy by those guides. These girls, barely even old enough to be considered young women, were seen simply as a means to an end, to a profit.

They finally arrived in a border region where they were ordered to get off the bus. They had to cross a jungle that limited the passage to Libya. The destination was Ghat, on the other side, located in Lebanese territory. The border was heavily guarded, so they had to hurry through the jungle and leave at the other end as soon as possible. At that moment, motorcycles started to arrive, driven by men of Arab features, all of them young. Their engines roared, and the noise pounded in the girls' eardrums as if they were thousands of drums beating in unison.

Each guide told the girls which bike to get on. As always, these were threatening orders. They were told to hold on tight to the bike because they would be riding at full speed and on terrain that was not smooth at all, with rocks, cracks, and dense undergrowth. There was no option to stop under any circumstances.

Aisha and her companions each mounted their assigned motorcycle. She was worried about Deborah. She was weak; she had not eaten anything for the last few days, and, above all, she seemed to have resigned herself to total apathy "Hold on tight. We won't stop to pick you up if you fall, so hold on to the bike's bars!" Ajani shouted at them, as always, with an intimidating tone. "Let's go!"

Aisha squeezed into the seat and grasped the bar that separated her from the driver with all her might. They looked at each other and wordlessly wished each other luck. The drivers started up with all the power they could muster, and some bikes even skidded on the way out. After ten minutes, they entered a dark, dense jungle, dark in every sense of the word. The branches of the bushes were hitting them from the front and from the sides, and they began to jump and skid continuously. The speed of the vehicles did not slow down at any time. On the contrary, it seemed that they even accelerated when there was more danger of crashing. The pilots were experienced in driving. They leaned the motorcycles and turned sharply as if they knew where the danger was coming from. They didn't warn the girls behind them but rather viewed them simply as luggage somehow responsible for their own security. Aisha kept her mouth closed to avoid biting her lip or any insect from entering her mouth. Her sole focus was to hold on. Her corneas became so dehydrated that she closed her eyes for a few seconds. An area of many bumps on the ground caused her to open her eyes quickly, and a pang of fear ran through his whole body. The image she could see was the motorcycle on which Deborah was riding and the girl shot out as if a catapult had launched her a long distance. An inert being in the air that did not even flinch, move her arms or kick the air.

"Deborah!"

Deborah's Story

Deborah was the youngest of six siblings—four boys and two girls. They lived in Mikang, a town in Plateau State, Nigeria. Its proximity to one of the main tributaries of the Niger River facilitated the agricultural wealth of the land. Almost all its inhabitants were cattle herders and farmers.

They had a small house on the outskirts of Mikang, enough to house the eight members of the family. They sold the products of the crops directly to the market of Mikang and in nearby towns. Deborah was almost eight years younger than the fourth brother in the family. When her mother became pregnant with her, it was a real surprise, as they thought she would have no more children. The others differed from each other by a little more than a year. Her sister, Esther, the eldest of them all, was fourteen years older and was left at home helping her mother with the housework as well as taking care of Deborah while her father and the boys all worked in the fields.

That state in northern Nigeria was one of the first to experience disputes between Sunni Islamists and Christians. Deborah's family were Christians, although they had never abandoned some ancestral, animistic traditions. Boko Haram's goal was to implant Islam throughout Africa, whatever the cost. As jihadist extremists they razed villages and stole everything in their rampage including kidnapping and murder anyone who resisted conversion. One of their atrocities consisted of kidnapping young girls, even pre-pubescent, forcing them to marry Muslims to increase the Islamic ranks while serving as sex slaves.

In early October was a busy time and the whole family went to the fertile land to plant cassava and corn, leaving just Esther to stay home and care for one year-old baby Deborah. They all left at dawn with the objective of returning at noon when Esther would have already prepared the food for them.

When they returned, exhausted from the morning's work, they entered the house and found it was in shambles with the tables overturned, the beds shattered, and shelves that once held groceries were now empty.

"Esther!" desperately shouted the mother. There was no answer.

"The child! Where is Deborah?" asked the older brother in a breathy voice.

They searched all that was left of the wreckage around the house and nearby, shouting their daughters' names. Silence. Suddenly, one of the brothers heard a moan in the area where his two sisters slept. He was right. He called the rest of his family to make sure. Under Esther's bed, they had dug a deep hole in the floor, covered with thick wood and earth, where they hid the money, they earned in the markets where they sold their products. They opened it quickly. Deborah laid there with a bluish tint to her face and hands from lack of oxygen. Her mother picked her up and carried her out into the open air, recovering quickly. But Esther was nowhere to be seen. On the front door of the house was a crude sign nailed with symbols they couldn't identify.

Days went by, and Esther was nowhere to be found. They asked in almost every house in Mikang. No one would talk. No one had seen anything. They went to the police. When two officers saw the paper nailed to the outside wall of the house, they looked at each other and told Esther's parents what it meant:

"It is Arabic. It means Boko Haram."

"No!" His mother could not get the sound out of her throat. It was almost a guttural scream full of anguish and desperation.

The ill fame of this group was already known; news of their devastating visits with the kidnappings of girls and young women had arrived from other cities. The policemen told him they would be vigilant and report it to their superiors but not to have much hope.

They returned to the police station almost daily to see if they had any news. On one of those visits, the squad chief said something that chilled them both:

"You have a little girl. They should think about her."

"What are you trying to tell us?" asked the mother.

"This is no land for girls, at least not as long as these monsters live and control it," said the policeman solemnly.

A year later, without news of Esther, they decided to emigrate far away. They had been told that things were quiet in Edo State, as far as jihadist terrorism was concerned, although employment was harder to come by. Fearing the same demise would come to their other daughter, they sold their land to adjoining neighbors, and with the money, traveled to Edo, settling in Ekhor, a village on the road to Benin City, an hour and a half from the capital by bus. They rented a one-story house with dilapidated but habitable areas. Two of the sons went to Benin City and found work as laborers in the cement factory. The other two started working as truck drivers transporting timber. The father found work carving logs to make support crutches for people with broken leg bones; it was a small factory, but it seemed productive.

Unfortunately, the family's opportunities came to an end when the cement factory laid off her two brothers, and the lumber transportation company was closed due to poor safety practices resulting in two accidents with three fatalities. Only Deborah's father was left with his work, which was becoming increasingly scarce. With some scraps of wood, he carved his daughter something like a doll, which her mother adorned with some scraps of straw. The money reserves from the sale of the land were running out. The mother found work cleaning a businessman's house in Benin City, but two meager salaries could barely feed seven people.

And so, the years went by in poverty. Many days they could not make one of their meals, and the children went out to the street to beg for something, but poverty was the way of life for almost everyone. Deborah grew up in this reality, reusing her dresses and adapting with patches to accommodate her growth. A local woman offered to teach her to read and write, free of charge, for which her parents were very grateful. In return, the girl helped clean the woman's house and prepared meals which also allowed the girl to take some leftovers home.

Deborah was transformed, little by little, into an attractive girl, with honey-colored eyes and curly hair. She was not very tall, but the boys in the area liked her. When she was fourteen years old, after meeting her friends for a chat and a walk, she found her parents at home talking to a lady, about forty years old, slender, and very smiling. Outside the house, next to the door, there was a boy, about twenty-five years old, leaning against the wall as if he was waiting for someone. Out of respect for her parents, she did not want to go inside. She approached the guy and asked him his name.

"Ajani," he replied without taking his eyes off the ground.

"You're not from around here, are you?" Deborah asked. She had always been very talkative and didn't hesitate to start a conversation with someone she didn't know.

"No."

"And what are you doing at my doorstep?"

"Waiting for my mother. She's in there," he pointed dismissively to the entrance of the house.

Mama Olawa had cast her net to the family. She would pay for Deborah's trip to Europe. There she would live in her sister's home, so they should be reassured that she would be protected and accompanied by someone they trusted. She would be hired to clean some luxury homes and take care of an old lady in one of them. They would pay a very good salary. The trip and the paperwork had a cost, a debt that the girl would pay from her salary: part to pay off the debt, part to send to her family, and part for herself. Everything was perfect.

When she left, the parents talked to Deborah and told her everything they had agreed upon with Mama Olawa. Deborah was very affectionate towards her parents and siblings; this was going to be very hard for her, to be separated from them, so far away, for so long. She burst into tears at the thought of parting from the company of her parents and siblings. Her mother consoled her, and her father made her see that the end of poverty in that family depended on her. The responsibility was enormous, and Deborah didn't know if her back could carry the weight. But her family was the most important thing in the world to her, so she accepted without objection.

A week later, they went to a rudimentary temple where the voodoo-juju ritual was to be held. Her father was her guarantor, and Mama Olawa was present at the ceremony. Deborah brought the personal offerings she had been instructed to bring. She was reminded of the terms of the agreement and the dire consequences if she did not fulfill her part.

Two weeks later, it was time for departure. Deborah spent most of the night crying in her mother's lap. At six o'clock in the morning, she was in front of the bus that Ajani had ordered her to get on. She was nervous, her whole body was shaking, and she feared something terrible, but all that was secondary to the grief of leaving her family. She got on the bus and sat where she was ordered. She couldn't hold back the tears. A hand took hers; it was the girl who was to travel next to her. Without saying anything to each other, Deborah rested her head on the girl's chest until she managed to calm down.

"My name is Aisha, and I am going to Europe to study."

Aisha's Story, Part II

"Deborah!"

She saw how her companion was thrown off, falling into the bushes. In that instant Aisha had to decide whether to let go of the bar that held her to the bike and help Deborah or continue to hold on with all her strength, and live. A muffled scream came from her throat, and tears began to well up in her eyes. She chose to live.

The air caused by the speed at which the motorcycles were moving quickly dried the tears on her cheek. An immense pain burned her chest, and grief stained all her thoughts black. She was sure that Deborah had let herself go. She was weak and very sad; it seemed that she did not want to continue the trip. She supposed that she let go of the bar of her motorcycle to leave her fate to destiny. No one stopped. Ajani had already warned that they would not stop under any circumstances, and he kept his word.

Guys like Ajani had no scruples, not even the slightest hint of anything resembling sentiment. That's why they were good at what they did. They didn't see people in those girls, only objects that were good for them to make money—lots of money. That's why they didn't need to care for them, be kind, or look after their emotions or needs. If they had to offer them as payment or if someone more powerful bought them, it was a business, just that. Beatings and rapes were nothing but a way to bend the will of the girls if there was any of that left in them at this point in the journey. After this "cargo" was delivered, they would return to Benin City and begin the journey of another shipment, just like that. That Deborah, or whoever it was, would fall off the bike and kill herself in some ravine hidden among the trees didn't stir heartstrings inside them. If they stopped to help her, the army or police could block them from passage to Libya, which would make the losses much greater; even their own lives would be in danger. One girl less was one less hassle, and one less gain.

They passed the jungle at full speed and reached a territory free of vegetation. They were in Libya and the desert quickly became the new landscape. In that country there was no stable government, and chaos was the way of life of its rulers. But this Nigerian mafia was well networked and had contacts that would ensure the safe transport of their smuggled goods, for a cost.

They continued the motorcycles, but no longer at such a high speed. The roads in the desert were perfectly recognized by the drivers, though to an outsider they were indiscernible. The first stop was Ghat, a flat city where not a single building stood out. Its houses blended in with the desert earth. A brownish tone dominated everything, even the air they breathed. They stopped and distributed the women in various houses. Aisha, her companions, and some girls from other guides shared a room with no beds, just some sacks on the floor that served as makeshift mattresses. They quickly grouped together and began to comment on the experience of the motorcycle ride. They all lamented what had happened to Deborah, and almost all thought she would not have survived the fall.

They were given some food and water. While their appetites were non-existent, they knew they needed to eat and the water was truly life giving.

In the middle of the night, Ajani quietly entered and, without a word, grabbed Aisha by the arm and dragged her out of the room. Out of the corner of her eye, she saw other guides doing the same with other girls. He moved her to another apartment. There were no words, no explanations. She was his, and he wanted to relieve his instincts and that's what he was finally going to do. Without further ado, he told her to take off her clothes, but she didn't even have time to do that as he lifted her dress, tore her underwear, and raped her. At first, she tried to resist, but the blows on her neck and the kicks on her belly made her give up. When he was done, he took away the bundle she always carried with her, took out her cell phone, and the food. He gave her back the empty bundle and pushed her with his foot as if she were a dog bothering him. She didn't know which was worse, leaving the house or staying there. She huddled in a corner of the room, still feeling the pain in her belly from the brutality of the sex and kicks he gave her to reduce her initial resistance. She went to grab her underwear, but Ajani grabbed her by one leg and dragged her back to where he was. He raped her again, but this time she had no strength to even attempt to resist.

The next day, the motorcycles were gone. They were loaded into open trucks with about fifty people. They drove across the desert day and night without stopping. Some of the girls asked to stop, but no one listened to them so many had no choice but to urinate on themselves. They only stopped after two days of travel. A little water, some food, and back to the truck again. The journey, under normal conditions, took about eighteen hours, but due to army checkpoints and guerrilla insurgents requiring bribes, it took them three days. Finally, they arrived in Tripoli where they were taken to a neighborhood on the outskirts of the city; it did not seem too populated, but fear was in the air. At any moment, from any place, a burst of gunfire, an isolated shot, or a hand bomb would break the latent silence in the streets. No one was to be seen; everyone was hiding in their homes. A person's life could be extinguished in a second if one dared to go out.

Before entering the city, they made them get out of the trucks. Ajani was nowhere to be seen, nor were the other guides. The girls did not know what to do; they grouped together in defense. The drivers, two for each truck, demanded that they pay them for the trip. No one moved. They began to search for the girls but found no money. It made them mad. Aggressiveness replaced their demands. They cornered them and started kicking and hitting them. They harassed Aisha and a girl from another group at the house entrance. They began to beat them mercilessly, as brutally as they could. One of the punches to Aisha's head caused her to fall and lose consciousness. Everything went black.

She didn't know how much time had passed when she came to her senses. She could hear indistinct murmurs as if they were people talking all at once. Her vision became clearer, and she could finally make out some of the guides pushing their girls away. She began to look in all directions, searching for Ajani, having become conditioned to follow his orders. When she turned her gaze to her left, she saw on the ground, near her, the girl from the other group, lying on the ground, motionless, her limbs outstretched, limp. Her eyes were open, and she could only see the white part. A trail of blood stained her shirt; blood was coming from her mouth. The position of her head made Aisha realize that her neck was dislocated.

"Come on, get up!" Ajani's voice was unmistakable.

"But the girl is hurt..." She still could not articulate her words well after he began to come to his senses.

"No. She's dead. They'll come for the body."

Nasha's Story

Ulegu was a village close to Benin City, barely forty minutes by bus, through one of the most chaotic roads in Edo State, characterized by people walking, old-fashioned vehicles that were mostly out of service, bicycles, ancient motorcycles, all mixed together, coming and going from Benin City. It had no market of its own. Goods were taken to the capital of Edo, and groceries passed through Ulegu on their way to other places. Rarely did a truck stop to sell food or raw materials to the inhabitants. Benin City was the reference point for them. There were only a few drinking establishments and a few huts where wooden figures or palm baskets were made, one of which belonged to Nasha's family.

Her parents married very young, not even fifteen years old. They both came from very poor families and continued to be poor. Three months before the ceremony, the young woman told her parents that she was pregnant by Keita, a boy she had known since they were children. Nasha's parents had built themselves a rudimentary hut; they had no income for anything else. Her father inherited the skill of weaving palm baskets, and it was his first job to provide the basics for him, his wife, and the baby. In those lands, having children was a gift from the gods, well, from God, although they knew that the ancestral divinities also had something to do with it. Thus, Nasha's parents had three sons within a year of each other. And, still breastfeeding the third one, she became pregnant again. When her mother went into labor, she could not go to the hospital nor call a doctor since they charged for deliveries. A healer from the village attended her in those circumstances, as she had done in the three previous deliveries, however in this case the fetus was breech; if she continued with the normal delivery, both mother and child could die. He took out of his bag a non-sterile knife and a piece of nylon, bought from some fishermen. He gave her a drink of infused herbs that numbed the senses but preserved muscular strength. He performed a kind of cesarean section, with the most rudimentary of tools. The child was born healthy, and the mother survived but could never be pregnant again.

Nasha grew up in poverty and breastfed for as long as possible since the family's income did not increase. The sale of the baskets was inconsistent and not a sufficient source of income to support a family. Sometimes, when her father exhibited the material at a flea market, he preferred to be paid in food instead of coins. The days seemed longer and longer. When they all finally went to sleep, Nasha's parents were breathing deeply, lying on the old mattress.

"One more day passed, and we are still alive," they said to each other every night before closing their eyes and surrendering to the night's rest.

The brothers began to work in the fields nearby that belonged to Saud, a well-known man in the area. He had a more than comfortable economic situation, some were suspicious of the origin of his income but of course no one questioned it publicly. The parents preferred that he paid their sons in food rather than money because it guaranteed they would at least eat. This man had two wives, both married in the Adventist Church and a traditional Yoruba rite. He had a reputation as a demanding and severe man; but he was also involved in the community and civic affairs. He frequently attended meetings and events of the Adventist Church, helped the councils of elders of the area and, of course, helped the police and political authorities of Benin. Though without any official title, he was indeed a man of significant influence in the area.

And so, the years went by. Nasha was already twelve, and her siblings continued to work on Saud's land without changing their conditions, but they were able to eat every day. Her father's eyesight began to fail which meant a significant decline in his basket production, so their financial situation began to decline even further.

Nasha was a sweet and pleasant girl and helped her mother as much as she could. At the age of twelve, she could neither read nor write, although the pastor of one of the Evangelical Churches in Edo State, from time to time, spoke to her about God and instructed her on some basic concepts of life—according to him, of course.

One day, Pastor Charles visited Nasha's family late in the afternoon and with hypnotic language that characterized his conversations, he proposed something different from the usual.

"Your situation is delicate; your family is barely surviving. Although God takes care of you and protects you from heaven, as His representatives on earth we must use all our strength to make our lives as prosperous as possible." He did not expect any answer, only that they understood his speech.

"Thank you very much, Pastor Charles," Nasha's mother interrupted, "but we're getting by. God keeps us going," she stated with a smile on her lips.

"But I have come to bring you a proposal that will alleviate the situation, I am sure." He made one of his strategic pauses. Saud offers for Nasha to live in his house. Of course, he will pay you a good price for her." Silence followed.

"But is it a marriage proposal?" asked the father.

"Not exactly. She would take care of his house, his children, and a little bit of everything. In exchange, he will have to take care of her in everything she needs."

"Do you bless this?" asked the mother.

"Of course, it is a tremendously generous act on his part. He is an exemplary person; he pays his tithe to the church and our daughter will be under a safe roof with food and clothing. In addition, if you accept, you also ensure that your sons will continue to work on their land and thus, continue to support this family. Of course, I bless this offer!"

Saud paid the family, through Pastor Charles, ten thousand nairas, equivalent to twenty-two euros. For them, that amount represented the family's earnings for more than a year of work. No one asked Nasha any questions and she simply obeyed because she knew she was helping to support her family. What she did not know at all was her new status as a "fifth wife." Men could have up to four "official" wives; thereafter, they were like maids in the house and bed of their buyers. That is why such a wife was "the fifth." However, even if they had only one wife, if another one entered with the conditions of servant-slave, she was considered a fifth wife. This was the case with Nasha.

She began her new journey somewhat intrigued but with caution. Her mother had told her about some things she had to do, which she had already heard about, but they had never been specific. She didn't like the idea, but it was all to help her family. Saud was away the day she arrived at the house. One of his wives met her with three small children around her. They commissioned her to make the meal that day; they wanted to test her. And she prepared it very satisfactorily. Saud liked her when he saw her, and that very night he wanted to enjoy her company. Nasha had never been with a man, but that didn't matter to him. He didn't plan to be the least bit careful. It was painful and, in a way, traumatic for a twelve-year-old girl in a bed with a man over fifty, who took no care for her. She did not scream when she felt the pain in her belly, but neither did she do anything to make Saud feel special. From that moment on, everything started to go wrong.

Nasha decided not to speak unless she was asked a question. She did the functions she had been given, including being grabbed by the arm, lying on the bed, and crushed by Saud's weight until he satisfied his desire. Nasha did dutifully complied with the sex but did so with the same mindset as that of cleaning the floor or preparing a dish to eat. One day they went to a church function, and Saud went to Pastor Charles' home, adjacent to the church building. He was there for almost an hour and afterwards the pastor found Nasha and took her to a room.

"How are you doing in your new home?" Nasha just shrugged her shoulders without saying a word. "Saud tells me that you cook well but that you don't give him all the satisfaction he wants, you know what I mean." She shrugged again, not meeting the pastor's eyes. "He says you don't get along with his women, that you don't even talk to them."

"I do as I'm told, isn't that what I'm supposed to do?" she said with a tone just short of contempt.

"Yes, but you are expected to put some passion into what you do. Well, hopefully, if you get pregnant, it will change things. Men like to see that they can father children." Nasha shrugged again.

Three years went by, and Nasha did not get pregnant, besides putting the same zero interest in everything, including Saud's increasingly infrequent requests. One day, a lady in her fifties, clearly overweight and sweaty, appeared at the house and asked for Nasha. She sat her down on a chair in the kitchen and got right to the point.

"Call me Mama Alossia. The master of the house is not at ease with you. I guess you know that. He was expecting someone nicer and who would take more interest in what he desires."

"I do what I am ordered to do," Nasha cut off without looking into the lady's eyes.

"I have agreed with the master that you are going to come with me to Europe," Nasha looked up to meet Mama Alossia's gaze and widened her eyes. "We will pay for your trip and take you to take care of some old people in their house. They are very rich, and besides, they have no descendants, so they will treat you very well."

"In exchange for what?" Nasha asked incredulously.

"To take care of these people. They need you very much. That's all. Mr. Saud has asked me for a favor, and I am only acting as an intermediary. Also, for your peace of mind, he has consulted with Pastor Charles, and he agrees. He thinks it will be very good for you. The expenses of the trip will be deducted from what you earn, but you will have money left for you and even some extra to send to your family."

The next day, Pastor Charles showed up to give his blessing. He made her kneel in front of him and, with both hands placed on her head, gave her God's grace for the trip and the rest of her stay in Europe.

One of Saud's wives accompanied her as she met Mama Alossia and handed over the little package containing a fingernail, blood from her last menstruation, and a piece of her underwear. A wooden image of the deity Olorum presided over the altar. She was reminded of her commitment of obedience to her guides, silence before third parties, and the delivery of the debt acquired for the journey. They threatened her with the consequences of not complying such as illness, personal and family harm, and even death. The voodoo-juju rite had fulfilled its mission: fear already lived inside Nasha.

A week later, at six o'clock in the morning, she was in front of the bus, following the instructions of Joseph, the guide appointed by Mama Alossia, with a promise to lead Nasha to a new life.

On the bus, she saw more girls, some older than her, some younger, almost children. Like all of them, she sat down and looked down. It was an order. It was her destiny: to investigate the void because it was the void that would shelter her every day and every night.

At the Niger border, she was dragged and beaten until she was convinced it was payment to let them go on. Three soldiers tore at her body and soul, one after the other. Returning to the room where the other girls were, she sat on the floor, leaning her back against the wall; she gritted her teeth with all the strength she had left to try to stop the cascade of tears her eyes were claiming. She continued to hope that this journey was indeed an open door to Europe, but she was sure it was also the hell of her life.

The motorcycle ride through the jungle that separated Niger from Libya was agonizing. Joseph's repeated rapes and beatings had sapped her will and body. The bumps on the motorcycle and the continuous back and forth were like daggers stabbing into her lower belly. She endured, as she had endured everything that had happened to her since her parents sold her. Yes, they gave her away in exchange for money, and that was something she had carried in her heart from day one. She never understood it, and now even less so.

In Tripoli, when the drivers who had transported them began to ask them for money, they were very frightened because these men did not seem satisfied with groping them or even raping them. In their faces, there was violent darkness, a murderous look, an absolute indifference to what happened to them. Indeed, she saw in their gestures the intention to do them unspeakable harm. In the melee of girls, all mixed among the different groups, she had grabbed the arm of one who was traveling with another group. They tried to defend each other from the blows of those men who were raging against them. They tried to defend themselves, to deflect the punches, to protect their bodies, at least the most vulnerable parts. She saw a punch hit the other girl in the head and watcher her fall senseless to the ground. Full of rage herself she kicked one of the aggressors in the testicles. In response another man delivered a sharp blow to her face. The dizziness was intense; she was unable to stay upright and fell to the ground, where everything became increasingly blurry. When she tried to raise her head, a kick to the back of her head made everything black.

Nasha's journey through this world had come to an end.

Aisha's Story, Part III

Almost two months had passed since that morning when she boarded the bus in Benin City. During that time, Aisha had witnessed the death of two girls just like her. She had suffered senseless beatings; and she had been violated more times than she could count.

Ajani told her that they would remain there for a long time, which she translated in her mind as a period in which he would offer her in exchange for perks, arranged payments, or who knows what else. The first few days were uneventful with her guide informing her one afternoon that they had to wait for the order to move to an undetermined port and cross the Mediterranean to Italy. Aisha listened to the explanations without moving a muscle on her face; she really didn't give a damn. She had not thrown in the towel, but her strength was weakening. It was almost like surrendering to her destiny, whatever it might be. But inside her, there was a small spark that kept her alive, the image of her daughter. What would become of her? Would she be well cared for? And, above all, when would she be able to hold her again? These uncertainties kept her will to live alive, whatever the cost.

One day Aisha started to feel ill; she felt feverish, her whole body ached, she coughed a lot, and her head seemed like it was going to explode. Ajani showed up one evening to once again take his own "payment" from her but when he touched her, he found that she was burning up and when he moved her she vomited on him.

A slap was the immediate treatment for her ills. However, for Ajani, Aisha was a valuable material since she was young and very attractive. Losing her would mean squandering a lot of money. That is why, just for that reason, he brought in a doctor who collaborated with the organization. He examined her and said there were two issues.

"This girl has pneumonia and should be on antibiotics." Ajani instructed him to acquire the medication and made it clear to Aisha the cost would be added to her debt.

"You told me there were two things. What is the second?"

"She is pregnant."

Pregnancies were frequent in these situations since none of the men involved in trafficking had interest in using a condom and the women had neither access nor standing to demand it. On many occasions they had someone hired by the organization who oversaw making sure that the pregnancy did not progress, with no concern for hygienic conditions or comfort of the patient. In some cases, girls did not survive. In other cases, as was the case with Aisha, it was in their interest for the pregnancy to continue, especially when they arrived in Italy because the pregnancy would slow down the process of deportation and repatriation. The child would be a very useful safeguard. Ajani was quick to make the decision.

"She must be cured and have the child there, on the other shore."

Three weeks passed, and with antibiotics and rest, her pneumonia largely subsided. The pregnancy continued. When she had carried her first born, Anatu, she remembered the sensations she felt in her body and her mind as pleasant as she felt every movement of the baby, marveled at every centimeter that her belly grew, and cherished every emotion that filled her heart. This time, it was different, constant discomfort, vomiting, headaches, and swelling in her legs. Above all, the reason for her pregnancy was different. Rather than being conceived in a loving relationship, this baby was conceived as a result of violent lust, and she had no way of even knowing who had impregnated her.

As her health was improving, she prepared to go for a walk, when Ajani suddenly came in and pulled her up by her arm.

"We're leaving now!" he ordered, shouting to the girls in his group.

"Where are we going?" asked one of them, to which Ajani did not hesitate to answer with a slap.

Again, they had to get into an open truck filled with fifteen of the girls who had left Benin City. Aisha did not even wonder what had become of the others; during her stay in Tripoli, she had no opportunity to speak with anyone except those who shared her room. They left at dusk. She could not calculate how long they were on the road or how many potholes they had to suffer, especially her. She could see that there were several other women who also were carrying babies.

They arrived at dawn on a beach. It was barely visible as it was a new moon, and the darkness was like a black cloak covering everything, including their souls. A small lantern carried by Ajani led them to the shore and a large boat. Silently, they began to climb in one by one, and a man inside pulled and pushed them as close together as possible.

"Hurry up! We must get out of here now. Hurry up, there must be room for a hundred people!" declared the man.

As the boat sailed, Aisha noticed one surprising detail: Ajani had not boarded. She did not know for sure if that was good or bad, although, with the experience of the last few months, she did not expect any positive surprises. It was the early morning of the thirtieth of July, and her destination could very well be the real gates of hell, thought Aisha. The sea was serene, which was a relief, however the boat would suddenly accelerate or slow down abruptly. The man ordered silence and looked through night vision binoculars. Some women vomited from the dizziness of the crossing, others reported stomach pains, possibly from the tension and anguish, and others were on the verge of falling into the water because they were too close to the edge of the boat. The boat was filled with complaints, moaning, crying as well as those who rode in silence, as many of these people, including infants and toddlers, took it almost like an adventure.

In the first light of dawn, they sighted a beach. The boat slowed down and stopped a prudent distance from the shore. The captain ordered them to get off since it was not too deep, and they could all get to shore. They all jumped into the water, some with more determination than others. Aisha had to be helped by another girl, as her belly was bulging enough to make it difficult for her to move with agility. The water was up to her neck, but she could walk with some ease. In turn, she helped a woman who was carrying her month-old son. His mother was shorter, and the water covered her, so she had to swim a little, while Aisha safely held the child. When they reached the shore some people with red vests approached them and helped them get out of the sea. There were tents further inland and tarps to sit on.

"Where are we?" asked Aisha to one of those people, grabbing his arm to get his attention.

"Italy. This is European territory. We will attend to you immediately."

It was a very common practice of the mafias that transported the victims of trafficking and other immigrants. They would leave them at sea, at a sufficient distance to be rescued by the humanitarian workers but far enough away to evade notice by the national police.

She looked everywhere anxiously, searching for any familiar faces besides the girls traveling with her. There was no sign of Ajani, Mama Olawa, or any of the drivers who had driven and assaulted the girls. She was alone. As she rested in the shade, nursing a bottle of water she had been given, she found herself cut off from the world. Uncertainty filled her old fears with new fears. Instead of any sense of freedom from being rescued she only felt more fear. No longer because she was being beaten or raped, but because she didn't know where, when, and how they would reappear. It could not end there, just like that. It was clear to her that the promises of a life in Europe to study were false. But also, Aisha was afraid all the humiliation and suffering she had already experienced would eventually return.

A woman in a red vest approached her and helped her up gently, something she had not felt from anyone since she had left her family. The five pregnant women were gathered to have a brief medical examination and to ask questions. They took each woman aside to provide privacy and the very first taste of restored dignity.

"We are volunteers of the Italian Red Cross. We are here to help you. What is your name?"

Aisha hesitated about what to say. Because of her oath in the voodoo-juju ceremony, she could not tell third parties about the trip or who was related to it. Nor could she say where she was coming from or where she was heading. She had never considered how difficult it was to answer that simple question. She took a breath and answered as if it was the most committed moment of her life.

"Vanessa… My name is Vanessa."

Aisha's Story, Part IV

The five pregnant women were transferred to Camp Hotspot, where they would remain until their illegal immigration cases were reviewed and their pregnancies were carried to term. A gynecologist examined them and established that all five were gestationally healthy. The camp was a luxury compared to all the places they had stayed during the African trip. Vanessa was struck by one detail: the absence of a distinct odor. During the journey, in all the means used and in the infectious places where they were, they could identify a specific smell, never a pleasant one. She remembered the scent of nerves and uncertainty on the first bus in Benin City, where all the girls emitted through their skin a perfume of hope, of latent restlessness for what would happen, of wanting to feel a change in their lives that would bring them hope to escape poverty. The smell of fear, a mixture of alcohol vapors, sweat, and violent sex, the smell of the soldiers taking their toll on the frontier, those wet and panting bodies. The smell of blood, from the beatings, and from the vaginal tears during multiple rapes. The intense, acidic stench of the back of the motorcyclist speeding through the jungle. And the smell of death, the soul of the deceased departing with the broken body left as a testament to her existence. But there, where she was now, she smelled nothing; it was a dense air due to the heat, but odorless.

They told her that they had to process her files and that this was a process that would take some time, but due to her condition, it was not a problem. She always answered questions with monosyllables and claimed that she did not understand what was being said, even though the questions were asked in perfect English, which was spoken in Nigeria. She said she spoke the Edo language. She didn't talk much, preferring to appear as someone who didn't understand, to prevent putting her foot in her mouth and giving out information that could be detrimental to her or her family.

The first few nights she was restless. It was strange that Ajani and Mama Olawa vanished. They were the architects of her trip to Europe, although she no longer doubted the deception and the kind of "help" they were going to give her. The day Mama Olawa went to see her father, the promises of studies and everything often surfaced to her mind. She thought of running away and making a life for herself, but she was afraid of the voodoo-juju threats. She quickly erased that idea and thought of asking to be sent back to Nigeria, but with this option she felt immense shame. It would be a stain on her family. Her father would not stand it, and how could she explain all that to her daughter and the girl's father? The fear, what that voodoo curse put in her body and her mind, paralyzed her.

Another afternoon, while resting on her bed, she wondered what would have happened if she had not been interested in learning if instead of listening to that child coming home from school, behind the curtain, she had continued with her homework or had gone with her friends. She blamed herself for what was happening to her. Because of that interest, Mama Olawa spun her spiderweb to trap her and wrapped her in a sticky thread that would immobilize her and not let her escape.

That morning, one of the pregnant girls told her about what she heard around, that they were tricked into slavery.

"Slaves?" asked Vanessa.

"Yes, and not only to work as maids or something like that. Sex slaves," the girl replied, slowly punctuating the syllables of those miserable words.

It was the first time Vanessa had heard that term. A shiver ran down her spine.

"We will do what we did during the journey, but with men who pay," said the girl.

"To earn money?" asked Vanessa, almost with fear.

"From what I have heard, they established a debt acquired and deceived our families. When you arrive at your destination in Europe, they inform you how much that debt is and how you must repay it." She imagined it that way because they made it very clear to her in the voodoo-juju ceremony.

"What happens when you pay it off?"

"The problem is that it gets bigger and bigger, and you never end up paying it off."

"How do you know all that?" asked Vanessa, intrigued.

"A girl who came in my group had contacts with an organization that orchestrated these things."

"So, if she knew, why is she here?" asked Vanessa in surprise.

"She was sold by her parents," said the girl.

There was a dense, suffocating, impenetrable silence. A lump in her throat prevented Vanessa from continuing to speak, and another in her soul prevented her from harboring any atom of hope for a happy ending to all this.

The human trafficking networks from Africa to Europe were quiet. Up to the time of Vanessa's arrival in Italy, the centers for the reception, recognition, and identification of African migrants were operated more by humanitarian organizations than by the police.

Politicians had not made the issue a priority to be addressed and therefore police agencies lacked the resources, protocols, and training to even attempt to combat the influx of exploited and trafficked individuals. Camps such as "Hotspot" were designated to provide support, but supervision was still not very tight, so members of the trafficking mafias could still move around these places with relative ease. In this way, they were spared the work and effort of keeping the people they trafficked hidden; that job was already being done by the authorities and the Red Cross. Then, after their basic needs had been cared for, the mafias would infiltrate the camp and retrieve their "property." This was the case with Vanessa.

She had already been in the camp for three weeks when one night, again a new moon night, a hand covered her mouth while she slept. At the same time, an African boy's face appeared before her eyes, telling her to calm down, that he was taking care of her. After the first impression, when her heart managed to reach a normal rhythm again, she went out with the boy, and he led her between the prefabricated huts, clearing knowing the way to go. They left the camp, and a dark brown car was waiting for them, with another young man at the wheel. They put her in the back seat, instructed her to lie down until they were out of the most heavily guarded area, and drove on with the lights off until they reached a side road.

"My name is Ajnam." It was obviously false. "We will take you to a safe place where we will give you a passport so you can travel. Give me the papers given to you by the Red Cross. I will keep them for you." His outstretched hand and threatening look left no room for doubt that this was an order not a request, so she reluctantly handed them over to avoid a slap, or worse.

"And where is Ajani?" asked Vanessa with all the uncertainty in the world on her shoulders.

"I'm guessing he was your African guide. Only we are here, but we work for the same... agency."

They arrived at an apartment in a nondescript neighborhood with few people on the street, all of them African or Arab-looking. She was deposited with two new men who told her to sit on a chair in front of a white wall, tied up her hair a bit, and took a picture of her. They quickly printed it out and added it to a passport they were reconstructing with her photograph.

"This is your passport, this is your plane ticket, and here is some money so that customs will believe that you are going to Spain for tourism. If they ask you, you just say you are going to study and do some sightseeing," they told her all this slowly, looking her in the eyes as if making sure she understood everything they were saying. "Do you understand?

"Yes," said Vanessa with yet another new fear rising within her.

"When you arrive, they will pick you up at the airport and take you to a safe place. Another thing, if you have any problems or get lost or get stopped before the plane takes off, as soon as you can, call this phone number "he gave her a piece of paper with a number written on it. "Ask for Mama Sarabi. She is your guide in Italy. Learn the phone number by heart. You won't be carrying the paper, so memorize it."

It was getting light. They gave her some breakfast and went back to the car that had taken her out of the camp. They drove to the airport and dropped her off at the gate.

"Remember everything we have told you," Ajnam told her before he got out of the car, "don't forget what you were reminded of at the voodoo-juju ceremony."

Her legs trembled as she approached the ticket counter. In a low voice, she rehearsed possible answers to probable questions. She could feel the beads of sweat running down her back, and the weight of her growing belly seemed to multiply. She passed the first test with flying colors: the boarding pass was in her hands. Secondly, she passed through the customs control without warning from the metal detector. All that remained was the police checkpoint. They asked for her passport, and the officer who was inspecting it, while glancing at the document, made a quick visual scan of her face, once, twice… he called a colleague, and she came out of the booth and stood behind Vanessa.

"Please follow me." He kindly led the way to a side door leading to a small office.

She walked in, and, without further ado, they began to ask her questions. Two agents, both women, talked almost at the same time. Vanessa burst into tears, helpless, defeated, holding her belly as if it would burst open. She could not tell on anyone, talk about anyone, or give any clue that would lead the police to the people who had brought her there. She just kept silent and cried. She was taken to the police station, where she was informed that she was being detained for using a false passport, not cooperating with the authorities, and being in the country illegally. A doctor came to see her and established that the pregnancy appeared to be in good condition. She spent the night in the police cell while the officers prepared their report. The next day she was taken to court, where she was met by a man who said he was her court-appointed lawyer. In the quick hearing of the case, the judge asked the parties (prosecutor and public defender) for information regarding the defendant, but they had little to offer since Vanessa continued to share very little. The judge had heard hundreds of similar cases; after further discussion between the magistrate and the two lawyers, the sentence was pronounced that the defendant would be transferred to the Women's Center attached to the Convent of the Nuns of Santa Maria in Rome.

For years, these nuns had been helping authorities and, above all, the women who had found themselves in such distressing situations. They decided to build barracks adjacent to the convent and provide care for all these girls. Authorities recognized the need to keep the women under control, and the nuns could thus fulfill one of their objectives: to help and protect the underprivileged. She would stay there until giving birth, and then the deportation process would officially begin.

They arrived at the Center, where a nun received her with great gentleness. She was escorted to a room with about twenty beds. She was given a nightgown to sleep in, a bag of toiletries, and was told that there was a bell in case she needed medical attention in the middle of the night. She was then taken to the dining room, where she could identify quite a few African women, young like herself, looking lost in nowhere. Nevertheless, as they entered, they looked at her curiously.

"Attention!" said the nun. "We have a new girl with us, her name is Vanessa, and she will soon have a baby, like some of you."

She sat down to eat and gradually connected with the other girls. Almost all of them told stories very similar to hers. They set out with the hope of a new life and found themselves in circumstances they did not know could even exist.

Life went smoothly in that Center as the nuns gave them meaningful work to do, and, in a way, some sense of normalcy began to return. It had been almost six months since she landed in Italy, it was Christmas, and the time there went by slowly and steadily. However, she kept thinking about her "contract" in Benin City, the fear came back to her, and she needed to make a phone call. One of the girls, after having gained Vanessa's trust, little by little, got along very well with her. They talked a lot, like when in her neighborhood, back in Nigeria, she met with her friends, although everything was different. In one of the conversations, the girl confessed to her that she had a hidden cell phone. Vanessa begged her to let her make a call. Of course, she let her do it.

"Hello?" said Vanessa when she heard someone answer the call.

"Who is it?" asked a woman's voice.

"I'm Vanessa. I'm asking for Mama Sarabi." A few seconds of silence seemed eternal.

"Good," the woman's voice said coldly. "It won't be long now until you have the baby. Stay there quietly until you deliver. When the baby is born, call me again. We'll contact you later."

At the beginning of spring, when everything started to bloom, her water broke while she was sitting in the cloister of the convent, basking in the silence. The doctor was called, and it was a quick delivery, in the same bed where she slept daily and without complications. A boy. She looked into the baby's eyes. He seemed to carry in his gaze the sadness of his conception, the anguish of his uncertain future, and the sorrow of knowing he was not entering the world as a new life should. Vanessa supposed none of that was possible in a newborn child, but she thought she saw it all.

Just as Mama Sarabi told her, two days after she gave birth, she called her again on her friend's cell phone.

"I've already had the baby; it was a boy and…" She intended to tell her what the newborn was like.

"Very well," Mama Sarabi abruptly cut her off. "Get ready to leave the Center. In a few days, we will come for you."

Indeed, she never knew how, but a few days later, a young man, African like the others, appeared in the middle of the night. Leaving that haven of peace with her newborn baby was difficult, but the fear of what would become of the voodoo curse compelled her to comply.

She climbed into a car, nondescript like the one that had transported her from the Hotspot Camp, with the child snuggled in her arms. They arrived at an apartment, where Mama Sarabi was sitting in an armchair waiting for her.

"We must be very careful. You will not be able to travel by plane, there are many controls, and they will miss your absence in a few hours," the woman told her dryly. "We will give you a new passport that they will not be able to detect at customs. You will go by boat."

"Where am I going?" asked a trembling Vanessa, still holding her son in her arms.

"To Barcelona. By the way," Mom Sarabi got up from the armchair, "the child stays with me. When you pay your debt in Spain, you will come and pick him up." She snatched him from her arms.

"But—" Vanessa hesitated.

"Don't worry. I will take good care of him. It is now too dangerous a burden for you to travel to another country. He will be fine. When you finish your engagement there, you will come back, and you can take him to your country or wherever you want."

She had been lied to so many times during the trip that she took those words as one more falsehood. Just as painful and cruel, just as lacerating to her soul, yet another one, and she was sure it would not be the last. Even though that child was not begotten willingly and lovingly, she was his mother, and the ties that bound her to him were as strong as their breakup was painful.

At the seaport, Mama Sarabi moved about freely. It was clear that this was not the first time she had done this, nor for the customs agents pretending to play dumb by looking the other way. The crossing lasted almost a full day. On the boat, sitting on one of the decks, she kept trying to make sense of everything that was happening to her.

As soon as they disembarked in Barcelona and passed through customs control without difficulty, a lady approached her, grabbed her energetically by the arm, and took her quickly to the arrivals area. Right there, another nondescript car opened its back door, and they both got in to quickly head for the Sants train station.

"This is your ticket," said the lady without showing any emotion. "You know what you must do and what you must not say under any circumstances. Remember what you risk if you don't comply. At your destination, you will be picked up, and you will be told what to do. Do you understand?" The lady's voice became threatening as she vocalized the question.

"Yes," Vanessa replied, in a fearful, trembling whisper.

She boarded the train wondering if it would be her last transfer or, as had happened to her until then, it was another stopover enroute to whatever destination awaited her. The train trip took six hours, so she had the opportunity to close her eyes and sleep for a few moments at a time. Each time she snoozed, the images piled up in a repetitive and disorderly mess in her head. They were always the same: her family, the voodoo-juju ceremony, the beatings, the rapes, the child, her daughter....

They announced over the loudspeaker that they were arriving at the destination station. She got up and got ready to get off.

As on previous occasions, this time, a man in his thirties approached her not far from the platform.

"Come on, Vanessa, you've reached your destination," he said without looking at her face.

"Do I have to go somewhere else?" she asked, afraid to hear the answer.

"No. Not for now."

Her next stop was an apartment in a ten-story building. It seemed too high compared to what she had known from her childhood. She was passed off to a man in his forties who indicated a chair for her to sit on and quickly began to give her instructions. She looked around, looking for someone with African features. Of the four people in that room, she was the only one.

"Give me your passport." She held it out to him, and he handed it to another man, who cut it with large, powerful scissors into five or six pieces. "This is your new ID." Vanessa reached out to take it, but he quickly took the document away. "I'll keep this one, and when you finish paying your debt, I'll give it to you."

"Debt?" She had already been told all about the debt, especially by her companion at the convent in Rome, but she wanted to know from the person who seemed to be responsible for it.

"Bringing you here, the expenses of your pregnancy, the payments to pass customs and some other things, add up to 35,000 euros. That is how much we have paid to bring you here and now it is time for you to start paying it back," said the man, leaning forward as if he wanted not one of his words to get lost in the space between them.

"But Mámá Olawa told me that she was bringing me here to study and that I would be living at her sister's house." Vanessa had already dismissed the veracity of all that, but she had to try. The response was a slap on her left cheek.

"Wake up! You owe us 35,000 euros, and you are going to pay it. You can't legally work here, so you'll have to serve us in our business. Don't play dumb. You must earn money with your body!" A shiver ran down her spine, even though she had foreseen this outcome, hearing the words spoken cemented her deepest fears. "We'll take you to an apartment where you will live with other girls. You don't have to pay for anything on your own. We'll buy everything you need and add it to your debt. Rent of the apartment is 300 euros every month, plus the food we buy you, the clothes, the medicines, and the temporary residence papers. Everything will be added to the debt, which you will have to pay with what you earn from the sexual services you provide...so the more you work, the sooner your debt will be paid. We will periodically tell you the balance of your account."

"And when will I finish paying?" asked Vanessa hesitantly.

"We will return your passport, and you will be free."

Free. That word was to be the essence of her destiny, her yearning, something for which she would fight day by day, man by man, night by night. Free. She had never believed that this feeling would paint the walls of her life. Despite her family's hardships, she would have never willingly agreed to working as a prostitute. Free. If she were not free, then her status was that of an enslaved person—a sex slave.

She arrived at the flat that would be her new home and was greeted by three girls. They welcomed her and saw from the moment she arrived, the same thing that each of them had felt on their own first day; the same sorrow taking possession of her soul, the same lost look, anxiously searching for eyes that would receive her and, above all, understand her. They understood her perfectly; she was the image of themselves a few months or years earlier.

They told her where she'd sleep, and each woman gave her a gift of a garment in preparation for her new job. Above all, they talked to her about how she should act, what she should do, the dangers to be aware of at the nighttime shifts at the industrial park. They schooled her in how to interact with other women and of course their clients, and shared strategies to earn money as quickly as possible along with ways to get out of compromising situations.

That night, she did not leave the apartment. She went to bed and slept as she had not done for many months, already more than a year. The next day was her first day at work and her body and soul would become a cash register with each transaction taking much more than it gave.

That next evening, she followed along with the other women and they explained that each nationality had its own area and that it was better for her to always be in their company to avoid unruly clients. They went by bus to the industrial park and stayed there for ten or twelve hours every evening. Vanessa was young and attractive, so clients frequently came to claim her services.

One night, a van appeared, and the girls joyfully went to meet it.

"Mommy! Daddy!" they shouted upon arrival.

"Who are they?" Vanessa asked one of her companions.

"Angels. You'll love them, you'll see."

Five people came out of the van and showed genuine concern for them as they offered drinks, some food, and a baggie filled with coveted hygiene items.

"You are new. What is your name?"

"Vanessa."

"Hi Vanessa, my name is Sara, and this is my husband, Diego. We are here to help you."

Juliet's Story

Juliet was born in Nigeria, in a suburb of Benin. Her parents, like most of the inhabitants of these slums, suffered economic hardship, but her mother was able to provide better than many from the sewing workshop she had in her home. Juliet learned the trade at an early age and was an invaluable help to her mother. As she grew up, she had the dream of having her own sewing store, a business that would support her and raise her economic status and provide a more comfortable living for her own family.

When she turned fifteen, as was the case in many families, her parents made arrangements for her marriage. Dembo was thirty-five-years old and part of her extended family. His first wife had died from tuberculosis a year earlier. It was well known that he drank too much but he also was wealthier than most so Juliet's parents believed he would provide well for their daughter and hoped a new bride would take away the strong appeal of alcohol.

Two days after the wedding, Juliet experienced the first signs of violence from her husband. When he came home from work and the food was not on the table, his complaint materialized in a slap that knocked Juliet to the floor. Her lip was bleeding profusely, and her head was pounding.

"You're a mess!" he yelled at her, looking at her cowering on the floor, "You're not doing anything right!

Juliet was strong, she had always faced problems head-on, but she was not used to such violence within the family. Dembo often came home at night reeking of alcohol and wobbling as he walked, stumbling over chairs. He would drop into bed and fall asleep. Those were the quietest times for Juliet because if he wasn't conscious, he couldn't hit her.

She did sewing work for the neighbors and that helped her save money to set up her own store next to their house. She grew in confidence and strength, the drunkenness and beatings made her tough, and she resolutely repelled her husband's blows more than once. Dembo would frequently not come home or if he did, fell asleep in the common room without even making it to the bedroom. One morning she noticed that the box where she kept her earnings was open and empty. That same night, when she returned home from work, she saw her husband rummaging through everything, taking the clothes out of the drawers and scattering them on the floor. He was drunk and was looking for more money to continue drinking.

He screamed obscenities at her, demanding to know where the money was.
"You've taken it all. There's no more!"
Dembo staggered as he walked, broke a glass vase in his wake, and headed out to her store. Finding no money there, he picked up a piece of cloth, clicked his lighter, and set fire to the fabric. The flames spread quickly, and her beloved store burned like a funeral pyre – exactly what it was, the death of her business and her hope for life.
Juliet couldn't stop crying. Her store had burned completely, there was nothing left to rebuild. As she sat and cried in front of the ruins of her tent, she felt a hand on her shoulder.
"Hi, girl, I'm Mama Olawa, I know what happened, and I'm here to help you."

As she had done on so many other occasions, Mama Olawa told this vulnerable young woman that she could help her, that there was plenty of work in Europe, and that she could recover financially there and help her elderly parents. She told her how much it cost to take her there and that she would have to pay back the money, but not to worry, she would be able to do it very soon. Juliet saw something strange in the whole proposal, but she had no choice but to accept. She was nineteen years old and knew she could not live under the harsh treatment of Dembo for one more day.
To seal the commitment, Mama Olawa took her to the voodoo-juju ceremony, and there, she signed her skin and soul to her doom.
Juliet was very beautiful, with intense, deep, hypnotizing eyes, a very striking body, and style when she moved. Mama Olawa realized this and planned the trip differently than she did with the other girls. She could get more money by selling her to the mafias that had the prostitution business in Spain, so she arranged for her to travel by plane. It was more expensive, but also the debt would include that increase in cost.
Juliet arrived in Spain, and there, her ordeal began. Instead of the recruitment office she had been told to expect, she found herself in a dark, sordid room full of old furniture. There an intimidating

Nigerian man spoke in her language and stated her debt was 10,000 euros and told her clearly how she was going to pay it back. He instructed a woman to give her clothes to start at the industrial park that same night. Juliet tried to protest, first with words and then an attempt to get away but the man's fist sank into her stomach, she fell twisted to the floor, and he bent down, grabbed her by the hair, and turned her head until he met her gaze with his own.

"Do you have any more complaints? No? Then get going and start earning money to settle your account."

She knew what the prostitutes practiced every day, she had seen them in Benin, and they commented on all the things they did to the men, but she never thought it would happen to her. That same night she was taken to the industrial park, along with other Nigerian girls. It was demeaning, dirty, and hurtful. She vomited twice and just kept thinking this was all a nightmare and she would soon wake up…

A Long Journey from Romania

Ciprian grew up in the small town of Ungheni, Moldova – very close to the Romanian border. From a young age it was apparent that he had a remarkable learning capacity and as he grew older his physical agility abilities became apparent in gymnastics and his engaging personality caused him to further stand out among his peers. From the age of ten, he was already showing signs of success in public school. By the middle grades he spent almost the whole day at the Vladimir Lenin Public School: in the morning, he attended mathematics, English, Russian literature, geography, history, science, and art classes; afternoon, he attended theater classes, where he was trained in modern stage acting techniques; around five o'clock in the afternoon, he went to a free public gymnasium very close to his home. Rare was the day he did not arrive home before seven o'clock in the evening. When he arrived, his mother had prepared some dinner for him.

Ciprian's mother was a simple woman who grew up in the interior of Moldavia. She married Mihail at the age of fourteen and moved to Ungheni after he got a job there as a driver for the local socialist party. He worked hard, so hard that some of his bosses asked him for special favors, such as serving as a cover for an unofficial meeting, a visit to comrades to satisfy their sexual instincts, or simply a private family trip. One day, in one of these unofficial tasks, he was caught in a trap; one of the party members told him that they had to go "warn" someone that he could not talk about the political regime in certain undesirable environments. They would visit him at night to convince him of the inappropriateness of his comments. Upon arriving at the indicated destination, his boss got out of the vehicle and asked Mihail to come with him. He knocked on the door, and out came a young man, about twenty-five years old, who was clearly surprised to see a party leader at his home at that hour. In a flash, he received three bullets in the chest and one in the face. Mihail was shocked, paralyzed, unable to breathe, his eyes wide open, unable to believe what he had seen. Without any gesture indicating anything different than his usual orders, his boss put his gun away and said, "Put him in the trunk. Let's take him to a place in town, where anyone who has thought of following the same path of dissidence can see him." He gestured with a nod of his head to the corpse lying on the ground.

"It will stain the car with blood," said Mihail, even now considering how to conduct his work in a professional manner, despite the shock.

"So, get some blankets from there to wrap it up…and hurry, we need to leave now!"

They drove to the bar where the man was known, under the alcoholic influence of a few drinks, to have criticized the party's behavior. The boss ordered Mihail to stop the car and dump the body at the entrance of the bar. He did so, and they left the place in a hurry. That night, Mihail arrived home and drowned his anguish with a bottle of vodka.

As time went on his boss required him more and more to participate in such duties well beyond his official role of chauffeur. The "warnings" took the form of beatings, the intensity of which was proportional to the type of "wake-up call" that was warranted. The sum of violence and vodka became an irremediable part of his personality and, more seriously, of his daily life. This included his wife. He no longer used words with her to get his way, only his fists. The beatings came for anything: a cold meal, a lamp that was out of place, an unmade bed, a dress that was too short or too low-cut, over-painted lips, in his opinion—anything.

One night, returning from one of his assignments, without saying a word, he forced himself sexually on his wife. This was a regular occurrence, but this time she became pregnant. Her condition calmed Mihail's fury for a time, but the violent storm inside of him eventually began and rage again and he was back to his old ways.

When she was eight months pregnant, a slap made her fall to the ground, and a trickle of blood began to flow between her legs. He was frightened and took her to the doctor's office himself. The result of that slap was the premature birth of their son, Ciprian. Another consequence to the violence was uterine damage that prevented her from getting pregnant again.

Ciprian grew up in an environment that could best be defined as sordid. A father who was rarely at home, and when he was, it would have been better if he wasn't. A mother who was overly devoted to her son, which many times became the cause of his father's bad temper. Ciprian grew as an explosive mixture of intelligence, artistic talent, and outstanding physical strength. In the first years of school, his intellectual side dominated. When he reached middle school, it was balanced with hard and intense gym workouts. At sixteen, he was a strong and attractive young man, with a trail of intelligence cultivated when he was younger and a special gift for acting, on and off the stage.

Ciprian could not stand seeing the bruises on his mother's body, the progressive forced aging of her face, and the fractures in her arms, which were always justified to the doctor as fortuitous falls. His mother would convince him to stay out of these situations, not to come between her father and her, in short, to look the other way. His pent-up rage grew more and more every day, and he feared that he could not keep it caged inside him. He would let off steam in the gym with the punching bag, the weights, or any exercise that served to release the seized strength in his muscles and the angst that weighed upon his heart.

That day in April, after a day as uneventful as any other, he returned home in the evening. He expected to see his mother preparing dinner and asking her how the day had gone. When he opened the door, none of that was happening. She had been raped by her drunk husband, and blood was gushing from her mouth. He dropped the bag of gym clothes and gave his muscles permission to let out all the rage he had been carrying inside him for many years. With a single blow, he knocked his father down. Mihail instinctively grabbed a kitchen knife to defend himself, but it did him more harm than good: Ciprian grabbed his wrist and twisted it until that sharp dagger penetrated his father's neck. Guttural gasps were the last thing mother and son heard from the monster.

"You have to get out of here, Ciprian!" his mother implored in anguish when she saw what had happened.

"No, mother, I will not leave you," said her son without showing any feelings of remorse for his actions.

"They'll kill you; you know it. You must flee! Give me the knife! I have nothing to lose. I will tell the police I killed him in self-defense. No one will be surprised. Go away while you can!" pleaded his mother.

Ciprian knew she was right. They hugged, and he left his house with all the speed in the world. He had once heard his father say to a comrade that the best way to get away from there was to cross the Prut River, that "it was very shallow, the water barely reached his knees." He would then soon be in the neighboring country, so that is what he did. He took his bicycle, went to the river and crossed to the other side, and soon entered Romania. He pedaled with all his strength to get as far away from the border as possible, as soon as possible. He hid in a forest and, still with his heart beating at full speed, huddled in some bushes for the night.

He could not sleep. Images filled his head. The beatings of his mother, the hatred that was building up in his soul, first towards his father, then towards the whole world. As scenes from his childhood flashed through his mind, he remembered a family that would spend two months in Ungheni every summer. He had become friends with the boy his age, Radu, and remembered that they lived in Timisoara, Romania, the second largest city in that country. Every summer, when Radu returned home, they promised that they would live in the same city someday. Timisoara would be his destination; he remembered the address by heart from all their years of childhood scheming. Before fleeing his home, Ciprian had taken money from the drawer where his father hid his earnings from the family, but which he knew perfectly well after spying on him on different occasions, and his cell phone.

In the morning he continued cycling on back roads until he reached Bacău. There he took a bus that took him far enough away from the area to, after several transfers, reach Timi□oara. There, he called Radu, and they immediately met in a café near his house. Radu had become the brother he never had; they told each other all their secrets from the innocence of childhood to a bit murkier in early adolescence, and now the darkest imaginable at the age of sixteen.

"I killed my father," Ciprian began the conversation in a low voice after the waiter walked away.

"What are you talking about?" Radu's eyes widened in unbelief.

He told him in detail what was going on in his family for as long as he could remember, something that, strangely enough, he had never told him during their times together in the summer.

"I need to live far away from there, and the first thing that came to my mind was to come to you for help," Ciprian spoke with a cold confidence.

"Some friends in their last year of high school are living in an apartment, and one of them has left. He is dropping out of school. I can talk to them and put you up there.

"But how am I going to pay for it?" asked Ciprian incredulously.

"My mother's family owns a large sawmill; you could work there."

Within a week, Ciprian was indeed working at the sawmill and sharing an apartment with three students. The salary was not much, but it was enough to pay his share of the rent and save for himself.

The next two years were relatively uneventful as Ciprian was forced to learn how to provide for himself. Life had started to become rather monotonous when one roommate left and Vlad, a boy of nineteen, tall, blue-eyed, good-looking, and with very polite manners, joined the group. Ciprian observed that Vlad did not fit in among his upper grade peers at the high school. He was sophisticated in his ways, he observed everything in a strategic manner, and he had a way with words that always seemed to work things out to his advantage. One night, while they were enjoying a beer in a relaxed setting, Ciprian finally approached him

"Tell me the truth, Vlad. You don't fit in a high school. Who are you really?" he asked, in a casual but convincing manner, remnants from his own days on the stage pretending to be someone he was not.

"My dear Ciprian," Vlad answered with an arrogant tone, "the school is a cage where there are many little animals just waiting for attention. I focus on young, innocent, love-struck girls. The ones easy to lead to thoughts of magical dreams where everything is peace, love, and happily ever after. It's not that difficult to make them fall in love with me; to become the Prince Charming of their dreams, that a fairy touched them with her magic wand and put in front of them the person without whom they could not live. Me."

"Ha-ha-ha, very creative of you, Vlad. I guess you'll be a romance novelist in the future." Ciprian held his bottle of beer out to him as a toast.

"You are wrong. I am a businessman who is going to make a lot of money. Listen to me—a lot of money," he slowly punctuated each syllable.

"I am not following."

"You see, I dazzle them, I lift them up to heaven in a cloud of infinite promises, I give them jewelry, trinkets really, but they are hypnotized and see what their heart and I dictate to them. I even talk to their family. I convince the parents that there is no one better for their daughter than this educated and well-positioned lad named Vlad!"

"All in all, a very well-planned deception. But for what purpose, just for the fun of it? How will you get rich?"

"That will happen later, with patience; haste is not a good companion for personal success. Once I have them trapped, I propose to them that we should go to another country, where the situation is better than here. They always accept. We leave, and that's where my profits start."

"I still don't follow," said a confused Ciprian.

"Upon arriving in our new country, I weave a tale of a business deal gone badly, that all our immediate resources have been lost in the unfortunate investment, and that we must find an alternate source of income to survive until I can make more networking connections and find new business partners.

By this time, they are so in love and devoted to me that they are willing to do anything to make "us" work. Now my question for you, young Ciprian...what is the fastest way to make money with these young, attractive, desirable bodies?"

"Prostitution," said Ciprian, as the mystery was finally revealed.

"Exactly."

Ciprian was no longer the good, studious, kind boy who lived in Ungheni. Everything that had happened, his escape, and the passage of time had transformed him. He had become self-absorbed and indifferent to the needs of others. He used his acting skills in his relationship with others, never allowing true connection or intimacy. He was not interested in the responsibility of a serious relationship with a girl, no matter how attractive or delicate she was. Sometimes he visited a brothel and had sex with a prostitute, never stopping to think about what was behind their scanty clothes, their lost looks, and their forced smiles. He simply unburdened himself through their bodies, and that was enough for him. What he was very much interested in was how to earn money without having to go to the sawmill every day for a half-decent wage and to use his natural talents in a more meaningful manner than physical labor. Vlad had just struck a chord in him, getting his full attention.

"Have you done it before?" asked Ciprian.

"No. I'm weaving my first spiderweb, and I already have the one who's going to get caught in it, a girl from high school." Vlad winked as he told him.

"So, how do you have everything so under control if you've never done it?"

"I know people. They have instructed me. They have been doing it for a long time. And I assure you, they are very rich." Vlad made the money sign with his fingers, rubbing together the thumb and forefinger of his right hand.

"I would like to meet them; could you introduce me to them?"

"Sure thing."

In a matter of days Ciprian had met Vlad's contacts. They saw that he had the right personality and abilities: good presence, polite, able to act convincingly and at the same time, cold, with no emotional ties and with physical strength, in case he ever needed it. They guided him through the business. The deal was half of what he collected with the first girl. It seemed fair to him.

He made some changes to the standard strategy but basically convinced himself that he was going to make a lot of money. He had no real regard for females, old or young, so it was an easy sell to convince himself that life was simply survival of the fittest and he had no problem looking out for his own best interests, regardless of the cost to others.

And so, he became a "lover boy."

Ionela's Story, Part I

Life in Arad was simple and peaceful. A small town, barely an hour from Timisoara by car, very close to the Hungarian border. In fact, from the Middle Ages until the end of World War II, it belonged to Hungary. Its inhabitants were friendly, quiet people who savored daily every serenity that their good climate and the surrounding nature gave them.

The Bogdam family was leaving the Orthodox Cathedral of Arad after attending Sunday morning services. The parents of the family were very devout and instilled the fear of God in their children, including belief in the supernatural, the immense divine goodness, and the protection that the angels gave to all the inhabitants of the earth. However, these principles had not managed to settle in the souls of their twin sons. While they respected the religiosity of their parents, for themselves they chose to follow communist pragmatism and materialism. The day after their eighteenth birthdays they became independent and moved to Timisoara to study, having earned state scholarships.

Ionela was different; very friendly, with a heart wide in generosity and deep in feelings. She believed in God, followed in her parents' moral footsteps, and dreamed of a future family and career. She was a very attractive girl with red hair, blue eyes, tall for her age, and with a smile that spread joy and optimism. Her parents considered her to be a dreamer but with her feet on the ground regarding her education and future. She wanted to be a nurse, an intention that she made known to her parents when she saw a television report that reviewed the work of these women in the post-war period, receiving the physically and emotionally wounded of World War II. It was clear to her—she wanted to help the sick. She would study to become a nurse.

Her father had been working in a textile factory for many years. His salary was enough to survive moderately well. Her mother helped-out in an old people's home. The pay wasn't much but provided enough to save some money for her children's education. The scholarship granted to her twins helped a lot so that they could enroll Ionela in middle and high school. She took advantage of this gift offered by her parents and repaid it by obtaining excellent grades.

One of the school's activities was forming friendship groups and imitating American university clubs or sororities. They met after school and organized reading sessions, debates, community service projects in the neediest neighborhoods, and parties once a month, where they listened to music from English bands, something forbidden for their parent's generation. In these meetings, they accepted boys and girls from outside their school, almost always relatives of the members of the group, or friends from the neighborhood.

She was sixteen years old, almost seventeen, when she attended a progressive meeting on the topic of relationships. All kinds of love relationships were to be discussed, and she longed to find her own Prince Charming. She dreamed of that ideal and was very clear that when she found him and they fell in love, she would give herself to him unconditionally, just like in all the pirated Disney movies she had seen.

At this meeting she noticed a new boy, older than her, handsome, elegant, and with good manners. He was tall and strong, but also gave an aura of gentleness. It was clear that Ionela was not the only young woman there that noticed his presence.

He came accompanying a companion, who introduced him to her at the end of the meeting.

"Ionela, I want to introduce you to a friend of my brother's, he is interested in participating in such social activities," at the same time taking her by the elbow to bring her closer to the boy.

"Hi, did you enjoy the meeting?" asked Ionela to break the ice.

"Yes, very much so. By the way, my name is Ciprian."

From the very moment they shook hands to greet each other for the first time, a kind of electric current passed from one to the other. They looked into each other's eyes, and Ciprian gave a look that was so deep and seductive it caused Ionela to tremble all over. She thought her legs were shaking in such a way that she would falldown. She stood unable to react, not letting go of his hand, looking at his face, smelling his cologne, feeling the strength in his fingers. Her companion realized at once that something was beginning, not surprising since she was also a girl with aspirations of falling madly in love.

A few weeks earlier, Ciprian had befriended the brother of Anna, Ionela's friend, and they frequently met for coffee, and eventually Anna was invited to join them. Thus, with subtle conversation, he learned which of her companions were strong-willed, which of them were romantic, which of them were intelligent and deductive, and how many of them were submissive or rebellious. Anna was ruled out because he needed her brother to guide her through that city and its possible new victims. He chose Ionela.

He began to subtly woo her, which was not difficult at all.

"Your voice is enchanting, Ciprian," she told her one day when he went to pick her up to go to the movies.

"Does it make you fall in love with me?" he asked with a tone of intrigue and seduction at the same time.

Every time he said such a phrase, the color rose in her cheeks. He knew how to dose them, to say them in a tone that separated them from the rest of the conversation, as a parenthesis, which only drew Ionela deeper into his lover's web.

When she turned seventeen, she wanted to invite him to the birthday party her mother was planning. The truth was that this idea was incited weeks before by him, little by little, until she was the one who proposed it to him. He went up to her family's apartment and introduced himself, displaying all the charm he could project.

"Nice to meet you." He shook hands with her parents with a slight nod. "I was really looking forward to talking to you in person. Ionela tells me so many wonderful things about her parents that I couldn't wait to meet these two wonderful people." Ionela's parents didn't know what to say as they were very humble and simple people and found themselves intimidated by Ciprian's flamboyant personality.

"And what is your job? What do you do for a living?" asked the father.

"When my father died, I took over part of the lumber export business," he said because his years in the sawmill had given him enough knowledge of the lumber business to be able to display some competency on the subject.

"And is it doing well?" asked the mother.

"The truth is that I can't complain. The earnings allow me to live comfortably."

"You are very young," remarked the father.

"I am twenty-three, sir. It might seem that I could not run this kind of business, but I have been blessed, and I think I have the intelligence to lead this company to a bright future."

Ionela's parents were delighted by this first conversation with Ciprian. What they lacked in sophistication they made up for in goodness and like any parent, they wanted the best for their daughter. Without expressing it explicitly, they gave their blessing to the relationship.

They were in love. Well, Ionela was in love. He played the role to perfection. Every day he gave her a flower, just one, which appeared in her locker at school—he gave it to Anna to put there—or on the table in the cafe where they went for a drink or, sometimes, he gave it to her himself, always accompanied by a compliment or declaration of his love for her, which she soaked up like a thirsty sponge.

As she had wished for years, when she met her Prince Charming, she would give herself to him unconditionally. And she did. One afternoon, walking along a bridge across the Mures River, south of the city, they came to a wooded area, far from any road where anyone would pass by. He stopped her, gently turned her so that their faces faced each other, and kissed her passionately. Any inhibition she might have had was lost in that moment and she gave herself over to desire. It was her first time, and it was much sweeter than her experienced friends had told her.

He behaved like the man she wanted to share her life with; he let her pass first when she came to a door, offered her bread at lunch, so she didn't have to reach for it, and kissed her just because, for no apparent reason. And they gave themselves physically to each other with the utmost delicacy and passion at the same time. She felt like the princess in the fairy tales she read as a girl; she was truly living a dream!

She finished her senior year just three days after her eighteenth birthday. They celebrated with her friends and their boyfriends. Ionela still wanted to become a nurse, and that is where Ciprian had to put all his efforts.

"Are you happy?" he asked her as they danced so close together that there wasn't room for a sheet of paper between them.

"Very much so. Now the road to my dreams begins." She pressed her cheeks against his.

"We are in Transylvania. Be careful at night. The count might visit you…" While whispering that intentional joke, he pretended to be biting her jugular.

"Ha-ha-ha-ha! You're so witty!" Ionela patted his chest, as she did every time, he played one of his jokes on her.

"I'm serious, there are a lot of vampires out there. Besides, with your beauty, they will approach you with sinister intentions. You are a very good person, and your heart has no limits, they could pierce it with evil arts." He was bordering on the limits of risk since he was describing himself, but he liked to play bluff.

"My heart is yours, and no one can harm it," was just what Ciprian wanted to hear.

He let a few days pass, but not too many, as she was determined to take the University of Timisoara entrance exams to enter the School of Health Sciences. He invited her to dinner in a small restaurant. He reserved a secluded table with light coming from a glass roof—a bottle of wine, a pleasant dinner, furtive caresses, suggestive winks.

"Ionela, I have a proposal to make." He took her left hand and caressed the back of it as he spoke to her.

"Tell me, Ciprian."

"You see, it is both delicate and important, what I have to tell you."

"You are intriguing to me. What is it?"

"The timber trade with Spain is booming, so much so that the company has offered to open a branch office there. That requires time and, above all, personal presence to control the installation and setup of the office."

"How nice, my love! I am so proud and excited for you!" She believed what he told her, even if he described that he had seen an elephant flying.

"You misunderstood me. I would be the one to go. The members of my family's circle have proposed that I should be the one to set up this branch. I have refused because I have told them of our love, and I refuse to separate from you. This would last at least a year." Ciprian pulled out all his theatrical artillery and manipulated his words so much that a tear almost came to his eye.

"But it's only one year, my love. It will pass quickly," She caressed his cheeks with all the sweetness in the world.

"This is my proposal - let's both go. It would only delay your entry into university for one academic year. It won't be a major disruption. Besides, as soon as I finish setting up that branch, we'll come back, and you can fulfill your dream of becoming a nurse."

"When do you have to answer to the company?" Ionela did not lose her angelic smile at any moment. She saw Ciprian's proposal as something positive for them.

"I should have answered by now. I told them I'd talk to you today." She squinted her eyelids and looked down at the tablecloth.

"Yes. We'll do that, my love. We'll go away. After all, it's just for a year…"

They talked to her parents and explained the situation to them. They understood it perfectly and believed it was a good thing for the couple's future because they assumed they would be starting a family soon.

"But I dreamed of you getting married in our Orthodox Church," her mother told her.

"Mom, get with the times. You know that a family can be formed without going down the aisle." She knew it would hurt her mother. "But we promise you that, when we come back, the first thing we will do is to prepare for the wedding." She looked at Ciprian for support.

"Of course, that's the first thing we'll do when we get back," he said with conviction.

"Well, we can only wish you good luck. God bless you," stated her father.

Ciprian pulled his strings. The organization would provide him with the necessary contacts in Spain to get an apartment and set up the strategy there. These services were estimated at three thousand euros, an amount he would pay as soon as the business began to produce profits. He knew that if he did not pay that amount in thirty days, they would visit him to remind him, in an unconventional way, that the debt with the organization had risen and added a broken bone or a beating so that he would not forget his commitment. Ciprian had crunched the numbers. The organization had shown him the way. He knew it was possible. Besides, his girl was attractive, had a desirable body for men, and, most importantly, was devoted to him unconditionally.

He was loaned an upper-mid-range car, which raised the price by another thousand euros. He would drive himself. He didn't want any more interference that would make it difficult for him to pay back the "loan."

He presented the trip as a premature honeymoon. Ionela could not sleep the day before the departure. She was leaving with her love, just the two of them three thousand kilometers away. It was a dream. She was easily convinced that delaying the start of her university career for a year meant nothing more than that—just a year—but if she compared it to what it meant to start a family with Ciprian, it was nothing.

He planned a route that would pass through European Union countries, and, above all, that would not leave the Schengen Area of free movement of people. Although she was of age and had her passport, he did not want any interaction with the police. They crossed the border from Romania to Hungary. For Ionela, this step was like crossing the barrier of her world and going out into infinity, so her heart skipped a beat when Ciprian told her that they were leaving Romania. He proposed that they should arrive in Vienna and spend the night there. It took them five hours to get there and Ionela was enchanted once again as they drove up to the hotel Ciprian had booked for them.

The second day of the trip was longer. They would reach Geneva but pass-through Germany, as he had been informed that in Italy, the controls had been tightened somewhat due to the recent influx of illegal immigrants. After fourteen hours, they arrived in the Swiss city.

On the third day, they crossed the Spanish border after a seven-hour drive. Earlier, they had stopped in Montpellier, famous, among other things, for oyster farming—a sign of luxury for any girl from a small town in Romania.

"We are arriving in Spain!" she said, opening the car window and directing her enthusiasm into the Pyrenean air.

"Many good things await us." Ciprian pulled her in and kissed her without losing sight of the road.

With his arm around her, his mind moved on to the next phase of the deception.

They arrived at their destination at night. They went upstairs and drank only a soft drink. They didn't feel like anything else, just to sleep. That's what they did, although Ciprian's brain began to work at full speed and with unusual intensity. He could not fail at this stage; he could not afford the slightest misstep. Time was running against him. When he got up, Ionela was already preparing breakfast.

"Good morning, Sweetheart," Ciprian came up behind her and kissed her neck.

"Hello, My Love." She turned and kissed him on the lips.

"I am going to meet with my contacts here right away to start getting everything in order."

"Okay. I'll tidy up the apartment and do our laundry." Ciprian noticed a cold sweat down his back.

He went to see the organization's contacts and asked about the next steps. They did not forget to remind him that if he took too long, he would not have time to fulfill his debt. He let the morning pass until noon and returned to the apartment.

Before entering, he ruffled his hair somewhat and changed his face to one that was both tense and anguished at the same time. He entered the living room and dropped into an armchair, hiding his face between his two hands.

"What's the matter, My Love?" she asked, frightened at the sight of him.

"The worst thing that could happen to me." He pretended to cry.

"What can that be?"

"The partners of the company have expelled me! They waited until they had me away to apply a clause in the firm's bylaws that allowed them to do so."

"But that's monstrous!"

"They are monsters. Yes, they are."

"What will happen now?" asked Ionela in anguish.

"I have been left with no company funds and no personal money. I had it invested in the company itself and have lost it all. This afternoon I have an appointment with one of the contacts from this morning. He promised me that he would help deal with this situation," said Ciprian, calming his demeanor.

"Well. You'll see how everything works out." She hugged him tenderly.

He waited until the afternoon, went to the mythical meeting, and returned around nine o'clock in the evening.

"Were you able to talk to that man?" Ionela asked as soon as he walked in the door.

"Yes, sit down. We need to talk," he replied with the utmost seriousness.

"Tell me, you're worrying me." Ionela sat down across from him.

"Things have become very dark. My contact told me that here the economic crisis has left many people on the street. There is no work for Spaniards, let alone a Romanian. He has called some of his contacts but nothing. Ionela, we don't even have money to go back to our country."

"We'll call my parents. They don't have much, but I'm sure they'll be able to help get us back home," she said, her eyes wide open.

"I have already called them," he lied, reacting quickly to Ionela's proposal. They can't do anything. In fact, they have their own financial needs. I couldn't ask them to sacrifice their own well-being for us, for me...it is my job to take care of you!

"There will be some way out!" said Ionela, trying to sound hopeful but clearly full of angst.

"Yes, my contact has proposed it to me, but you must agree because you are part of the solution. You really can be the solution." He stared into her eyes as he said these last words.

"Me? What do I have that could help?"

"Your body."

"Ciprian, are you telling me to prostitute myself?" She drastically lowered the tone of her voice as if she didn't want anyone to hear her utter those words, not even herself.

"You don't have to look at it like that. It's only temporary, while we get enough money to reactivate our own business, help your parents—really, I've seen them in need of help—and return to our country to start a new life. Besides, you will start a nursing career, and everything will be just as we had hoped and planned. It's only a matter of a year or so. My contact told me what you can earn, and we could solve everything in that time." Ciprian supported this story with more theatrical displays of a trembling voice and forced tears.

There was a silence between them so dense that it could be cut with a knife. Ionela silently pondered what that proposal meant—sleeping with strangers, without any feeling, simply sex in exchange for money. She didn't want to admit what the women who do it are called. She would be a whore. She almost burst into tears, but if Ciprian said it was the only solution, it would be for a reason. He would never force her to do that if it wasn't the very last option.

"Don't worry, my love. You know I'll do anything for you. I promised to give myself entirely, unconditionally. I know it is temporary. I don't know how to act, I have never done it with strangers and in an insensitive way, but I will do it. Besides, if that's how you think I can help my parents..."

Ciprian felt the knot in his stomach unravel, replaced by a sense of victory. He had managed to deceive her, and most importantly, she was in love and would not give up or escape from his web. He became quite pleased with himself, like a hunter who had successfully caught his prey. In this case the trophy would be in the form of a human cash register, ready to collect all the money that he had positioned them to collect.

His contact had promised him that an experienced prostitute would instruct Ionela on everything related to her new occupation. The next day they met with a woman who was not only a prostitute - deceived, raped, and assaulted, but who had become an active member of the Romanian mafia. When she paid her debt, she joined the organization. She gave her some suggestive clothes and indicated that, with the body she had, she was going to collect a lot of money. Ionela was astonished. Everything was new to her. She had never gone out on the street with such tight clothes, such heavy make-up or such a suggestive look. The woman instructed her to acquire a working name; Spanish men liked to remember an easy name and that she would have no difficulty pronouncing the next time she showed up there claiming their services.

"Andrea was my grandmother's name."

Ciprian explained to her when they left that she should give the money she earned each day to him and, if he had to be absent, she should deposit it in his checking account. He would oversee sending money to her parents. He also had to take away her cell phone so that she could not contact her parents since he would contact them. He gave her a capped cell phone, i.e., she could not make international calls. What she did not know was that in the beginning, whatever she earned to cover Ciprian's debt to the organization would be collected by that woman, and then two-thirds for Ciprian, and one-third for them in payment for controlling her and helping her in case she got into trouble.

The next evening Ciprian took her to an industrial park, where the mafia had told him to go. For the first two days, he stayed nearby so that she would feel more at ease, but after that, she stayed there alone, with two or three companions. As the mafia had predicted, she was demanded by many clients, and she gradually hardened to the point of feeling absolutely nothing while men satisfied their sexual desire. When she finished with a client, she always repeated to herself that this was temporary and would save Ciprian, her parents, and herself.

Andrea had earned six thousand euros in the first month of work alone, enough to pay off Ciprian's debt, unbeknownst to her. From then on, he was earning between nine and twelve thousand euros every month. He explained to Ionela that she had to pay the rent for the apartment—one thousand euros, according to his lies—plus electricity, water, medical insurance, immigration papers, transportation, to send part of the money to her parents, pharmacy expenses, condoms, lubricants, mouthwash…and after these expenses, they barely had four hundred euros left.

She believed everything Ciprian told her; she was in love. She had given herself to him completely and unconditionally.

Magda's Story, Part I

Ciprian bought himself a laptop, as he explained to Andrea, to keep the accounts and try to find contacts to create a new business and get them back on track. He always spoke in the first-person plural, as if he were also a victim. He stayed at home with his computer or went to a coffee shop, always with it under his arm. Andrea did not question that dependence on the computer screen—she believed him.

He wasn't really looking for contacts for a traditional business, but rather he was planning the expansion of his current one. He didn't want to move from where he and Andrea were. He couldn't risk her getting suspicious and stumbling upon the truth. He had to keep her close and well-controlled. The mafia was lending him that part of the control in exchange for a third of the profits, but he didn't want to let go too much of the rope that was bringing in so much money.

"How was your day, My Love?" Ionela entered the apartment just as Ciprian was starting breakfast.

"Nothing too significant."

"There you go," She handed him some bills. "I earned three hundred euros today."

"All right, sweetheart. I'm still looking for potential partners."

"On the Internet?" He pointed to the laptop on the table.

"Yes, today everything is done through the Internet."

He chose three dating websites that offered, for a small fee, the possibility of finding a partner. They sold the idea of putting an end to loneliness and finding the love of your life. They didn't check anything, so you could invent the character you wanted or that best suited your interests. And Ciprian could do it from their apartment without leaving Andrea's side. It was perfect.

He created a different profile on each website. In the first one, he was a thirty-five-year-old Spanish doctor, a specialist in cardiology, who worked in a well-known hospital and who had been divorced for six months. In his preferences, among other more banal things, he indicated that he had always been very interested in Eastern European culture, especially in Romania, which is why he preferred female applicants from that country. According to his profile, he had no children and enjoyed a more than acceptable income. He took some photos of himself in casual clothes; Ciprian was handsome and would certainly attract women. He was looking for a woman between eighteen and twenty years old; for his interests, they had to be of age to travel without problems.

On the second website, he was a young man, twenty-five years old, who oversaw his parents' business in the textile sector. He spent a lot of time at work, and that gave him little chance to go out with friends and meet people, especially women; in fact, he had never had a formal girlfriend. The reference to Romanian culture was repeated verbatim from the previous profile. He also took several photos of himself in more youthful clothes.

The third personality was more sophisticated. He described a man in his thirties, heir to an aristocratic family. Obviously, he did not mention his name, finances, or job other than enjoying life, travel, and parties. As a further snobbery, he again indicated his interest in Romania. The photos were taken, in this case, next to a high-end car exhibited at a trade fair in the city.

With each profile came a line and hook filled with bait and the hope that he would soon snag the next right catch.

"Ciprian, I'm on my period. I don't think I'm going to work today." Andrea came out of the bedroom looking tired, with dark circles under her eyes and no desire to do anything.

"What did Jasmin tell you about these days?"

"To put cotton balls in me and change them after each service," she repeated as if it was a lesson learned by heart.

"Then do it. Think of your parents... and our future together." Ciprian said with a sincerity that was truly irresistible.

Andrea returned to work that afternoon at the industrial park. One more day, one more night. She was a more educated young woman than most, but Ciprian devoted himself daily to envelop her in the dream of love, and she fell for it every day. He understood what the Spanish people said about a person in love, that "love is blind, it dulls the senses and the mind." He wasn't going to argue with that, especially if it brought him the benefits.

He started monitoring the three profile pages that same night. He got no response, but he started looking at the profiles of others. Romanian girls appeared dominated his search results and he couldn't help but wonder if others were more truthful than he had been or if they too weaved their own tale. Except for three or four who did not seem right at first glance, all the others he saw were likely to fall into his nets. He had to be patient. He hit the like button or match for about thirty candidates. Now, he had to wait for some of them to respond to one of his fake profiles.

Andrea arrived at five in the morning. She was especially tired, with an uneasiness in her eyes that was not lost on Ciprian.

"What are you doing up so early?" she asked him as she literally fell into an armchair.

"I couldn't sleep and got up to keep looking for something on the Internet."

She glanced around the room out of the corner of her eye and saw that the bed was perfectly made up. She supposed he had made it up when he got up. She didn't have the strength to think otherwise or any reason to doubt him.

"How did it go today, Andrea?" Ciprian was only interested in the money. He didn't care about her.

"Good." She obediently handed him the money she had earned. "By the way, you never call me Ionela anymore," she said with evident sadness.

"Well, I like Andrea, and it's better not to have two names."

She was silent and went straight to the shower.

> "Hello, my name is Ivanka, and I am Romanian, from Bucharest. I have seen your profile, and I liked it very much. I don't know if, because of the time difference, you will be awake, but you can read my message when you wake up. I am very interested in the European aristocracy, and that you belong to it. In my country, you can't say it openly; that's why I do it through the networks. I like your physique. You are very handsome. I hope you like mine. I studied high school,

> but I didn't enter university because my father died last year, and I must work to help my mother and my brother, who is still in high school. Well, if you want, you can answer me, and we can talk more about you. Thanks for liking my profile."

It was starting to work. The first interested party didn't look bad. Surely, more would come. The profile of an aristocrat could be attractive and appealing, although it would be the most challenging to fake, but he was not going to rule out any possibility. He would be patient. He would wait for other messages, although he should not neglect the ones sent to him. He had to stay in control of each interaction, and without Andrea getting suspicious or starting to ask questions.

> "Hello, what a pleasure to meet you! I have been looking for an interesting man in Spain for a long time. I have read a lot about your country, and I have a huge collection of photos downloaded from the Internet. I'm looking forward to meeting Spain and you, of course. My name is Lenuța, and I am from Cluj-Napoca, a city in the north of Romania. If you choose me, I will compensate you for all the time you spend in the textile business. As you will see, I have a good body, and I will be able to make you forget any worries. Please reply to this message. We can be very happy together."

Ciprian immediately deleted this profile from his list. Too straightforward, there was nothing to believe that she was a submissive young woman likely to fall into his trap. No, she did not serve his purposes.

Quite a few messages followed, some more likely than others. He would reply to some of them but without appearing too interested, simply leaving in the air the possibility that he was to her liking or that perhaps they could continue to correspond to deepen the relationship.

After a week of messages, Ciprian was somewhat discouraged and was on the verge of abandoning the idea of expanding his business interests in this manner. He believed it was possible, even more so in these times when young people were so dependent on social networks. But so far, no girl on the list of his favorites met the profile he wanted: submissive in character, hopelessly romantic, free from the bounds of family, and who could travel three thousand kilometers to fall into the arms of her beloved.

In the meantime, Andrea continued to provide a considerable source of income. He maintained the magic thread that bound them together, that was what she believed, and she was still convinced that she was helping her parents and Ciprian. He gave her regular updates about his business prospects which kept her committed to doing her part.

He would tell her that he called her parents from time to time and that they were happy and could send them money. They were sorry that they couldn't talk to her, but they understood that she was very busy. Andrea didn't want to call them so she wouldn't fall apart in front of them, and he wouldn't allow that call because it could uncover the plot or at least raise suspicions.

One day, when she was returning from her day of sexual services, and Ciprian had gone downstairs to buy some food, Ionela did what she never thought she would do—she looked at her beloved's laptop. She knew she was entering the forbidden territory and feared that Ciprian would be angry if he noticed. But she had to do it. Her strength had begun to waiver and some doubts fluttered in her mind. She walked over to the computer and opened it in fear.

Once, he told her that he always set the same password for applications, "radu23," in deference to the name of a childhood friend in Moldova. Ionela tried that password. And it worked—not everything about Ciprian was calculating and mysterious. He also had some flaws. She detected folders of money accounts, some online games, a directory of names, e-mails, and some other unimportant things. But she saw some icons, three to be precise, with the names of webpages she had heard about from some friends at the industrial park. Without hesitation, she opened one of them and entered the same password. In an instant, everything inside her collapsed.

At first, she thought it was a way to pass the time, to make himself the attractive man who needs to be flattered. It couldn't be anything else. Not her Ciprian. She couldn't ask him either, because he would be very angry, for sure. She wanted to trust, but a thick cloud settled in her head, a cloud that didn't bode well. She closed the laptop and decided to try to forget what she had seen. But the cloud took possession of her reasoning.

Days passed, and Ciprian was on the verge of giving up and moving on to a new strategy when he opened a message and was pleasantly surprised.

> "Hi. My name is Magda. I am eighteen years old, and I live in Iași, near the border with Moldova. When I saw your profile and saw that you were a doctor and such an attractive one, my heart skipped a beat. Since I was a little girl, I have been enthusiastic about doctors' stories, I have watched all the TV series about hospitals, and I have always dreamed of marrying a doctor. I would not be able to practice medicine. I am very moved by illnesses, and I am sure I would suffer a lot from the calamities of the sick, but if my husband were a doctor, he would tell me the stories of these people as if they were a novel. I am very romantic. I believe in pure and lifelong love. I have never had a boyfriend, just some crushes. Well, if you are interested, write to me."

When he read that this girl lived near the border with Moldova, a strange feeling ran through his body. It was true that Ciprian's change of character made him cold and calculating, to the point that he had not contacted his mother since he fled his village. He didn't know if she was arrested, but he didn't care. He was obsessed with money and how to earn even more.

He didn't know why, but he had a hunch that Magda might be his ideal victim. He had to explore that intuition. He would try throwing her a romantic hook to see how she would react.

> "Hello, Magda. I loved your message. I really liked your profile, I find you a very attractive girl, and I think you have a very good heart. Really, seeing the preferences and tastes you put in your profile, we have a lot in common, besides the love for medicine. I am also very romantic. I believe in love, although I recently got divorced since my ex-wife fell in love with another man. I have always been interested in Eastern European culture, so you could enlighten me. I don't know why, but when I saw your photos, something happened inside me, like a click, maybe it could have been Cupid, who knows... I would like to meet you in person. Would you come to Spain?"

His spiderweb was ready to receive a girl who had all the characteristics of being caught. More messages were exchanged, daily texts were written, more and more intimate and seductive. Of course, she told him she would come to Spain to meet him. She was a motherless girl, her mother died in a traffic accident, and her father remarried a distant cousin; they lived in an apartment next to some elderly relatives. If Magda left there, it was not likely that her family was going to claim her back. It was perfect. Besides, there was the factor of a grieving father staying in Romania, which could be a reason for coercion, in case she put up too many objections to his plans. He decided it was time.

> *"My dear Magda, I am going to be straight with you: I think I have fallen in love with you. What I feel when we write to each other, what happened to me when I saw your photos, the very special feeling that flows between us, I don't know, many things lead me to think that this is love. I can't promise fairy tale life, but I will do what I can to offer the closest thing to that. Maybe we won't feel the same when we see each other in person, but I propose that we should try. If you agree, I'll pay for the plane trip, and you could stay at my house, it has plenty of room. Are you willing to take a chance on me?*

Ciprian had already coordinated everything with Jasmin, the mafia member who was already managing Andrea and would take care of Magda. He would sell her to her for two thousand euros plus ten percent of the daily earnings. The expenses of the trip would be paid by the organization and come out of his profit.

"Ciprian, do you still love me?" Andrea asked him while they were having lunch in their apartment.
"Of course, I do, my love," he lied with an ever-convincing tone.
"You're not hiding anything from me, are you?" she said, staring into his eyes.
"What do you want to tell me, Andrea? He put on an expression of contrariness.
"Nothing, forget it," she finished as she saw his face turn to anger.
She got up and headed for the shower, getting ready to go to the industrial park. She usually arrived around five-thirty. Ciprian was puzzled by Andrea's reaction, he didn't know what to attribute those questions to, but he feared she was asking too many questions. He would have to keep a close eye on her, as well as talk to Jasmin to get her to control her movements even more.
"I'm going to drive you to work today," he said as he put on a sweater.

"Work? You call what I do work?" The tears begged for permission to come out of her eyes, but she immediately swallowed them.

"It's a figure of speech. Think of it as our future and your parents' future."

Andrea's reaction was not going out of his mind. Who did she even think she was? He left her in her area and went to talk to Jasmin. He explained what had happened.

"Don't worry, we will intensify our control," Jasmin reassured him, "but isn't the new one arriving this afternoon?"

"Yes, indeed! I'm going to the airport right now." Ciprian got into the car and headed to pick up Magda.

He recognized her immediately from the photos on the contact page. She was tall, curly-haired, and even more attractive than the pictures, with honey-colored eyes and insinuating lips. He felt a little sorry for what he was about to do for a moment, but it only lasted a few seconds. He quickly saw her as if she were the euro symbol walking toward him.

"Hi, Ciprian!" They gave each other two kisses on the cheek.

"How was your trip, Magda?" he asked as he took her suitcase.

"I'm tired, but the flight was not too long."

During the walk, they spoke little. She wasn't sure how to break the ice and he, really knowing where they were going, didn't want to give her too much conversation either. He didn't want any preambles. They wouldn't do any good. He no longer needed to be attentive to her. At that moment, she was just a body that he was going to sell, charge for it, and benefit from part of the proceeds. It was now the job of the organization to convince her and from what he had seen with other women, he was sure they would do so at any cost.

They arrived at the house and Magda was surprised by the place; the photos on the profile showed a modern, spacious house with a swimming pool and a large living room. This was nothing like that but rather a narrow, old building, dark even on the outside.

The first thing that caught Magda's attention was the smell of the place. Something that mixed dense and hot air, cheap perfumes, and tobacco. They reached a room at the end of a narrow corridor, and there sat in an armchair, behind a shabby table, a man of about fifty, flanked by two other stocky men.

"Sit down, Magda," he ordered.

"What am I doing here?" She looked in all directions, not really knowing what she was looking for, perhaps Ciprian, but he was hiding in a dark area of the room.

"You are going to work for us," he didn't beat around the bush. "You'll see, I'll explain it to you very clearly: every day, you'll go to the bar of this club, and you'll attract the clients who enter; you'll make sure they order drinks and extend an invitation to you, then you'll go with each one to the room we'll assign you, and you'll satisfy their sexual desires; they'll pay for the drinks and for the time they spend with you. You already have a debt with us, corresponding to the value of your trip. In addition, you will pay fifty euros a day for the use of the premises, ten for washing the sheets and towels and of course, you will hand over to us what you earn each day. We will subtract all that from your debt and, when you are earning a considerable amount of money, we will give you something to send to your father in Romania, if you want.

Magda was petrified. She kept looking for Ciprian; he had deceived her. He had sold her to those idiots! She didn't believe she was living that moment. It was all a dream that would pass as soon as she opened her eyes. But no, everything was a cruel reality.

"Who are you to talk to me like that?" Magda began to get up from her chair, raising her voice higher and higher.

The answer was not long in coming. The man also got up from his chair, took two steps towards her, and slapped her in the face, which made her sit down again. Magda began to cry desperately.

"My name is Dumitru, don't forget it," he said with a slow drawl while he tightly grabbed the girl's jaw.

"I'm not a whore!" she managed to articulate, despite having her face immobilized with that sweaty paw.

Another slap abruptly silenced her scream. A trickle of blood began to flow from the corner of her lips. He grabbed her shoulders and forced her upright in the chair.

"This is just a small preview of what can happen to you if you don't do what we tell you to do. You will be whatever we tell you to be. Get it into your head that you are mine, and I can do whatever I want." Magda was so filled with fear that she couldn't help peeing herself. "Now, Jasmin will give you precise instructions. By the way, we know everything about your family. If you do anything that displeases us or refuse to work for us or try to run away or talk about us to third parties, we will show you a video in which you can see how your people will be tortured until they wish for death."

With her cheeks red and swollen and pain in her soul difficult to measure, she was pushed into an even shabbier room with a precarious bed, a rickety bookshelf, and a low stool. She was pushed and fell onto the bed, which gave off the same smell she detected at the entrance to the club. She was left alone, but after a few minutes, Dumitru entered, closing the door behind him, ripped off all her clothes, and raped her as violently as he could. Her initiation had begun.

"This is what the men who come here want, this is what you are going to offer them, and this is what they are going to pay you for," he said with a tyrannical tone. The man knew that bending a girl's will was a necessary first step towards compliance. "By the way, here you won't be called Magda anymore, now you will be Lupita, which the clients like better."

When that monster left the room, Magda shrank in on herself, naked, dirty on the inside, hurt on the outside, crying non-stop, and completely unsure how she had stepped into this hell.

For Ciprian it was business as usual and the cash from both his investments was coming in nicely. Lupita was under the control of the organization, but Andrea's reactions began to worry him. Jasmin told him at the club not to worry, to keep showing her love. They would let him know if they noticed anything unusual.

That night, while Andrea worked at the industrial park and Lupita wanted to die at the club, he deleted each of his dating profile pages. There was no longer any trace of them; they had fulfilled their mission. He leaned back in his chair and smiled in satisfaction. He never thought it would be so relatively easy. But greed is infinite in evil humans, so his head already began thinking up another scam to increase his abundant income. Being a lover boy is going to turn me into a rich man, he thought as he began to laugh out loud.

He sent a message to Andrea on her cell phone, telling her that he would come for her at five in the morning. He had to show her more details to calm her possible doubts. When he arrived at the industrial park, Jasmin called him. She had to talk to him.

"Ciprian, I think Andrea may be pregnant. I am a woman, and I know how to recognize the signs. I've been pregnant myself on three occasions." She had climbed into the passenger seat and started talking without even saying hello. "Besides, I have ears everywhere, and they talk about everything."

"Are you sure?" he asked incredulously. "We use condoms, and I'm sure she doesn't allow any man not to wear one."

"Do you always use them with her?"

"Almost always," he acknowledged.

"Well, something has to be done because I'm pretty sure she is."

Ciprian picked up Andrea, and on the way to the apartment, he noticed a concerning look on her face.

"Is something wrong, Andrea?"

"Take today's money." She handed him the euro bills.

"You can give it to me at home. I want to know if something is wrong with you. Lately, you've been more irritable, and you don't look so good."

"I'm pregnant," she looked down as she began to cry.

"But you use condoms, don't you?"

"Yes, it's yours, Ciprian." Although he suspected it, he feigned surprise.

"It is true that sometimes we have not. It's just that now is not a convenient time to have a baby. We need more money for our future. We already talked about it. A child would complicate everything. It's just not the right time, Andrea. It would be better to talk about it when we go back to Romania. I think you should end the pregnancy." Andrea couldn't stop crying.

"I'd like to have it and leave all this behind," Ciprian braked and pulled the car over to the shoulder.

"My love, you know why we are doing all this." He used the first-person plural to refer to what she was doing. "It is essential to continue for a while to ensure our life together, and then we will have as many kids as you want." He held her in a tender, though, inauthentic embrace.

"I know," her answer reassured Ciprian.

Jasmin arranged everything. They had a doctor with a malpractice record who did such favors for them. The abortion was performed in the basement of her own house, in deplorable hygienic conditions. She bled profusely and had to use several packs of gauze to stop the bleeding. The mafia was quick to remind Ciprian that these expenses and the days she did not work were to be paid to the organization.

"I know," he replied resignedly.

From that day on, Andrea's contagious smile, her joy, her enthusiasm, and even her spark for life we lost. She still loved Ciprian, but the suspicion that he was hiding something from her was growing.

Ciprian started taking her to the industrial park every night, at least at first. He encouraged her to return to work three days after the abortion. One day he decided to take a walk around the club where Lupita was. He entered through the back door and approached the room from a dark hallway where he could not be seen from where the girls and potential clients were. He saw her. She was at the bar with a man who could be twice her age; she was wearing a tight skirt that covered the bare minimum.

"How is Lupita doing?" he asked the room manager.

"She resists. She doesn't quite obey orders. We have had to motivate her two or three times. Dumitru also visited her one day in her room to remind her what she must do. I think they called a contact in Romania, and he went to the house where her family lives, photographed them coming out of the house, and the boss showed her so she could see that we knew where they were and what could happen to them. Since then, she has been more cooperative."

"How is her income?" asked Ciprian, unfazed by what he had just heard.

"I guess it's still a little scarce, but it will increase, for sure. She's a girl that customers like, and as soon as she softens her pride, she'll make a very good profit," he said with conviction.

"You can't see the bruises," said Ciprian.

"Hurt can be without bleeding. I guess you know that."

"Yes, I know."

They kept her in a back room of the club when she was not working, not yet daring to move her to the floor with other girls for fear that she might try to escape. They preferred to keep her on a short leash until she surrendered her opposition, although that was happening day by day. They had not yet paid Ciprian his share of Lupita's daily income; he had agreed with Dumitru that they would do so at the end of each month. Then he would see the girl's productivity.

Katerina's Story

Ciprian's ambition was growing by the day. Andrea brought him a considerable economic benefit. He had her under control; although nothing was the same anymore, he would hold on to her as long as he could. Lupita finally gave in to the beatings and the threats to her family in Romania, convincing her that she had no way out, at least for now. She began to generate decent income for the organization and Ciprian. But all that was not enough for him. He wanted more, so he began to devise a third strategy of deception, one he was taught in Romania.

"You are good, Ciprian. You have convinced two girls who have transitioned well. It was a risk, and you took the plunge. You have a good future in this business," Jasmin told him over a drink in the club room where Lupita was.

"I like difficult challenges; besides, they pay off well in the end."

"You can expand your investments."

"I am working on it."

"Have you thought of anything yet?" asked Jasmin.

"I have something in mind." He didn't want to give too many details.

"I have spoken with Dumitru, and we want to compensate you for your success and encourage you to continue with us. We could come to a partnership agreement."

"I am listening," he gestured with his glass to Jasmin's face as a sign of inviting her to state the proposal.

They reached a pact. It was beneficial for him to have good relations with the organization because he was sure he would earn more than on his own.

As he said goodbye, he saw Lupita coming out of a room. He approached her, not sure why he did it. He was going to ask her something inconsequential, to break the ice, but he didn't have time. She slapped his face and went on her way. Ciprian touched his cheek. He could still feel Lupita's fingers and, above all, the anger he saw in her face upon receiving the blow. He shook it off and simply walked away.

Lupita had been taken to the floor where the girls were crammed together. A floor inside the building they called home, of about eighty square meters, where twelve girls of different nationalities (Colombian, Croatian, Moroccan, Venezuelan, Spanish, and now, Romanian) all lived together. Just inside the entrance of the flat were two triple rooms with four girls waiting to be assigned to a client, and further inside a series of bunk beds where they rested, if they could: a bathroom and little else. Lupita was assigned to the bottom of a bunk. When a client arrived, he would choose, and a manager, who was once one of those girls, would direct her to a room on another floor, where she was to perform the service. Everything was cramped and both the lighting and the air circulation were poor. She was struck by the expressions of the girls who were there, almost all of them very young: they would not make eye contact with her. When Lupita entered for the first time, they all continued with what they were doing, almost always looking at their cell phones, but none of them raised their eyes to even notice her.

Ciprian was ready to enact his next deception. He took advantage of Andrea's return from the industrial park when she was tired and had little emotional strength to put up any resistance to his suggestions.

"Good morning, Andrea." He stood up and kissed her, to which she didn't even respond.

She handed him the money, as she did every morning, the twenty- and fifty-euro bills.

"Sit down for a moment. I want to tell you something."

Andrea obeyed mechanically.

"Please be fast. I'm dead tired."

For a moment, Ciprian doubted if that "dead" had a double meaning, but he didn't dwell on it for more than a few seconds.

"You see, there is going to be a trial in Bucharest about my family's company. I haven't told you anything because I didn't know how the matter would evolve, but part of the money I have spent on a lawyer so that I could sue in order to recover my position. Apparently, the trial proceedings start next month, and the lawyer recommended that I should be there from the beginning of the process. So, I was thinking of going next week and staying until the end of the trial. If it goes well, we could come back immediately, start a new life together, get married, and have children." Andrea noticed a certain spark of hope in her heart and opened her eyes with interest.

"Is there a chance of success?" she asked.

"The lawyer told me that it is quite likely."

"Then go, Honey." This was just the hope that she needed.

They agreed that she would continue working until he returned since they were not sure of winning the trial, besides there would be expenses from the lawyer and Ciprian's trip; obviously, he exaggerated all the theoretical expenses. Whatever she earned each day, she would give to Jasmin. She knew where to deposit it to get it to their accounts. Of course, Ciprian had urged the mafia to intensify their control over her while he was in Romania. The right time came, and he left to return to his country a year and a half after he had begun dating Ionela.

He had previously contacted Vlad, the boy who had initiated him in this business. He recommended going to a city not too big but far away from places where anyone would recognize him. They agreed upon Re□i□a, a small town with car and chemical factories and lots of young people, including girls who had to give up their studies and go to work. It was an ideal location to find a girl between sixteen and eighteen years old, emotionally vulnerable, and with limited education.

Ciprian flew to Bucharest and from there traveled to Reșița by bus. He rented an apartment on the outskirts of the city and spent his time visiting the cafes and pubs in the city center. He was on a mission everywhere he went, seeking to identify potential prospects for his next victim. It didn't take him long to find her. After two weeks, he spotted three young, pretty girls at a bar. After confirming that they didn't seem to be with boys, he casually approached the bar to order a drink, intentionally standing closer to them than necessary.

"Waiter, give me a light gin and tonic, please."

The three of them turned their heads to see who was talking. As women can do, they exchanged glances and without a word agreed that they should engage with this handsome, young stranger. He noticed their interest and responded accordingly.

"Hello, girls, would you allow me to buy you a drink?" he said with a broad smile.

"What is your name? We haven't seen you here before," said one of them.

"My name is Ciprian. If you accept my invitation, I can tell you my whole life story." They all laughed openly at the joke.

"Okay, we accept. But you will tell us about your life, right?" The taller, black-haired girl winked at him as she answered.

Ciprian hoped to discern if one of these three was a potential candidate, so he was willing to put all his theatrical expertise to use. At first glance, he liked all three of them physically. One, tall and black-haired, another one shorter in stature but with attractive curves, and the third, about 5'7", red-haired and beautiful eyes. The third had not uttered a word so far, which led Ciprian to think she was shy. He liked her.

"My name is Alina," said the tall, black-haired girl.

"I am Ioana," said the shortest girl in turn. The third one did not say anything until Ioana hit her with her elbow, prompting her to speak.

"My name is Katerina," she said while blushing intensely.

As the conversation unfolded, the possibility that Katerina was the ideal candidate was taking shape. She hardly spoke. She blushed every time he said something about her beauty or her eyes. She maintained a posture that was not at all upright, as if she wanted to hide even from herself and, from what little she said, he deduced that she belonged to a humble family, so she had to work in a factory producing chemical products for the automotive industry.

"I am from Moldova. There I worked as a carpenter with my father." He chose the woodworking industry again. At least he knew the ins and outs of that business. "But I outgrew it and, together with my mother's brother, we founded a transport company and have three vans. Now I'm here looking for potential customers for the business."

They all engaged in cheerful conversation until closing time. The girls said their goodbyes and as they were leaving, Ciprian grabbed Katerina's arm and pulled her away from her friends.

"I'd like to meet you another day, just the two of us," he said in a low, somewhat whispered voice.

"Okay," she replied, but keeping her gaze at the sidewalk.

"Tomorrow around eight o'clock?" Ciprian didn't want to waste any time.

"Good. I get off work at five o'clock."

"See you tomorrow."

Another web for another girl...now to see if he would once again catch his next prey.

They saw each other the next day, and the next, and the next...every evening, they would meet to talk, and her interest in him increased every day. Katerina told him that she lived with her mother and was an only child. Her father left home when she was born, he didn't want to have children, and her mother chose to have her. They never heard from him again, nor did they ever try to contact him. Her mother was very young when she had her—fifteen years old. Her mother worked very hard at cleaning houses and received some help, making just enough for the two of them to survive, barely. As soon as she was of age, Katerina was hired in a chemical factory in the automotive industry (windshield wipers, antifreeze, brake fluid...), and she had been there for two years. Between what she earned and her mother's, they earned about six hundred euros a month, but that was still very little to live on.

Ciprian shared fabricated details about his life and emphasized his willingness to emigrate abroad where the income could be higher.

Little by little, they approached more intimate and personal conversations about feelings, dreams, their shared romantic natures, his hope of finding a good woman to share his life with and form a family, and other parts of possible future. And then came the moment of the kiss, the caresses, the desire, and the physical, and emotional surrender. Once again, Ciprian was a convincing actor and easily seduced the young woman.

In the bedroom of his apartment, lying together after making love, Katerina told him for the first time that she had fallen in love with him. She wanted him to meet her mother. He gladly accepted.

"Mom, this is Ciprian." They were holding hands.

"Katerina has told me wonderful things about you." He shook the woman's hand with a slight nod of his head and a gracious smile.

"My mother's name is Viorica."

"You are so young, if I may say so," Ciprian said in true appreciation of her attractiveness.

"Not so much. Thirty-three years old, just turned thirty-three," she replied shyly.

She did not look as old as she confessed. Tall, dark, deep-set black eyes, a very shapely body, although he noticed that her hands were cracked, surely from all the house-cleaning work. Ciprian thought that mother and daughter constituted a banner pair of women.

"It is striking that, being both so beautiful, your hair and eye color are so different," Ciprian asked, intrigued.

"My father had red hair and green eyes," Katerina replied, although she showed almost contempt when mentioning her father.

"And how have you not remarried, surely there have been men who have shown interest?"

"I know my daughter told you about her father. After that, I stopped believing in men."

It was helpful to hear the mother's perspective on men, and a good warning to bring an end to that topic.

Katerina was madly in love with Ciprian. He was leading her more and more to where he wanted her to go, and she let him. One day, sitting on a bench on a promenade lined with leafy trees, he started to reveal the plot he had been planning.

"Business here is not developing as I had hoped. There simply are no clients looking for new transportation services," Ciprian explained to her in a dismayed voice.

"You mean you're leaving?" Katerina quickly questioned.

"I don't want to leave you, my love, but without money, we can't form a family and plan a future."

"I'll go with you anywhere, even to the end of the world!" she said resolutely.

"You would really be willing to do so?"

"Of course." Katerina squeezed his hand as a sign of her firm decision.

"I have heard that in Spain things are going much better than here, the minimum salary for any job is around a thousand euros a month, and there are offers for carriers, even if they are modest like me. I think Spain is the best option I have."

"You mean that we have," she said.

They spoke with Viorica, and she gave her blessing, hoping for a better future for her daughter. She had never seen her daughter so in love and determined to follow him. They discussed the possibility of Viorica joining them in the future once they were settled, but for now she would remain at her job as she was able to earn enough to support herself. Ciprian had caught Katerina in his web, now to put her to good use.

They followed the same route he used with Ionela. They arrived in Spain, where Ciprian had rented a small furnished apartment in the same city where he lived with Andrea, but in the opposite part of town. They settled in, and he went out to look for work, or at least that's what he told her.

He went to see Dumitru and informed him that the plan was still on track. It was just a matter of weeks, and Katerina would be working for them. The Mafioso was pleased with Ciprian's work. He saw in him a good lover boy for the business and together they were an increasingly profitable team.

He let a couple of weeks go by, making Katerina believe that he was looking for jobs for the two of them since his Spanish skills were stronger. Every day, he came back to the apartment and, in a despondent voice, kept convincing her that the situation was not as "pretty" as it was portrayed. She did not lose hope. Two weeks passed, and nothing.

"We need to talk, Katerina," he told her one evening as he invited her to sit with him on the couch.

"Tell me, my love."

"This is not what they said. Here, too, the economy has almost collapsed. Even the biggest companies are closing their branches in Spain. They are not hiring anyone, they are lowering salaries, and everyone is telling me that this is not temporary but that it is going to last for a very long time," he explained.

"So, what are we going to do?"

"I have given it a lot of thought. I have talked to some other Romanians who live here, and they are in the same situation. They have all found a temporary solution."

"What solution is this?" she asked with interest.

"Their wives started working in a club. This business has not suffered from the economic downturn, they are still open and with important profits."

"As a waitress?" Katerina asked.

"Well, serving drinks, having them with the customers, making them spend and…"

"Sleeping with them," she cut in, knowing full well what that kind of job in a club was like.

"My love, it is the only thing to do. We have no money left. I thought we were going to find work quickly. Instead, there are only dead ends. This would be a solution, even if it was temporary. Besides, it's not making love to a man. It's just cold sex without any feelings. We can earn enough money and set up our own transport business rather than trying to get hired by others. To do this, we will have to buy a van. Remember, I sold what I had to pay for the trip and the apartment."

Katerina noticed how she could feel the strong beating of her heart but the rest of her felt immobilized. The last thing she had planned in her life was to be a whore. If she accepted, she wouldn't be able to talk about it with her mother or her friends. No one. From that moment on, she had to deceive, lie about everything, make-believe that she worked in a very important company in Spain, in short, and fake her life before the rest of the world. But her love for Ciprian and the direness of their circumstances led her to accepting this new path, believing it would indeed be a temporary detour before they could get back on the road to their future.

"All right, I'll do it for you, for us," she said with resigned sadness.

Little did Katerina know that what was to come was not just renting out her body but would feel more like selling her very soul.

Ciprian took Katerina and accompanied her to a club different from the one Lupita was at; there's no way he could allow his three "dupes" to discover one another. Jasmin was once again there to bring Ciprian's latest catch into the fold. Katerina received yet another shock when she was told that she would be living there with the other girls to eliminate the rent for their apartment. Ciprian would occupy a room in a nearby apartment that he would share with other men in the same circumstances. These arrangements were presented as the norm and Katerina had no real option other than to accept it. Jasmin said she would keep their passports safe. While the financial arrangements were managed the same as with Lupita,

Jasmin explained it all to them as if it was new information to both, another convincing tactic to deceive her.

"Put these clothes on and get to work," Jasmin prompted her.

"By the way, your name is not very easy for the Spanish to pronounce, so it will have to be changed."

"I would like Elena, like my maternal grandmother," she said.

"Okay, Elena is fine. Come on. There's no time to lose."

She hugged Ciprian, and they kissed.

That same night, Elena received her first client.

She began to bring in decent money. The color of her hair, the beauty of her eyes, and her attractive body excited many clients. Jasmin was satisfied, and every week, she settled accounts with Ciprian. It had not been a bad idea to have him for the business. For his part in the ongoing charade Ciprian just had to visit her from time to time, sleep with her, and tell her how much he loved her. He had given her a cell phone, knowing she would not reveal anything when she called Romania because shame would prevent her from doing so. In view of her mother and friends, she was employed in a pharmaceutical factory in Spain.

Ciprian called Andrea every two or three days. He would let her know that he was in Romania and inform her how the legal proceedings against the company were going. Of course, he described a tedious, long and complicated investigation. From time to time, he would send her photos, taken when he had been there to discover Katerina. They showed cars with Romanian license plates, a building with a typical Romanian style, or a bar with a name in Romanian. He gave them out little by little, making them look like they were made in real-time. Andrea would tell him that she missed him a lot and encouraged him, trusting that soon all this would be remembered as a bad dream. And while she still sounded optimistic on the outside, more and more of her soul was dying on the inside.

Jasmin informed him that all was well with Andrea. She looked less active, her face aged as if at least ten years had passed, and her walk was not as lively. She was keeping up with clients, and that was what mattered. She didn't contact anyone other than her companions at that traffic circle in the industrial park.

He then approached the club where Lupita was.

"My dear Ciprian!" Dumitru got up to shake hands with him. "How nice to see you!"

"Likewise," he sat down in a chair, shabby like everything else there. "How are things going?" He meant Lupita, of course.

"Good, good. We no longer must remind her that she works for us. Apparently, she has learned that it is not in her best interest to protest or resist because the reminder on our part can be painful. Do you want to see her?"

"No." He unconsciously brought his hand up to his cheek.

"She has realized that this is her destiny and that her mission is to pay her debt, although she is unaware of the lies about it. Do you already have something in mind for the next one?"

"I'm planning something..."

Three months went by, and Ciprian had three sources of income, imported from Romania: one at 66 percent, one at 33 percent, and one at 50 percent. He was earning about ten thousand euros per month. While very profitable, he wanted to increase that amount and he knew how to do it.

From time to time, the police raided the clubs and the industrial parks. This time, they were after a network trafficking Nigerian women to use them as sex slaves. Dumitru got a tip-off that, at the same time, Romanian organizations were also sniffing around. One day, he received a call warning him that they were going to visit some clubs in the city center, which was surely related to some lead they had. The next day, the same informant told him that the Donatello Club was on the list.

Dumitru took immediate action. Ciprian and all the women recruiters were ordered to stop any activity for a week; Jasmin was told to distribute the girls from the Donatello to other properties owned by the organization; finally, he planned for Donatello to get cleaned up and appear to be an establishment drinks and only drinks. That same day, Jasmin was accompanying Andrea to their hired doctor due to persistent pain in her lower abdomen caused by a kick from a dissatisfied customer. Jasmin received a call informing her of Dumitru's orders, waited for the doctor to examine Andrea, took note of the painkiller to be purchased, and of the recommendation that she should not work in the industrial park for a few days. With the urgency of Dumitru's order and all the moving pieces, Jasmin made a quick decision that did not account for all the potential outcomes.

"The doctor says not to work for a few days, so we'll set you up on one of the floors of a club downtown." She had her mind on how to distribute the girls at the Donatello more than on what she was saying to Andrea. These women were just pieces on a chess board that needed to be moved strategically. Though Jasmin had once been one of those pieces herself, her circumstances had improved greatly in this role, and she had long ago hardened her heart.

Jasmin told the manager of the girls of the club to distribute them to other properties while she would dedicate herself to giving the place the appearance of a cocktail bar. As chance or providence would have it, Andrea, Lupita, and Elena ended up at the same club, La Casa Malva.

The activity at La Casa Malva continued as usual and just incorporated the new girls, except for Andrea, who would only be there while her abdominal pain improved. Like a magnet, the three Romanian girls were grouped together in two bunk beds, next to a Colombian girl. They began to talk and share their experiences. The time they had been working in the trade had taught them to trust no one, absolutely no one, so none of the three gave out names, places, or dates. They spoke of impressions, emotions, and how they coped. They did not know why, but, unlike the other girls who lived there, who seemed to function without any expression of emotion, they had the need to talk to each other, to share what their souls had experienced since they arrived in Spain.

The police inspection was carried out just as Dumitru had been tipped off. After two days, the girls went back to their places of work. Andrea, Lupita, and Elena exchanged their phone numbers, which they agreed to memorize in case their cell phones were taken away, which happened periodically.

Ciprian began to carry out his next plan. He would visit Elena from time to time and lie to her about everything he was doing and thinking. Every time they saw each other, they ended up in bed. He used condoms in hopes of avoiding catching anything, but he also pierced them to allow his own semen to escape. After two months, Elena fearfully announced to him that she was pregnant. Ciprian did not show any feelings. She asked him what she should do. He told her that she should have it, that they would figure it out.

During her pregnancy, she did not stop working, and some clients even found it morbid to do it with a pregnant woman, so they paid more. Marcos was born a plump boy, smiling from the moment he was born, healthy, and with facial features and expressions that made Elena have no doubts about who his father was.

Ciprian acted quickly. He called Viorica and informed her about the birth of their son. He proposed that since they both had such good jobs that she should join them in Spain and instead of cleaning houses, she could care for her grandchild.

"Don't worry, we are doing well and have money saved. We will send you the plane tickets, and you will live with us here," Ciprian lied to her over the phone.

"What joy!" she said.

Ciprian went to see Dumitru. They had agreed that they would take care of the child. He would serve as a bargaining chip to keep Elena chained to them for a long time.

"The organization will have a very attractive woman in her early thirties. He showed her a picture of Viorica.

"Well done, Ciprian, you're a pro!" Dumitru patted his back as a sign of satisfaction.

Andrea had just received a call from Ciprian from Romania. He was still lying to her. All the same, routine conversation. She had lost all enthusiasm. She no longer believed anything, even more so when she had heard Elena and Lupita's stories that sounded so similar and had ended in the same hell hole. She was smart, and her head began to tame her heart. She was sure: everything was a deception, from the first minute to the end. The three Romanian women talked frequently, each time they gave each other more details, except for names. They were softening their initial protective shells and, at the same time, opening their eyes to reality.

While Andrea was awaiting the arrival of a client who frequented her weekly, her companions were suddenly on the move.

"Here they come!" said one of them. "They're coming earlier today."

"Mommy!" said two of them enthusiastically.

"Hello, good evening," said Sara, as she opened the van door and stepped out with her loving smile.

Andrea felt a palpitation inside her. It was as if an unexplainable force was pushing her towards the light that was in front of her eyes. She approached Sara and looked around to ensure no one was suspicious.

"Mommy, I want to talk to you." Sara took her by the elbow and led her to the side of the van while Diego and a woman from the team handed out the kits, water, and something to eat. "I need your help."

"Okay, I'll call you tomorrow, and we'll meet." Sara had the phone numbers of all of them. "Don't worry."

"I have two Romanian colleagues who also need your help," she said while showing her contacts on the screen of her phone so that Sara could copy them.

"No problem, we'll talk tomorrow." Sara took her hand, and with the other, she caressed her right cheek, a welcomed affection for once.

"Thank you so much, Mommy. We will be grateful for the rest of our lives."

"There is always a way out. You just need to have the courage to go for it. We will be there."

A Long Journey from Latin America: Gabriela's Story, Part I

Gabriela was intellectually curious. She must have inherited it from her mother. She came from a middle-class family that valued education and upon graduating from high school she enrolled in the School of Medicine at the Central University of Venezuela in Caracas. She was excited to embark on this next phase in her life, but she was also increasingly alarmed at what was happening in her country as a result of rampant corruption in the government. Just before the school term was set to begin, the issues of the nation became very personal. The Bolivarian government expropriated her parents' hardware business when rumors had spread that they favored the political platform of the opposing party.

Despite the set-back, Gabriela began her studies with enthusiasm, but the mood at the university was soon disrupted by a wave of anti-government rebellion brewing among a sector of politicians and students. The university budgets and scholarships were reduced. Demonstrations began, and Gabriela was in all of them, hidden from her parents because she knew they would suffer even more if her involvement was discovered.

It was at one of these demonstrations that Gabriela's life began what would become a downward spiral from being enrolled in a university to being enslaved on the streets as a prostitute.

The planned march would lead to the doors of the Attorney General's Office to present their demands to the authorities. It was a student protest for economic improvements and investment in the university, but the political implications were much greater, including the request for the release of fourteen colleagues arrested in protests of previous days.

The leaders of the demonstration had instructed the students that if their peaceful protest became violent, everyone should return to their corresponding buildings on campus and lock themselves in as a passive protest. Things did indeed deteriorate with violence on both sides, and Gabriela went with others back to the School of Medicine building. But instead of a safe retreat, the students found the police and paramilitary groups there waiting for them. Banging, running, shooting in the air, and arson ensued. Gabriela was trying to protect herself, and as she turned to avoid a direct hit to her face, she fell to the ground, right where an incendiary bomb had just exploded. She felt a burning in her left hand, but her goal was to run away from the disaster.

She returned to her house to find only her father, Armando, home. He was greatly alarmed to see his daughter's hand and the panicked expression on her face. Her father quickly washed her wound and soaked it in aloe, then wrapped it in a bandage. He calmed her down, and she explained everything that had happened.

"Don't come back to the university for a while. They may have recorded you. I'll talk to some of my contacts and see what they can do," he tried to reassure her with his words and gestures, although inside, he was trembling right along with her.

"It's getting worse and worse, Dad!" she cried in his arms in clear despair.

Armando spoke with men he knew who confirmed that the authorities had recorded the people who participated in all the protests. Gabriela had to leave the country as soon as possible or she was likely to be arrested.

She remembered Liliana, an older childhood friend who shared her troubles and joys. She knew that she had moved to Spain when things had first started to deteriorate in Venezuela. Her parents had mysteriously disappeared, and her family was told that they had been found burned to death on the outskirts of Caracas.

Gabriela scrolled through her phone and found her old friend's phone number.

"Hi Liliana, it is Gabriela," she began to cry as soon as she heard his voice on the other end of the line.

"Gabriela, what a joy to hear from you, love!"

Liliana's Story

With coffee in one hand and his tablet in the other, Diego scrolled through the morning headlines. An article caught his eye and then landed heavily upon his heart. While he was aware of the raid that had previously occurred that got over fifty women away from the clutches of one human cartel, he knew that they each represented hundreds of women in that region alone that were still trapped in slavery...truly, the tip of an evil iceberg.

Four women who were prostituted in apartments in San Sebastian have been freed by the National Police in an operation in which ten people have been arrested, four of whom have been imprisoned, accused of being part of a criminal organization.

As reported by the police in a statement, at least fifty-two women were allegedly exploited by this mafia gang, which recruited its victims in Venezuela under the promise of a decent job with which they would pay the debt of 4,500 euros. However, the women were forced to prostitute themselves during the ninety days of their legal stay in Spain and were continuously monitored by video surveillance cameras, which were controlled by those in charge of the women through cell phone applications.

The search of the apartments where the women subjected to sexual slavery were found resulted in the seizure of cash, firearms, and knives. But Agent Montalvo's attention was drawn to a notebook that was inside a bedside table. She opened it and found that it was a yellowish diary, with a dirty cover and a pen attached to the top. Once at the police station, her superiors asked her to read this diary carefully in case it could provide additional information to the investigation.

(May 22, 2013)
From the very moment Hugo Chavez ascended to the presidency of Venezuela. It was clear to me that our family was in danger. When the organizations opposing the regime became public and known internationally, my parents put themselves on the front line of action with them. That is why, the day they disappeared, I knew I would never see them again. I immediately called my closest relative, my mother's cousin, a supporter of the Bolivarian Revolution, who did not hesitate to advise me to leave the country as soon as possible. I went to his house. He gave me some money

and told me that he would contact me by cell phone when he heard from my parents.

The call came a few days ago. My parents were murdered. I am an orphan and will soon be a refugee as I flee the only land and life I have ever known.

I have no documents. I left them in Caracas in a hurry. I cannot cross to Colombia via the Simon Bolivar International Bridge as there are National Police checkpoints everywhere. I have no choice but to go to the guys who help with crossing and even though I must pay them twelve thousand pesos, I have no other option. I have been warned that the crossing of the Táchira River and then the trails to Cúcuta are full of very dangerous traffickers. Many of them are army men. May God protect me.

(May 24, 2013)
I was very scared to cross the river. The guy who was helping me already had a rope fixed on the other bank, and I held on for dear life to keep from being swept away by the current. I arrived soaked, trembling, and fearful. I'm already in Colombia, I don't know if I'm safe, but at least I don't feel the breath of the Chavista paramilitaries on the back of my neck.

(May 28, 2013)
We left Cúcuta three days ago and arrived in Bucaramanga. I am faint. My whole body hurts. I was told that some people have set up their houses to shelter women and children coming from Venezuela and traveling on foot from Cúcuta. They say that at least they give shelter and some food to regain strength and continue each one to their destination. I hope they will receive me in one of these houses.

(June 1, 2013)
The owner of the house where I am staying is a good woman. She allowed me to stay for up to five days. She has given me clothes provided by families who find it painful to see us in these conditions.

Today a woman from around here was talking to me. I think she is a lawyer, at least that's what I wanted to interpret, although she didn't really tell me clearly. She told me that things are much better in Spain, that there are jobs, and that she has contacts that would give me a position as a caregiver for the elderly in a nursing home. Apparently, she belongs to an NGO that helps women like me. Thank goodness these people exist. I thank God that I found this woman. She is taking care of my travel and will get me a new passport. I accepted.

(June 11, 2013)
Her name is Belinda. She moved me to her house, and I am staying there until I get the papers to go to Spain; she is even willing to accompany me. I have asked her about other women like me, and she has told me that they are a large group that distributes aid, so they will help as many girls as possible. By the way, the day after tomorrow, we leave for Spain, the Mother Country.

(June 15, 2013)
I am already in Spain. We are in a small roadside hotel. The trip has been long and tiring, but Belinda has told me many things about this country and has softened the discomfort of twelve hours of flight.

She gave me fifteen hundred euros to carry in my purse because at customs, we will say that we are tourists, and you need to carry cash to prove it. When I got to the hotel, I gave it back to her.

Tomorrow we will be picked up by car and moved to the place where I will live and work. I am nervous. I have sent a message to my uncle to tell him that I am in Spain. He has asked me not to communicate with him because it is dangerous for both of us.

I miss my parents dearly! It is hard to say I miss my country and community because with the civil war there it is not the same. I am convinced that this is the beginning of a phase in my life with a lot of uncertainty but with excitement and hope.

June 25, 2013
Everything was a pure lie! There was no NGO. There was no intention to help, everything was a lie! From the first word to the last, from the kindest gesture to the most treacherous smile. All of it!

When I arrived at the destination indicated by Belinda, the lights of the city were mesmerizing

We arrived at a small hotel, not centrally located, but it seemed clean and comfortable. We slept pleasantly. I wrapped myself in those sheets as if they were the most beautiful party dress in the world. That was the last night I rested. The next morning, I went to Belinda's room, but she didn't answer. I thought she was still asleep and went back to my room. I got a huge shock: inside, two men and a woman were waiting for me. She was sitting on the edge of the bed; they were on either side of the room.

They made their intentions clear to me from the very first sentence.

"You owe us 4,500 euros for the trip, the passport, and the risks we took bringing you here," the woman said.

"Where is Belinda?" I asked anxiously.

"It doesn't matter. We have paid your expenses, and you have to pay us back."

"But I don't have any money. What Belinda gave me, I gave back to her."

"You will work in a club. You will give pleasure to the men who ask for it, and the money you earn will go to pay your debt," she explained to me nonchalantly.

"I am not a whore!" I tried to leave the room, but a slap from one of the men threw me against the wall and immediately pressed me by the neck with all his strength.

"We all have some slut in us." She got up from the bed and closed the door from the inside.

While one of them held me, the other ripped my clothes off. The woman watched and as brutally as they could, they raped me. While one held me down and prevented me from resisting, the other groped and penetrated me. Then the other.

In those moments I felt like I was having the most real nightmare I had ever experienced, but I also felt a numbness. It was as if my body and my soul were separated.

"Tonight, you start work," the woman said as the men left the room.

I have not been able to write a single word since that day until today. And I still find it hard to hold my pen steady to capture what I went through. But I must do it. I must believe that in the near future, someone will read it and make these bastards pay for what they did to me that night and all the days that followed.

I am being claimed by a client of the club. Tomorrow, I will continue writing about what has happened to me.

(June 26, 2013)

They took me to an apartment in a suburb. As I entered, three young girls looked out. I noticed their zombie-like faces, expressionless, staring blankly. It was noon, and they were trying to recover their strength from the previous day (I could tell very soon that they were doing between fifteen and twenty services a day) to continue that same evening.

I was given a single room, but it was very small.

"Don't even think of talking to anyone, not even those bitches!" the man who took me shouted, with the clear intention of threatening me and warning the others of what would happen if this order was not complied with.

"I am in pain," I whispered because I couldn't get my voice out of my body.

"So, take a pill and get dressed for tonight." He tossed me a tiny pink and green dress on the bed, a very small bra, and a black thong.

Before leaving, as a warning, he pointed to a small camera located in a corner of the ceiling and signaled me with his fingers on his eyes as if to warn me that we were being watched. They took my cell phone and passport.

I had been isolated, raped, and thrown into a cesspool where I would be a money-making scrap, nothing more than that.

The first night at the club, I was unable to accede to the desires of three men who requested my services. My whole body ached from the rape and beatings. I had to assimilate what was happening to me. At that moment, I saw no way out, but I had to come up with an escape plan. They didn't give me a chance. The club manager approached me and took me to a room, holding my arm tightly. I remember it as if it happened a minute ago.

"I have been a whore like you. I always will be, even if I don't let them use my body as they please. I also had a debt, and I paid it off by forgetting that I was a person with feelings, emotions, and a soul. Take my advice—get as much money as you can to pay off your debt as soon as possible. If you try to resist there will just be more beatings and pain so you might as well accept things as they are and make the best of it, otherwise you may become hopeless. If you reach that point, suicide is the best way out. I used my agony to my advantage and look, now I make enough money to live very well."

"But you are one of them!" I glared at her.

"Survival, Liliana, survival…"

Agent Montalvo participated in many raids, mostly drug raids, but it was the first time she had been involved in a case of trafficking of women for sexual exploitation. That night, she arrived home, took a shower, had dinner, and lay down on the bed looking at the ceiling, the words she had read in that diary still echoing in her head. She wanted the night to go fast so that she could continue reading the next day at the police station.

(Dec 15, 2013)

I can't get used to this. I suppose I never will, but I have managed to anesthetize myself, to let my body be touched by dirty, rough hands of all kinds, to let them squeeze my breasts as if they were going to milk a cow, to let them violate me in every way imaginable.

I know how to control the impulses of the most violent ones, even if some of them have managed to slap me or kick me because I didn't want to do something that I found intolerable.

I have paid part of the debt, but it grows when the Mafioso feels like it. As an excuse, they said that the fixed price for using the club has gone up a bit, the antibiotic has cost too much—ten times more than it really was— that this week, the clients...—they called them clients! —were not satisfied with me, which meant the imposition of fines for poor performance. That the papers for staying in Spain had to be renewed... And so many other lies. If things don't change much, I will finish paying off my debt in a couple of years. And then...who knows.

(Dec 25, 2013)

I have just been informed that I still have two thousand euros to pay. I have given up. I can't take it anymore. I know I will never get out of this life. My colleagues say that my shoulders have slumped, and I drag my feet when I walk. They don't know that I gave up on life if you can call it life.

The words of the club manager that first night are still going around in my head. The mobsters had somewhat relaxed the pressure on my work, and although I had been moved from club to club every so often, I was now back in the first one, next to that woman. She had been diagnosed with breast cancer, and it is growing rapidly. She called me and shared that she was going to die soon and that she had given my name to the boss to take her place. Why not? I could help the girls, but I would also add to the gangsters' wallets.

(Jan 5, 2014)

They did not accept my mentor's proposal. I still have two thousand euros in debt. It never goes down. I need to pay it however, I can and get out of here. I don't want to help anyone anymore or plan anything. I just need to get out, break away from this and try to rebuild myself, even though they already warned me that this was impossible. But there must be a way out somehow, a door, no matter how small.

They gave me my phone back. They knew I was already too exploited. I have been avoiding clients whenever possible, so I think they gave it back in hopes of putting some life back in me.

(Feb 10, 2014)

I'm still swimming in the dreariness of the clubs. At least I don't get transferred from one to another. I am no longer being raped by ten or twelve men every day. I really cannot. According to the gangsters, at this rate, I won't pay my debt for a long time because the fines for "lack of productivity" equal what I get every night from those I do service.

I drag my life along as if someone were pushing me to continue, even if that someone is nothing more than my own instinct of self-preservation, which I feel less and less. I almost don't care if it all ends here.

(Feb 14, 2014)

Today I got a huge surprise. I was resting, trying to get my body back together from the night before when I received an unexpected call. It was Gabriela, a little girl I knew in Caracas. I went with my parents to the parties organized by hers. She was younger than me, but we were the only girls close in age, so we spent considerable time together.

She burst into tears as soon as she heard my voice. Apparently, history repeats itself. Nothing has changed except now she is the one who must get out. I have shown her joy at hearing from her, but the truth is any sense of joy is gone from my heart after enduring the endless nights in the clubs. I'm emotionally numb, but she has no idea. And the worst thing is that I don't care. I don't give a damn about the rest of the world.

The police officer closed the diary and imagined for a moment the ordeal that girl must have gone through, how she must have gone from a quiet and comfortable life to becoming a 21st century slave.

Agent Montalvo hated those men at that moment. If she could, she would subject them to the same humiliations they induced in others. But she was a police officer, and she had to have a cool mind to analyze what she was reading and be able to extract data that would help imprison these animals. And she still had to read the last part of the diary…

Liliana & Gabriela's Stories, Part II

"Gabriela, what a joy to hear from you, love!"

"Liliana, I need help," she said in an anguished, pleading tone.

"Tell me, what's wrong?"

"I need to leave the country. Things are very bad here. With the death of Chavez, nothing is over, Maduro continues in the same line, and people are dying.

"No wonder, those murderers will not stop until they exterminate all Venezuelans," said Liliana with almost no intonation in her words.

"I am in a group of students who organize demonstrations to improve conditions at the university, though truth be told, we are trying to push back against this oppressive regime.

"You wanted to study medicine, didn't you?" Liliana asked, remembering.

"Yes, I was enrolled in the School of Medicine, but the authorities know I participated in protests and I need to leave the country. I remembered you; I knew you went to Spain, and I wanted to know if you could help me to go there too."

"I don't know, let me think..." The woman was caught off guard by this request. She couldn't order her thoughts so quickly. "Could you call me in an hour?"

"Yes, of course. What are you working on in Spain?" asked Gabriela innocently.

"I'm a secretary in a company," That was the first thing that came to her mind at that moment, and that's how it came out of her mouth. "Call me in an hour, and I'll tell you something." She had to gather her thoughts to come up with a coherent answer, especially one that would not give away her real situation.

A vibration of her cell phone was the signal that she had received the expected message after her most recent conversation with Liliana. It was the online reservation of a plane ticket. She would be boarding at La Chinita International Airport in Maracaibo because she needed to avoid the capital's maelstrom of Caracas. She would have to endure nine hours on second-class buses on back roads to get there. Liliana told her that she would pay the fare, they would handle all the expenses from Spain. Liliana's contacts also made arrangements with a local man in Petare to forge a passport for her.

Liliana told her not to worry when she arrived in Spain and that she would provide her with housing and a job taking care of the elderly.

The plan was for her to arrive at Madrid's Adolfo Suarez Airport, where she herself would be waiting for her and would accompany her to Galicia, where she would have her job.

They landed in Madrid, and she could not help but feel free. Once through passport control, as she stepped into the common area of the airport, she knelt, covered her face with both hands, and began to laugh uncontrollably. It was a way to get all the accumulated tension out. Oh, how she wished her parents had been able to join her!

When she got up, she saw Liliana and ran to her. They embraced one another and the floodgates opened, and Gabriela cried tears of both grief and relief. Landing in a country seven thousand kilometers away from home and finding a friendly face was priceless for Gabriela. Liliana hugged her, but she didn't shed a tear. She simply didn't have any left.

They left the airport lobby and headed for the parking lot, where a man behind the wheel of a navy-blue car was waiting. He greeted her with a subtle gesture, just a slight shake of his head. Both friends sat in the back seat, and without asking, the driver started their journey. They had five hundred kilometers of road ahead of them. They only stopped halfway to use the facilities and get some water.

The tension of the trip and the fear of being detained before arriving in Spain took its toll on Gabriela, who fell asleep in the car from the halfway stop to their destination. They drove through narrow streets, blocks of apartments six or seven stories high, nondescript, without green areas, but she was already familiar with this type of housing in her native Caracas. They stopped in front of one of those buildings.

"Well, this is where you'll stay," Liliana told her as she pointed to the doorway.

"Thank you so much, my friend. I will never forget your help. Where are you staying?" asked Gabriela, a bit surprised.

"In a hotel. The driver will escort you to the apartment. We'll talk tomorrow," Liliana wanted to say goodbye as soon as possible.

They gave each other two kisses, and the driver motioned for her to enter the door. He followed behind her, and they took the elevator to the third floor. As they got out, he stepped forward and knocked on one of the four doors. A woman of about fifty opened the door, tall, with an austere expression, a dark complexion, and brown hair tied up in a well-organized bun.

"Come in, Gabriela," she indicated as she looked her up and down.

"Thank you." Gabriela turned to her companion to thank her for his service, but he was gone.

"This will be your room," a woman pointed to the third door along a long corridor, "leave your things there. We will come and talk to you."

Through the walls of her room, she heard voices coming from multiple televisions, which made her assume that there were more people living there. Carefully, she opened the door a little and saw the lady who received her, sitting at the end of the corridor, in what she guessed was a living room, in an armchair facing the rooms. She gave the impression that she was guarding her doors, but she immediately thought it was just her imagination. But who would come to talk to her? She said, "We will come," meaning not just her.

After half an hour, the door opened without anyone knocking. In walked a stocky man, about forty years old, with a face that was threatening just by looking at him. Behind him appeared the lady who had received her.

"My name is Andres, and hers is Daniela. You left Caracas in a hurry, and we brought you here. That cost a lot of money. The trip, some bribes, your passport... We paid for it, and you must pay us back."

"But I don't have any money! Liliana told me that—"

"Shut up and listen!" Andres put his face right in hers and fixed his gaze on Gabriela's eyes while holding her face tightly, painfully squeezing her cheeks. "Get this number into your head: four thousand euros. That's your debt to us!"

"Well, when I start working, I will pay you back that money, little by little," she answered in a trembling voice. Her whole body was shaking.

"From this moment on, you work for us. Tonight, you start in a club. Drinks, chats, and bed. Do you understand?" He kept his gaze fixed on Gabriela's eyes.

"No way, I'm not going to sleep with anyone for money!" she said, offended, but a slap in her face prevented her from finishing any argument she might have made.

"Daniela is going to give you clothes for work, which you will pay for with the debt, so get used to the idea. By the way, we have located him." He threw on the bed a picture of her father leaving work. The date was marked on the picture. It was from two days ago.

"What have you done to him, you sons of bitches!" she raged, grabbing Andres by the arm, who easily got away from her and threw her to the bed.

"Nothing yet. But if you don't obey, I'll show you a picture of him that I guess you wouldn't like." Gabriela began to cry inconsolably.

A slammed door was all the farewell Andres offered her. In the hallway, he ordered Daniela to get her ready to go to the club that afternoon. Gabriela curled up on the bed in the fetal position, closed her eyes, and began wishing and praying that this nightmare would end. She couldn't let them do anything to her father, but she couldn't prostitute herself either. It was contrary to her principles and her faith. And then there was Liliana. How could her friend have done that? She could not find an explanation. She thought they had been real friends. Perhaps she had changed so much that she could have become evil and cruel. She had to call her and talk to her. She grabbed her purse and looked for her cell phone. She couldn't find it. She realized that, at some point, they had taken her phone and her passport. She was alone, with no one to turn to, at the mercy of a mafia that trafficked women. In a medical psychology class at school, she had been told how these networks about how unscrupulous people of an evil nature used women as pieces of meat that, through sex, brought them large sums of money.

She had a debt, Andres made it very clear, and they would do everything possible to collect it. If she died because of some intimidating beating, it didn't matter—it was a small loss compared to everything that came into their coffers. Had Liliana fallen into that spiderweb as well?

(Feb 15, 2014)

"I called my mentor. I told her my plan. She took a good look at it and got me an appointment with the boss. I think I was convincing. It hurts to remember the conversation."

"I can bring you a Venezuelan girl. She is a childhood friend of mine. She is very pretty and has a very nice body for men. She is desperate to get out of there, just like I was. I told her that I am a secretary for a company and that I could get her a job as a caregiver for some old people," I explained.

"Well, I see you've learned your trade, Liliana. I'm starting to like you as a club manager. You're cool and don't mind betraying a friend. I guess you want something in return…"

"Pay off my debt. According to you, it is two thousand euros. If I give a new prospect to you, we could put an end to all this," my legs were trembling, but I had to show confidence in my proposal.

"Would you like to be in charge of the girls in one of our clubs?" he asked without taking his eyes off me."

"No. I just want to pay off the debt and leave."

"Good. It's a deal. When you deliver her to us, I'll tear up these papers." He showed me some sheets of paper with numbers and a sort of accounting table.

(Feb 21, 2014)

Yesterday, I betrayed Gabriela. I left her in the hands of these heartless people. I know perfectly well what is going to happen to her, I already went through that, but it is my life or her bitterness. I chose the first option. I remember her as a strong, determined girl with strong character, she can handle this better than I can. Besides, if she has stood up to the evildoers of the Bolivarians, surely, she can find a way to escape this. At least I want to believe that she can.

On the trip to Vigo, she told me that she finally felt free. Now I am the one who is really freeing myself from the demons. I have to think about how to put myself back together, look for the broken pieces in every corner of my existence, and put them back together in the right order. I approach it like when I used to do puzzles as a child: first the pieces that form the frame and then...I will have to trust my intuition. Although I think fitting the pieces together will be much more difficult than the ones Gabriela and I used to do together when we were young.

Daniela entered the room and threw some pieces of clothing on her body. Gabriela took them in her hands, looked at them, and said to herself that she would have never bought them at any flea market in Caracas. She sat down on the edge of the bed.

"Daniela, I don't want to prostitute myself," she said with a pleading look.

"Wash yourself, put that on, and put this in your bag," she gave her a package that left no doubt of its contents; they were condoms, "you'll need them."

"I've been tricked. I didn't want this!" A fury filled her face.

"They can do you a lot of physical harm. Think about it. They can make you wish you had never uttered a word. Give up and surrender. You have no way out. Pay the debt, and you will come out of this as whole as possible. Learn from your friend Liliana," counseled Daniela.

That was it. Now she understood what had happened to her friend. Possibly she had been forced or was so desperate that she had no choice but to do it.

She put on the clothes and looked at a small mirror in the room, not recognizing herself. A semi-transparent top showed off her breasts, tight shorts so tight she thought they would cut off her circulation, and underneath a black thong. Daniela came in and urged her to leave. In the hallway, she saw other girls dressed like her. She went to talk to them, but a strong hand squeezed her arm.

"Nothing is said here, you have nothing to say to them, and they have nothing to say to you. Silence will be your language. And when you return, go to your bedroom. Just know that there will always be someone watching over you so that you don't go out or talk. Understood?" Gabriela nodded.

They arrived at the club, Sherezade.

"You know what you must do. We'll tell you the prices to charge; for the rest, just do what the men paying ask you to do."

"I don't want to!" Gabriela dared to say to the club manager, who responded with a slap that knocked her down onto one of the well-worn and dirty cushions.

"At the end of the workday, you will give Shalma—" another false name that belonged to a woman who was sitting on a stool in a corner of the bar— "what you have earned.

Gabriela observed that the other women went about their business as automatons that seduced the men who came in the door and then spread their legs for them to unload their family or work frustrations or simply believe they were the king of the universe. Some could not hide a scar on their shoulder, a lip that had been split, or a lump on their back; one of them showed a slight limp, and another one disguised with her hair a clear sign of a burn, like the one she had on her hand and that Daniela decorated with a handkerchief as a bracelet and an excessive load of makeup. You didn't have to be very smart to know how and who could have inflicted those injuries.

With the first client who claimed her, she resisted, and that provoked an additional morbid curiosity in him, which meant that the penetration was more violent, the groping even more unpleasant, and the hair-pulling even more humiliating. That night, she had to endure it all with five different men. That same night she began to draw in her mind an escape plan.

Agent Montalvo turned page after page of that diary, but there was nothing else. She did not write again about her life, nor anything that would indicate anything about what happened to Liliana from that day on. It was as if her existence had ended suddenly or, on the contrary, another life had begun at that very moment. Perhaps she was getting herself together somewhere in Spain, or perhaps she had left the country for who knows where. She went to the residence where the liberated girls were staying and asked them about Liliana. None of them knew anyone by that name. The agent showed them the diary. They looked at each other, and no one had seen it before. Only one acknowledged having seen a book, which could be that one, in the drawer of a bedside table in a room of the club. She couldn't read, so she put it back where it was, over three years ago.

Montalvo left the residence and returned to the police station. She sat down in front of the computer to write her report. She stared at the screen and said in a low voice:

"I hope, wherever you are, you find yourself putting the pieces of your puzzle together. May you succeed, Liliana."

The second night at the club, one of the Colombian girls felt sick, her belly ached, and she was dizzy. Gabriela accompanied her to the bathroom, and in the few minutes they could be alone, she learned that there were organizations that attended to the trafficked women, provided them with help for their hygiene, health, and opened some doors to facilitate their exit from these networks. The Red Cross came around, but there were also other smaller associations, not so well-known to the public, that also participated in providing this assistance. This girl was menstruating and had just performed a service with a not-so-sensitive client. She needed to stop but was not allowed to. Gabriela had a painkiller in her purse. She gave it to her so she could endure the rest of the night.

On the floor, they were watched day and night. There was always someone at the end of the corridor to prevent them from leaving the rooms. They had to open the door and ask permission to go to the bathroom. If they needed to go to buy something in the nearby stores, another person would replace Daniela, who then accompanied the girl. She would pay, but she would write it down in the girl's debt, of course.

When she had been there for ten days, she realized that most of the time, it was Daniela who oversaw the surveillance. She supposed that, at some point, sleep or simply drowsiness would distract her; she would occasionally take a nap in that armchair. That was her chance.

At the club, from the second day, Gabriela indicated had been charging her clients five euros more than she was ordered to pay. She ran the risk that one of them would complain to Shalma, but it was the only leverage she had so it was worth the risk. After fifteen days of torture, Gabriela had four hundred euros saved without the knowledge of the mafia.

In her room, she had a cloth bag with the essentials for a few days; some underwear, a pair of sunglasses, a couple of T-shirts, some toiletries, and a cell phone that had been given to her so that she would always be in contact with them. On the afternoon of the sixteenth day of her ordeal, after lunch, Daniela began to doze off. It was just at that moment that Gabriela opened her door and realized that it was her moment. She grabbed the bag, walked out slowly, shoes in hand so as not to make any noise, and made it to the front door of the apartment. She stepped out onto the landing, but just at that moment, the elevator stopped on that floor. A cold sweat ran down her back, but she ran down to the bottom flight of stairs. She huddled in the corner and heard someone exit the elevator, open a door and close it. Gabriela continued speeding down the stairs until she stepped out onto the street. She looked in all directions in case she saw a car waiting for someone, but thankfully she was the only one in the neighborhood at that hour.

She put on her shoes and ran straight for the bus station. At the entrance to the ticket counters, she looked carefully at the schedules and nearby destinations. She saw that there were three buses leaving practically at the same time: at 15:35 to Valencia, at 15:40 to Madrid, and at 15:45 to Seville. That circumstance favored her since, when they noticed her absence if they went to that station, they would have doubts about which of the three she could have boarded. For no real reason, she chose Seville.

She pulled out her ticket and climbed into the assigned seat on the bus. As happened before, when she boarded the plane in Venezuela, her chest tightened until it almost prevented her from breathing. She anxiously turned her attention to the entrance to the bus, looking at her cell phone clock every ten seconds. Finally, it started up and pulled away. She shrank back in her seat to lessen the possibility of being identified from the outside. They left the city, and that again provoked the same feeling of freedom as on the plane. But this time, she was forewarned. That feeling was no security at all.

She arrived in Seville, and the first thing she did was go to the cafeteria to eat a sandwich. She hadn't eaten anything since she left the apartment in Vigo. Once she had regained some of her strength, she looked at the departure notification panel. She chose the exact place where she had decided to go. As she was about to go to the ticket counter, she noticed two tall, strong, South American-looking guys looking for something or someone; they were looking at everyone, staring at the faces of each of the people who were quietly waiting for their bus to leave, seated on the benches in the hall. She feared the worst and rushed to the ladies' room, entered one of the stalls and although her heart was pounding like a herd of stampeding bison, she managed to control herself to the point of barely breathing. They opened the bathroom door, and she could already imagine the end. She closed her eyes and prepared to surrender. But it was just a woman who was going to use the restroom. She let a few minutes pass and went back out into the main room. She didn't see the men, nor did she notice anything unusual. She pulled out her ticket and hurriedly boarded the bus. As she left the city, emotional and physical exhaustion caused her to fall fast asleep.

Upon arriving at her destination, she found the cheapest hotel she could and once settled in her room, called a Red Cross hotline. The person answering told her they periodically visited an industrial park where prostitutes gather. Gabriela wrote it all down and determined she would go there on Friday, two days from now. When she went out to buy some food it seemed to her that everyone was watching her. She knew she was being paranoid, but she also knew she had to stay alert.

Between the expenses for lodging, food, and the bus tickets, she calculated that she had enough for a couple of weeks.

On Friday she went by bus to the industrial park and located the women, grouped together by nationalities. She managed to find out where the Latin American women congregated. When she arrived, she recognized a familiar accent.

"You are from Venezuela," she said to a girl who looked even younger than herself.

"And you too," she replied coldly, not trusting anyone who approached her and didn't ask for sex.

"Does the Red Cross come through here?"

"Yes."

"I have been told that they come on Fridays," Gabriela said, hoping for confirmation.

"Sometimes," the girl was beginning to feel uncomfortable; while she was talking to this woman, no clients approached her, and that prevented her from getting money for her debt.

"I would like to talk to them…"

"Then get out of here and wait over there between those containers. You'll see the van when it arrives," she pointed to an area away from her.

"Thank you."

She waited there until two in the morning. They did not come. The girl told her that they didn't always come. When the girl returned from her last service, Gabriela approached her.

"They won't come today, will they?"

"I don't think so," she continued with her disinterested attitude. "Sometimes, they have an emergency somewhere else and can't go to two places at once. But they'll be here next week, sometimes even on weekdays. Why do you want the Red Cross?" she asked as Gabriela was about to leave.

"I want to get out of all this. I've escaped," Gabriela replied.

"Do you have a cell phone?"

"Yes," she showed her the device.

"Then copy this number. Mommy will help you."

"Mommy? Who is Mommy?"

"They come on Fridays, alternating with the Red Cross. They are good people. They treat you as human beings with feelings and a soul. They hug you, comfort you, and listen to you. They can help you," she showed her the number, and Gabriela copied it immediately. "Call her. She will answer, for sure."

"Thank you very much. I will do it. By the way, what is your name?"

"What difference does it make…?"

She decided to wait until the next morning to call that Mommy. She went out for coffee at a nearby cafe. When she returned, the manager of the boarding house handed her an envelope. She took it and was startled to see her name written, simply Gabriela, underlined with a double line. She asked him who had brought it, but the man simply shrugged his shoulders and continued watching a small television in his cubicle.

She rushed upstairs and opened it with trembling hands. A piece of paper written in capital letters left no room for doubt.

"You sneaky whore, we've got a fix on you! You'll never get away from us again. We'll give you three days to come back, or we'll come and show you what we're capable of doing to a woman who has betrayed us."

In the envelope was also a photo of her father, the same one from Vigo, with a red X drawn over his image.

She thought that if something had been done to him, the photo would not be that one. On the other hand, she reread the note and noticed the phrase "we have located you." She quickly looked at her cell phone and realized that they had given it to her and surely, they were tracking her location. She didn't hesitate for a moment. She left the cell phone in the room and took the bag with the few things she had taken with her since her departure from Vigo.

Gabriela asked for a nearby phone booth, and immediately went to call the number that girl had given her the night before.

"Mommy?" she asked brokenly when she heard a woman's voice answering the call.

"Yes, who are you?" asked Sara on the other end of the line.

"My name is Gabriela, and I need help," she said, fighting back an avalanche of tears.

"Don't worry. Where are you now?" Gabriela gave her the address where the hotel was.

"I ran away, but they tracked my cell phone."

"Leave the cell phone there and go to a church behind the place where you are now. We are coming for you. Don't move from there."

She did as Mommy had instructed, and forty minutes after the call, an older couple came in and approached her.

"Hi, Gabriela." They sat on either side of her. "My name is Sara, and this is my husband, Diego. We're going to get you out of here, and everything will be fine, you'll see." She took her hand, which produced in her a feeling of peace she couldn't define.

"Thank you, Mommy. I'm so bad." Tears began to fall down her cheeks.

"Don't worry. There is a way out of all this. Even this hell has an exit door."

Cecilia's Story

Cecilia had proven to be a difficult girl to have in the clubs. She complained about almost everything and frequently rebelled if she was moved to another club. On one occasion, she even slapped Felipe when he told her that she was not performing as she should and that she was being fined five hundred euros. After several slaps and an excessive push that made Cecilia fall to the ground, Felipe violently violated her. She screamed, she resisted, but that only made the penetration more ferocious.

After finally being fed up with her, Felipe sold her to a pimp from Vigo, Andres "the Galician," for six thousand euros. She would stay with Daniela, the caretaker of the apartment where she would live with other girls with whom she could not communicate, until she finished paying her debt, which now amounted to six thousand euros.

They took her to a club, and there, she did what she had been doing since Felipe and broke her in. Two months went by. Cecilia no longer protested so much. Her fortress had been broken.

One night, a new girl showed up. She was introduced as Gabriela. A couple of days later, she was feeling sick, her belly ached, and she was dizzy. She was menstruating and had just performed a service with a not-so-delicate client. She needed to stop that night, but she was not allowed to. Gabriela accompanied her to the bathroom. She had a painkiller in her purse; she gave it to her so she could endure the rest of the night.

It was clear to her that Gabriela wanted to escape and would do everything possible to do so.

"There is an organization, like the Red Cross. They help girls like us. Apparently, they take care of us and give us a lot of love, besides offering us a way out of this world, at least that is what some of our colleagues who have worked on the streets have told us," Cecilia explained.

"Thank you very much, Cecilia; it could be a good option," Gabriela answered with a thoughtful expression.

When Gabriela ran away, Cecilia did not have the courage to accompany her. She really didn't have the strength for almost anything. At first, they thought that some of the girls had helped her escape and increased the control over them. They swore they had nothing to do with it, but that did not free them from a fine of five hundred euros each.

Despite the lack of energy and mental fatigue, Cecilia began to think about the possibility of doing what Gabriela had done. But she had her daughter, Valeria, to consider. Although she knew the basics of reading and writing, she wanted to put her feelings on paper for her daughter's sake in the future.

"We cannot lose hope in getting out of all this, even if we have lost our strength."

"God hears us."

Cecilia was no longer the same. No one was the same as the girl who arrived a few years ago. She offered sex like the one who sells candy—a sweet for the one who buys it and bitter for the one who makes it. Her earnings were considerably reduced. She almost didn't care. She knew the debt would never end, or perhaps it would end just the minute before her destruction as a person. The pimps know when that moment comes, and far from giving the girl her freedom, they simply sell her. That's what Felipe had already done once, but this time, fate was smiling on her as she was sold to a club where they had told her about the existence of those earthly angels that could help her to get out and start to put her life back together with her daughter.

"Hi, Mommy!" she could hear from her bunk.
"Who is Mommy?" she asked a companion.
"Come out and see."
"Hi, you're new, aren't you?" asked Sara with a sweet look full of understanding.
"Yes, my name is Cecilia, I am Colombian, and I have a daughter who is with the bosses," she wanted to quickly explain her situation, to attract Sara's attention.
"Are you all right?" she asked as she took her trembling hand.
"No, I am not."
"Give me your phone number," she said quietly, behind the other girls' backs.
"Will you call me?" Cecilia asked as she discreetly showed her the phone screen.
"Of course. You won't be alone anymore..."
A Long Journey from Morocco:

Shamira's Story

Shamira was full of joy, vivacity, and compassion from a very young age. She was tall for her age, and her reddish and curly hair, which, together with her caramel-colored eyes, made Shamira a very attractive girl.

At home, she was her mother's helping hand in daily household chores. Much of the time, it was just the two of them, as her father spent long periods of time on the fishing boats. Despite this, they lived modestly, without great hardship, but were at the mercy of the results of the fishing seasons.

Shamira was trained in everything related to the Islamic religion at school, as was the case with all the children. The customs, the rules, the divine, and the human. The role of women was not discussed, it was simply their duty. According to the teachers' interpretation of the Quran, men and women were not equal. The woman was the property of the man, who was a supreme being of creation and her purpose was to satisfy him in everything he asked for at any given moment. Some were seeking to transform the status of women, which would lead to greater equality with men, but this was not adopted in schools.

When she turned fourteen, Rachid's family made Amina aware of the need to find a husband for Shamira. She was not ready to plan such things, so he always changed the subject and ended with a "we'll see." Her daughter's natural beauty grew with her age. Her hair could be a lure to the lasciviousness of Moroccan men if it was not for the fact that she always wore hijab.

She turned nineteen, and her parents made her a special meal with dishes they knew she liked and allowed her to invite some friends. Lamb tagines, salad, and pasta. She was happy. She didn't need anything else. Three days later, her father boarded a Spanish fishing boat and announced that the fishing would last about a month. Everything was going smoothly, at least, she felt and saw it that way

One evening at about six o'clock, there was a knock at Rachid's door. It was a foreman from the port, and he was bringing her the worst of the news.

"The boat your husband was on has disappeared at sea. An unexpected storm hit them, it seems, and we don't know anything. They have gone out to look for it, but nothing is showing up on the radar."

Amina was overwhelmed, and darkness set upon her. Every time Rachid went fishing, she dreaded this moment. She knew it could happen someday. Shamira, her daughter, was behind her, some distance away, but she heard everything. She shrank back just like her mother. Amina adjusted the veils on their heads, and together they set off with the foreman to the port of Agadir.

Both Amina and her daughter refused to keep the mourning period dictated by the Quran, of four months and ten days at the home of her late husband's family. They moved to his house, wore a white robe for three days, and for the rest of the mourning period, they dressed ostentatiously, without adornment, only adorned with their sadness, their memories, and the hope that Rachid would be in a place where Allah would protect him until the end of time.

According to Islamic tradition, Rachid's family would take care of both women, to preserve the dignity of the man's family. So, little by little, they returned to the routine. Mother and daughter were very close, even more so after the death, and it was Shamira who took more and more care of her mother, reversing the role she assumed since her birth.

One afternoon, Maryam, a woman living in Inezgane, a village very close to Agadir, visited them. She knew Rachid's family indirectly and had found out about his death.

"I join you in remembering Rachid. He was a good man," she began her visit, to the surprise of Amina and Shamira.

"Thank you very much. Yes, he was. A good father and husband. Did you know him?" Amina asked curiously.

"Through my husband. I had business in the port of Agadir, and that is why I knew about him. I did not want to let any more time pass before coming to give my condolences."

"The sea has stolen him from us," Amina lamented.

"I guess Rachid's family is taking care of your needs, right?"

"Yes, of course," said Amina.

"We live in difficult times, not only in Morocco but in most of the world. I worry about the young people," she looked directly at Shamira, "and how they will get ahead."

"It's true. They're going to have a hard time the way things are going," said her mother.

"I have a daughter, now twenty-nine years old. When the economic crisis started, some friends insisted she should go to Spain to work in a stable family business that had not suffered from the economic situation. She has been there for two years and lives much better than here, earning two thousand euros a month, about twenty thousand dirhams. In addition, she can continue her studies in Spain. I thank Heaven for having had this stroke of luck when her friends contacted her," Maryam recounted at length.

"And could my Shamira do that?" Amina asked with great interest as she grabbed her daughter's forearm.

"Of course, if you are interested, I could help you make it happen," she replied with some enthusiasm.

"Could you really do it?" asked Shamira.

"I have already done it with other people in the area. They are delighted there in Spain. If you want, I can call my daughter and ask her if they could accept Shamira in the job where she is."

"Yes, please," answered Amina.

When they were left alone, Amina held her daughter by the shoulders.

"This is an opportunity that you should not miss. There is no future here for people like you, intelligent and eager to learn and work. Let's wait for that woman to call us and tell us what you should do."

"But mother, I can't leave you alone. You are old, and the daily chores are hard," disagreed the daughter.

"Don't worry; your uncles protect us, and they will continue to do so with me when you leave. You must continue your studies, and you will make much more progress there than here. You have your whole life ahead of you, and you must take advantage of this opportunity. That's all there is to it."

The next day, they received a call from Maryam. She told them that she had already spoken to her daughter and that her bosses were willing to receive Shamira. The trip, the residency papers, and the house and food for a year would cost six thousand five hundred euros, about seventy thousand dirhams. She could take care of all the paperwork. She knew it was a lot of money, but she urged Amina to talk to Rachid's family, who had an ancestral obligation to provide for her niece's education and future.

She did not delay talking to her brother-in-law.

"It is a lot of money, Amina. I don't have that much. Besides, I must support my family. You know that my two children are still in school, and my brother lives with us; he cannot lead a normal life. God has taken care of him for many years," said Rachid's older brother, Youssef, in response to what Amina proposed to him for her daughter.

"I know, and I appreciate everything you are doing for us. I only look out for my daughter, for her sake, for her future."

"We can ask for a loan from the bank. Maybe they will give it to us. The director has business with the family and is a good Muslim. Let me try," said Youssef.

Three days later, he had the money in the bank. The director had known Youssef since they were children. They had always dreamed of founding a spice company and imagined exporting spices all over the world. The death of Youssef's father prevented his dreams from coming true. He had to take care of his mother, his sisters, and his handicapped brother. Nevertheless, the friendship between the two friends would last forever.

"Take, Amina," he gave her an envelope with the money inside, "and may Allah, the Gracious, the Merciful, guard and guide Shamira on her journey through this life."

"He will pay you back in spades, Youssef."

Maryam organized everything. She explained in detail to Amina the route her daughter would take, how she would go, when she would arrive and when she would be able to speak to her again. The first step was to travel to Tangier to go by boat to Tarifa, arriving on Spanish soil. Amina handed the envelope with the money to Maryam, and Maryam did not even check its contents; she simply put it in her purse. She wished Shamira the best of luck and predicted a fortunate future for her.

The Strait of Gibraltar was drawn in her mind as a bottomless abyss, as something she had to cross in one leap and savor everything on the other side, take the opportunity to study, and get a job for her future and that of her family. It was clear to Shamira that, one way or another, she had to pay back to her father's family all the money they had given her for her. She even planned to pay back some of the money to Youssef whenever she was able to spend some time with her mother again.

She carried in her hand luggage—she was told that in Spain, they would provide her with more clothes—the essentials to subsist for a few days: some clothes, a bag with toiletries, a small wallet with her identity documents, passport, and visa papers to enter Spanish territory, and a cell phone. She said goodbye to her mother, promising her that he would call her often, that she would send her money as she earned it and that she would return during vacation periods to be with her. She wished her all the good that life could give her and all the health that the Almighty would be good enough to grant her. Amina hugged her and cried with much emotion, a feeling of doing the right thing for the sake of her daughter, it was what she and her husband wanted, and now she had to fulfill what they had planned almost from the moment of her birth. She was left with the thorn of not having arranged a good marriage, but that would come at the right time.

At eight a.m., there was a knock at the door. Two boys helped carry her luggage, though it was scarce, and they left quickly for their destination. She was in the back seat. They did not engage her in conversation but just talked to each other about soccer matches and the like. Shamira rode with a shared sense of uncertainty and excitement as she imagined what her future would look like. She was told only that in Tangier; a woman would give her suitable clothes and instructions on how to cross the Spanish border.

The trip took eight hours, along a road that ran parallel to the coast for most of its length. They went directly to the Quartier Berouaka, a central district of Tangier. In a two-story house, a woman was waiting, dressed in a black kaftan (the typical dress of Moroccan women), that covered her mouth with a black veil. The two boys left without saying anything, and the woman motioned for Shamira to follow her.

"Take off your hijab and your kaftan. I will give you appropriate clothing to cross the border without attracting attention. Remember that the moment you get on the boat, you must adopt a European image, both in appearance and in how you express yourself."

Shamira obeyed without any resistance. She wore a dark green kaftan with discreet black embroidery on her chest and a string at her waist; she wore a black hijab on her head, her face uncovered. She did not take her eyes off the ground.

"First of all, don't lower your gaze—" she lifted her face and her chin" —in Europe, women look everyone in the eye. You are going to be European, so look straight ahead."

She looked around and saw that they were alone, with the door closed. The woman noticed and assured her that there was no one else in the house. Shamira began to remove her clothes slowly: first, the hijab, shaking her head to loosen her reddish, wavy hair; then, she loosened the string at her waist and removed her kaftan, which the woman picked up to fold. She had on her left a chair with western clothes: jeans, a light blue blouse, a fashionable bra, sunglasses, designer sneakers (fake, of course), hoop earrings, a pendant necklace, and underwear.

As she was putting on her new outfit, the woman continued to give her instructions.

"Don't be hesitant to answer at customs. You are going to visit some friends on the Spanish coast, you will take the opportunity to go sightseeing—you have permission—and they will pick you up in Tarifa. Talk to the police officers in a respectful way, but don't keep your eyes on the ground. Fix your eyes on their faces and be resolute in your answers. If they ask you if you are going to work in Spain, tell them that you are only going as a tourist, but if they offer you a job, of course, you will legalize your papers immediately, but that is not your intention."

Shamira finished putting on her western clothes. She had a strange feeling. Her pants were tight, the bra squeezed her breasts and gave her a feeling of suffocation, the slippers from home were much more comfortable than those sneakers, and she felt out of place without a veil, with her hair in the air. She approached a mirror and looked at the girl whose image was reflected in the opaque glass. She analyzed her from top to bottom and smiled, although she had the impression that she was looking at a woman from one of those magazines that she saw, from time to time, on the sly at school.

"You look perfect," said the woman, looking at her from a distance.

"I'm thirsty. Could you give me some water?"

Her throat had gone dry. It was undoubtedly that a certain aura of intrigue and of doing something not quite legal filled her doubts. But Maryam had already warned her about all this and explained that the border authorities were wary of Muslims entering Europe, possibly because of the recent jihadist attacks in Germany.

Everything was ready. The two guys who brought her from Agadir came to pick her up and took her to the seaport. They gave her the boat ticket to Tarifa and told her that two other men would contact her on the way. They told her that one would introduce himself as Mohamed and would accompany her to her destination in Spain.

She passed the police and customs control without any problem. She listened to all the recommendations given to her by the woman from Tangier and did not have the slightest issue. Despite this, every question, including a glance, from the policeman provoked the perception of a drop of sweat running down her back from her neck to her waist. She breathed a sigh of relief as she sat in the ferry's common room, noticed how her muscles relaxed, and the tension in her neck disappeared completely.

Thirst returned to her mouth. She went to get up to the small bar in the center of the room, and at that moment, a man approached her.

"Hello, Shamira. I'm Mohamed." He sat down opposite her. "How are you? Everything went well, I see. Well, you've already got one foot in Spain. Only the other is missing." He smiled a forced smile.

"I was going to buy a bottle of water. I'm very thirsty," she told him, standing up.

"Don't worry. I'm coming. Would you like some tea?" offered Mohamed kindly.

"Yes, please." She looked into his eyes, remembering the Tangier woman's recommendation.

Mohamed was a man in his mid-twenties, tall, handsome, and well-groomed. As they drank tea, he spoke to her about the goodness of the climate in southern Spain and the excellent quality of life in that area, the job opportunities, and the acceptance of people like her at the University of Arab. Shamira began to feel dizzy. She held tightly to the arms of her swivel chair, believing that it was the movement of the boat and her seat that caused her lack of stability. She rubbed her eyes but it did not help. She looked at the glass of tea and saw its edges rippling. Mohamed was still speaking, and she heard his voice, but she could not distinguish the words and understand the sentences. She noticed a general sluggishness in her body and a lack of strength and desire to move. She closed her eyes and fell asleep

"Shamira, wake up." Mohamed grabbed her arm, shaking it a little, to wake her up from sleep. "We are arriving in Tarifa. You have fallen asleep. You must be tired from the hustle and bustle of the day."

"Have we arrived?" She was still not well, still drowsy and lacking strength.

She believed that the boat's oscillating movement in the harbor gave her that feeling of instability as if she were floating in the air, but at the same time, all the objects around her were also floating. She let Mohamed know, but he only replied that she must have been seasick on the boat, that this was normal. She struggled down the stairs, helped by the two men who accompanied her, they carried her luggage, and between them, one on each side, they held her to give an impression of normality. They arrived at the exit of the port of Tarifa, and there, an eight-seater cab was waiting for them.

"Make yourself comfortable," Mohamed told her as he opened a side door of the vehicle and helped her get in. "We have a two-hour drive ahead of us."

Shamira sat in the last row and her mouth felt dry, very dry, pasty, almost preventing her from uttering a word.

"I am thirsty. Do you have water?"

"Yes, here you are," Mohamed took out a thermos of tea, preparing a glass for her to drink.

She was so thirsty that she drank it all at once. Her mouth got wet, and she felt better. She leaned her head against the backrest and closed her eyes. She could remember almost everything that happened to her from the time she left home until she got on the boat in Tangier. From then on, everything was hazy. She entered intense drowsiness and surrendered herself to sleep once again.

It could have been a minute or a whole century; it didn't matter. She had no notion of time. It could have been at the exit of the port of Tarifa or in a secluded area of El Bujeo or in some place on the way, or when arriving in Huelva; it didn't matter. She had no notion of space. It could have been the two companions or only Mohamed or the three of them, together with the driver or even more men who joined along the way; it didn't matter. She was not aware of what was happening around her. It could have been in the same cab or in the middle of the field or on a bed or on the floor of a house; it didn't matter. She had no memory to recall it. She could have resisted, or they could have held her down or simply taken off her clothes without difficulty; it didn't matter. She had no will. It could be that they thought she liked it or that she felt aroused by being groped or that the multiple penetrations throughout the night seemed little to her, or that it didn't matter where they were performed; it didn't matter. She moved unconsciously to the voice of her masters. It didn't matter how, where, and how much; she, Shamira, was not there.

> "I don't remember anything, just getting on a boat in Tangier. They offered me tea; I'm sure of that. I drank it because my mouth was dry. I drank it all. From then on, nothing. I can't give any details, neither specific people, nor places, nor time that passed. Only loose, blurred, distorted images come to my mind. I don't know if it was real or if I dreamed it, but a thousand ghosts passed before my eyes, faces of demons with deformed features, laughing, screaming, and emitting monstrous sounds from beyond the grave. One face, then another, and another, and another…different demons, but all were equally harmful. I remember that every time a new face appeared, I felt intense pain, sometimes sharp and sometimes dull. I felt my belly pierced by a thousand daggers, sometimes as if I had been given a sharp blow in the middle of my stomach; everything burned, my belly, my legs, and my breasts. I noticed how my mouth bled. A warm liquid ran down my neck. Above all, my soul ached, an infinite pressure that did not let me breathe. All I remember is having a nightmare, the most horrible nightmare of my life, something like entering directly into the bowels of hell."

She woke up in a dingy room, gloomy, with peeling walls, the ceiling black from humidity, and the mattress gave off a strong and unpleasant odor, like dog urine. She opened her eyes and tried to visualize that dive. She could hardly move, her thoughts were tangled together, she was unable to focus.

She struggled to stand and stumbled over her own feet, almost falling, staggering to catch herself on the edges of the table. Everything weighed on her. Even though she was thin, it was as if her body had thickened, and her skin had swollen. She looked down at her hands and saw how the moisture had settled between her fingers, felt warmth on her face and neck, and noticed her clothes were wet from perspiration. Pain was present from the neck down. She opened a rickety door and entered a small room where there was something resembling a sink and a toilet. As best she could, she poured water over her body. She felt the coolness of that liquid, and she wanted to get rid of all the secretions that covered her legs and her most intimate parts.

Her mouth burned and felt extremely dry again. It hurt to move her tongue inside. Without thinking, she took the pitcher that was on the table and drank directly from it. It was sweet, like the tea infusions that her mother used to prepare for her at home in Agadir. She drank a good gulp until she was satiated. Feeling weak, she rested her trembling arms on the bed and lay down, naked.

She thought she had fallen asleep, although she had no notion of the time that had elapsed or of anything. Suddenly, the door opened, and a woman entered without saying a word, threw clean clothes on her, and went out the same way she came in. Shamira felt numb; she had no will of her own.

She slowly dressed and sat down on the edge of the bed. The woman who had brought her the clothes came back in, now with a small tray containing a sandwich, an apple, and a yogurt. She put it on the table and left without a word. She took the tray, placed it on her aching thighs, and ate its contents, only then realizing how famished she was.

At dusk, when the light began to draw reddish traces in the sky, the door opened again, and two men told her to get up, that they were leaving.

"Where are you taking me?" she asked hesitantly.

"We're going to grow strawberries." They both burst out laughing.

In Huelva, she was taken to an apartment in a neighborhood almost on the outskirts of the city, far from the visitors who were looking for sun, food, and the beach. They took her upstairs and left her in a room at the end of a small corridor. When she entered the room, the effect of the drug she was being administered subsided somewhat so that Shamira's senses were able to respond somewhat better to the dreary surroundings that were imposed on her as a dwelling. Nevertheless, she was in a constant state of confused fogginess. They knew what they were giving her, and the exact dosage needed to achieve their purposes: to have her "high," to have her obey and prostitute herself almost unconsciously, yet with the strength to perform satisfactory sex for those who paid for it.

"Here you will live. Here you will receive customers and give them everything they ask for. We will come daily to collect the money you earn, and we will give you food and clothes. Do you understand?" Mohamed reappeared, but he was no longer so friendly. Now he was giving orders.

"Yes," she said without reasoning, without will, without understanding what she had said yes to.

"By the way," he turned from the door before leaving, "you are Fatima here. Your real name doesn't attract potential customers."

"Fatima," she repeated automatically.

Shamira's Story, Part II

Mohamed left the apartment, and she was left alone in that sad, dark room, on a mattress on which hundreds of men would have fornicated, under a lamp that more than lighting seemed to watch over the girl who was imprisoned there: she was a prisoner whose future consisted of being exploited, sullied, vilified and assaulted.

Moroccans, Portuguese, Spanish…they all worked in the strawberry fields, some clandestinely, others with contracts, and a few with legitimate jobs. The majority were Moroccan women, especially those with children, whom they left behind in Morocco. They were the ones chosen because this ensured that they would return without causing problems. Men worked to control the women's groups in the greenhouses and performed some of the more labor intensive and complex tasks. In these places, there was always some element of the mafia that had the girls enslaved.

The next day Mohamed returned to check on her. Shamira was less sleepy than the previous days, but still lacking in self-will. He told her the price of the services and gave her a bag of clothes suitable for the work. That same night, a seventy-year-old man entered her room and abused her. When he left, her body was sore, her soul broken, and she could only vomit.

She continued to be drugged daily. She became constipated for two weeks, so she had to go to a doctor, in the service of the gangsters, to apply enemas that increased the pain in her anus, already torn apart by the beasts. The doctor told Mohamed that they had to reduce the dose of the drug or it would cause intestinal paralysis. It didn't matter to the mobster, but the woman was providing the network with considerable profits, so he listened. As a result, Shamira's level of consciousness increased somewhat, and she was able to reason sometimes without being hurt by her thoughts.

> "I felt more awake, and at times, I could think and understand everything that was happening to me. Yes, I managed to integrate into my conscience that I was prostituting myself. I did not know how long or how many times; everything was clouded in my memory. I only remembered faces that appeared around me, some names that I could not identify, and that dull pain that did not leave my belly and sometimes my whole body. With my senses more awake, I tried to ask for explanations from Mohamed, the one who often visited me to take the money or to take me to the bar where he offered me as sexual merchandise. The answer to my questions was a clear threat: they knew where my mother and the rest of my family lived, and if I did not cooperate, they would pay dearly. I had no choice, no strength, and no will to react."

One night a Moroccan guy in his thirties appeared in her room. He arranged for her services in the bar where Mohamed's contacts were. This encounter would prove to be very different from all the others she had endured.

He was one of the privileged strawberry workers who had a contract. He came from Morocco to claim a job offer in Huelva. Of course, it was not an official work visa but through mafia groups that swarmed the country. The State Security Forces had identified two ways of obtaining work in the Huelva greenhouses: the crop managers themselves, who went to Morocco to carry out recruitment of temporary migrant workers (almost all women), and the mafia networks, which generally hired men who paid for the opportunity for a job during the strawberry picking season. The police had well-founded suspicions of some collusion between these networks and the land managers, but rarely took any proactive action to intervene.

Ahmed arrived in Spain with a forged, temporary residence permit. Obviously, that had a price: two thousand euros. According to the indications of those in charge of his transfer, he went to a plantation managed by a Spanish family, whose eldest son took them in to work the crops. Several Moroccans, Ahmed among them, settled in a ramshackle house near the work site, where eight men lived together in four patched bunk beds and a filthy bathroom for all of them. They were paid thirty euros a day, but they were happy because they knew that many compatriots, almost all of them arriving by boat, crowded the traffic circles to beg for a job from the foremen who came every morning in open vans, offering wages of twenty euros.

Ahmed was willing and adapted to the hardness of the work. He did not protest. He carried out his work without complaining, which was rare. He learned to tolerate the xenophobic atmosphere of the area and had already been warned that years ago, campaigns of harassment and violence had been launched with the slogan "Hunt the Moor" on the grounds that the region was increasingly occupied by Moroccans, Malians, and Senegalese, among other nationalities; in fact, when Ahmed arrived in the Huelva fields, three out of every ten salaries paid in the area were for African immigrants.

And so, he, due to his organizational skills and ability to help his colleagues, made the owners' sons notice him. He demonstrated his skills in more complex tasks than just picking strawberries and after a year, they offered him a contract to be in charge of a group of workers, which he accepted immediately and increased his dedication to the productivity of the employees.

He used to meet up with other guys his age to get together for tea or to help in some of the many stores run by Moroccans to transport goods. In this way, within a year, he had paid off his debt to the mafia that brought him here. One Friday afternoon, having just collected the week's wages, several of them went to a bar located on the outskirts of Huelva, frequented by compatriots. There they noticed that at a table, they were making deals to visit prostitutes. The men were encouraged to take advantage of the opportunity, and three of them took the plunge. They agreed on the price and sent each one to a different house.

Ahmed had a sensitive nature. He was able to perceive the emotional state of others and always tended to try to help whomever he saw in need of a shoulder to cry on or ears where someone could unburden himself. Already in Morocco, his mother had perceived this quality in her son but warned him that it could turn against him. Emotional sensitivity was easily confused with sentimentality, and this, in men, with homosexuality. But he could not help it. He knew how to grasp the suffering of others.

He climbed the stairs of that house and knocked on the door that had been directed to.

"Fatima?" he asked at the sight of a shadow that remained motionless, leaning against the door jamb.

"Yes, come in," she opened the door a little wider and led the way inside.

She stood at the side of the bed. She was beautiful, in a long, flowered robe open wide, exposing her body in only pink underwear. Her curly reddish hair inspired in him an intense attraction, her caramel eyes immediately spoke to him of mystery, but it was the sadness of her gaze, the emptiness between her pupils and what they expressed, that caused Ahmed to take notice. She stood there, as if she were a wax figure, almost without facial expression. She held an insinuating pose, but it was not natural, but rather forced. Her body seemed in total disconnect from her mind.

"Don't you like me?" she asked when she saw that he didn't move. "Is it the first time?"

"No... it's just... I don't know... you're very beautiful... but..."

"Do you want me to do something special for you?"

Fatima took off her robe to ignite some excitement in the man. She approached him and began to remove his shirt. She took his hand, brought it to her breast, and her other hand began to fiddle with Ahmed's belt buckle. He quickly pulled both her hands apart and grabbed her shoulders.

"No. You're very beautiful, you'd be able to excite me, for sure, but I can't take advantage of you. You're not well. Are you sick? Are you taking any pills?"

"What are you, a doctor? Why are you asking me these questions?" She was getting impatient and uncomfortable.

"Don't worry, I've paid for your services, but I'm not going to sleep with you. I just want to talk."

"That's all I need!" She laughed a somewhat grotesque and emotionless laugh.

Ahmed had heard of some substances used by pimps to keep the girls high, to make them obey without their own will. He knew that they were specialists in controlling the dosage and the effects they intended and thus kept them in a continuous state of intoxication.

He scanned the room and stopped at a small table in the corner.

"Is that the jug you drink from?" He pointed in the direction of that corner.

"What do you care? You're weird as hell!" Her voice was shaky, and she mixed one word with the next.

"I beg you, don't drink any more from that jug!"

"I still remember, albeit with gaps, that evening. At first I thought Ahmed was gay. He kept looking at me, but not like the others. I don't know; it was as if he knew what was wrong with me. I didn't treat him well that day. I made fun of him and almost threw him out of there. He only wanted to help me! He's a good man. I can never repay him for all he did for me."

Shamira's Story, Part III

He promised her that he would come back, that she should not worry, that he would pay for the visits so as not to arouse suspicion and that he would bring her food and toiletries. He did not demand anything in return.

"I only ask you not to drink any more from that jug. I will bring you bottles of water."

Fatima showed neither appreciation nor rejection. She simply listened to him and put her flowered robe back on. But she was a little more alert, and that allowed her to somewhat understand what Ahmed was telling her.

"You don't deserve to be here. You must get out of this hellhole," he told her before leaving the room.

Fatima continued with her routine, beasts in the afternoon and at night, visits to the bar, and more beasts in her bed or in some back room of the premises. She didn't stop to think about what that man suggested to her. She didn't care much either. She kept drinking from that jug.

Ahmed, however, could not stop thinking about her. He had seen in her eyes that emptiness that told him that she had been forced to be there; she did not deserve that life, and he was going to do everything possible to get her out of all that garbage and back to a normal life, even if he had to face the whole mafia in the area.

He returned two days later and exchanged the contents of the jug for mineral water. He brought her food, shower gel, and some intimate hygiene items, which he got from a Spanish co-worker who asked his girlfriend. Fatima thanked him.

"Why are you doing this?" she asked Ahmed, staring into his eyes.

"Because I know what suffering is. I experienced it in Morocco. I know the contempt for the women of our compatriots, and I don't want you to waste your youth walking slowly towards death," he answered, staring at her dilated pupils.

"Why me?"

"Simply because I was assigned to you that night, I came looking for sex," He lowered his gaze, feeling ashamed for having even considered it.

On the one hand, he regretted having gone to seek pleasure with someone who was a victim of trafficking, but on the other hand, he was glad to be able to help get that girl out of hell.

"By the way, my name is Ahmed. What is your real name?" he asked, knowing that Fatima was a false name.

"I don't remember…" she wasn't lying.

She listened to him as attentively as her foggy brain would allow. He made a point of coming by every morning, clandestinely, to change the jug so as not to allow her to continue to be drugged. Every two or three days, he paid for a service but instead just talked to her and gradually led her to the conviction that she could get out of that non-life existence.

The withdrawal of the drug from the water made her recover areas of her mind that had been totally dormant, her memories anesthetized, her emotions muzzled, and her self-esteem sunk. Little by little, she began to recall her former life.

> "Conversations with Ahmed opened my eyes and began to make the possibility of being able to leave a reality. I liked talking to Ahmed; he was entertaining and cheerful, but when he wanted to convey something serious to me, he knew how to talk to me so that I could interpret the meaning of what he was proposing. He wanted me to improve, find myself, stop being Fatima, and return to my original self. According to him, I had to press charges against those people, tell my case to the police and take the final step towards my freedom. But my family depended on me not taking that step. It was not going to be easy."

Her awakening to the real world and conversations with Ahmed were the spark that ignited a different attitude from that day on. She began to voice complaints to Mohamed about the conditions in the apartment and refused to have sex with some old and decrepit men on several occasions. She knew that she had her mother's and her family's life under her responsibility, so she did not want to push too hard. Besides, she couldn't reveal she was no longer under the effects of the drug, so she was disguising her true state. Mohamed responded to her first refusal with a slap and began to fear that Fatima would try to escape. He sent two henchmen to guard the house day and night. After a few days, he moved her to another apartment, where Ahmed could not go, simply because he did not know where she went.

They noticed her change, so they had to take more drastic measures and turn the screw that kept her working for them, and they knew exactly how to do it.

A common fact in all mafia networks trafficking women for the purpose of sexual exploitation was to keep the girls' tethered to their origins, specifically with their closest relatives and children, if they had any. They did not try to maintain an emotional relationship but rather one of blackmail and threats. The local elements of these networks, those who oversaw the initial deception of the girls and their families, carefully collected information that made the girls weak: the status of their parents, addresses, telephone numbers of the closest relatives, possible illnesses of someone close, emotional dependence of their contacts, etc. All this data was transmitted to their superiors, who always had them in the chamber in case the girl showed any kind of rebelliousness or even an attempt to escape.

It was simply enough to show them a photo of their father or mother leaving their house in the city where they lived or to show them some object from their home, one that they could only have photographed if they entered the most intimate part of their homes. In the case of Moroccan women, it was even simpler, a phone call, a phone message, a post on some social network addressed to young people close to the victim; a simple "your sister works as a whore in...", "your cousin is bought for a night in bed for thirty euros..." or any message of this type. It was enough, they would quickly go and tell the head of the family, and he would order compliance with the Islamic rules—religious trial and death.

A message, just one, closed the doors to return to their country, rendering them a wanderer all their lives, enslaved people in a prison from which they could never leave and which no one from their family would be able to visit. In fact, they would not even want to go near. Mohamed began to think that such a threat might well be necessary to get Fatima under control.

It was a Thursday afternoon. It had rained during the morning, leaving a smell of wet earth in the field. In the village, however, it produced only street streams of dirty water and garbage. Ahmed's inability to contact Fatima caused them to drug her again, not as intensely, but enough to have her will numbed. Mohamed intimidated her to emphasize she had to comply with whatever he ordered. That night, he sent her a burly man in his forties. He raped her in violent and cruel ways, and then left without paying. He didn't have to—it was a blunt warning from her pimps.

The next day, in the field where Ahmed worked, they were talking about the prostitutes in the area. Each one gave his opinion about the ones they visited. Ahmed could not escape the curiosity and approached those who were commenting jocularly about it.

"She came three times in half an hour," bragged one of them.

"But they're faking it! You're a fool!" They all laughed at their companion's story.

"I like Dina. She makes you feel like Superman and always with a smile on her face," said another of them.

"I had the time of my life with a girl called...Fatima, I think that was it," Ahmed embellished the story to see if he could get some information. "The thing is that I haven't seen her for a long time, and I would like to see her again to get to paradise." They all laughed again in unison.

"Yes, Fatima, a whore who works for Mohamed, she does great, especially because she always seems to be hung, and she likes it. She lets herself do everything," said one of them quickly.

His blood ran cold. He had not heard from her for a week since they had moved her from the apartment, he could not find her, and he was anguished. He even thought that they had taken her from Huelva or, worse, that they may have given her too many drugs.

"They moved her to another apartment, and now she receives clients at the Casa Naranja," said one of them, "I have already been with her there."

A stroke of luck led him to find Fatima. He said nothing, but that same afternoon, he tried to contact her.

He scanned the street and saw that it was unguarded. He cautiously went upstairs and rang the doorbell. On the second ring, he saw that the door was not locked, he simply pushed it a little, and it opened. She was lying on the bed, shreds of clothing clinging to the blood flowing from some wounds on her chest, her face was bruised, and her lip split in two. Her legs were spread open, a trickle of blood running down her thighs. She had no expression. Her gaze, or what was left of it, was lost in the void.

"What have they done to you?"

Fatima did not answer. Her eyelids half-open, Ahmed thought she hadn't even noticed he was there.

"Let's get out of here. This has gone too far."

He fetched a towel, and with soap, he cleaned her wounds and removed the traces of blood. He dressed her as best he could because she offered no help whatsoever, and with difficulty, he carried her by the waist, afraid that she might fall limp. He feared that Mohamed's people would see them, but he could not leave her there in that state. He had dressed her in an inconspicuous dress, a pair of sunglasses, and a French-style cap that she had in her closet. Ahmed had called his Spanish partner, the one who had provided him, through his girlfriend, with the intimate hygiene products. He had no objection, his girlfriend was at home, and he could go to help Fatima.

Every corner they turned was a reason for fear of meeting someone they did not want to run into. Every human voice they heard was an alarm signal. Ahmed could feel his skin wet with sweat from the effort he had to make to keep Fatima in an acceptable condition to walk and from the anxiety of being seen. Finally, they arrived at the house. Her partner's girlfriend took care of her, took her to the bathroom and helped her shower, and applied antiseptics to her wounds and ointment to her bruises. After a while, they both came out of the bathroom, and Ahmed made them some hot tea. Fatima began to regain an acceptable state of consciousness.

"Who was it? Mohamed, I'm sure it was that beast." Fatima extended her hand to Ahmed in denial.

"It was a warning" —her voice was trembling, and it was difficult for her to articulate words because of a bruise on her lower lip— "they do not take no from anyone, much less from me. They threatened me, and this was their way of making sure I got the message."

"We are leaving! We'll go to the police. This is too much..."

"I must go back to the apartment. My mother, my family...they are in danger if I run away!" She kept sobbing, her breath and voice cracking.

Two days later, she showed up at the bar in front of Mohamed. She still bore traces of the violence she had suffered, but Ahmed's friend's girlfriend applied make-up that partially concealed the bruises. She knew the risk, but she was going to play one last card. Ahmed, his friend, and his girlfriend talked a lot with her. They made her think that it could have been just a threat, very violent, but maybe it was a bluff, and they would not actually do anything. Yes, she would try confronting Mohamed. Besides, Ahmed and his friend would be nearby, keeping an eye out in case things got ugly in the bar.

"I can't do it anymore. I'm not going to do it anymore!" Fatima was angry and with her gaze fixed on her controller's eyes.

"Are you sure?" A twisted smile played on Mohamed's lips.

"So, this is the rebel of Agadir. Well, well…"

It was a female voice. A woman appeared at the back of the bar. She was of medium height, brunette and very dark eyes, made up and wearing a dress that could only be found in high end stores. She was about thirty-five years old and left no room for doubt—she was in charge there.

"Mohamed has already told me that you often rebel, and I just heard that you want to leave." She brought her face just inches from Fatima's. "Do you know what you are exposing yourself to?" she asked her dismissively.

"I know you have threatened me with harm to my family, but—"

"No, daughter, no," the woman put on a very serious expression, "we're going to destroy you. You're not going to be able to go back to Morocco for the rest of your life!" She raised her voice to show authority.

"But—" She put a finger to her lips as a sign to order her to be silent.

"Mohamed, tell her what we can do."

"It's very easy, remember your cousin Abdel?" Fatima feared the worst. She thought they had done something to him.

"Yes."

"Well, we have his phone number. He uses WhatsApp." He started to scroll number after number, slowly—and write—the text while telling Fatima, "'Hi, Abdel. Your cousin Shamira works as a whore in Huelva, on the street…'" He stopped writing.

"No, please!"

"Shall I hit the send button?" Mohamed put his finger on the symbol on the phone screen.

"No, please!" Her voice was weak, pleading, defeated.

"If you ever rebel again or complain or try anything you know we don't like…" The woman ran one of her red enamel nails across Fatima's cheek. "You know that in Morocco, this behavior is not forgiven, and if you go back there, you know the punishment—stoning."

"No, please don't do that!" Fatima begged.

"Well, you know what you have to do…" she said as she headed for the exit door.

"You heard her," Mohamed told her." Maryam's daughter does not forgive such nonsense."

Maryam…the woman who had deceived her and told her that her daughter worked in a business in Spain and was doing very well, that her bosses would take her in. Fatima noticed that her muscles and mind gave out.

They won.

> "The world collapsed just at the moment when I determined to stand up to them. Ahmed had convinced me. He had done everything he could to make me brave. He had made the decision to go to the police and denounce everything that had happened to me and what was happening in Huelva. I already knew who was behind the network and how they treated the girls, who the woman was who tricked the families into bringing their daughters. I was already ready to denounce. But they had just put a noose around my neck, loosely, and if I made any sudden movements, the knot would tighten and squeeze my neck until it prevented air from entering my lungs. If they sent that message, that alone was enough. It was the burden that would prevent me from returning to Morocco with my mother. They would not accept that I had done those things. I would be the dishonor of the family, a stain that could only be erased with my own life."

They had just made it clear to her that she did not control anything in her life, that whatever she did, she was trapped in their nets and would have to do what they ordered her to do. She told Ahmed and the couple who were taking her in everything that had happened in the bar. It was words mixed with tears, bitterness wrapped in helplessness, emptiness.

"They won't. I'm sure they won't send that message," Ahmed said emphatically.

"They are evil; if Fatima escaped, she would be a voice calling out to the others, and they wouldn't allow that." Ahmed's companion saw it clearly. "You only have one way out—prosecute and never see or speak again or return to your land."

Fatima was plunged into a deep silence, an abyss in which there was no light. She fell silent, stood up, and prepared to leave the house. Neither Ahmed's pleas, nor the couple's calls for her to think before making any decision, could prevent her from returning to the bar and once again surrendering her body and soul to those monsters.

But the vermin, once they have prey in their jaws, do not let up in their determination to continue tearing their victim apart. They knew how to do it with Fatima. And they did. Mohamed wrote the WhatsApp message and sent it to Abdel. Just a short text without giving specific data. They knew it would be enough for those people.

It was immediate—Youssef's son read that little text with astonishment. He was old enough to know what it meant, according to Quranic Law, so he quickly showed it to his father. The latter hurled all the expletives he knew and swore by the memory of his ancestors that his niece would pay dearly for this affront. And if the religious authorities so ruled, Shamira's life was worthless.

Amina, Shamira's mother, had just read the message and her eyes seemed to pop out of their sockets. She was pulling her hair, trying to tear out all her hair in one gesture. She was beating her chest and belly; regretting having given birth to that rebellious woman. In front of her brother-in-law, she beat her head against the wall, and in a violent gesture, she tore her clothes, thus expressing all the rage, hatred, grief, and anguish that her chest contained.

"This cannot go unpunished, Amina!" Youssef shouted.

"May Allah decide the fate of my daughter!" replied his sister-in-law but knowing inside that storm which was to blame for it all.

She fell backward to the ground and began kicking in the air, convulsing and screaming as if possessed by an evil spirit. Her brother-in-law called his wife and children, who were waiting outside the house, to restrain Amina. Suddenly, she got up and stumbled into the kitchen, grabbed a knife, and headed for the exit.

"Maryam, you devil of a woman! You have brought misfortune to my family! I'm going to kill you!"

"What are you going to do, Amina?" Youssef was trying to hold her down to prevent her from achieving her threat. "Stand in front of the door, don't let her go out!"

> "They showed me the text sent to Abdel and had no qualms about letting me know that my family, including my mother, had already read it. Now, I really had no way out: my mother would be devastated, and my uncle would cry out for my death as soon as I set foot in Morocco. I had two conflicting forces inside me. On the one hand, the pain of knowing the hell my mother must have inside her heart; on the other hand, the clear evidence that I would be a migrant all my life, which forced me to watch out for the police because if my papers were not in order, I would be sent back to Morocco, headlong to a death sentence. Ahmed did not turn away from me. That was my only hope to go on living, even though for me it was no longer life as I had known it."

She returned to the apartment from which she fled. Mohamed visited her and, in a blasé manner, made her see that it was the best thing for her. She settled into silence, into the absence of words, emotion, and of any expression that would indicate that something was alive inside her. Ahmed again brought her food and, as he was sure of what they were doing, bottles of mineral water. The truth is that they no longer needed the scopolamine to make Fatima do her part. They knew she could not do anything else or go anywhere else.

She wanted Ahmed to come and see her, and sometimes they would even meet somewhere to sit and talk. She often went to where the crops were, and there, under a tree, they would spend part of the morning. She could not disappear for long because Mohamed and his henchmen would find her and would have no scruples about hurting her mother as the next form of punishment.

Ahmed gave Fatima a sense of peace, disconnected her from her anguish. But she could not erase the darkness that had invaded her mind, the feeling that she had no control over her life, that each day was simply the consequence of a route that had been designed for her, another piece of hell whose flames were fanned by other people. She was incapable of anything but the passage of time and the slavery to which she was subjected.

He tried daily to encourage her and at the same time, to convince her that she had to prosecute these scoundrels. It was useless despite all his attempts.

Shamira's Return

Ahmed woke up at dawn, and his first thought was about her. He had tried every day, trying different approaches that he thought might cheer her up and turn her life around. It didn't work, but he persisted. As he did every morning, he lay in bed staring at the ceiling as if that might inspire him to try a new tactic. Suddenly, as if the sun had entered through the solitary hanging light bulb, his mind lit up. He jumped out of bed, dressed quickly, and went out determined to give his latest idea a try.

He knocked on her door with the certainty that she was awake, she hardly slept, which added to her sense of hopelessness. She opened the door, knowing it was him. Every morning, he came to see her before going to work in the plastic covered strawberry fields.

"Come with me, today I have to go to the warehouse to pick up a new forklift to take to the crops," he said to her as he handed her a dress he took from the closet.

"A forklift? I don't know what that is," she answered reluctantly but began to dress.

"In Spanish it's called *torito*. It looks like it has horns and charges when the driver orders it to."

In his position of responsibility, Ahmed could enter the warehouses without asking permission, to take or leave material from the agricultural work. They pushed open the metal doors and entered a large warehouse full of boxes that would be used to transport the fruit when it was ready to be picked. On one side, there was a kind of small tractor with its lifting shovels perched on the ground.

"Let me introduce you to the little bull," Ahmed told her, adding a touch of dramatic flair.

"What is it for?" she asked him without showing much intrigue.

"It has levers to go forward or backward, a steering wheel to tell it which direction to go, and paddles, the horns I told you about this morning; they pick up the boxes and lift or shift them. I'll show you."

Ahmed climbed on the little bull, started it up, and moved toward a pile of empty containers. She gasped when she saw how fast the contraption was moving. He picked up some boxes and moved them a few meters.

"Come on, you try it," he offered with a smile but with doubt she would want to.

"I don't think I can."

"You can. Come on."

She climbed in, and Ahmed stood beside her, giving her instructions on how to handle it. She moved the lever forward and gently pressed the pedal, as he had told her, moving forward slowly. That was the moment when Ahmed stepped aside and let her decide how fast to go and in which direction.

Suddenly, something inside her crackled and made her suddenly wake up. She was able to be the one to decide which way the little bull should go. No one was giving her orders. She was able to go forward or backward whenever she wanted, to go right or left with a movement of her hands. But, above all, she felt that she could make a decision, and it was so. For the first time in a long time, she had some semblance of control. She stopped dead in her tracks, jumped off the little bull, and ran to embrace Ahmed. She began to cry desperately, releasing all that was inside her.

That morning, her heart began to beat with a different rhythm. That morning, Shamira re-entered her soul. She decided to come out of hell to embrace her destiny and be rid of Fatima once and for all.

> *"I will never forget that day. It was the turning point that marked the before and after of everything. I will never be able to thank Ahmed for coming up with the idea of that vehicle. I lack words to express what I felt, to notice that the lever responsible for the forward or reverse gear was a continuation of my hand and that it only acted if I ordered it, in the direction I wanted, that the turn of the steering wheel determined where the lift went, but the important thing is that this turn depended on what I wanted to do, that it stopped or accelerated only when I stepped on one pedal or the other. For the first time in a long time, I felt that I could control something; that my will began to run through my veins as if it had never been there, that I could hope to be master of my own life. I stopped dead in my tracks, jumped up and ran to embrace Ahmed, cried as much as my heart could, and emptied my insides, all at once, of all the fears that gripped me.*
>
> *'Ahmed, my name is Shamira.'"*

"Good morning. What can I do for you?" asked a policeman at the door of the central police station in Huelva.

"We want to file a complaint," Ahmed replied.

"At the end of the corridor, my colleague will attend to you."

"Thank you."

"What do you want to report?" asked a young policeman who oversaw processing the reports.

"I have been enslaved. I want to press charges against those who did it," said Shamira with a firm, convincing voice and staring at the agent.

They took her statement and shared the information to their superior. He called a contact at a shelter, and they activated the usual lines of action so that they could come to take Shamira in and get her out of that hell.

Claudia answered her local contact on the other end of the line and shuddered as Shamira's story was told. She was used to dealing with terrible stories, some of them surpassing any fiction in a horror novel, but this one especially touched her soul. She did not hesitate.

"Take her to the Casa Del Embalse. I will leave immediately."

Diego's phone hadn't stopped ringing for an hour. He was in a meeting and answered the call when he finished.

"Okay, Claudia, we'll go as support."

"The local team is still being formed, and there are still few of them; besides, we have another rescue coming up this very night."

"Don't worry. We're on our way. "

Diego and Sara helped Claudia in Shamira's case, and close cooperation with the police made the process successful. Claudia arranged a safe place, where they could not find her until the trial. The agents would begin their investigations based upon what Shamira told them and hoped to dismantle the trafficking network that brought her and enslaved her in Spain.

When they were driving home, Diego received a call from the Government Delegation telling him that a Moroccan woman had contacted the social services to ask for help. They had the phone on hands-free, so Sara was able to hear the woman's story. Of course, they were going to help.

Sara called the Red Cross team with whom they were partnering. They needed support from someone who knew the Arabic language, as it seemed the woman spoke little Spanish. They arranged to meet the next day. When she hung up the phone, Diego could not help but comment.

"Have you noticed, Sara? Now the government is asking us for help," he said with a wry smile.

"We must be doing something right," replied Sara with a similar expression on her face.

Fadhila's Story

Marrakesh, where Fadhila was born, was very influenced by Quranic law; ironically it was also where they were most ignored. Tourism was the primary industry and young people were quite drawn to the Europeans and their freedoms and customs.

Fadhila had a large family, but they were neither close to one another nor devout in their Muslim faith and practice. The teens often visited the luxury hotels to learn about cultures beyond their own traditions.

On her group outings, Fadhila met Youssef, a young man five years older than her, though he had little education or vocational skill. What he lacked in a career he made up for in charisma. It was easy to attract Fadhila, to get her where he wanted her to go, and convince her that they were made for each other. It didn't take him long to seduce her during a visit to a wooded area on the outskirts of the city. Subtle caresses, fleeting kisses, and sexual arousal were enough to bring them together on several occasions. Youssef knew how to do it perfectly. It was not the first time. It would not be the last either.

Fadhila did not menstruate for two months in a row, which was very unusual for her. She first shared her pregnancy with her aunt, who was her close confidant, and then Youssef, who quickly disappeared from her life. At seventeen, she became a mother; insulted by part of her family, ignored by another, abandoned by the father, but welcomed by her aunt. The baby was a boy she named him Brahim, and her aunt, who had the reputation in the family of being something like a seer, predicted the boy's future.

"He will bring you trouble, Fadhila, a lot of trouble."

Djamel was a man of thirty-five who agreed to marry Fadhila. He would not recognize Brahim as his son, but he accepted that his wife brought an unwanted burden i*f*nto the marriage. Life in Morocco was not easy because such a non-traditional family was not socially accepted. People criticized Djamel for marrying a "tainted" woman, but they managed to keep themselves insulated from the comments. What they could not avoid was the world economic crisis, which greatly affected Morocco. At that time, Fadhila became pregnant and had a baby girl, whom Djamel adored.

Adding to the criticism of their union and financial difficulties, the two decided to move to Spain. Fadhila turned twenty-three the week before they left. Their minds were made up, and they soon moved to the European peninsula. At first, it was the couple and their daughter, but she wanted Brahim to live with them. It was difficult because Djamel did not recognize him, so the legal procedures were more complicated. In any case, her husband made no effort to facilitate the necessary paperwork and navigate the bureaucracy.

They moved to the South of Spain, in an area where tropical fruit crops proliferated, in plantations covered with plastic, and where Djamel found a seasonal worker position. They settled near the greenhouses in a humble but comfortable house. One morning, after seeing her husband off on his way to work, she received a letter from the Kingdom of Morocco. She had enough permission to be able to take Brahim with her, at last!

She managed to reunite her family, and lived a rather normal life, at least for the next three years. Brahim was not a model boy; Fadhila's aunt, who acted as the boy's mother for years, first sensed and then verified that his veins were full of aggressiveness and often got into fights with the neighborhood kids. His friends were not exactly models of virtue either. They committed petty thefts and sold and smoked herbs. Many nights, he would return home with dilated pupils and clearly under the influence of the drugs; if he was reproached for something, the answer would come in the form of smashing any object within his reach. Djamel could not stand it, and Brahim's behavior undermined the family peace to the point that the father was increasingly away from home. Eventually Djamel's infidelities resulted in their separation.

Fadhila looked for work cleaning houses, but people took advantage and paid her a pittance, knowing she was desperate and would accept anything. The economic precariousness and Brahim's daily behavioral problems drowned her in anguish more and more each day. The straw that broke the camel's back came one afternoon when there was a knock on her door. Her son was in serious condition in the hospital. A street fight, resulting from a drug deal, escalated to the point that a kick in the face caused the rupture of his right eyeball. They feared for his life at the hospital, but managed to save his life, but not the eye, which was practically shattered. The police intervened and Brahim was placed in a Juvenile Center.

Djamel could not stand it any longer. He could not see his daughter growing up in that environment. He asked for custody and was granted it. Fadhila was left with the responsibility of her son and broken with grief at the separation from her child.

Brahim was only in the juvenile detention center for six months, after which he was released, but under the watchful eye of social workers. He went back to his old ways: drugs, fights, assaults on his mother.

Just a few days after his recovery and release from the detention center, his violent nature erupted towards his own mother. "Give me more money!" Brahim held a knife in his hands, its edge pressed against the skin of his mother's neck.

"Stop it! I don't have any more money!" pleaded Fadhila. "Please calm down!"

"Bitch, give it all to me, or I'll kill you!"

After several violations of his parole, a judge ordered Brahim's deportation back to Morocco. The family did not hesitate to blame Fadhila and it gave them yet another reason to disown her.

After Djamel had left, Fadhila found no other way to support herself but to sell her body. Her son was demanding more and more money every day. Her income was not even enough for food. It pained her to make this decision, she never thought she would find herself in this situation, but she could see no other way out of this narrow, dark, and oppressive dead-end.

All sorts of men would come to the industrial park to seek out the services of a prostitute. From freight truck drivers to CEOs of corporations, Fadhila endured unimaginable humiliations and violence from many of them. One night she met a man named Angel, and he seemed different. He continued to seek her out every time he went to the city, and he wasn't rough. He wanted sex, yes, but he didn't demand too many strange things from her; she didn't even dislike having sex with him.

One night, after having sex, he asked her to move in with him at his house on the coast. Anything sounded better than her current situation and having to endure prostituting herself to all kinds of men and still having an insufficient income.

"Are you sure, Angel?" She needed to be sure of what he was proposing.

"Completely."

Upon arriving at his destination, Angel became a demon. It had all been an act, an intentional deception to get himself a private sex slave and labor slave. He forced her to clean everything the way he wanted. Nothing seemed right about what she did, neither the food, nor the cleaning, nor the tidiness. He began to call her derogatory names and would not let her go out alone. He even locked the door from the outside when he was away on business. The verbal assaults soon became physical with slaps, shoves, and neck squeezes a regular occurrence. It went on like this for two years. She did not attempt to report to the police for fear of reprisals and deportation and because she had nowhere to live or work. In early 2018, a neighbor, taking pity on her, informed her of a job as a live-in maid in an inland town.

She did everything she could to placate Angel and her scheme worked as he soon let his guard down and Fadhila took advantage of the unlocked door to get away and pursue the job. It was an under the counter job, paying just 400 euros per month, but she would live in the same house where she would provide her services. Again, she had to accept that she was not able to refuse a job, even without knowing the people she would be assisting

Rafael was seventy-three years old and lived alone. From the first day, he complained about how she did everything and in his most cantankerous moments a push or slap would be added for emphasis.

But her surprise came when sons, daughters-in-law, grandchildren, and other people began to parade through the house. They all made demands, they all gave her orders, and they all complained about her work. From the time she got up at dawn until she fell asleep on her bed well into the night, she did not stop working for the whole clan, receiving degrading treatment on many occasions.

"Come, woman, go to bed with me tonight. I'm horny." Rafael opened his bedspread for her to enter after having called out to her.

"No, Don Rafael. I am not going to do that."

The screams were heard in the adjacent houses as she fought to resist but the elderly man was strong enough to force himself upon her. The next morning Fadhila confronted Rafael.

"I can't go on like this. You hired me to take care of you and your home, not your whole family."

"You will serve everyone! Who do you think you are?" he shouted at her as he pushed himself up on the arms of his chair to get up with threatening gestures.

"I can't take it anymore…"

"Well, you know what? I need your room for my eldest son with his wife and son so you can be on your way now. By the way, I don't have any money to pay you."

"You owe me for three months!"

"Well, you're not going to collect it. Get out!"

Fadhila did not stop crying for hours. At the end of the morning, Rafael came to the bedroom and told her that he had spoken with an acquaintance from the same village, Jacinto, sixty years old, who lived alone and needed help in the house. The Covid-19 pandemic forced him to be confined to his home, and Jacinto had no one to bring him food and help him around the house. Between her lack of legitimate working papers and the limitations caused by the global pandemic, Fadhila had few options and so reluctantly accepted this opportunity to at least have a place to live.

Rather than a refuge from the indignities she endured with Rafael, the same patterns soon emerged with Jacinto, and in fact were exacerbated by the confines of the national health restrictions. Sexual demands were frequent, and she was subjected to all kinds of humiliations. One afternoon, a young man appeared at the house. He introduced himself as Jacinto's nephew; he was drunk and contravening the rules of the Covid-19 confinement. When he saw her, he became infatuated with her and showed up every afternoon at the house, drinking and smoking marijuana. The nephew soon joined his uncle in taking advantage of her in every way.

Fadhila was desperate, despondent, with no hope for anything, certain that she had no way out. When the stay-at-home orders were lifted, Jacinto sent her to the store to buy alcohol for them. It was as if she had been released from captivity but was also given the threat of death for any misbehavior before she left the house. Arriving near the grocery store, she saw a local policeman talking to a social services guy from the town hall. She went into the store, bought two bottles of gin, and when she came out saw that both men were still there. She looked in all directions to make sure no one was watching her. She crept over and touched the policeman's arm and soon began to cry inconsolably.

"Please, I need help; I can't take it anymore; save me, I beg you."

Invitation to Seattle

Sara and Diego lived just blocks away from the Mediterranean Sea in a small coastal town that drew retirees and tourists. They had family and friends and community – everything a retired couple would wish for. They had always been active people with lifelong histories of serving people. Diego had the heart of a pastor, the personality of an evangelist, and the charisma of a preacher. In his younger years he had traveled the world with Billy Graham Ministries and in his later years had faithfully served a local evangelical congregation very near where he grew up in southern Spain. Sara had an entrepreneurial spirit and was the kind of person who knew how to get things done and make things happen. The mission trip to India had made such an impact on her and it had soon spread to Diego and together the couple had made a commitment to fight for justice for the enslaved women for as many days as they had left in this life.

Sara's compassionate nature meant that she took the well-being of each girl they interacted with very personally. Whether on the streets or over the phone, she was often trying to speak hope and do everything possible to solve their problems. That had a price: it was taxing to both her mind and body. Diego feared that all those sleepless nights, those taken-for-granted anxieties, would take their toll on Sara's health.

"They are like my daughters!" she exclaimed in a conversation with some relatives who did not understand her dedication to doing all she could do to bring even a small sense of relief.

While the couple was fueled by love and passion, they were also weary from the long days, the never-ending needs, and the emotional weight of it all. Although the needs were great, they knew that they could not meet them all and that they needed to pace themselves and their little team of volunteers to avoid burnout...easier said than done.

During one of their weekly FaceTime calls, Diego's brother Damian proposed, "Come to Seattle; it's been two years since we've seen each other. You can get some rest, and we can get together."

"Yes, I think we will. We could use a week's rest," his brother replied.

Indeed, the time away was just what their bodies and souls needed, although they had no idea that this would be yet another trip that would change everything...

During the ten-hour flight, they finally had time to process some of their experiences as well as discussing potential new strategies that could move them closer to their goal of getting some of these women off the streets for good. Since they started going out to the industrial park, they had learned a lot about the world of sex slavery and some of the darkest aspects of human nature. Until they had seen these things with their own eyes and heard these stories with their own ears, they had not believed that such evil was possible.

"Do you think prostitution can be abolished?" asked Diego, although he knew the answer.

"Well, rather than prostitution being a moral issue, it is more of a political one," answered Sara. "The conservatives have lived well with the existence of that underworld, and you know what they say about it being the oldest profession, not to mention the social dynamics of power, control, sex, and money. Politicians are not going to wear themselves out, nor lose votes, trying to abolish prostitution."

"But the leftist politicians are fighting to unionize prostitutes!" Diego interjected with signs of anger, "rationalizing that this is just another job, like any other, that they are voluntary workers. Politicians and average citizens don't take into account that most of the sex workers are slaves and that they don't choose their trade voluntarily, that they are forced to sell their bodies because they have to pay their captors and their owners." Diego was disgusted to say it that way but couldn't find another way. "They don't care about the enslaved women; they don't want to lose votes over that issue either."

They had attended conferences and round table discussions on the abolition of prostitution in Spain, but always came to the same conclusion of the difficulty involved.

"If there was no demand, there would be no business," said Sara, closing her eyes as if aware of the giant in front of them.

Diego reminded her, "That is why we must focus on the education of the youth. You have seen the number of young people that come to the industrial park."

Diego began to doze but while also tired, Sara could not get Violeta out of her mind. The previous month, in their last two outings to the industrial park, she had not been at her traffic circle and even more odd were the excuses offered by her colleagues.

The following day, they had gone to her house, seeing that she did not answer her calls or the messages Sara left on her phone. She lived with her boyfriend, a Romanian guy, good-looking and outgoing. They had seen him several times in the industrial park, near the place where Violeta offered her services. She was also very extroverted. She had no qualms about going out to meet the team, and, as soon as they got out of the van, she gave each of them a hug, especially Sara. They went up to the apartment and their knock brought the boyfriend to the door.

"We came to visit Violeta. We haven't seen her around for a few weeks," said Sara.

"She is in bed," he pointed to a room dismissively, "she has women's days, you know, but this time, it lasts long...."

They rushed in and saw her lying on the bed, cringing, with her hands holding her belly and moaning softly. When she saw Sara, she burst into tears. They hugged, and she could see a bruise on her left forearm.

"How did you get this, Violeta?" asked Sara.

"I ran into the door, Mommy, really," she replied with a less than convincing voice.

Diego put his hand on Sara's shoulder and squeezed to get her attention to where he was looking. The sheets were stained with blood where her thighs were. Sara uncovered it and checked the size of the bleeding.

"Have you had an abortion, Violeta?" Sara stared into the girl's eyes.

"I, Mommy... it's that... you don't understand..." At that moment, she writhed in pain.

"We have to take her to the hospital," she directed her penetrating gaze at the boyfriend who was standing in the doorway, "without waiting any longer."

Violeta's boyfriend shrugged and said, "I don't have money for that. I can't pay the doctor," as he left the room.

Without further ado, Sara and Diego grabbed her, put on a gown that Sara found in the closet, and left for the hospital emergency room.

She had become pregnant, by her boyfriend or customer, she could not know. Pregnancy meant less work, less income, and delayed earnings for her boyfriend. She wanted to go ahead with the pregnancy, but he would not consent. The argument was violent. He forced her to go to a man who provided these services to the prostitution mafia, without asking, without any legal accountability, and in unsuitable hygienic conditions with inadequate resources.

It was past midnight when they finally returned home after the exhausting ordeal at the apartment and hospital. "This time, we managed to save her, but next time..." Sara sighed.

"Do you remember that time in the industrial park when we saw how she covered her thighs, and you took her hands off to check the bruises?" Diego recalled.

"Of course, I remember, and how she denied it all...."

Eventually Sara, too, succumbed to her own weariness and got a few hours of sleep before their plane finally landed in Seattle. The reunion with Damian was comforting as they were able to talk about everything they had experienced and were feeling. While they had shared much with him over the phone and video calls, being able to unload it all in person was in and of itself a form of therapy.

Damian listened attentively and saw in what they were doing the start of something very big that was being done by a very small group. They told him that they wanted to expand on what the Red Cross was already doing, to take the necessary next steps to get women closer to freedom.

"David and Goliath!" He wanted to give graphic form to what Sara and Diego were telling him.

They burst out laughing, as they had already discussed that simile between the two of them on several occasions: a small team

(David with his slingshot) against a giant that vast and deep mafia (Goliath) that controlled the whole dark and cruel world.

The couple visited the church where Damian was the pastor of Global Missions, and they shared about their work in Spanish while Damian translated. Of course, they also toured the city and took in the sights.

"Tomorrow, we are going to have dinner with a friend of mine. You will like her, and she speaks Spanish almost perfectly since she was in Spain as an exchange student in college.

Meeting Laura

Laura's sense of adventure and achievement had been evident since childhood, so it was not surprising to those who knew her well when, just after graduating from high school in the Seattle area, she set off to Spain as part of an educational and cultural student exchange program. Though she had traveled very little, she had a strong attraction to all things international and embraced the opportunity to learn a new language and experience a new culture. She had studied some Russian and French in high school, but the Spanish language was new to her; however, her gift for language acquisition and the immersive experience of living with a host family and attending classes soon resulted in the ability to communicate with others. After the year in Spain, she returned to the United States to continue her studies at the University of Washington. In high school she had intended to study medicine in college, but after experiencing life overseas she knew that she wanted every opportunity to explore the world that she could get and so she focused on International Studies and Business. After two years of study, another study abroad opportunity became available, and she spent another transformative year in Argentina and returned to the States with not only amazing memories but fluency in the Spanish language.

She was anxious to complete her final year of university so she could embark on an international career when her life took another unexpected turn. Daniel was not only tall, dark, and handsome, but he had a personality and similar sense of adventure that drew the couple towards one another. He was also as practical as he was German, so while they were committed to one another, marriage was delayed so they both could build their careers. Laura began working for a technology company as their distributor to Latin

America, which afforded her many opportunities to travel for business and, when his own job in finance would allow, Daniel tagged along.

While Laura both loved and excelled at her job, her growing family and her husband's stable career led to her step away from the corporate world and invest herself in her home, church, and community. If there was a bake sale, or a PTA meeting, or a neighbor in need, Laura was there to help and serve. Having three kids in three years meant she was also constantly on the go with their various activities.

Laura and her family were also very involved in a local church where Damian served as the Global Missions Pastor. As their kids got a little older, Laura and Daniel enthusiastically joined an opportunity to be a part of a family mission trip to Nicaragua. While they had continued to travel quite a bit for vacation as a family, this international opportunity to serve and to use her language skills to be a part of something bigger than herself, with more eternal value than her business career, was just the spark she needed to rekindle her dream of having an international impact and now the bonus blessing of having a Kingdom impact.

Over the next few years, she continued to be involved in supporting the Global Missions efforts in their church and developed a close friendship with Damian as they shared not just Spanish language but appreciation for the culture. When the opportunity developed for Sara and Diego to visit and share about their outreach work in Spain, Damian immediately thought of Laura. With her gift of hospitality, sense of adventure, and her passionate and authentic personality, he knew she was just the right person to connect with this new opportunity.

Damian was right, Laura was moved as she heard about the work the couple was doing on the frontlines in Spain to fight sex-trafficking and soon she and Damian came up with the idea to host a "Dinner with a Purpose." The plan was to extend an invitation to couples and individuals to come to their home for an authentic Spanish dinner, featuring tapas and paella, and to hear a brief presentation about the work that the couple was involved in. Laura and Daniel would open their home and donate the food and Damian and his wife, Camila would prepare and serve it. Each person would pay a minimum amount for the delicious meal with the opportunity to give more generously with all the money going to the couple as a blessing.

Twelve people accepted the unique invitation and enjoyed a delicious meal and wonderful fellowship. After dinner, Diego shared about their work and Damian translated his account into English. For most, this was the first time that they had heard the term sex-trafficking and were shocked to hear of the harsh realities experienced by the women on the streets. Those in attendance gave generously with great respect for what Diego and Sara had been called and committed to doing.

Diego and Sara were overwhelmed with gratitude by the support Laura had so graciously shown them and as a way of thanks they invited her to lunch with Damian. Laura took advantage of this more intimate gathering to ask many questions and of course no translation was necessary as her own Spanish skills quickly returned.

She was stunned by everything she heard from that couple.

"That's unbelievable and awful!" Laura exclaimed with tears in her eyes.

"I would say, the cruelest of hells," answered Sara.

Sara was much more comfortable speaking in this smaller environment and went on to tell Laura more details about what they were starting with the girls, their goals, and expectations. They also told her how lucky they were to have met Claudia and the opportunity to join the network of after-care homes. Laura was moved by compassion by all she had heard and being a woman of action, she was determined to learn more and find out what she could do to support their courageous work.

"I have to go there and see firsthand everything that you have shared."

"Whenever you want, Laura, we will be happy to show you what we are trying to do."

Sara had no idea at that moment how everything would change after Laura's visit in just a few months.

Traveling Home

Sara and Diego were both rested and reinvigorated following their trip to Seattle. To have the opportunity to bring awareness to the horrors of sex-trafficking and to receive the support of others, all the way across the world, brought much encouragement.

"Laura seems to be very interested in what we are doing." Sara commented as she settled into her seat on the plane that would take them back to Spain.

"I don't know if it's that, or if we've awakened her need to know a world she had no idea existed," Diego said as he buckled his seat belt.

"Do you think she could help us?" asked Sara with a hint of hesitant hope.

"I don't know how she could, but maybe God knows," replied Diego.

The trip was smooth, at least until their first stop, in Miami. They had a four-hour layover, so they decided to stretch their legs with a leisurely stroll through the terminal. As they walked, Sara began to share her ideas for new strategies to implement upon their return.

"I think we need to more boldly make deeper connections with the girls, to encourage them to imagine what it could look like for them to get away from this life of bondage."

"I agree, but remember, Sara, what we have always said, this is like trying to get a child to do something we want them to do, it has to be their will, without pressure, but with a strategy to get them into a situation where they feel safe with us and trust that we can help them to leave that life." Diego reminded her of the precept that had been so clear to them so many times.

"Of course, but it would be like helping them get closer to the exit door, almost without them noticing, with love and acceptance, but still feeding their curiosity to open that door and believing that it is not completely closed."

After getting their steps in they found seats near their departing gate. Diego hated just waiting and was quite anxious to start the next long leg of their journey. Living on their retirement pensions, while also self-funding the work with the women meant that they needed to be good stewards of their money. In this case it meant that the cheapest ticket had also been what seemed like the longest ordeal possible as they traveled from Seattle, to Miami, to Paris, and finally back to their local airport in Spain.

Near them sat two women. One was about fifty years old, very well-groomed and made up, with manicured nails and designer clothes. The other was in her early twenties, tall, slender, with soft features and a golden complexion; her hair was curly, almost raven black, and her eyes had a special, almost magical, emerald-green glow; she was young and beautiful. Both spoke Spanish but clearly of Hispanic origin. Possibly from Colombia, thought Diego. Or Venezuela, guessed Sara. It was impossible to determine their nationality just from their dialects. What began as an innocent attempt to discern their country of origin based on the Spanish spoken between the two of them in conversation took an unexpected turn as the content of their conversation became clear.

"I'm really looking forward to arriving. I'm sure my life will change completely. I'll finally be able to earn the money my parents couldn't get for my studies, and hopefully even earn enough to help them out, said the young woman to her older companion.

"Of course, you will! You'll see that when we get to Spain, and I take you to the old people's home where you are going to work, your life will turn around, and nothing will ever be the same again," the woman replied, reaching out her hand and taking the girl's firmly in hers.

Sara couldn't help but notice a strange feeling, an intuition that had been developing since they had begun to learn about the life and stories of the girls in the industrial park and the clubs.

Sara held her husband's hand tightly, and he squeezed hers. They both knew what the conversation meant, and an irrational, anguish-filled shiver ran down their spines. They both immediately remembered the South American girls. They looked at each other, knowing that the same people were in their minds at that moment, similar tragedies with a common ending.

Their relaxing vacation was coming to an end sooner than they had ever imagined.

"Let's notify the customs police, Diego."

"Yes, let's go."

New Year, First Rescue

They returned from Seattle with the bittersweet taste of a very pleasant stay combined with the unsettling encounter at the Miami airport. The two were quickly right back where they had left off and that Friday night once again were out at the industrial park.

Christmas holidays were coming, and they thought they should do something special for the women since they lived far from their families and could not celebrate together. Sara and Diego sought out to find something, even if seemingly insignificant, that they could give to each woman. A basket with perfumes for Mercy, a dress that some woman from the team gave them as a gift for Doris, a doll for Nicoleta's daughter, a scarf for Raluca's neck, black patent leather shoes for Valentina and earrings for Teresa.

On Three Kings' Day they approached the area where many of the women lived, their van loaded with gifts.

"Mommy! Daddy!" They came out to meet them dancing, shouting for joy.

"The Three Wise Men are coming!" said Diego when he saw their reaction.

The expressions of gratitude were so emotional and authentic as the women accepted not only the tangible gifts with appreciation but were overwhelmed by the act of being seen and cared for by another human being.

At least for that brief time it seemed that the emptiness in their eyes was filled with life, with that life they longed for outside of there as if those miraculous people granted them the magic of giving them back their very being and identity. It surely brought them closer to Sara and Diego; the intended safe place where they might truly consider the possibility of getting out of this life.

At that time Sara and Diego did not have a strategy for how to get a willing woman off the streets. They were simply happy to see that they were bringing joy to the girls.

The nights in the industrial park were hard, not only because of the conditions of prostitution but also because of the especially cold winter. One week the small team of volunteers changed their routine and went to the clubs first. A young woman had phoned Sara that afternoon. She could hardly understand her in between her sobs, but Sara knew she needed to talk to her. They arrived at the club where Habiba was offering her services, and that night Sara asked Diego and the team to let her go upstairs alone. Diego was uneasy about this, but he knew better than to argue with Sara once she had made up her mind about such things. When Sara arrived at the room where the girls were gathered, waiting for the customers, she asked for Habiba since she did not see her.

"Is Habiba working?" asked Sara, pointing to the area of the rooms where they were entering with the client.

"She didn't come today," one of the girls answered.

"Is something wrong?"

"I don't know. Akram, the pimp in charge of her, came and told the manager that she would not come today and needs to be replaced."

Sara went outside and tried to call Habiba's cell phone. Nothing. The line was off or out of coverage. Alarms went off inside her, but there was nothing she could do.

The team moved on to the industrial park. That night they arrived around eleven o'clock. It was cold and drizzling. The girls sheltered under a roof or tree the best they could. They also moved non-stop, appearing to be doing a tribal dance, anything to warm up. If they saw a potential customer, they quickly went out and displayed their bodily charms to attract them. When they saw the van with the banners on each side, they did not hesitate. They went quickly to meet them, ignoring the rain.

"Hi, Mommy!" they said almost in unison.

They had to be careful with what they talked about; one of them was almost always designated as the link with the pimps, forcing them to always keep their cell phones on to hear any conversation or incident that happened in that group. It was something that Sara and Diego insistently repeated to the team members to keep in mind.

"Be careful what you talk about, do not get carried away by wanting to offer excessive sympathy and affection that makes you say something suspicious. They will not hesitate because they will know who she is, she will disappear, and they will take her to another city, and we won't be able to rescue her if she decides."

The team handed out the kits, recorded the names, gave them hot cocoa and some food, and opened a box where they had folded individual blankets to protect them from the cold. The women were especially grateful that night as they welcomed the brief respite from their forced work.

They drove the usual route, and the blankets were enthusiastically welcomed in all areas of the industrial park. That night there were many girls, possibly more than on other days. They even had to make a second round when they saw that there were more joining from the secluded areas where they had been having sex with the men who had picked them up. It was almost two in the morning, but they were determined to make a connection with every woman that they possibly could.

"Mommy, can I have some hot chocolate?"

Helen was Nigerian and her story was typical of so many others they had heard. Extreme poverty in her village, the mafia connected scout specialized in detecting potential victims, approaching the family with a job proposal and a life full of hope in Europe, the conditions of the debt she would incur if she accepted, the benefits of earning a consistent salary and being able to help her family, the acceptance of the proposal, the voodoo session and the commitment to be chained to the ceremony and its consequences if she did not comply with the conditions of the verbal contract accepted, the hellish trip through Africa, the mistreatment along the way, the rapes before reaching the Mediterranean, the arrival by boat to the Spanish coast, the slavery to which she was subjected to pay an ever increasing debt, the destruction of her person, the feeling that she had lost the rudder of her life, the perception that the abyss was getting closer and closer…the awakening when she realized that there were people who wanted to help her and at the same time gave her love, something she had not felt for several years, the turns she had to make in her head before arriving at the decision, always risky, to take the step that could take her out of that spiral.

"Yes, of course. Come to the van, and I'll give it to you," Sara noticed something different in her expression. For a moment, she thought about the possibility of being in front of her first rescue.

"I'm determined," Helen almost whispered to Sara, making sure no other girl was around, "I want to leave."

She almost spilled the cup of hot chocolate. Sara knew how to stay calm on the outside, even if a storm was raging inside her but now, she could not prevent her lips from trembling, her hands from losing coordination, her heart beating faster than normal, and her pupils dilating.

"You go on as if you had told me nothing. Before you return to the house, a man from your own country will visit you and give you instructions. Listen to him and do as he say."

"Yes, Mommy, I will." Helen returned with the rest of the girls to the corner where they usually waited for the customers.

"Well, Diego," Sara took her husband's elbow and pulled him towards the van and turned to the team members who were out that night.

"Let's go, the kits are all gone - Marian, Angel, we're leaving."

As soon as the van started, Sara announced that Helen wanted to get out. Marian couldn't help but let out a shout of joy, she was the most expressive of them all, and Diego felt a strange sensation go up in his chest and into his mouth.

They were facing the long-awaited hope of their first rescue.

As soon as they turned into the exit of the industrial park, Sara ignored the fact that it was 2:30 a.m. and immediately called her contact, a local Nigerian pastor. The operation was underway.

"We have a girl who wants to go out. It's Helen. She's with the Nigerian girls on the corner of Hortensia Street. I told her to expect that a Nigerian man would pick her up this very night. The man awoke his wife and put together a plan while they were getting dressed.

She then called Claudia.

"Claudia, sorry for the time of my call, but we have the first girl who wants out. She is a Nigerian named Helen. She's scared, and another time she told me that she was very controlled. We need to get her out quickly. It's happening right now. Where do we take her? Okay, I'll let you know how the rescue goes. Yes, don't worry, I'll inform the police right away."

It was quarter-past three in the morning when they arrived back to their home after dropping off their team members. Sara was on the phone, waiting for a call from her contact to receive instructions. In the meantime, Diego prepared some bags with food, sandwiches, bottles of water, caffeinated drinks, and some pieces of fruit they had in the fridge. Their intention was not to stop until they reached their destination. They knew it was possible that they might be pursued by the pimps or their henchmen. They had no idea what they were facing, but they intended to go all out and would try with all their might to succeed in the rescue. Diego noticed that the van's gas tank was not full; without delay, he went to a 24-hour gas station and filled it. When he returned home, Sara had already received the long-awaited call from her contact.

"They've contacted her and have a plan. We must go to her house to pick her up. She will be expecting us at seven in the morning, in less than three hours," Sara announced.

Sara called Claudia and the police. Everyone was informed. The rescue was underway.

"We'll have to sleep, even if it's only for a couple of hours...."
"Do you think we are going to get any sleep?"

She was right, even Diego, infamous for the ease at which he could doze off, could not settle his mind and body enough to get any sleep.

Helen lived in an apartment in a town about thirty kilometers away. They loaded the van and headed out. Sara couldn't quite settle into her seat. It was not yet dawn; in January, it was usually about an hour later. That benefited them, as they would have a twilight that was beginning to lighten, and at the same time, it was a dark cloak that provided some protection. As agreed, they stopped at the corner of the building at the beginning of the street, turned off the engine, and remained there for five minutes. They watched for any unusual activity. Sara noticed a girl with dark sunglasses, jeans, a brown sweater, and a partially open coat peeking out of the doorway where Helen lived; she was carrying a small travel bag slung over her shoulder, and as she got out, she looked directly at the corner where the van was waiting.

A fleeting thought brought to Diego's mind those thrillers in which a team of some secret agents had to pick up one of their own on the run from their captors. Tonight, he imagined he was a more mature version of James Bond, Ethan Hunt and Jack Bauer – and the very notion filled him with a surge of youthful energy that combated his fatigue.

Diego's hand trembled as he grabbed the keys in the ignition, he feared a scene like the one in so many spy movies he had seen, but reality did not surpass fiction. The engine started the first time, and he tried to drive as casually as possible. Helen climbed into the back seats of the van, where, at Sara's request, she lay down without saying a word. Her breathing was labored, no less than that of her rescuers, but she concentrated all her fear on the back of the driver's seat, staring at its texture and trying not to make the slightest sound.

Sara kept looking around, trying to look for moving shadows or figures. Diego was sweating as he feared at any moment, a car would come out to block his exit, or some guys would jump on the windows and shatter them to force him to stop. But neither of those possibilities occurred. They left the neighborhood and headed straight for the highway. They wanted to get away from there as soon as possible.

Helen remained down until Sara told her she could sit up. Diego was constantly looking in the rear-view mirror. His heart raced every time he saw two lights behind him, like two eyes that were staring in his direction. He slowed down, and the vehicle following them passed and continued their way. A deep breath followed the overtaking, but he did not let his guard down. He was nailed to his seat, and his hands clung to the steering wheel as if he wanted to prevent it from escaping or rather so that he would not lose his strength.

Another two lights, the same fear, the same reaction. Again, he slowed down, but this time the vehicle following them did not overtake them. The car slowed down and was still behind them. Sara noticed and did not know what to say. Diego took an exit, the first one in front of him.

"It's gone!" said a relieved Sara.

The unexpected exit added an additional ten kilometers to their trip before they could get back to the right highway. The constant glances in the rearview mirror, the sidelong observation of any strange movement, and the permanent tension in each and every one of their muscles did not cease for a moment.

Sara had asked Helen for her cell phone. They already knew that these were tracked so they could be located anywhere. With a pointy gadget, she opened the cover of the device and took out the SIM card. Earlier, she had given Helen a pen and pad to write down any numbers in her address book that she wanted to keep. She put the card in a zip-lock bag and handed the phone back to Helen.

"Please, Helen, tell me if you have another phone or another SIM card, it is very important that you don't keep anything that could facilitate your location. You know they can do it, and the consequences would be terrible, you know that," Sara warned her.

"I swear that's the only cell phone I have, Mommy, I swear."

The first beams of reddish light announced that the new day was dawning before their eyes. The three passengers had similar sensations: a mixture of adrenaline gushing through their arteries, worry about what might happen, and fear of being intercepted by the mafia. That mixture kept churning inside each of them for the entire trip.

They prepared everything so as not to stop along the way. When they had been traveling for four hours, they grabbed some sandwiches and bottles of water from some of the bags. But with the anxiety of being the first rescue, they did not think about the most basic things: they had to empty their bladders and refuel the vehicle.

Diego was annoyed to have to accept that they had to stop, but of course they had no other choice.

He took the next exit and pulled into a gas station. Even there he took in his surroundings and considered the quickest exit if he had to get out of there in a hurry. Sara and Helen headed for the restroom, and Diego set about filling the tank. Diego kept looking in all directions, vigilant, cautious. Two cars arrived, both of which pulled up to the pumps behind him. Diego's pulse quickened as he saw two men get out of the first vehicle and a man and a woman get out of the second. The woman and one of the men entered the gas station store, where the restrooms were located. Diego feared the worst. He was shaking and did not know what to do. He didn't do what a secret agent would do, but a man with a family to save would do - he locked the car and hurried inside and straight towards the restroom. There he saw Sara, who was frightened when she saw the look on her husband's face.

"What is it, Diego?"

He turned his gaze to the suspicious couple, who were taking a package of cookies, a bar of chocolate, and two bottles of water from the shelves.

"Where is she?" Diego didn't even want to say Helen's name.

"In there," she pointed to the door of the ladies' room, "but she's taking too long."

They looked at the newcomers and went to check the restroom. The wait took forever. Diego came to think that the other two men might have entered through a back window and captured her inside. He looked toward the pump area but couldn't see the vehicles from there. Sara kept knocking insistently on the door, not wanting to name the girl, and Diego went outside until he could see that the two men were at the pumps filling their vehicles. This brought a little peace, but he did not let his guard down. Sara couldn't hold on any longer and turned the bathroom doorknob with all her might. Luckily, it hadn't been repaired for years and gave way quickly to Sara's thrust. She found Helen sitting on the toilet, sweating and with tears in her eyes.

"Mommy, my belly's upset…"

"Don't worry. It's the nerves and tension of it all but try to be as quick as possible."

Diego kept watching. He did not trust those people at all. He calmed down somewhat when he saw that they were leaving and returned to the highway. Helen finally came out, and the two women got back into the van while Diego returned to the restroom for the chance to finally relieve himself. After returning to the car, Diego drank a bottle of water in one gulp. His mouth was a desert, and his heart a rattling earthquake.

They arrived mid-afternoon at the after-care home. Claudia was waiting at the door. They got out of the vehicle, and a woman helped Helen with her travel bag. All three of them were exhausted. Helen turned and hugged Diego, crying as she thanked him. Then she extended her arms to Sara, and they melted into a long embrace, both crying with all their might.

"Thank you, Mommy. You have given me life. I will never forget it," said Helen between sobs.

"Thanks to you, Helen, you have been the first. You have given meaning to our work." Sara couldn't stop the tears from running down her cheeks either.

"Congratulations, you made it!" Claudia congratulated them.

At first, they thought of leaving the girl and returning immediately, however their muscles and sleep deprived eyes did not agree with their idea.

"Is there a hotel near here? We can't go back now. We need to rest.

Half an hour later, they entered room 312 of the Horizonte Hotel. They went like zombies to bed and dropped all their weight on the mattress and quickly fell asleep and did not wake up once during the night.

The next morning, almost as if nothing had happened, they got into the van and returned home. On the way, they reviewed things that had been left half done before the rescue and impending appointments. Then they began to talk about how everything had unfolded so quickly and what they had learned from this first experience of extracting a woman from the chains of bondage. They also said a prayer of thanks for protection, for Helen's future, and for the next opportunity…

Laura's Visit

"Butterfly!"

It was Sunday, the only day they could get some rest to regain strength unless they received a phone call from one of their girls with an urgent need. Diego had just dozed off in his favorite armchair when he was startled by Sara's exclamation.

"What do you mean butterfly?"

"The name of our group."

Sara had been thinking for some time about the possibility of giving their team of volunteers a name that would identify them, give them personality, and describe their purpose. The simile of butterflies and their metamorphosis had come to her mind that afternoon when she had seen it in a documentary on television. The analogy perfectly described what they did. The girls began their first years of life like caterpillars coming out of the egg, trying to develop a normal life with their dreams, their joys, and their sorrows; in the middle of the development, while they crawl trying to subsist and participate in the work of the family, they are taken and convinced of the goodness and the future of entering the chrysalis that they offer them, a kind of paradise where they will solve all their problems and hardships; that chrysalis really becomes their prison, a place with hard, impenetrable and indestructible walls, no matter how hard they try, the walls do not give way; they promise them that if they comply with their orders, they will be able to leave, but that moment never comes.

That is the point at which they intend to intervene - piercing the chrysalis little by little, filling it with care, and drilling a window through which to enter, stretching out their hands and giving the vulnerable being inside some hope that one day they will gradually transform into a beautiful and free butterfly.

Diego agreed that the imagery made sense, though of course he had to joke about the implications towards his manhood if he were being referred to as a butterfly!

It was just two weeks after they adopted the name Mariposa that Laura arrived. Since the couple had visited Seattle, Laura hadn't stopped thinking about everything they had shared. She was anxious to see for herself what the world of trafficking looked like.

It was bitterly cold and wet that February evening, the kind of weather when you didn't feel like going out for a walk in the street all bundled up, let alone stand on a street corner barely clothed. The team had gathered in the small office area and Laura took in all their preparations of hygiene kits, food, hot cocoa, and some warm clothes and blankets.

Luisa and her nineteen-year-old son Roberto were the other members of the team that night. His mother had begun volunteering and told him about what she saw. He honestly couldn't believe what she had described until he saw it himself. At first Diego and Sara were unsure about having an attractive young man as part of their volunteer team, but they soon saw the value of showing the women that not every man sought to take advantage of them.

Before they climbed into the crowded van, Diego prayed a blessing over their evening, and they took their traditional team selfie.

Sara explained, "I usually do most of the talking with the girls while the team members pass out supplies and record their names." But the Nigerian girls speak better English than Spanish so perhaps if you introduce yourself as a friend who has joined the aid team, maybe some of them will share more openly in English. Get them to do as much of the talking as possible; they will know what is or isn't safe to say."

"Okay, I'll try," said Laura. She was someone who was always up for being stretched outside her comfort zone, but this was taking things to a whole new level!

When the van arrived, the girls quickly approached, showing their joy for the visit and welcoming the help. Sara introduced them to Laura, a new member of the team.

"Hello, my name is Laura. How are you? It is cold, isn't it?" said Laura with a sincere smile.

The girls looked at each other, surprised that the woman was addressing them in English. Most of them were able to communicate sufficiently in Spanish, but in English they were able to express themselves more freely. They quickly surrounded Laura and seemed to enjoy just chatting about basic things. As they were getting their drinks and hygiene kits, one of them grabbed Laura's arm and pulled her away from the others.

"I need help. I want to be taken out of here; tell Sara, please." She looked nervously in all directions. She knew they could be monitoring her conversation.

"What is your name? I need to know to tell Sara."

"Lilian, tell her that I am Lilian. She knows who I am."

Laura's legs were shaking. She couldn't believe that the first time she went out on an aid mission, she was going to be the recipient of a call for help, for a rescue. As soon as she got into the car, Laura looked through the window of the van and winked at Lilian. It was a sign that she would fulfill her assignment.

Her voice trembled. She could not articulate Spanish sentences well, even though she spoke it almost perfectly. She told Sara about her short conversation with Lilian. A spark went off inside Sara, the prospect of their second rescue in two months. She immediately called her Nigerian contact again. They were to wait for her instructions. In the meantime, they continued their normal route through the industrial park, visiting many other women on that frigid night.

Laura practiced the same tactic with the Romanian girls but did not achieve the same success as with the Nigerian girls. She thought she had done something wrong, but Diego pointed out that what happened with Lilian was not a frequent occurrence every time they went out. The Romanians also tended to be more reluctant to trust them and it was more challenging to communicate due to language barriers. After visiting the group of Romanian girls and explaining each girl's story to Laura, they went to the clubs and prostitution houses where the trafficked women both worked and often lived.

They arrived at a four-story apartment building in the center of the city. It was typical for that area, a bit old, not very well kept on the outside, but it did not look out of place from the rest of the apartments with shops underneath them along that street. Security cameras were clearly visible that allowed the managers to see who was calling and decide whether to open the door or not. They went up the first flight of narrow and steep stairs. In the end, on the left side, there was a solid metal door; it was closed. Sara told Laura to look at that door. In a low voice, she told her that she would tell her why later. They continued up to the second floor. Sara entered and warmly greeted an elderly woman with dyed hair and a face furrowed by time and hard living. This woman was the Madame who managed the house and the girls. With Sara, she felt understood or at least listened to and she seemed to welcome the visits almost as much as the women. Sara told her that a new member of the team was joining her this evening.

Laura entered the room through an opening Sara had made in a plastic fringed curtain. What she saw literally took her breath away. Before her eyes was a scene she would never forget: three girls, almost girls, with their headphones on and their gazes fixed on their cell phones, expressionless, they did not even flinch at the entrance of the person who was going to attend them, they did not change the direction of their eyes, imprisoned in the screen of their cell phones; another one was coming out of a room, separated from the main room by a curtain already worn out from opening and closing so much, it was a girl who clearly just woke up, still a little disoriented and fixing her bra; another one was also coming their way from a side corridor. Laura took a step forward and could see inside a room with two unmade bunk beds, recently used, where the girls were resting between customers. The Madame's cell phone buzzed, prompting her to get the attention of one of the girls with headphones. She was wanted on the third floor, in room number two. She then returned to her post on the rickety armchair with a worn yellow bedspread over it.

Laura was taken back by how lifeless these women were as if they were robots as they all seemed to just function in an automatic, dutiful state. Sara asked the names and the nationalities of each one: Laly from Venezuela, Marian and Dulce from Morocco, Sofia from Colombia, Clara from Romania, Rosy, who did not want to say where she came from, although Sara knew she was from Morocco too; and so, on up to twelve girls, plus three others who were in rooms with customers.

Sara thought of Habiba, that Moroccan girl who called her crying and then disappeared. She asked for her, but the girls literally pretended to not even hear the inquiry, they did not even look at her when they heard Habiba's name. Sara was worried about what might have happened to her. No one knew anything, or at least no one was going to say anything, and it seemed no one wanted to know anything.

As Laura stepped out onto the street, she had to lean against the van. She was nauseous, almost vomiting right there on the sidewalk. She was breathing deeply and felt her heart racing.

"They are girls! They are just girls!" That was all that she could say. She had two daughters of her own who were not much older themselves and all she could think was that these girls had moms and dads too. Laura was one who had always worn her emotions on her shirtsleeve and now she was overwhelmed with an intense mixture of anger and sadness. No part of her could comprehend how this was happening right here in front of her.

The team returned to the office, unloaded their supplies, and then Laura joined Sara and Diego at their home. Even though it was well past 1 a.m. and all were tired, Sara had learned the importance of allowing those who visited the streets to have a chance to process what they had experienced while it was still fresh. They talked for almost an hour with Laura asking many questions, seeking to understand all that comprised the sordid world of sex trafficking. She could have kept going, but eventually she realized the older couple was clearly exhausted and needed to get to some sleep. They exchanged hugs and Laura retired to the guest room in their modest home.

No sooner had she closed the door than the floodgates burst, and uncontrollable tears ran down her cheeks. Not only was she overwhelmed, but she felt very alone. Though she had debriefed with the couple in Spanish, she still felt a need to process what she had just witnessed with those who were not accustomed to what she had seen; she needed to feel the comfort of home. Looking at the world clock on her phone she realized that it was daytime back home in Seattle, so she began texting with her husband, Daniel. She didn't even know what or how to say anything about what she had experienced or was feeling, so she just said that she had returned from the night on the streets with the team, that she was safe, and that she was overwhelmed by what she had experienced. It was comforting to connect with him and getting an update on the kids at home helped settle her. Soon she realized how emotionally and physically exhausted she was, said goodnight, and was thankful that sleep came quickly.

The next day Laura asked Sara five times if she had already been called in for Lilian's rescue. Sara told her that each situation was unique and had to be handled with great discretion and just the right timing.

Laura was restless, she wanted to experience a rescue firsthand and see the young woman again. Sara and Diego had to attend to some family matters, so Laura had some down time by herself. She got out her laptop and began researching and reading everything she could to increase her understanding of how sex trafficking had become a global industry where so many suffered at the hands and will of others purely for their financial gain and sexual satisfaction.

She had assumed that learning more would better equip her to know how she could help, but the more she learned the more discouraged and defeated she became. Again, she felt compelled to process what she was feeling with someone who, even if they couldn't understand, would at least care. She kept an eye on the clock and when she figured her best friend Amy, a single mom, had put her kids down to bed, she began messaging her, hoping to connect. Amy had been anxiously awaiting word from her friend on how she was doing. The two messaged away for quite some time and Laura shared via text just some of what she had seen and how she was feeling.

The next day came, and it was time for Laura to return to Seattle. As they drove to the airport she went with her luggage and a weight inside her named Lilian. She made Sara promise to keep her updated on what was to transpire. Just as they were headed towards the terminal, Sara's phone rang. It was her contact. Everything was set for that very afternoon. Laura so badly wanted to cancel her ticket, but she had to be in Seattle the next day and could not delay her return. The flight seemed endless; she anxiously wanted to land and call Spain; she desperately wanted to know the outcome of Lilian's rescue.

As she was about to board, she hugged Diego and then Sara one last time.

"I am going to get involved in this. Knowing this world and what you are doing for these girls has given me a storm in my soul. I must do something. I must help you from Seattle." Laura knew she could not unsee what she had experienced on this trip, and she knew that she had to do something, anything, to help.

Lilian and Friends

Sara and Diego agreed that they would pick Lilian up in a square near her house. They prepared everything, just as they had done for Helen. They alerted the police about the rescue, who agreed to discreetly provide protection for the operation. They arrived at the scheduled time, did a reconnaissance of the area, but everything seemed quiet. They stopped at a corner of the square, anxiously waiting for Lilian to appear, but the surprise came when Lilian appeared in front of the car, and she was not alone.

"These three companions are coming with me.

The couple exchanged an affirmative nod with one another and quickly loaded them into the van and got out of there as fast as they could. When they decided they were out of danger, Diego called the police. One of the girls was a minor, so she could not be rescued like the other three; the police would have to take care of her. It was one of the main points Claudia emphasized when she instructed them on rescue protocols. They were to have the police as their allies. The volunteer team was to be the eyes of the agents on the street, and they were to be the ones to ensure the safest possible rescue and to oversee arranging for after care support in Spain.

Diego oversaw the contacts and the relationship with the police forces. He would inform them of suspicious vehicles on the outings to the industrial park or of unusual attitudes in the girls or in their controllers at the clubs, and of course the plans for a rescue. When notified of a potential rescue, officers would check that the woman was free of any pending court case, cover the rescue, and follow the rescued girl's vehicle at a certain distance until they had left the area. All this gave Sara and Diego a certain peace of mind, although the fear of an ambush by the gangsters or a kidnapping of the rescued girl was always there just below the surface.

The State Security Forces had developed various action groups in response to the increase in certain types of crime. One of them was the trafficking of women for the purpose of sexual exploitation, for which it organized the structure of the *Unit Against Immigration Networks and Documentary Falsification* (UAINDF). The Civil Guard also operated in these matters through the Women-Minors Team (WMT) for the fight against gender violence and violence against minors. The women were interviewed in-depth; it was necessary to know the authenticity of their intentions to leave the mafia networks. The agents had access to the results of these interviews, but what they were most interested in, as was everyone on the team, was to dismantle these complex networks and save as many women as possible, as well as preventing new ones from being enslaved. While there are these governmental agencies and other NGO's such as the Red Cross intending to help women trapped in sex-trafficking, the resources are limited, and the needs are beyond both measure and imagination.

Juliet's Rescue

Sara and Diego agreed that though they never would have imagined saying yes to a four-woman rescue, the success they had with getting Lilian and her friends off the streets and away from their traffickers gave them confidence to press even deeper into relationships with women they hoped would also find that courage. In short order they were once again enacting their rescue protocol and bringing freedom to one more life.

"If only they all had the same capacity as Juliet," an UAINDF agent commented to Diego in one of their many meetings.

"But this woman is special. She has strength of character and a strong memory, unusual for victims."

"Yes, the truth is that she had no qualms about launching all her own artillery against the mobsters."

"If only they all had her courage!"

On the third day, it was clear to her that she could no longer tolerate this life of slavery. She was determined to use her will and her wits to find a way to escape this hell or die trying. One of Juliet's characteristics was her good memory; back in Benin at her shop she hardly wrote anything down because she kept everything in her head. She found a used notebook and a pencil where she was being kept and began to write down everything, from the departure from Benin to the smallest detail of each day: names, routes, apartments, girls, frequency of transfers, meeting places, new faces…

When she first saw Sara and her team, she suspected this was her best shot at getting out. She was connecting with Sara little by little, cautiously; she knew that one of the girls was always given the duty of informing the pimp of everything the other girls did and talked about. Even when Mariposa's van arrived, she knew that the one in charge of controlling everything dialed a phone number and kept the line open so that they could listen to what was being talked about on the other side. But one night, that girl happened to be with a customer while Sara, Diego, and two other members of the team arrived. Juliet knew it was time to muster all her courage and take this leap of faith in hopes of landing in freedom.

"Mommy, I want to get out of here, and I'm going to report them all." Juliet didn't look distressed or nervous. She simply fixed her gaze on Sara and spoke to her with determination.

"All right, Juliet, let's get the rescue underway. Someone will be here later to give you instructions."

They rescued her without major problems and when they arrived at the after-care home Claudia told Juliet she could take some time to just rest and recover before contacting the authorities and beginning the process of getting her papers in order. However, Juliet was indignant from the moment she arrived.

"I am going to press charges against them. I want them to all rot in jail. I want them to pay for what they have done to me and to all the women they have enslaved!" She showed them the notebook. "Here I have everything written down, everything."

"All right, Juliet." Claudia tried to calm the desire for revenge that oozed from the girl's pores. "We'll try, but we must be cautious so that everything goes well. We will talk to the police."

The officers assigned to her case listened attentively. She was a unique source of information as she had the facts down in detail. The process of reintegration into a normal life continued, but the prosecution of the pimps became an obsession for her. The police checked some of the notes Juliet had in her notebook and were able to give credibility to the information she provided.

From that moment on, UAINDF, Civil Guard, and police from other countries were on the move. They were on the trail of a network trafficking Nigerian women for the purpose of sexual exploitation, and Juliet made it possible for them to go directly to the core of the mafia leadership. They managed to tap some of the ringleaders' phone lines, and Juliet was able to translate everything. When the time came, she filed an official complaint, and a raid was carried out in several Spanish cities. Fourteen members of the network were arrested and brought to justice. Thirty girls were freed from their enslavers in various parts of Spain. Juliet became a protected witness in the trial.

The dismantling of the mafia network, the release of the girls, and the satisfaction of seeing their traffickers convicted, formed the basis for Juliet to advance in her new life by leaps and bounds, of course, without forgetting the work of Sara, Diego, Mariposa and Claudia, and their team. After the court case was completed, her counsel asked her what she wanted to do with her new freedom and future.

"My dream is to have a sewing shop." She couldn't stop a tear from running down her cheek.

"You shall have it," said Claudia, while affectionately squeezing her hand.

Juliet's next step of freedom was to place a phone call.

"Mommy, I did it!" Sara had to pull the phone away from her ear because of Juliet's loud exuberance.

"What a joy!"

"If it weren't for you and Papi, none of this could have happened. Who knows where I would be now!"

"With your strength and determination, you would have succeeded, sooner or later, I am sure," assured Sara.

Laura's Next Adventure

Laura landed in Seattle, and as soon as she could turn on her cell phone, she checked her WhatsApp messages and then immediately made a call. At Seattle-Tacoma International Airport, it was 6:45 p.m., in Spain, it was 3:45 a.m.

"Sara, you rescued Lilian!"

It took Sara a few seconds to get herself together. She was sound asleep, and the ringing of her phone made her jump, as it did every time it happened at that hour. Usually, it was some girl in danger or needing to be rescued. Despite the early hour she was pleased to see it was Laura.

"Yes, Laura, we did it!" Sara had sent her a picture she took of Diego and her with Lilian.

Laura's heart was overwhelmed with joy to hear the news and to know that she had played even a very small part just by showing up. It wasn't until she realized it was the middle of the night in Spain that she apologized to Sara for waking her and said goodbye. As she made her way to customs and passport control the tears of joy continued to flow and she wondered what her fellow seatmates had thought of this Spanish-speaking American crying happy tears following a phone call…

Her husband picked her up at the airport and she did not stop talking for the entire 45-minute ride home. Daniel was used to Laura's enthusiasm for getting involved in advocacy efforts and he sensed that this trip was going to be the catalyst for yet another endeavor; little did he know what the adventure ahead would look like for both of them.

Laura and Amy met for coffee soon after she returned home and once again, she unloaded not only all her experiences in Spain and her deep emotions, but also her desire to find a way to do something to make a difference and help support the work of Mariposa. Amy was an educator and the prospect of helping young women a world away appealed to her own sense of purpose. When she saw the excitement in her friend's eyes and the determination in her heart, she knew that something was sure to come of this and she committed to joining the cause.

A few days later the friends gathered for dinner and Laura told Daniel and Amy about an idea that had come to her while in Spain. The three were avid cyclists and often rode together, which was what had sparked Laura's idea...to organize a cycling tour to Spain where participants would enjoy the popular sport and beautiful rides while also raising funds and awareness for Mariposa. In faith, they both agreed to join in planning and promoting the trip, though none of them had any previous experience with international cycling trips or developing a fundraising campaign. It was in these moments of doubt that Laura would remind her teammates that if Sara and Diego could figure out how to do all that they had to build relationships and get women off the streets, surely, they could manage to find creative ways to use what they loved to fight what they hated.

In just over a year from her first visit to see the work of Sara and Diego firsthand, Laura returned, leading a team of nine road cyclists who had committed to pay all their own expenses as well as fundraise donations from friends and family to support the frontlines work of Mariposa. In designing their cycling jerseys, they had matched the nature of the cycling adventure with the goal of those involved - Ride for Freedom. The team cycled by day, and then took turns in small groups to join Sara and Diego for visits to the industrial park and clubs, giving them their own firsthand look at what sex trafficking looks like. Every person was greatly impacted by what they experienced and like Laura, returned home with an intention to continue to support the work and fight for justice in some manner. In fact, Ride for Freedom 2018 was such a success that another team of cyclists returned in 2019, a third team in 2022 (after a two-year delay due to the pandemic), and the intention of future trips.

Damian consulted with Laura and Amy as they were planning for the Ride for Freedom cycling trip and provided them with both encouragement and advice from his own experience in organizing many international trips. It wasn't long after they had committed to planning the cycling trip that Damian and Diego proposed another fundraising and awareness idea to the two women. Since the initial "Dinner with a Purpose" had been such a success, they thought a larger Spanish-themed event would draw even more people and increase the potential for fundraising. Diego shared that a group of artists were willing to come together to "Paint for a Purpose" and then their original watercolor paintings would be donated to Mariposa and then brought to Seattle area and sold at an art show with the funds going to the anti-sex trafficking organization.

Laura and Amy were committed to supporting Mariposa and didn't want to disappoint the two men that they held in such regard, but they also were clueless when it came to knowing anything about art and while they had attended many philanthropic fundraising events as guests, they had zero experience planning them. The greatest challenge they perceived was going to be convincing people to come and support an organization halfway across the world that they had never even heard of on behalf of a cause that few people had any real awareness of. It was agreed that they would appear more legitimate if Sara and Diego attended the event and Damian came up with a brilliant idea that would surely draw people; he used the event as a pseudo 60th birthday party and invited everyone he knew. With such charisma, charm, and a vast network there was a great response to the invitation. But while the "Birthday with a Purpose" theme would draw the people, it also meant that they had just four months to pull it all off that fall while also planning the Ride for Freedom trip for the coming spring!

Thankfully Damian was not only a pastor but a gifted artist, so he recruited others to manage the art aspect of the event while Laura and Amy managed the venue, ticket sales, rentals, food, and entertainment. They found a local caterer who specialized in authentic Spanish tapas to go along with the art, but it felt like there was another component missing…wine! Washington State has a flourishing wine industry and Amy knew of a local winemaker who specialized in working with organizations to design custom labels to promote their cause while enjoying great wine. They chose four wines and designed four different labels to promote the four aspects of Mariposa's work: Relief, Rescue, Restoration, and Relationship.

The women reached out to others in their shared communities and managed to recruit a small but dedicated volunteer team to help with the event. Thanks to Damian's birthday promotion and the encouragement and support of so many of their own friends, that first Taste of Freedom event drew over 250 people who enjoyed a delightful evening out while also growing in their awareness and offering their financial support to continue the anti-sex trafficking work.

Sara and Diego were filled with gratitude for all the work the two women had done and all the people who had given so generously. And much to their surprise, what Laura and Amy assumed would be a single event has become an annual tradition for the last six years, even surviving two years with pandemic restrictions.

All this resulted by the formation of a group of volunteers in Seattle, people who contributed what each one knew how to do. And just as Sara and Diego's work has been likened to David fighting Goliath, the volunteers in Seattle often reference their own meager contributions to the cause as offering up their "fish and loaves" knowing that it takes a Divine Blessing to multiply their humble efforts.

Seattle's financial support provided Mariposa with peace of mind and, above all, an increase in resources to help the girls. All expenses were documented, and every euro was well spent. Thanks to the financing, they were able to secure a larger office space where they could expand their services to include receiving donations of food, clothes, medicine and other much needed items. This expansion began as a blessing but proved to be a prophetic necessity as the organization that was so well connected and positioned to respond to the needs of the women as Spain was so greatly impacted by the global pandemic.

Since those first years of research, learning, and eventually developing established rescue protocols, Sara and Diego have been contacted by other likeminded citizens throughout Spain, asking them to come to their cities to train others to replicate the model as more awareness of the evil and injustice of sex trafficking is taking place.

Thanks to a group of people in Seattle, another group in Spain could do and will continue doing all the good that goes into turning those imprisoned chrysalis into beautiful and free butterflies.

Fadhila's Rescue

"Claudia, we have a Moroccan woman ready to leave. She is in an agricultural town and is in danger, we must get her out immediately."

"Both our after-care houses are full, but I will talk with another organization doing similar work and see what I can arrange," replied Claudia.

A few minutes later, Claudia confirmed that they could receive the woman and gave Sara the address. At the same time, Diego called the police in that area to update them on the situation; he was informed of the mafia network active in the town and the dangers involved in taking someone they had enslaved out of there, especially if her captors believed she would turn them in.

The local policeman who had first contacted Fadhila provided her with a cell phone so that Sara could talk to her and share the plan. An animal stable on the property provided the perfect place to make the phone call away from the ever-watchful eyes and ears.

"It is very important that you stay calm. They must not realize that you are planning something," Sara insisted several times. "We will pick you up and take you out of there, don't worry."

Diego had spoken with the local police who would assign two plainclothes officers in an unmarked car. They would be stationed at the entrance of the town, in a discreet area, but with easy and quick access to the center where the extraction would occur.

"We will come for you just after dawn on Saturday morning. You must be ready to go and be sure to hide and mute your phone."

On Saturday morning, Sara and Diego arrived at the outskirts of the town, where they had arranged to meet the plainclothes officers. They were told to keep one of their cell phones with their phone number on the screen so that if there were any threats, they would only have to press the call button, and in two or three minutes, they would be there to help them.

"Where are you now, Fadhila?" asked Sara as they started to slowly drive down the street into the town.

"At the door of the church, in front of the fountain." Her voice trembled so strongly that you could hardly understand what she was saying.

"Listen well, Fadhila, there is no fountain in front of the church." They knew the village. "Look around and tell us some other landmarks."

"I don't know, there are three streets that lead to a square and the church…" she couldn't finish. She began to cry in desperation, fearing that it wouldn't work out.

"Fadhila, talk to me!" The interrupted call signal sounded in Sara's cell phone earpiece as if it were an alarm that did not bode well.

Within seconds, they had received a Google Maps location from Fadhila.

"Come on, Diego, let's go get her!"

When the app indicated that they had reached their destination, there was no one there. It was clear that they had made a mistake. Their already heightened anxiety began to grow as the danger of raising suspicions with their vehicle or of being located and captured was increasing. They closed the app and began to drive directly to the two squares that the town had, but they did not see her at either one. The local policeman had taken a picture of her and sent it to Sara's cell phone and Sara had memorized her face and was looking for her on every street corner and doorway or hiding in the bushes. Nothing.

"Did they take her?" asked Diego fearfully.

They were just about to circle back out to the outskirts of town when they saw a woman crouched behind a traffic sign at the end of one of the streets.

"It's her, stop!"

"Come on, Fadhila, get in quickly!" Diego urged her while looking everywhere in case someone might follow them.

They headed towards the highway and saw that the undercover car had followed them for quite a distance until finally they sped past and gave Diego a nod.

The trio arrived at the train station, and there Fadhila, much calmer, thanked Sara and Diego. The planned train soon arrived, and Sara joined Fadhila to escort her to the safe house while Diego returned to the car to begin his four-hour drive home. Though weary from the early morning and all the adrenaline, he was also invigorated by such a sense of purpose. He had much time to think and pray as he drove and he couldn't help but wonder how this had become his life, and how he wouldn't trade it for anything else.

A Second Life for Helen

That morning had dawned with threatening rain clouds. But, as if a premonition, a sign of all that the last two years had meant, the sky began to clear as the clouds scattered to let the beams of light reach the surface of the skin of a woman who had gone from hell to the kingdom of hope.

"Look, Helen, this is a sign that indicates the light that will mark your life from now on. Do you remember Moses when he opened a path in the sea so that the Jews whom the Egyptian soldiers were chasing could cross over? Well, the demons chased you for years, they tried to destroy your soul, but your decision, your perseverance, and everything that has happened in these two years have managed to open the waters of life for you to cross and reach the Promised Land of your new life. The demons will drown as they try to come after you. Look at the sky; that is what it is trying to represent." Claudia hugged Helen.

It was time to embark on a new life, so she took one last look at those who had done their best to help her and headed firmly and eagerly to her destination.

That afternoon, two years ago, Helen was rescued and taken to the after-care home. There she was left to rest for a couple of days. She needed to rest and get used to the idea that everything was going to change. She would be living with six other Nigerian women. Claudia's team had learned that grouping women together with the same ethnic background was beneficial to their recovery, but that it was also necessary to separate women who had been enslaved together as their shared past often brought toxicity.

A social worker and a psychologist interviewed her to get an idea of Helen's mental health. Little by little, they gained her trust. They had listened to many girls with similar stories, but each was unique and personal. She then underwent a full medical examination.

Her new companions gave her a warm welcome, like the one they themselves had received from their predecessors, showed her the rooms, and told her their stories, similar, but at the same time different. They helped her see that there was a way out and that she had made the right decision.

Claudia, the social worker, and a policewoman from the Central Immigration Networks Unit met with Helen to explain her legal rights. Helen's passport had been taken. That was something that all mafia networks did, knowing that stripping away their legal identity made them even more vulnerable to controlling their bodies and wills.

"Helen, we are going to explain to you the legal possibilities that you should take into account," Claudia began to explain. "Whichever one you decide, we are going to help you to get legal paperwork to stay here in Spain. I want you to be sure of that."

"You see," the policewoman interjected, "we value very much what you have done and the steps you have taken, and we are going to support you in everything. You have two alternatives. One option is to press charges against those who brought you here under false pretenses and those who enslaved you here through prostitution. When you file a complaint with the police and identify yourself as a victim of trafficking, an investigation will begin with the hopes of bringing the pimps to trial and hopefully dismantling a network of those who are trafficking in women for sexual exploitation. It is a difficult step, but it would speed up the process of your legal documentation in Spain.

The second option is to apply for refugee status. The procedure is slower, and we would not be able to prosecute your exploiters."

"You should think about it very carefully, Helen," said the social worker, "The law on the rights and freedoms of foreigners in Spain and their social integration gives you three months to think about the possibility of filing a complaint. You can take advantage of the law without pressing charges, but you must think about the other women like you who could benefit from your action and be freed from slavery. Do you understand?"

"Sort of," Helen replied hesitantly.

"Don't worry," Claudia reassured her, "we will be with you along this journey, whatever path you decide."

While the legal process was underway, Helen took Spanish language classes while also participating in trauma therapy and other social service supports to help in her recovery. After a few months in the home, she participated in an art therapy workshop put on by a group of women from the Ride for Freedom cycling team who had come to the after-care home to learn about the program and provide support to the women.

Sara and Diego continued to keep in touch with each of the women that they had rescued, and one day Helen received a phone call that helped make one of her dreams come true.

During her time in the after-care home, Helen was often seen styling the hair of her housemates and showed a true gift for it. She dreamed of becoming a hair stylist and working in a salon—legitimate work so that she could support herself. The dream became reality when Sara called to share that her brother-in-law, Damian's church near Seattle had recently completed a campaign to raise funds to provide vocational training for women rescued from sex trafficking and Mariposa would be able to sponsor Helen's enrollment in the program. She was thrilled at the opportunity and proved to be a diligent and talented student.

After a year, it was time to take another step towards independence. Helen joined three other women at the same stage of recovery, and they moved into an apartment that Claudia had arranged. They each were required to contribute 120 euros a month for rent and utilities. From training they received, each learned how to make handicrafts out of wood, cloth, wool, beads and other materials, which Claudia and her team sold at charity markets or to people who knew about this work.

But it was not all easy sailing. Helen and the women were integrating into society, but they were also exposing themselves to its dangers. One morning Claudia came to the apartment to see how everyone was doing, but Helen was not there. She had gone to the market early, but had not yet returned; it was strange, as it had been three hours, and she had never been so late. Claudia called her cell phone, but a recorded voice indicated that the phone was turned off. Claudia had a bad feeling. It was not the first time; it had happened on a few other occasions. She called a social worker with connections to law enforcement and who specialized in these cases.
"It has happened again. It's Helen."

A few days earlier, Helen had returned from the salon where she was continuing her training as a hairdresser. Like every day, she returned cheerful, singing. She was aware that her life was entering a new chapter, that she was getting a second chance, that she was becoming a person again, and that she was rebuilding the puzzle of her existence. As she crossed the street that led to the little square where her apartment was, a man was coming out of a bar in the area. He was Nigerian and immediately noticed Helen. The woman had changed her look considerably and he thought he could be mistaken, but no, it was her, he was sure. With great caution so as not to be discovered, he followed her until she entered the doorway of her house. He removed the cell phone from his front pocket and made a call.

"I just saw your girl, the one who escaped. She is in an apartment right in front of where I am. I'm sending you the location."

The pimps who had enslaved her sent two henchmen to the address where their contact had seen and followed her. They waited to study her movements and decided to act that morning, just as she was on her way to the market. As she left the building, the two men approached quickly with the car, and without giving her time to react, one of them grabbed her and pulled her inside. He gagged her while the car drove through the streets towards its dangerous destination.

Claudia was desperate. They could not find her in the places where Nigerian girls had been taken on other occasions. They didn't know where else to look. They informed the police of the disappearance, but now there was nothing more they could do. This frustrated the team enormously. It was as if their work was all for nothing, but, above all, they feared for Helen's life.

Three days later, she appeared back at the apartment. Claudia was quickly called and came immediately to the apartment and saw Helen packing a suitcase.

"Helen, what happened to you?"

As she turned, Claudia saw a face full of despair and bruises and she also noticed that Helen was wearing a pendant around her neck representing a god used in voodoo-juju ceremonies.

"They activated their voodoo oath!" Claudia exclaimed.

"I must comply. I am sorry. My family and my life are at stake. I am going back to them. The debt has increased tremendously."

"No way, Helen! We will not let them enslave you all over again!"

It had happened before, and they were ready with a response. She took Helen firmly by her shoulders and met her eyes.

"Do you trust me, Helen?" She crumbled at the question.

"Of course, I do!" The tears were flowing.

"Look me in the eyes. We will deactivate the voodoo, and you will be free of your commitment to the gods forever."

Claudia called her Nigerian contacts in the city. She explained the situation to them, and they acted on other occasions. They took Helen to a healer who knew all the incantations and ceremonies to deactivate a voodoo-juju oath, not only that, but also to reverse it against the inducers of the oath. That was how Helen was released from her oath before the gods and how her pimps were made to suffer its consequences. Claudia did not ascribe to these beliefs, but she had learned that in Nigerian culture it was often a necessary step to fully free a woman from the emotional bondage that remained.

Helen moved to another apartment, far from where she had been, but convinced of the effectiveness of the ceremony that counteracted her voodoo-juju oath. Once again, she settled into an apartment with new roommates and enrolled in a new vocational school to finish up the last bit of her training. Thankfully it was not long before a local hairdresser offered her a position and the blessings continued when her documents came through and she was a full-fledged legal resident.

While working at the salon she met a man who showed sincere interest in her. He was five years older than her, had a stable job, and faithfully attended a local Nigerian church congregation. As their friendship soon took a romantic turn, Helen told him her story. She didn't want any more deception in her life. If he stayed with her, it would be because he loved her, not out of pity. That was how they deepened their relationship to the point of considering life together.

Claudia's team continued to support Helen's next steps towards independence by finding an affordable apartment and gathering furniture and decorations for it. The evening before moving in, they arranged to meet her at Claudia's house.

"Here, Helen," she handed her an envelope, "so that you can start your new life; the rest is up to you."

Helen could not hold back the cascade of tears. Tears that for once were not preceded by suffering, slavery, beatings, or degradation of any kind. No, this time, they were tears of pure joy and gratitude for this second chance that life was offering her, that Claudia's team had made possible for her. She also remembered who had first given her affection, trust, and love; those people who led her to the conviction that she could get out and, who, in fact, rescued her from hell. Her angels, Sara and Diego.

"Mommy, I've got a job!" she shouted when she called Sara that afternoon. "And I have a beautiful apartment, thanks to you!"

"You don't know how happy I am, Helen!" Sara couldn't hold back a few tears of joy.

Shamira's Trial

When Sara and Diego first shared the details of Shamira's story with Claudia, she immediately grasped the complexity of the case. She arranged for Shamira to be placed at a safe house very close to her own home, as she wanted to handle the case personally. In addition to the usual protocol with rescued girls, Claudia sought a lawyer for Shamira's legal proceedings against her pimps; she would assist her in her statements to the police, in the process of obtaining residency status, and in the trial that would most likely take place.

Shamira told the police everything she remembered although parts of the story were missing because of all the drugs they had forced upon her. Despite the many gaps in her memory, she was sure of what had happened. As her lawyer explained to her, the problem was that this was not enough evidence for indictment. In effect, she was told that she could not legally prove that she was a victim of trafficking, although she could still press charges against Maryam's daughter for sexual exploitation.

"I don't care! I want to see her in jail!" Shamira exploded when she learned of her situation.

"There is a problem," his lawyer told her, "Regarding the trial—you will not be able to be a protected witness."

"What does this mean?"

"You will have to be in the courtroom in front of them, and you will not testify from a place where you cannot be seen, but you will have to do it in full view of everyone. In addition, you will have to enter the courtroom through the same door as them."

"But how can it be like that!" Diego stood up indignantly from his chair. He couldn't understand the situation, even though Claudia asked him to be calm. "Doesn't the victim count for anything? Is this what you call justice?"

"I know, but it is the law; the accuser must face the defendant," said the lawyer, trying to calm Diego's irritation.

But the police and the lawyers did not know Claudia's determination when something was unjust; she kept calm and remained convinced that Shamira would be protected. Together with the lawyer, they raised all kinds of claims, appeals, and documents. Ahmed even mobilized anyone who had had anything to do with Shamira, from Tarifa to Huelva.

In the end, with the help of the police, they managed to protect Shamira and, most importantly, she didn't have to see Maryam's daughter and Mohamed face to face.

Claudia, Sara, and Diego were determined to do all they could to protect Shamira from any more trauma than necessary as she would be testifying against her traffickers and her story becoming a matter of public record.

The police parked the van outside the hotel where they were staying. The side windows were dark and blocked the view from outside the vehicle. The four of them got in and together they drove to the courthouse, Shamira holding firmly to both Claudia and Sara's hands. They parked where they could see the entrance to the courthouse; in this way, they could choose the best moment to enter the building.

From their vantage point they watched as Maryam's daughter arrived. Sara commented that she looked more like a guest at a wedding than a defendant: elegant dress, heels, hairdresser, and a fancy manicure. This comment gave them all a laugh that helped ease their nervousness. At her side were two men in dark suits, likely her lawyers. Behind them, about ten meters apart, Mohamed entered alone.

"Now is the time, Shamira," said Diego.

"Try not to look at them directly. In case your eyes meet, don't let yourself be carried away by all the evil they have done to you. Remember that the goal is that they do no more harm to you or anyone else and that the verdict is guilty," Claudia told her, looking straight into her eyes.

As they awaited in the small hallway for the ceremonial opening of the courtroom doors that would indicate the proceedings had begun, the police officers kept Shamira at one end next to a staircase, keeping her back turned. A partition separated her from the others, but she could still hear the familiar voices. Diego noticed her awareness and quickly began talking about rather random and irrelevant topics, but it was just the distraction that everyone needed, and the gentle strength of his fatherly voice drowned out the din just a few meters away.

At last, the bailiff entered the hallway, announced the case, and opened the courtroom doors. An official showed them where each party was to sit. Shamira was seated behind a large, opaque partition, impossible to see through. From that moment on, everything began to boil inside her. She had to hear repeatedly that she did it voluntarily, that she was paid 90 percent of what she earned, that she did it willingly, that no one held her back, and she was even offered housing at no expense. She only looked up once. She wanted to locate Ahmed. He was her support, the one responsible for giving her the strength to be there. He was at the end of the room, he wanted several times to get up and attack Mohamed, but he managed to control himself.

Both defendants denied the charges the prosecutor had made on Shamira's behalf. The young woman even declared that she did not even know Maryam, her own mother. She knew nothing about drugs. She insisted she ran a legal nightlife business, nothing more.

The defense lawyers argued to bring as much attention as possible to the drug induced gaps in Shamira's story in an attempt to discredit her accusations. Their own argument was that Shamira had fabricated this story to obtain legal status in the country and in hopes of gaining economic advantages as a victim.

When Shamira was not herself testifying, she sat there with a crestfallen countenance. Sara noticed that she was also writing something down on a piece of paper, but she couldn't see what exactly. It could be a way of isolating herself from everything, or she was taking notes in case she was asked questions later.

Finally, the judge announced that the trial had ended, and court was adjourned until a verdict was ready. Quickly, her lawyer, Claudia, Sara, and Diego tucked Shamira out of the courtroom, surrounding her to protect her from the proximity of the pimps and their lawyers. When they made it behind the partition in the hallway, Shamira leaned against the wall and they could see the tension start to ease from her body, but not her mind or soul. She said goodbye to Ahmed, and they gave each other a silent embrace, full of gratitude and sweetness.

Sara and Diego escorted Shamira outside into the bright light of the beautiful late afternoon while Claudia was going over things with the lawyer. Across the street was a park and boardwalk alongside the sandy shore of the Mediterranean. Claudia had called and said it would be about thirty more minutes before a van would be ready to drive them back to the safehouse, so they walked over and found seats on a wooden bench. Shamira noticed the hardness of the seat and thought of how it represented so much of the hardship she had experienced since leaving her home in Morocco.

She opened her purse, took a piece of paper in her hands, folded it, and placed it in the palm of her right hand. Sara signaled for Diego to give them some space which he was thankful for, so he could get some walking in after already sitting so long in the courtroom. He was anxious about the outcome of the verdict and walking at least gave him something to do.

Sara took Shamira's arm with affection, hoping to convey strength, security, and a lot of love. The woman noticed it immediately, turned her face, and made a gesture of gratitude. Sara asked her what was on the paper she was clutching in her hand. With tears in her eyes, she showed her. It was a simple drawing with black lines, representing the image of a witch.

Sara recognized the symbolism and the very personal evil that it represented in Shamira's life. She drew her phone from her pocket and messaged Diego to find some matches or a lighter somewhere nearby and come back to join them. Diego thought the request an odd one, since none of them smoked, but he had learned that his beloved wife did everything with intention, so he knew better than to even ask and quickly set out to complete the task.

The first bar he stopped at had matches, so he returned promptly with them in hand, curious to see what Sara was up to this time. As he strode toward them the women stood up and Sara led them on a walk to the shore. Sara held her hand out and Diego passed along the matches. Sara held them up to Shamira and she understood perfectly what she intended to do. In fact, she was looking forward to it. She walked to the shoreline and set on fire that witch who had ruined her life. The sea foam kissing their feet and the gentle swell made the ashes disappear quickly.

They burst into tears and held each other closely. The door to her private hell was closed, and she was finally out. As they returned to the sand, Sara instinctively turned her gaze to the sea. From the place where the ashes had met the sea, a group of butterflies in a beautiful array of colors was flying up into the sky.

These were colors of hope.

Two weeks later, Sara and Diego knocked on the door of the aftercare home where Shamira was living. Claudia had been anxiously awaiting their arrival so that together they could share the exciting developments with Shamira.

"Hello, what a joy! How are you, Shamira?"

"Good, good, I am much better now. Claudia and others in this house are helping me so much. I am starting to believe that I can take back control of my life. But I do have a very deep sorrow…."

"Your mother?"

"Yes," Shamira could not hold back her tears.

"Well, I think Sara and Diego have some news that will ease that pain."

Shamira opened her eyes as wide as she could.

Claudia had understood the importance of a meeting between mother and daughter as part of Shamira's healing. She had been determined to find a way to make it happen and had asked Sara and Diego for help.

"You are going to see your mother," said Sara.

Shamira's tears flowed freely and soon they all were overwhelmed with emotion themselves.

Finally, the woman asked, "When, Mommy?"

"Very soon, have some patience." Claudia hugged her tenderly. "As you know, you can't go back home. You wouldn't exactly be welcomed or safe, so we are preparing a transfer of your mother to another city, and you will see each other there."

"Thank you, thank you!" Shamira kissed Claudia's hands, filling them with tears of gratitude.

Once Shamira had regained most of her composure, it was Diego's turn to share the next piece of news.

"Shamira, there is even more to rejoice and give thanks for today. The judge issued the verdict today: those responsible for enslaving you have been sentenced to jail."

At this news Shamira sank to her knees and then collapsed into a ball as words in her native dialect flowed from her mouth along with what seemed like an endless flow of tears.

The process had been neither short nor easy. Shamira had made the decision to try to fight her own battle with Goliath with only a few small stones in her hands. She had fought against a society that refused to see what was happening in their own dark alleys, a justice system that placed considerable burden on the victim to prove her own innocence despite all her suffering, and the actual abusers who had stripped away all her dignity for their own profit and the warped pleasure of others.

The Pandemic

It was a typical Tuesday morning in March and Diego was reading the news on his tablet while drinking his coffee, his daily ritual. The health situation was going from bad to worse. The cases of patients infected by the coronavirus were multiplying every day, and so were the deaths. The local hospitals were overwhelmed, and reports were coming in from similar situations around the globe.

"Sara, the government has declared an emergency health crisis and ordered residents to be confined to their homes except for the most essential needs!" Diego declared. As it so often did, Sara's mind went not to her own comfort but to concern for the women they had grown to love. "But what will happen to our girls?" she asked anxiously.

"The same as with the rest of the population who will have to work from home: they will not be allowed to work in the industrial park."

"I am sure the authorities are not going to protect them. They have not done so in normal times, much less in these circumstances. This complicates things for us, but we will find a way."

"Especially because we will not be able to access them as easily as in the industrial park. In the clubs and apartments, they are more guarded, and it will be more difficult to establish contacts that lead to a rescue."

"Call the UAINDF; tell them that we are planning to come to take food and cleaning supplies to the vulnerable women and that we need them to facilitate our movement around the city because we will continue to do everything possible to take care of them and provide rescue when we can."

He made the call, the agents set to work and, within a few days, obtained official permits allowing them to move around the city. They also notified the local police in each neighborhood to ensure their free movement and protection.

Sara began messaging the girls to get their addresses and quickly established the food delivery routes. It was an arduous task and not without health risks. They handed out masks and sanitizer along with food. At first, they used their own money to purchase the groceries, but before long they activated others in their network as well as humanitarian groups and were able to procure donations. Many in the social services world were quite impressed at their ingenuity and ability to find a way to provide for these otherwise ignored members of society, these vulnerable women and children.

Sara used these opportunities to share that it was the trust earned through relationships that opened these doors that were otherwise closed tightly.

In addition to the news reports, Diego regularly scrolled through his Facebook feed and could see the toll this virus and all these mandates were having on the lives of his friends and family, not only in Spain, but all around the world. He thought about what the girls must feel, locked up with even more limits on their freedom and still expected to serve clients in an even more clandestine setting. They were always at risk of contracting sexually transmitted diseases and now they had even less access to condoms, as well as the added risk of being exposed to the COVID virus, with no access to medical treatment.
The UAINDF agents had told him that pimps were redistributing the girls to the apartments they had in the city as well as other places outside the watchful eyes of those enforcing the travel restrictions. All this complicated Mariposa's ability to support the women they had developed relationships with.

Unlike all their previous rescues that had been interviewed, planned and most often executed with the awareness of the police, these unusual times brought unexpected opportunities.
A Nigerian girl, who lived with four others in an apartment in a suburb, signaled Sara with her eyes as she was handing them a box of food. Sara understood her perfectly. At that moment, the companion who was in contact with the pimps was not in the apartment. Sara was always quick to think on her feet and to get the girl alone for a minute she used an animated voice to bring attention to a broken bookcase on the far side of the room and instructed Diego to go over with the girls and look to see if he could fix it.
"Mommy, I can't take it anymore. I want to get out…."
She had no choice. That was the moment. Quickly, she took the girl by the arm and told her to gather only the most essential things in a bag and quietly go to the stairwell. She joined the bookcase repair conversation to buy the woman just a few precious minutes.
Once she'd seen her slip out the front door, she began saying her goodbyes to the women and promised to bring the necessary tools to fix the bookcase on their next visit, then grabbed Diego by the hand and headed towards the door.
Instead of returning to the elevator, Sara guided them to the exit door leading to the stairwell and whispered, "Diego, Nala is coming

with us." Discussing the matter was not an option, so both quickly shifted into their rescue protocol mode.

The three walked down the five flights of stairs as quickly as their bodies would allow and in silence other than the heaving breathing coming from under their medical masks. Once to the street level, Diego exited first to unlock and start the car, then quickly returned to the door and said, "Come on, let's go! Get down in the back seat. I've seen movement in the area, and I don't like it at all."

They left the neighborhood in a hurry. When they arrived at their office, Diego called the UAINDF immediately and explained the unexpected outcome of what was supposed to be a routine food delivery.

Like everything else in their lives, the strict public health measures brought many complications. The UAINDF was able to arrange the necessary paperwork that would allow Sara and Diego to transport the woman by car to a safe house because the trains were not running, and buses only provided very limited service for essential workers.

Claudia had located a place for the woman, but all three would be required to provide documentation of a negative COVID test before they arrived, much easier said than done. Sara began gathering some supplies for their long drive, while Diego began making phone calls to his contacts in search of someone who could arrange the necessary tests and send the results. After encountering several dead ends, his prayer was answered when a friend who worked as an administrator in a local clinic returned his message and said she could make it happen, and she did.

Nala was the first to be rescued in times of pandemic, but she was not the only one....

Failures Also Count

Not every rescue results in a happy ending.

Once the months of house confinement elapsed, the restrictive measures were relaxed and the girls began to move around a little more freely, although with a strict timetable for their stay in the street, the so-called "curfew" at 11:00 p.m.

One Friday Mariposa team members were delivering food to different apartments when Sara received a call that there was a Moroccan woman in one of the apartments who asked for help. They immediately changed their route and headed for the location. They climbed a narrow, poorly maintained staircase, reached the door, and heard shouting with some crashes between the words. They knocked insistently, and a tall, wiry, middle-aged man with pronounced dark circles under his eyes opened the door. His Argentinian accent was unmistakable.

"What is going on here?" Sara gave him no option to avoid answering the question.

"Nothing, these two are crazy," replied the man, almost reluctantly.

"Come on; you're coming with us!" Sara immediately identified the Moroccan girl and urged her to go with them.

Without giving the man any time to react, and in the intimidating presence of Diego, they took her away quickly. Once in the car, on the way to a place where they could establish the rescue protocol, the girl told them briefly what was happening.

"He is a bad man. The other girl is Nigerian and has a son who lives with us. In addition to exploiting and prostituting us, he humiliates us, beats us, and rapes us at his pleasure. He got angry with me, and this afternoon, we were fighting about it."

"Well, don't worry. Are you sure you're wanting to get out of this?" asked Sara.

"Of course!"

They prepared the whole operation, calling the UAINDF and Claudia, and purchasing train tickets. Sara would accompany her to the safe house on the now functioning trains. They could not travel until morning so they found a modest hotel where she could spend the night.

During the ride in the van, Sara noticed that she kept chatting on her phone. She feared it was the Argentinean man threatening her if she left. They got the girl settled into a room, and Sara returned home with Diego. She worried that this man would not leave the woman alone.

They picked her up at half-past seven, as they had arranged the night before. Diego took them to the train station and left them at the entrance to the platforms. Once again, the girl did not stop chatting on her cell phone. Sara was starting to get irritated by her behavior. They got on the train, and during the whole trip, she got up several times to go to the bathroom, always with her cell phone in her hand.

When they finally arrived at their destination the woman said, "I'm sorry, I can't. I don't want to leave. I want to go back."

Sara wanted to shake her and make her see that this guy was manipulating her, but one of the rules they were clear about in Mariposa was that they would only help and rescue the girls who agreed to go on their own free will - the decision had to be theirs.

She took a deep breath and closed her eyes to control all the emotion inside her.

"All right, let's get your return ticket."

Four hours later, they were on their way back home. She kept chatting the whole way, and Sara had to contain her anger again. Diego knew what time Sara was coming back and went to pick her up. She had not called him. Her anger and indignation did not let her. They arrived and approached the place where Diego was waiting for her.

When he saw Sara's face, he knew something wasn't right. She always came back from those rescues looking happy, smiling, and relieved. Not this time. The answer came when Diego saw the face of the Moroccan girl among the arriving passengers.

Without a word to either of them, the girl walked to a side door where the Argentinian was waiting for her. He threw his arm around her shoulders, and they left as if nothing had happened.

They never heard from the Moroccan girl again.

Sowing and Reaping

As the months of the pandemic continued to drag on, so did their routine of handing out food and supplies. During their visits to the industrial park, they found the number of women on the streets had decreased. However, upon resuming regular visits to the clubs they learned that many of the women had been relocated to private apartments. One of the blessings of the pandemic was that it opened doors for food delivery that allowed Sara to keep in touch with women as they were moved around by their controllers.

One January morning the news headlines from Diego's morning reading ritual once again became the catalyst for supporting the most vulnerable in their community. An immigrant settlement in Almeria (an agricultural area a few hours away) had been destroyed in a fire that took the shacks—all of them—in one night. One person was seriously injured, two slightly injured, and hundreds of people were left without a roof over their heads. The Mariposa team set to work immediately. Leveraging all the contacts they had, they asked for donations of clothing, blankets, and basic supplies to help those who already had so little and had now lost everything including their shelter. The response was overwhelming with donated blankets, coats, pajamas, sheets, and other supplies. Sara and Diego took the items to the temporary shelter in Almeria that had been set up by the Red Cross and were moved by the gratitude expressed by so many. Not only were they blessed to see the response of the immigrants, their hearts were overjoyed to see the generosity and goodwill of others in their community who were also compelled to do what they could to help those in need.

A week later a news article stated that the fire investigation had revealed that it was indeed an act of arson. Apparently two Moroccan men had come to the settlement to find prostitutes and when one of them was dissatisfied with his "service" they decided to set her shack on fire which quickly spread and led to the great destruction. The men were not caught, but their actions had come to light when they were bragging about their deed at a bar in a town several miles away.

Like the pandemic, the fire opened an unexpected door of access that allowed Sara and Diego to build trust with people in Almeria. The seeds of clothing, blankets and supplies that were planted in those days later led to ongoing relationships and ultimately the reaping of rescues as women reached out seeking a means of escape.

Late that spring another one of their freed butterflies told Sara and Diego that the wonderful Spanish man she had met wanted to propose to her. But the problem was to honor her Nigerian culture. It was important for her that he get the blessing of her parents.

Tanisha said to them, "Here, you are my parents. Would you meet with him?"

"Yes, of course," they replied in unison.

This was not the first of their rescued young women who had come to them with a prospective beau, and they had learned that the most loving thing to do was to speak truth to any concerns they had because some of those relationships had ended very badly.

On the agreed evening, Tanisha showed up at Sara and Diego's house with her boyfriend. In his nervousness he repeatedly tugged at his shirt collar with shaking hands and sweat dripping everywhere.

"Meet Jorge."

"Nice to meet you." Diego shook his hand, and Sara extended the traditional Spanish greeting by kissing him on each cheek.

"I would like to seek your blessing for my relationship with Tanisha," his voice was trembling.

"Do you have good intentions with her?" Diego sounded very much like any father concerned for the wellbeing of his daughter.

"Of course! I love her with all my heart and wish to marry her."

"Well, you have our permission." Sara was about to laugh. She had never seen her husband in those circumstances and with that paternal demeanor. "I only tell you one thing, if you hurt her or don't treat her well, you will have to deal with us."

Jorge shook his head in full affirmation.

Tanisha jumped out of her chair, full of joy. She hugged Jorge and then Sara and Diego. They shared a celebratory toast together along with a few traditional tapas that Sara had prepared for the occasion and then the happy couple said their goodbyes.

After they had left, Sara and Diego recounted to one another the details from Tanisha's story and rescue: the hardships she had to suffer from Benin to the Spanish coast, the aggressions and scorn, the objectification by the pimps, the deceptions, beatings, rapes, and every other indignity that is experienced in exploitation and slavery.

To see her now, so happy, content, with a new life, master of her destiny, having regained the sparkle in her eye, all that was priceless. Getting to share in this special moment today as if they were blood family, brought a deep sense of satisfaction. If even only for that one redeemed life, it was worth everything they were doing.

No sooner had their reminiscing and celebrating this joyous occasion come to an end and soon they were already thinking about what they had planned for that Friday. Which girls in the industrial park and at the clubs were most receptive to potential rescue and who needed any kind of specific help.

They prayed for Felisa, the Colombian girl who had become pregnant and had not told her pimp for fear of reprisals. She did not want to have an abortion, but she was certain he would demand it.

Sara gathered the documents she had prepared for Amelia to present at the Civil Registry in pursuit of legal residency.

Diego was rummaging through their donated items in search of a stuffed animal for Susana. She was devastated by the news that her young son in Nigeria had recently died of an illness. Diego remembered that Susana loved stuffed animals. He was debating between a bear in one hand and a puppy in the other when he heard Sara calling to him.

"Diego, we have another girl who wants to get out! In fact, it's Felisa, the one who is pregnant, and we were just praying for her earlier." He chose the puppy, put down the bear, and stood up to begin the rescue protocol.

Sara brought him up to speed regarding the details and together they looked over the calendars on their phones to strategize a plan.

Diego suggested, "If we arrange to do the extraction on Wednesday morning, we could reach Madrid by the evening, and we were already hoping to make it up there on Thursday to celebrate The National Day Against Human Trafficking."

"Great idea!" exclaimed Sara as she gave her husband a kiss; a show of affection less about passion and more about shared purpose and partnership.

The Flutter of Butterflies Gather

As the nation's capital, the city square in downtown Madrid was the ideal location for the largest anti-trafficking campaign. At 9:00 a.m. each organization began to set up their information table with various posters and informational brochures along with pendants, bracelets and bags made by survivors with the intent of raising funds to help more women.

As usual, by 10:30 a.m. the city square was full of people – from those who passed through every day as part of their daily commute to those out for a leisurely mid-morning walk, to the throngs of tourists who were finally returning after most of the travel restrictions had finally been lifted.

Claudia and a network of volunteers from her church located here in Madrid were the main organizers of the annual event that had come to fruition as a result of her advocacy with various political contacts. While the Spanish government still had a long way to go in addressing the complex issues surrounding sex trafficking and exploitation, she was optimistic that they were making progress and increasingly welcoming the efforts of NGO's and faith-based organizations. Those with firsthand knowledge of the nature of the global crisis well understood that it would take a united, global effort with a commitment of both governmental resources and societal pressures to one day bring it to an end.

The primary goal of this public event was to bring awareness to the common person in hopes that more people would truly see the plight of so many women and the proliferation of evil embedded right in their own neighborhoods.

"Look at the posters!" said a lady to her teenage daughter who was accompanying her: "'No deal with trafficking,' 'Human beings are neither bought nor sold,' 'Breaking the chains,' 'Don't feed the slavery of women,' 'Slavery in the 21st century,' 'I am not for sale'...."

"That refers to prostitutes, doesn't it?" said the teen.

"Actually, all this refers to slavery. You see, the evil that allowed the degrading ownership of other human beings all the way back in ancient times is not just a historical tragedy, but one that is more pervasive today than ever before."

"Didn't you volunteer with one of those organizations?"

"Yes, and I still do. That's why I brought you here, so you could learn that at the same age as you, there are hundreds of thousands of girls who suffer from this scourge, without options to live a life like yours, without the possibility of defending themselves from traffickers and pimps. Come, let's go meet some people who are fighting for justice for these women."

"Wow, I had no idea! Ok, but are they prostitutes or not?" asked the daughter, still stuck with her preconceived stereotypes.

"You will be able to answer that question yourself by the time we leave here today. And as you're walking around, listen carefully...try to hear what rises above the murmur of people. That strange yet beautiful buzzing, that's the fluttering of butterflies, women who stand here today with new-found freedom and beautiful rebirth."

The previous afternoon, Sara and Diego had successfully delivered the Colombian woman to the designated safe house. Thankfully the rescue had been one of the most uneventful with no surprises or unforeseen elements. They had spent the evening catching up with friends who lived in the city and then took advantage of being in the capitol to take care of some business matters that morning.

At 11:45 a.m., they began walking up the Carrera de San Jeronimo. The temperatures were quite warm for this time of year already. As they approached the square, they began to hear a murmur in crescendo, almost tribal. They looked at each other with their characteristic complicity and quickened their pace, despite the heat.

As they entered the square they took in the grand sight of several tables representing different organizations, many staffed by young people. This brought them great encouragement because they believed that for trafficking to stop it would take this next generation of young people making a stand and forcing an end to the demand so that there was no longer any profit in providing a supply. It was this belief that fueled the awareness efforts that took them into schools and universities all over the country to lead assemblies and workshops on the topic.

They sensed the fervor building among the crowd and then right as the first toll of the noon bell rang out from the cathedral, dozens and dozens of women raised their fists and shouted, "We are not for sale!"

This powerful scene was repeated with each bell toll and after the twelfth and finally ring, a collective cheer went out from the hundreds who had gathered. Music filled the air, and a group of local boys and girls began to perform a choreographed dance they had clearly been practicing for this event.

"That's what I call a flash mob," said Sara to a surprised Diego.

"How beautiful to see all of these people, especially the young ones!"

Their hearts were already overflowing from the purposeful energy all around them when Sara exclaimed, "Look, I think I recognize Aisha, over there, to the right of the group!"

The dance routine and music had attracted an even greater crowd, so they were unable to move that direction. A deafening applause arose from all over the square and again, many more people had emerged from side streets to check out what was happening. The mayor and two associates ascended the small platform that had been erected and began speaking to the crowd, proclaiming his support for these anti-trafficking organizations and then introduced two women who then read what is known as a manifesto – essentially a scripted statement that summarized the issue and extent of the trafficking of women for sexual exploitation and made a proclamation to bring an end to this form of slavery of the 21st century. Another thunderous applause came in response, followed by more upbeat music and a very organic outbreak of dancing and celebrating, of which the Nigerians present were clearly the energetic and enthusiastic instigators.

Sara was excited and, at the same time, overwhelmed. She looked around at all those groups of people who had organized themselves into different teams to help the enslaved women and she was especially struck by the presence of large organizations like the Red Cross which appeared in the media, those that had strong structures with many people and means. She felt small; Mariposa was like one small stone surrounded by massive boulders. Although she never regretted anything they had undertaken, she could not help but feel like her efforts were insignificant in comparison.

A hand rested on Sara's left shoulder. She turned immediately.

"Claudia, so good to see you!" They gave each other a warm and extended hug.

"Well done on rescuing one more life, my friends! I've heard that Felisa has already settled in well at the assigned house."

"And what a tremendous job you have done at coordinating all of this; it is amazing!" said Diego.

"Yes, let's hope that more people become aware that this slavery exists and that they are closer to it than they could even imagine."

Together they began walking towards the information tables, but before they had gone twenty meters...

"Mommy!"
"Aisha!"
"Mommy! Daddy!"
"Nasha!"
"Mommy!"
"Andrea!"
"Daddy!"
"Elena!"
"Mommy! Daddy!"
"Marissa!"
"Mommy!"
"Violet!"
"Mommy! Daddy!"
"Cecilia!"
"Daddy!"
"Lupita!"
"Daddy, Mommy!"
"Helen!"
"Mommy!"
"Shamira!"
"Mommy!"
"Fadhila!"
"Mommy!"
"Nala!"
"Daddy! Mommy!"
"Tanisha!"

More girls approached, some with small children in their hands, one of them with a baby in her arms. They surrounded the couple, jumping for joy, shrieks of laughter, and a friendly competition for hugs as each woman wanted to embrace the first two people who had opened their door to hope, to a new life. For each of them, Sara and Diego were their mother and father, yet they did not even know one other.

"How do you know my mommy?"
"They rescued me. Did they rescue you, too?
"They saved me too!"
"We are all their daughters?"
"Yes, all of you," answered Claudia, who was also overwhelmed at that moment at the magnitude of what this humble couple had accomplished in such a short period of time. Over her many years she had worked with several organizations, including those well-

known ones that had just minutes earlier cast a shadow on Sara's perspective of their work.

For the first time in four years, I was aware of what we had done. When we rescued a girl and left her in a shelter, as soon as we got in the car, we always said, 'Let's go for the next one,'" and so we did. We didn't realize how many there were; each one was a world, a story, a life, and we would go all in until we managed to save her. But today was different. We are a small team, but being surrounded by all the girls, my legs trembled, and I blushed so much that I thought I was going to faint. We did everything discreetly, taking care not to be seen, almost without being noticed, and in doing so we exceeded all our expectations. We were thrilled as never before. They were our girls, our girls."

"But how many of you are there?" Sara meekly asked.
"There are fifty-four women and four children, Sara," Claudia informed her. "David is very powerful, even if he is facing Goliath."

Sara and Diego let themselves be carried away by that tide of women and allowed every hug, every tear, and every expression of gratitude to penetrate every part of their beings and settle with such satisfaction in their very souls.
Unknown to Sara and Diego, Claudia had organized a meal for all of them in a space rented for the occasion. When they arrived, all the women were waiting for them with a big sign: "You are our parents. Thank you."
"Take a picture with me!" one of the girls shouted.
"Me too!" protested another.
Hundreds of photos were taken, but the smiles came naturally. Claudia enlisted the help of her husband (a local police officer) to get the attention of everyone and bring them together for a group photo.
"We will keep this photo in our hearts until the last of our days," Diego told them aloud.
At the end of the meal, one of the girls raised her voice to propose a toast.
"Let us raise our glasses to toast Mariposa, who has given us a new life."
"Cheers to them!"
Without planning it, in unison, Sara and Diego replied at the same time:
"For you and your futures!"

The woman who had brought her daughter visited each of the information tables and talked to the people who offered all kinds of insight and information. They also had the opportunity to talk with several women including a Nigerian, then with a Colombian, a Romanian, a Moroccan... The young woman opened her ears to everything they said, and her eyes were opened to see that these women represented such a very small fraction of those who remained trapped inside the evil chrysalis of their bondage, women with no real hope for being set free. It was a very special day for the teenager. When she arrived home, she was exhausted, not just from the heat but from the heaviness of all she had seen and heard. She realized she could not unsee and unknow what she had experienced, in fact she hoped that the spark for justice that was lit inside her that day would never be extinguished.

"Now you can answer the question you asked me this morning," her mother reminded her, "are they prostitutes?"

"No, Mom," she took a moment to answer, "They are people, just people. Just like you and me."

In the hustle and bustle of the celebration, still in the throes of excitement and overflowing joy, Sara noticed her cell phone vibrating in her pocket. She pulled it out, but it was impossible to hear what was being said. She got up and left the room in search of a quieter setting. Several moments later she returned to the table and put her hand on her husband's shoulder.

"Diego, we have another girl who wants to get out."

"Let's go!"

Made in the USA
Middletown, DE
26 October 2022